LIFE FOR A LIFE

T. FRANK MUIR

LIFE FOR A LIFE

A DCI GILCHRIST INVESTIGATION

ACADEMY

CHICAGO

Copyright © 2013, 2015 by T. Frank Muir
First published in the United Kingdom in 2013 by C&R Crime
An imprint of Constable and Robinson Ltd
This edition published in 2015 by Academy Chicago Publishers
An imprint of Chicago Review Press Incorporated

Chicago Review Press Incorporated
814 North Franklin Street
Chicago, Illinois 60610
ISBN 978-1-61373-324-0

Library of Congress Cataloging-in-Publication Data
Muir, Frank (Crime novelist)
Life for a life: a DCI Gilchrist novel / T. Frank Muir.
    pages; cm
ISBN 978-1-61373-324-0 (trade paper)
1. Police—Scotland—Fiction. 2. Murder—Investigation—Fiction.
I. Title.
PR6063.U318L54 2015
823'.914—dc23
            2015007779

Cover design: Joan Sommers Design
Cover image: © Marek Ševc, courtesy of 500px, Inc.
Interior layout: Nord Compo

Printed in the United States of America
5 4 3 2 1

LIFE FOR A LIFE

1

She stumbles across the lawn, pushes through the gap in the hedge.

She has no time, ten minutes at most, probably much less.

Beyond the hedge, overgrown grass, dead and flattened for the winter, clings to her shoes. She kicks her way toward the low garden wall, grips the snow-freezing stones, and pulls herself up and over.

In the blackness, she lands awkwardly, sprawls onto her stomach with a force that brings a hard grunt to her throat. She picks herself up, risks a quick look behind her.

The gable wall of the cottage is already fading into the freezing darkness.

He is not following. Not yet.

But he soon will be.

She thinks of knocking on someone's door but knows this part of Scotland beds early. And he could return anytime, catch her in another house, then where would she be?

Better to run into the darkness.

Her high heels sink into the ground, slowing her down, and she slides a hand the length of her bare legs and removes one shoe, then the other. She grips them in her hands, shivering from the cold, and runs into the night. She does not know where she is, or where she is running to, but the faintest smell of the sea, and the whisper of distant surf, pull her on.

He will not expect her to flee this way. He will waste valuable time searching the housing estate, driving the streets, hunting her.

And if he finds her?

Just that thought has her throat constricting with fear, her lungs pulling for air. She chokes back a sob, risks another glance. Behind her, lights fade into a ghostly glow, and she realizes that mist is falling.

Thank God. At least He is looking out for her.

That thought gives her hope.

The wall appears out of the empty darkness, like a barrier to block her escape. But again she hauls herself over, lands on a gravel pathway, the stones small and sharp enough to cut into her bare feet. She cleans mud from her soles, slips on her high heels, and jogs as best she can into the ice-cold breeze. The mist changes to the finest of snowflakes that thicken as she runs on. From behind, she hears a thump, imagines it is him slamming the cottage door shut. Another hard sound echoes in the darkness.

Is it his car? Is it an engine firing up?

She reaches down for her shoes, snaps off one heel, then the other, and throws them into the darkness. Without heels, she runs faster, her feet thudding the gravel path in a steady beat, reminding her of days at her school in Rzeszow, pounding the track. She wishes she was there now, wishes she had never met Anna, never listened to her dreams of starting a new life in a new country.

The snow is thickening now, flakes landing in her eyes, flying toward her like some spinning vortex. Despite the sweat on her brow, her arms and legs feel frozen dead, like limbs of ice. Her lungs breathe fire, and her chest pulses with an ache that makes her want to stop.

But she can't stop. She must keep running.

She will need to find somewhere to hide, someplace warm, or she will freeze in the bitter winter cold. She presses on, not knowing where she is going, knowing only that if she does not turn back, she will find her haven. She will at last be free.

Free from the pain, the insults, the inhumanity.

Free from the constant fear of death.

Free from him.

2

Tuesday morning, four days later
St. Andrews Memorial Hospital

Detective Chief Inspector Andy Gilchrist flashed his warrant card at the nurse. "Won't be more than five minutes," he said.

He found Detective Inspector Stan Davidson asleep, one of two patients in a small ward outfitted for six. He pulled a chair bedside, gave the mattress a gentle shake.

Stan stirred, opened his eyes, took a few seconds to come to and say, "Boss?"

"Got it in one."

Stan tried to shift himself but stopped short with a grimace.

"Bit sore?" Gilchrist said.

"And then some." Stan gritted his teeth.

"Would be worse if they didn't have you doped up."

"Help me up, boss, will you?"

"Stay where you are, Stan. You've got twenty-six stitches. Best if you don't move."

Stan gave a welcoming nod and seemed to deflate under the sheets.

"You'll be out of action for a week or two," Gilchrist said. "Give you plenty of time to do your Christmas shopping. Not that I'm looking for much." He waited until Stan offered a half smile. "Just the usual. A pint behind the bar. But make it a Deuchars IPA this year."

Stan frowned. "What brought that on, boss?"

"Thought I'd give the Eighty Shilling a miss and try something different. Talking of which . . ."

"I'll be good as new after the New Year, boss."

"I'm counting on it, Stan."

"I've never missed a day, boss."

"I never said you had. But while you're lying in bed pretending to be ill, life goes on. It's the festive season, Stan. Nothing but drunk-and-disorderlies and a thousand Breathalyzers. You won't be missing much."

"What about the new DS?"

"Starts tomorrow."

"So she'll stand in for me?"

"As a temp, Stan. Don't worry."

Stan nodded, as if in thought. "From her file, she looks like a cracking bit of stuff."

"You worried that I'm going to prefer her to you?"

"Well, she is better looking than me."

"Maybe she'll fall for you, Stan. With your charm and your blond looks."

"I'm too busy for birds, boss."

Gilchrist pushed his chair back and stood. "I've spoken with Dainty," he said. "He assures me it's an old photograph, and a cracker she's not. Well, not to look at anyway."

"Don't tell me she's trouble."

"Dainty didn't say that."

"Is that why she's transferring from Strathclyde?"

"Apparently not," said Gilchrist. "But time will tell."

Stan held Gilchrist's gaze, then said, "What are you looking at, boss?"

Gilchrist peered closer. "Are you losing your hair, Stan?"

"Piss off. I've nearly been stabbed to death, and you're asking if I'm losing my hair? Yes, I'm losing my hair. I'll be pure bald by the time I'm as ancient as you."

"Touché," said Gilchrist. "But then you won't have to worry about going gray." He waited a couple of beats, then said, "The name's Stewart Donnelly. A right nasty piece of work. We have four eyewitnesses who've given written statements, all confirming the attack was unprovoked."

"Well, that's a start," Stan said. "And has Donnelly explained why he jumped me?"

"Said you provoked him. I know, I know, settle down, Stan, it's only his story. He'd say black was white if it got him off. He's got form. Lots of it. Apparently he was over from Dundee to celebrate being released on bail."

"You're kidding."

"I kid you not, Stan old son. You were attacked by a career criminal."

Stan frowned. "What about the other guy? His mate? What's he saying?"

"Name's Craig Farmer. Says he pulled Donnelly off you. Which was lucky for you. But he's not Donnelly's mate. Says he doesn't know him. Met him in the pub for the first time that day, although Donnelly says otherwise." Gilchrist checked his watch.

"Got to go, boss?"

"Could give you a kiss good-bye, if you'd like."

"I don't think my stitches could stand it."

"We don't want you popping any sutures."

Outside, a gray sky threatened snow.

Gilchrist pulled his collar up and strode to his Merc, remote in hand. It irked him that he had not been altogether honest with Stan. Not that he was being deceitful, rather that he felt there was no need to trouble Stan over personal thoughts and concerns.

Donnelly's mate, the man who had pulled Donnelly off Stan, arguably saving Stan's life, had traipsed along to the station as requested, given his name—Craig Farmer—signed his written statement, then returned to his B and B, Arran House, in Murray Park. Except that when Gilchrist checked in on him earlier that morning, Arran House had no record of a Craig Farmer staying over, or of anyone else who fit his description. Nor did his name tie up with his driving license registered with the DVLA.

Which only raised more questions in Gilchrist's mind.

Questions he knew from experience he would need answered.

DS Nancy Wilson eyed the recorder on the table and said, "DCI Andy Gilchrist has joined the interview." She glanced at the clock on the wall, recited the time, then said, "Once more for the record, Mr. Donnelly has turned down his right for legal representation during this interview. Is that correct, Mr. Donnelly?"

"Yeah."

Nance flipped through her notes, found what she was looking for. "Because, and I quote, solicitors are nothing but expensive, useless wankers that know fuck all."

"That's what I said."

Gilchrist leaned forward. "You do realize that an assault with a deadly weapon on an officer of the law is a serious offence."

"Yeah."

Gilchrist nodded to Nance, a sign for her just to get on with the interview, get it over and done with.

"You came over from Dundee for the day, just to have a couple of pints with a mate of yours," Nance said. "But he's such a good friend that you don't know his name."

"Don't *remember* his name. There's a difference. I'm hopeless with names. If I don't write them down, they're gone. Poof. Just like that." Donnelly snapped his fingers and gave a shrug of puzzlement.

"That's not what your mate's saying."

"He wouldn't, would he?"

"Why wouldn't he?" Gilchrist asked.

"Cause I'm a nutter, see? A right fucking nutter." He grinned at Gilchrist. "No one wants to associate themselves with a nutter, do they now? And that's a good word that is. Associate."

"Good at English, are you?"

"Yeah. Here's another good word. Unpredictable. How's that for English?"

"Full marks."

"Yeah. Ten out of ten, and all that. But unpredictable's my middle name."

Nance could not resist the opportunity. "I predict you're going back inside," she said.

"Good. Yeah. I like that. Three square meals a day. No matter what the fuck I do." He grimaced at Gilchrist. "Beats coming to work every fucking day. I mean, look at the pair of you. What you earn? Not a lot by the fucking looks of it."

"Handy with a knife?" Gilchrist again.

"Too true, mate, I'm real fucking handy."

"You said DI Davidson provoked you." Gilchrist shook his head. "I don't think it would take any provoking to get your attention."

"Yeah?"

"Yeah, like your mate just happened to tell you that DI Davidson worked for Fife Constabulary."

"Maybe."

"How did you get to St. Andrews?"

"Like I said, my mate drove me in his car."

"And dropped you at the Golf Hotel? Where did you go to first?"

"First?"

"Over from Dundee? Straight to the Golf Hotel? Why?"

"I was thirsty. I wanted a beer."

"We've already got someone checking out CCTV footage. We'll find out what time you crossed the Tay Bridge, when you got to St. Andrews."

"And we'll pick up your mate, too," Nance said.

"Yeah, sure you will."

Gilchrist could tell from Donnelly's smirk that the man knew more than he was letting on. But Gilchrist also knew they could interrogate Donnelly through to midnight, and all they would be doing was massaging his ego. All of a sudden, he felt as if he was through with it all, through with interrogating thugs who cared less about their own lives than the lives of others, through with the pointlessness of it all. He pulled the file toward him and said, "How old are you? What, twenty-seven? And you've been incarcerated . . ." He glanced up. "How's that for a big word?" then ran a finger down the page, working out the arithmetic. "Fifteen of your twenty-seven years." He looked at Donnelly, not sure what to expect, but the smile came as no surprise.

"Like I said, I like it inside." Then something died behind Donnelly's eyes, and he said, "Maybe your associate, Mr. DI Davidson, just happened to be in the wrong place at the wrong time."

Gilchrist thought he kept his surprise hidden. He knew now that he was being toyed with, that Donnelly was not the dumb thug he painted himself to be. "So you stabbed him on the spur of the moment," he tried, "so you could spend some more time in jail?"

Donnelly sniffed, livened up. "Yeah, clever you."

Gilchrist pushed himself back from the table and stood. What was the point of it all, when you had thugs like Donnelly who did not fear the wrath of the law but welcomed it, a way to secure a roof over their head, three free meals a day, and a bed at night?

"Fancy a bit of sun?" he said to Nance.

She hesitated, but only for an instant. "South of France for the weekend?"

"I'm thinking somewhere warmer. Like the Caribbean. Swim, sail, soak up some sun, share a few cocktails." He glanced at Donnelly. "Pity you won't be able to do that for some time," he said, "lie on the warm sands of some golden, sun-drenched beach."

"Don't like the sun, can't stand darkies, and I hate the fucking beach."

"The sand gets in your butt crack?" quipped Nance.

Gilchrist shoved his hands into his pockets. "The Caribbean might be full of shaded people," he said to Donnelly, "but it beats masturbating to four walls or having your cock sucked by your cellmate." He smiled at Nance. "Want to discuss holidays over a pint?"

"Sure."

When Gilchrist left the interview room, he excused himself from Nance and visited the Gents. He was relieved to see the place deserted, which gave him time to pull himself together. Donnelly's smug voice came back at him—*the wrong place at the wrong time*—repeating itself like an echo that whispered and resounded and refused to fade.

Gilchrist had not told Stan of his fears. But he felt sure Stan would work it out for himself, once he healed. He eyed the mirror, ran the tap, splashed cold water over his face, trying to cool a guilty heat that flushed his face.

The wrong place at the wrong time.

Christ, it didn't bear thinking about.

3

Tuesday night
The Stand Comedy Club
Woodlands Road, Glasgow

Gilchrist thought she looked small onstage, not diminutive—
her baggy top suggested otherwise—more like she was out
of her depth, in unsafe waters, a swimmer struggling against
a rip current that changed direction without warning.

The rough Glasgow accent cut through the ambient din
once more.

"Is that the best you can dae?" he roared. "C'mon, it's
time to get aff."

"Isn't it past your bedtime, sonny?" she railed back at him.

"Goin to bed? Are you interested?"

Pint glasses chinked in drunken victory.

"Only if your old man's at home," she retaliated. "But if
he looks anything like you, I wouldnae let any of my sheep
near him."

A surge of laughter, a ripple of hard applause, drowned out
the man's response. For a moment, it looked as if he would

rise to his feet and stagger to the stage, but a hand on his shoulder from a man as wide as he was tall and a whisper in his ear suggested otherwise.

"And talking about sheep," she went on to mild laughter. "How many of you here like your whisky?"

Several hands lifted in unsteady embarrassment.

She spread one arm wide in mock surprise. "Is that the best youse can dae?" she mimicked. More arms lifted.

Gilchrist noted the loudmouth now sat silent, a scowl on his face, his mates subdued beside him, half-empty pints perched on the table, behind which the oversized man in his oversized suit stood guard.

"That's better," she said. "I know youse like your whisky. You're Scottish. Right?"

She waited a beat for a nonresponse. Beads of sweat glistened on her top lip. She was struggling to win the crowd, maybe losing more than she was winning over.

"And we all know what whisky's made from," she went on. "And it's mostly water." She strode across the stage, then back again, as if she had now discovered the power in her legs. "And where does the water come from?" she shouted. "The hills," she answered, then stopped and faced the audience. "And what's in these hills?" A pause, then, "Yes, you're allowed to say it," she egged on an elderly couple at a front table. "That's it, dear. Sheep," she concluded for them. "That's right," she said. "The hills are alive with the sound of . . . ?"

A woman near an exit sign chuckled, more in sympathy Gilchrist thought.

"Sheep shagging." A voice from the back.

"Close," she said. "Try sheep shitting, and sheep pissing." She faced the audience and nodded to a table by the corner of the stage. "So next time you take a sip of the amber nectar," she said to them, "give a thought to all these sheep."

The audience laughed. Someone shouted, "Go Jessie," and Gilchrist noticed the fat man was clapping the loudest. Jessie looked out across the pond of faces, as if imagining she was in the London Palladium, or maybe wishing she was somewhere else, somewhere far from that night's thankless audience. Then she smiled as her gaze settled on a young man—more boy than man—standing alone at the rear of the hall.

A quick wink, then back to the audience. "That's it," she said. "You've been a fantastic crowd." A wave of her hands. "Thank you, thank you. And good night."

Gilchrist clapped as well, a grin tugging his lips, as she strode off the stage as if she had just been called back for her third encore.

She almost bumped into a man in denim jacket and jeans, who spread an outstretched arm behind him as they passed on the stage. "Give a big hand, ladies and gentlemen, to Jessie Janes," he shouted. "Gun-toting, joke-toting Jessie Janes."

Gilchrist watched Jessie step from the stage and work her way along the edge of the room, applauded by some as she passed their tables, ignored by others. As she neared, he stepped from the shadows.

"DS Janes?" he said.

"And you are?" But before Gilchrist could respond, Jessie shifted her stance, almost turning away from him, and half-whispered, "Shit. Here comes Jabba the Hutt."

"Problems, Jess?" said the oversized man.

"Just having a chat."

The man nodded, gave Gilchrist a hard stare. "You look familiar," he said. "We met before?"

Gilchrist shook his head. "If we had, I'm sure I would have remembered."

Jessie coughed, put her hand to her mouth.

The fat man squared up to Gilchrist, eyes twin raisins in a suet pudding. He wore his clothes well for a big man. His gray suit looked brand new, his white shirt starched and large enough to limit neck folds at the collar. An aromatic fragrance spilled off him.

"Fancy yourself as laugh-a-minute?" the fat man asked. "Want five seconds of fame behind the stage?"

"Steady on, Lachie, he's only—"

"I know what he's only doing."

Gilchrist recognized him then—DI Lachlan McKellar of Strathclyde Police, plus ten stones of flab—more tubby than fat when they first met fifteen years earlier. He must have spent the bulk of these years stuffing his face with lard.

"Andy Gilchrist," he said, offering his hand. "DCI. Fife."

McKellar ignored Gilchrist's hand. On the stage behind him, the next act, a skeletal man with stick legs and hands of bone, was fiddling with the mic to a wave of light applause. Movement to the side distracted Gilchrist, and a young man with dirty-blond hair—the boy at whom Jessie had winked—nudged into Jessie's side for a quick hug, then shrugged her off and mouthed in silence as his fingers flicked and his hands moved with the speed of an expert sign linguist.

Jessie responded with signs of her own, then faced Gilchrist and held out her hand. "Didn't expect a welcoming committee to come and fetch me," she said.

Her hand felt warm and dry, despite the flat act on stage. "Thought I'd come down and take a look," Gilchrist said.

"To see what making a fool of yourself looks like, you mean?"

Something in the tone of her voice warned Gilchrist not to challenge her. "I'm also a part-time scout for the Byre Theatre," he joked, and pushed past the moment with a smile.

But Jessie's face deadpanned, and she turned to the boy. "What d'you think of my new boss?" she asked him. More signing that coughed up a raspy chuckle from her. "Robert says he likes you," she said to Gilchrist.

"Nice to meet you, Robert." Gilchrist held out his hand.

Robert touched it, then stuffed his hands into his pockets.

McKellar slid an arm around Jessie's shoulder, his grip tight enough to prevent her wriggling free. "Nice talking to you again, DCI Gilchrist. But we have a reservation at the Park."

Gilchrist nodded, was about to walk away, when Jessie shrugged McKellar's arm from her shoulder and grumbled, "Give me a minute."

Robert seemed to understand before McKellar, who paused for a moment, then brushed past Gilchrist with a move so sudden that he bumped him against the wall.

When McKellar and Robert were out of earshot, Jessie said, "Sorry about that. Lachie can be a nasty shite when he puts his mind to it. Gives me the creeps when he acts like that."

"Seems possessive," Gilchrist said.

"He's looking to trade in his wife for a younger model."

"You?"

"I heard you were good."

"And you don't have it in you to tell him you're not interested?"

"Oh I've got it in me, all right," she said. "Don't you worry about that. But Jabba doesn't understand English. Maybe I should tell him to fuck off in Huttian, or whatever the hell they talk in."

"Which is the reason you've transferred to St. Andrews?"

"One of them."

"And the others?"

"Don't ask."

Gilchrist nodded as her eyes darted left and right, as if expecting some ghost from her past to manifest from the shadows. But he guessed it was more basic than that.

"It's no-smoking," he tried.

"Don't rub it in. I'm trying to give up."

"Join the club."

"A right fine pair we'll make," she said, then gripped his arm. "Look. I'm not always this dizzy. Just not feeling right at the moment. With the move and . . ." A glance at McKellar. "It's important for me, for Robert, that this new job works out. I won't fuck it up, I mean, I won't let you down," then added, "Sir."

"Trust is important," Gilchrist said.

"You can trust me, sir."

"And honesty."

"Cross my heart and hope to die."

Gilchrist let several beats pass. "What did Robert really say?"

"Thought you looked a bit of a plonker," she said.

"Plonker?"

"Well, wanker."

"That's better. No more lies?"

"No, sir."

"Good," he said, and smiled. "We'll make a right fine pair indeed, then."

4

Gilchrist had Nance chase down Donnelly's missing associate.

When the call came into the station at 10:13 AM, Nance was no further forward.

"Whereabouts on the Coastal Path?" Gilchrist asked, and jotted it down. "Are they still there?" He flagged Jessie, and she caught his eye, puzzled. "Tell them to stay put. We're on our way." He pushed to his feet, pulled on his leather jacket, Jessie by his side as they swept through the station and out the door into North Street.

"What's the rush?" Jessie gasped, as she struggled to keep up with him.

"A couple walking their dog found a woman's body," he said.

"Dead?"

Gilchrist glanced at her. "A woman's body usually means she's dead. Yes."

"So she's not going to get up and run away, then?"

Gilchrist eased back on his stride. "Sorry," he said. "Force of habit."

"Habit? Sounds like the East Neuk's the murder capital of the world."

By the time they reached Gilchrist's Merc, Jessie was breathing heavily. She stood back as he pressed the remote, then opened the door for her.

"Thought the last of the gentlemen vanished with the cowboys," she said, sliding into the passenger seat.

"You look as if you could use a hand," he said, and closed the door on her.

Jessie fiddled with her mobile while Gilchrist worked his Merc onto Abbey Walk, and neither of them spoke as he powered through the double roundabout and accelerated onto the A917. Gilchrist waited until he passed Kinkell Braes Caravan Park before flooring it to seventy, then said, "Hard night last night?"

"Does it show?"

"I'd say you're looking a tad rough around the edges."

"Where's a cowboy when you need him?"

He gripped the steering wheel and eyed the road ahead. "You found a place yet?"

"Nothing permanent. A friend, Angie, is putting me up."

"Robert, too?"

"No, I stuck him in a bin back in Glasgow."

He glanced at her.

"Of course, Robert, too. He's my son, for God's sake. You can't just wake up one morning and throw him away."

"Although sometimes you'd like to?"

"Speak for yourself."

"Just asking," he said.

"Well ask something sensible."

Gilchrist chose silence and nudged the Merc up to eighty.

"You're not convincing me she's not going to get up and run away," Jessie said.

Gilchrist eased his foot off the accelerator. "So, after your night out with Slim at the Park, when did you get up here?"

"In time to make it to the station for 8:00."

"You always like to cut it that fine?"

"Only when I can't get rid of Jabba."

Gilchrist glanced at her. "Sounds like he stayed the night."

"Yeah, he did. First I went on top, then he went on top. What is it with all the grilling? My personal life's personal. So why don't you stick to solving murders, and mind your own business?" She grasped the dashboard as the Merc powered through a bend. "And slow down, will you? You're making me feel sick."

Through the village of Boarhills, the road turned into a single-lane dirt track. Gilchrist followed it all the way to the seafront. He parked on the grass verge and pulled up his collar. Hands of ice slapped his face from a bitter east wind. He trudged toward the Coastal Path in silence, Jessie breathing hard behind him.

"Sorry," she said.

"What's that?"

"You heard."

He stopped then and faced her. She pulled to an abrupt halt, eyes wide, like a deer caught in headlights. She looked not only cold and tired but something else that he could not quite put his finger on. "It's your first day in a new job," he said, "and I'm giving you the benefit of every doubt."

Silent, she nodded.

"But I'm curious as to why."

"Why what?"

"Why you're behaving the way you are."

Her lips tightened, and her eyes creased. She blinked once, twice, and he thought he caught a flicker of fear shift across her face. Then she shook her head.

"We'll talk about it later," he said, then strode toward the waiting couple.

The SOCOs had not arrived yet, and Gilchrist flashed his warrant card.

"Clive Watkins," the man said. "My wife, Jayne."

Gilchrist nodded. "Who called it in?"

"I did," said Mrs. Watkins. She fingered her hair. "But it was Skip who found it, the woman's body I mean."

As if on cue, the black Labrador lifted his eyes and gave a tired wag of his tail.

"Where is she?" Gilchrist asked.

"This way."

Mr. Watkins led them along the Coastal Path, nothing more than a foot-worn grassway that looked icy enough in white stretches to demand crampons, until they reached a point where the trail narrowed.

Watkins faced Gilchrist and said, "She's down there."

Gilchrist glanced at his feet, at black leather shoes in need of a polish, and stepped into long grass whitened with snow and frost, Jessie close behind him.

They found her about twelve feet from the path, facedown, bedded in snow. Skip's paw prints trailed across her back. From the path, unless you knew the body was there, you could pass it every day until spring. It had snowed the last four nights but one, and even from where he stood, Gilchrist could tell the body was days old, maybe even a week.

Watkins looked down at them from the edge of the path. "Do you take Skip for a walk daily?" Gilchrist asked him.

"We do, but we haven't been along this path since November."

Christmas was less than three weeks away. Only someone walking a dog would have any chance of finding the body. "End, middle, beginning of November?" Gilchrist asked, just to test the possibilities.

"Twenty-third. Jayne's birthday."

Gilchrist nodded, turned away.

"Are you thinking what I'm thinking?" Jessie asked him.

"Depends what you're thinking."

"That she could have been lying here for a couple of weeks?"

"Somebody would have reported her missing."

"Maybe," Jessie said. "Maybe not."

Gilchrist frowned at the body. Even with her face hidden, he could tell she was a young woman, no more than a girl, probably mid- to late-teens. Could a teenager be dead for a couple of weeks without anyone noticing her missing?

"She could have tripped and fallen," Jessie said to him.

Gilchrist looked back up at the path at Mrs. Watkins turning away as if embarrassed to be caught talking on her mobile. He estimated the drop in elevation to be ten feet, the spot where the body was found to be distant enough from the path to lie unseen, and far enough from the water's edge to be untouched by even the highest tides and the wildest seas. He eyed the path again and in his mind's eye watched a young girl trip, roll down the hill, and . . .

"Running along in the dark," Jessie said. "Then you trip all of a sudden. Crack your head on the way down." She looked across the rocks to the sea, gave a shiver against a sudden breeze. "Knock yourself unconscious," she said, "and you'd freeze to death out here in less than two hours."

"Running?" Gilchrist said to her. "Why running?"

"Check the heels."

Gilchrist bent down, brushed snow off the woman's feet. Not running shoes but red high heels without the heels, evidenced by a square base where the fall had torn them free. Or had they been ripped off to make running possible? And bare legs, too, no tights, woollen or otherwise. Behind the left knee, the blue-black stain of a tattoo in the shape of a broken heart could have been mistaken for a bruise. He noticed, too, that the skirt was short, halfway up her thighs, and finished off with a red belt as shiny as plastic to match. And her white blouse, thin enough to raise goose bumps in the summer, did little to hide the stain of a larger tattoo that spread across her shoulders like a pair of wings. He pushed himself upright.

"What do you think?" he asked Jessie.

"How does the East Neuk shape up for prostitution?"

"It happens."

"I'll bet it does." She sniffed, rubbed a hand at her nose. "Is it always this cold?"

"An east wind," he said, then stared off along the Coastal Path. "What was she doing here?"

"Any brothels close by?"

"In St. Andrews?"

"I'd say that's where she was running to. Wouldn't you?"

Gilchrist tried to visualize the body falling off the path, rolling down the slope. But tumbling head over heels did not compute. Her body was lying in the direction she had run. He looked back along the path as it trailed the coast, back toward Kingsbarns. Although he had walked the Coastal Path several times when he first married, he had never traveled its full length—from Newport-on-Tay to North Queensferry on the Firth of Forth. He pulled his collar tight to his neck. Gusts of wind raised spindrift from the sea like mist. Christ, it was cold out here. Too cold to survive in a summer blouse and bare legs—

"You seen this?" Jessie said.

She had brushed snow and frost from the woman's arm, to expose a hand with fake fingernails, red to match her belt and shoes. One of her nails was missing, the middle finger of her left hand, probably broken off in the fall. As his gaze shifted to her wrists, a frisson chilled the length of his spine. He knew what it was but felt compelled to ask anyway.

"Some sort of bracelet?" he tried.

Jessie fiddled with the knotted rope, ran her fingers along its short length to a frayed end. Then she stared up at him. "I think you've got some serious shit going on up here."

5

Jessie was still taking statements from Clive and Jayne Watkins when the SOCOs arrived and spilled from their white Transit van like students at a beach outing. Gilchrist led them to the body, but the ground was too uneven, and the wind too strong, for them to erect their Incitent. They were in the process of roping off the path and slope when a black Range Rover eased in behind Gilchrist's Merc.

He watched the door open and a pair of green Hunter Wellington boots reach for the ground, followed by the suit-clad legs of the forensic pathologist, Dr. Rebecca Cooper, who had taken over after old Bert Mackie retired six months earlier.

She gave him a warm smile as she shook his hand. "We must stop meeting like this," she said. "Why don't you just ask me out?"

"I don't think Mr. Cooper would approve."

"Mr. Cooper wouldn't know," she said, then looked beyond him. "What have we got?"

Gilchrist explained his thoughts as he escorted her along the path, where she then faced the wind in that imperious manner of hers that he found attractive. Her blonde hair

whipped her shoulders, long and thick with a natural curl—
not tight like a perm but loose and soft. He had run his fingers
through it once, and he struggled to shift the image.

"Who's the new face?" she asked him.

"DS Janes. Transferred from Strathclyde."

"First name?"

"Jessie."

"Jessie Janes." She almost laughed. "Isn't she a bit young
for you?"

"Everyone's a bit young for me these days."

"That's what I like about you."

"That I'm becoming old?"

"That you're an older man." The bluest of eyes held his
for a tad too long, he thought. Then she turned and marched
down the slope.

Off to the side, Jessie closed her notebook, and Clive and
Jayne Watkins departed on their unfinished morning walk,
holding hands in mutual comfort, Skip nose to the ground,
tail brushing the grass with renewed vigor, it seemed.

"Anything of interest?" he said to Jessie.

She shook her head. "They live in Kingsbarns. Retired.
Moved up from England four years ago. Why do they do
that?"

"Do what?"

"Make fun of the Scots, then when it's time to retire, come
and live amongst us. We should put a gate at the border."
She raised her hand, ran it along an imaginary sign board. "No
English welcome. Stay out." She chuckled. "Or better still.
Exchange rate—two English pounds to one Scottish. That
would keep 'em out."

"Got something against the English?"

"World Cup, 1966. You're old enough to remember it."

"And you're not," he said. "Which proves a point."

"What point?"

"That children are influenced by what their parents tell them."

He thought it odd how her lips tightened—not just pursed as if silenced but white and bitter as if reining in her anger. Too late, he realized that he knew nothing of her upbringing, knew only what he had read from her police records, and from his call to DCI Peter "Dainty" Small from Strathclyde HQ—*Reliable, rock solid. Bit of a tongue on her, but so do most women. She won't let you down. I'd recommend her.*

"Looks like I stuck my foot in it," he said.

"Forget it."

"I would like to," he went on, "but if we're going to work together, I'll need to know more about you."

"Why?" she snapped at him. "So you won't stick your foot in it again?"

Her snap of anger surprised him. "Look—"

"I said forget it."

His escape route opened in the form of Dr. Cooper, who was making her way back up the slope. She reached out for a helping hand, and Gilchrist obliged by pulling her up and onto the path.

She offered her hand to Jessie. "Rebecca Cooper," she said. "Call me Becky."

Jessie reciprocated with a firm grip. "Jessica Janes. Call me Jessie."

If she caught the cynicism in Jessie's voice, Cooper smothered it cleanly. "I'd say our young woman's been dead for several days." Her gaze shifted from Gilchrist to Jessie, then back again. "Body temperature's close to zero. Skin's frozen solid from the ice and wind. She has a nasty cut on the right temple, but I won't be able to determine cause of death until she's on my table."

"Anything else?" Gilchrist tried.

Manicured fingernails pushed through a layer of windswept curls. She shook her head, as if to tease him. "It's interesting that she's not wearing any knickers."

"Why's that interesting?" Jessie said.

Gilchrist caught the challenge in her voice, but again, Cooper glided over it.

"It could give some lead to the cause of death," she said. "Any knickers close by?" She held Jessie's fierce gaze with a steady stare of her own. "Which might have been where she spent the last moments of her life." She faced Gilchrist, as if she'd had enough of Jessie. "Although I suspect she wasn't murdered."

"Why?"

"Her calves are covered in minor bruises and scratches, which could have been caused by walking through grass or bushes—"

"How about running?" Jessie said.

"Of course." Then back to Gilchrist. "Did you notice her heels are missing?"

"We did. Any thoughts?"

"I'd be searching the path for the missing heels." Back to Jessie, with a gentle smile. "She might have broken off the heels herself to walk, or run, and if you find them, it might give some indication as to where she came from."

"Thanks. I'll remember that." Jessie turned away and walked toward Gilchrist's car, her mobile already at her ear.

"Bit touchy," Cooper said.

"She's not a morning person."

Cooper smiled. "It's almost midday. Want to buy me lunch?"

Gilchrist grimaced at Jessie. "Could you handle both of us?"

"Spoilsport. I'll get back to you as soon as I've got something on our young woman," she said, then added, "And Mr. Cooper is flying to Italy for four days, leaving first thing tomorrow morning."

"Business trip?"

"Who knows. Maybe he's got a sultry Italian mistress waiting for him. And I might need company of my own." She tossed her hair, teasing him further, then mouthed a kiss and said, "Ciao."

Gilchrist watched her stride toward her Range Rover and give a curt nod and a tight smile to Jessie as she passed. Jessie stretched her lips in response.

Gilchrist refocused on the SOCOs, watched them sift and filter their way through the frosted grass. The temperature felt as if it had dropped another degree or two, and he tugged his collar tighter around his neck. The wind was now subdued in that sudden way that seems unique to Scotland, and the SOCOs were discussing erecting an Incitent. Overhead, the sky hung a painted gray, as still and lifeless as a frozen lake. Even the sea looked oddly calmer, its beaching waves puffing mist in tired gasps. Behind him, the rumble from the Range Rover's engine faded from his senses. He almost jumped at the sound of his name.

"Andy?"

He was struck by how pale Jessie looked.

"I know it's my first day on the job," she said, "but I need to get home. I'm sorry."

Without a word, he strode to his Merc, keys already in his hand, beeping the remote.

As he eased the car along the track, he called the station and organized a search of the Coastal Path. "We're looking for a pair of high heels, not the shoes, just the heels, likely red, but could be black. On the Coastal Path between Boarhills and Kingsbarns for starters. And have Jackie find out if anyone has been reported missing in the East Neuk over the last week. Girl, short blonde hair, average height, average weight, mid- to late-teens." He hung up and said to Jessie, "Can you talk?"

"Of course I can talk. I'm talking now. Right?" She glared at the passing fields, white from patches of snow and hoarfrost, and waited several beats before saying, "I'm sorry, I don't mean it, it's just . . ." She shook her head.

Gilchrist held the wheel in a tight grip in the pretense of negotiating a bump in the track. "I can't help if I don't know what the problem is."

"You don't want to know," she said. "Believe me."

"Try me."

She faced the window again, stared outside long enough to make him think she was not going to share her troubles with him. Then she said, "I suppose it's bound to come out sooner or later."

He thought silence his best option.

But still she waited until they were beyond Boarhills and back on the A917 before she said, "It's my mother. She's here." She shook her head, dabbed a thumb into the corner of an eye. "One day in St. Andrews and she's already found me."

"Found you?"

"That's one of the other reasons I had to leave Glasgow."

"*Had* to leave?"

But Jessie seemed not to have heard. "She's a fucking bitch of a woman. I swear, if she ever tells Robert"—the anger in her voice left Gilchrist in no doubt that whatever she was about to swear to would happen—"I'll have her. I'll tear her heart out with my bare hands. I'll do time for her. I promise you that. With maximum fucking pleasure."

"So you don't like her, is what you're telling me."

Jessie glared at him, stunned for a moment, as if he had slapped her.

Then she chuckled and said, "I think I'm going to like working with you."

6

Gilchrist parked curbside at Forgan Place.

A woman in her sixties, with silver hair in a wild bun fraying at the edges, looked as if she was trying to reason with a uniformed policeman—PC Grant McLay—by the front door, her face flushed from cold or anger, or maybe a lifetime's worth of alcohol.

"Wait here," Jessie said and rushed from the car.

Gilchrist watched Jessie push herself in front of the policeman and flash her warrant card. Then she grabbed the woman by the arm and jerked her onto the lawn. Not good. Not good at all. Gilchrist opened the car door, stepped into the midday chill.

"Here," the woman cried. "You're hurting my arm."

"I'll hurt a lot more than your arm, you drunken old slut."

"As if you've never had a drink, or done a turn for—"

"Shut it." Jessie tugged her farther onto the lawn. "What're you doing here?"

"I'm here to see my grandson."

"You're violating the non-harassment order, you stupid old cow. You're not allowed within fifty yards of him. I could have you jailed."

"It only works in Strathclyde." The woman fumbled in her handbag. "We're now in Fife." She removed a single sheet of paper and waved it at PC McLay, then at Gilchrist. "See? It disnae work here." Then back to Jessie. "I want to talk to my grandson."

"About what?"

She seemed confused for a moment, as if trying to find the trick in the question, then recovered with, "About what grandmothers talk to their grandchildren about."

"Which is?"

"That's my business."

"I'm his mother, and I'm not going—"

"And I'm his grandmother, and I have—"

"Listen to me, you drunken old slag—"

"Who're you calling a slag? You watch your tongue, you heathen bitch—"

Jessie slapped her then, a quick swipe with the right hand that left her looking every bit as stunned as her mother.

Then Jessie's mother turned to Gilchrist. "Did you see that? That's assault, so it is."

"I'll take care of this," Gilchrist said to PC McLay and stepped onto the lawn. "Get in the car," he said to Jessie.

Without a word, Jessie did as she was ordered.

"What's your name?" Gilchrist asked.

"Are you gonnie charge her with assault? She cannae go running around hitting—"

"Name?"

She patted her bun, sniffed at the air. "Jeannie Janes."

"And you are Detective Sergeant Janes's mother?"

"Oh, Detective Sergeant. Listen to that." Then she scowled at him. "Where's your notebook? Shouldn't you be taking down notes?"

"You're not listening to me." He repeated the question.

"I am. Which makes me Robert's grandmother. And I have a right to see my own—"

"Let me see the order."

She handed it to him and watched him in silence. She slid her gaze to the Merc and smirked at Jessie in the front seat.

"Why was this granted?" Gilchrist asked.

She poked a finger at the order. "See what it says? It only works in Strathclyde."

"You're still not listening to me, Mrs. Janes. I need you to listen to me, and I need you to answer my questions. I could take you down to the station if you'd like, let you phone for a solicitor of your choosing. But that takes time and costs money. So why don't we just have a friendly chat on the front lawn like two sensible adults?"

She narrowed her eyes, and some hidden knowledge shifted behind them. "I might have known it," she said. "She's screwing you, isn't she? No sooner does she move up here, than she's fucking putting it about, the wee tramp."

"Let's try this for the last time," Gilchrist said.

"Did she charge you for it? Eh? Fucking trollop. Look at her, sitting there in that flashy car, tits all bunched up like she's selling it. Fucking bitch is what she is."

Gilchrist turned to PC McLay, signaled him over.

"Lift her," he said to him.

"What? Wait a minute. What for? You cannae just come prancing along—"

"Disturbing the peace," he said.

As he turned to walk back to his Merc, he noticed movement at one of the upper windows and caught Robert's eye for a fleeting moment before the boy's face slid from view.

*

"Would you like me to hand in my notice?" Jessie said.

"That's up to you," Gilchrist said. "You did strike her. I can't deny that."

"I was hoping you missed that."

"PC McLay and half the street saw it."

She buried her head in her hands. "What have I done to deserve a mother like that?"

"She's lifted," Gilchrist said. "Want me to follow through with the charges?"

Jessie shook her head. "I just want her to stay away from Robert. She's a bad influence."

"You'll need to do better than that."

"I can't tell you," she said. "Please understand, Andy. It's deeply personal."

Gilchrist tried to decipher her look, then said, "Tell me you're clean."

She glared at him, anger furling her brow. "What d'you mean *clean*?"

"That your reasons for keeping your mother away from your son are aboveboard."

She snorted. "They're *well* aboveboard. They're so far aboveboard, they're up here," she said, her knuckles rapping the cabin roof.

"In that case, you should apply to have the non-harassment order amended to include Fife. You don't have to press charges, just have the incident noted."

"That'll take ages."

"I'll talk to Clive. He owes me one. Meanwhile, I'll have one of our boys in blue keep your mother busy for an hour or so. After that, we'll have to charge her, or let her go."

Jessie nodded. "Let her go. I need to talk to Angie when she gets back."

"Robert's at home by himself?"

"Angie's had to step out to the doctor. But Robert's mature for his age, and I haven't had time to arrange for tutors—"

"That's not what I meant," Gilchrist said. "Robert could have let his grandmother in."

She shook her head. "He doesn't know who she is."

"He doesn't know his own grandmother?"

"That's what I said. And besides, he wouldn't have seen her at the door. He spends most of his time on his computer, writing. He wants to be a comedy writer. He's writing short sketches and jokes to begin with—"

"I hope he didn't write the joke about the whisky and the sheep."

Jessie chuckled. "It's got potential, that has. Just needs work. That's what Robert told me last night. Which is why I do the occasional stand-up spot at the Stand. Tuesday nights are for beginners. It's not for me. It's for Robert. To let him check out his jokes."

Gilchrist said, "He seems bright."

"As smart as they come." Her lips pursed, and she brushed a hand across her face. "If he could hear he could be anything he wants."

"Isn't he already doing what he wants? Being a writer?"

"His dream is to be a stand-up comedian," she said. "But how can he, when he can't speak properly, or can't pronounce his words like any normal person? The audience would roast him alive."

"Speech therapy?" Gilchrist tried.

"Where do you think my money goes?" she snapped. "I could have bought the bloody clinics outright with what I've spent on therapy." Her voice softened. "That's what's hard," she said. "Robert's got nothing to compare the sounds to. He's been deaf since birth."

"Which in a strange kind of way is good."

"*Good?* How would you like to live your life in total silence?" she said. "What kind of a prison sentence is that?" Then she softened again. "He's just a wee boy trapped in his own silent world. He doesn't know what a guitar sounds like, or a piano, or what the Old Firm crowd's like when a goal's scored. He's never even heard me tell him I love him."

Gilchrist let several seconds pass. "What I meant," he said, and hoped she would not see that he was still rooting around for answers, "was that he can't hear whatever it is you don't want his grandmother to tell him."

"Tell him?"

"You swore you would have her if she *tells* Robert, I think were your words."

"You don't miss a trick, do you?"

"Neither do you."

She stared out the windscreen, then shifted her gaze to the front door. "He lip-reads," she said. "He doesn't need to hear her."

"What about mail? She could write to him. Or text him."

"She can hardly speak English, let alone write it. And I'll be buggered if I'll give her his phone number."

"Can she speak Huttian?"

Jessie chuckled. "Now there's an idea. Turn Jabba loose on her." Her face darkened once more. "That's another one who can't take no for an answer." Then she grabbed the door handle. "Let me do a quick check on Robert," she said and, without waiting for an answer, slipped into the cold air.

Gilchrist waited until she stepped inside before he called. Thirty seconds later he was through to Dainty. "What can you give me on a woman by the name of Jeannie Janes?"

Dainty said, "I was wondering how long it would take you to call."

7

Jessie reappeared at the front door, which brought Dainty's call to an end with the promise to e-mail Gilchrist a copy of what he had on Jeannie Janes. Jessie hustled into the Merc, grinning as if she had just won the lottery.

"That went well by the looks of things," he said.

"He's a wee darling. I just love him to bits." She waved at the window as Gilchrist turned left into Shoolbraids.

"So he didn't talk to his grandmother?"

Jessie winced, then turned her attention to her mobile.

Five minutes later, Gilchrist parked outside the station in North Street.

"I'd like you to meet Jackie," he said, and pushed through the door. "Do you fancy a cuppa first? Lipton's. Best I can do for you."

Jessie blew into her hands. "As long as it's hot, it could be cat's piss for all I care."

"Or sheep's?"

"Bugger off."

Jessie's mother was in interview room 1, with PC McLay having the unenviable task of questioning her. Gilchrist stuck his head in, ignored the splutter of curses, and nodded to McLay that he needed to talk to him.

In the hallway, Gilchrist said, "We won't be pressing charges. Send her on her way," then added, "Did she drive up from Glasgow?"

"Came by bus. Said she used her bus pass."

"Lying bitch."

Gilchrist and McLay turned to Jessie.

"You have to be sixty to get one of these," Jessie explained. "She was born in '58. You do the sums."

"Can you show me the bus pass?" Gilchrist asked McLay.

"I had a look through her handbag when she was booked in, but I couldn't find it," McLay said. "She said she must have lost it."

Gilchrist glanced at Jessie, then said, "Give me a minute."

When he entered the interview room, Jeannie patted her bun and snarled a smile. "Nice eyes," she said. "And no wedding band. You no married?"

"You have a bus pass," Gilchrist said.

"And I like the jacket. You no a bit upmarket for that piece of shite out there?"

"Let me see your bus pass," he pressed.

"Think I musta lost it."

Gilchrist leaned closer. "When you find it, use it to return to Glasgow. One of our officers will arrange a lift for you to the bus station."

"I'm no ready to go home."

"There you go again. You're not listening."

"And neither are you. She's filled your ears with shite. That non-harassment order disnae work up here. I'm sick and tired of trying to tell youse lot—"

"You're not going to be charged with breach of the peace."

"Aye, that wee bitch knows better than to try that."

"We could charge you with fraud instead."

She stilled for a moment, her eyes flickering with uncertainty, then said, "You're fucking at it."

Gilchrist held out his hand. "Bus pass."

Her face darkened. "I've no got one."

"I thought you came up on the bus."

"Aye, but I paid my way."

"I can easily check that out."

Her lips pursed into a tight line.

Gilchrist smiled. "So, we have an agreement then? You buy a ticket to Glasgow, and we don't charge you with fraud." He waited for a reluctant nod before pushing to his feet. "I'll have someone drop you off at the bus station."

In the hallway, he explained to McLay, then nodded for Jessie to follow. He led her to a room at the rear of the station. A wooden desk choked the space. A pair of crutches rested against the wall to the side. A wide-screen monitor hid a small woman with a freckled face and a head of hair as thick and dark as rusted wool. The screen reflected its image on her dark-rimmed glasses. She looked up and smiled at Gilchrist as they entered.

"How are you keeping, Jackie?"

She opened her mouth to speak, then seemed locked into silence.

Gilchrist introduced Jessie, then said, "This is Jackie Canning, Fife Constabulary's most brilliant researcher."

Jackie mouthed a response like a dying fish. Jessie smiled and nodded.

"If it's been printed, written, or exists anywhere on the planet," Gilchrist pressed on, "Jackie will find it. Which is why we're here."

Jackie looked at him, waiting for her command.

"I'll have Nance give you photos of a woman we found on the Coastal Path earlier this morning. See if you can match her to any missing persons. You may want to start searching for anyone who's been reported missing in the last six months."

Jackie eyed the screen, her fingers flitting over the keyboard as he spoke.

"Try limiting the ages to between, say, thirteen and eighteen. If that's too wide, narrow it down to Scotland only. And if you could band them together in age groups and region, that would be great. Let me know if you get a match. OK?"

With her eyes to the screen, Jackie nodded.

In the corridor, Jessie said, "What's with the crutches."

"Spina bifida," Gilchrist said. "But her mobility's amazing. She throws herself around on those things like they're another pair of legs. But she suffers from cerebral palsy, too, and it's her speech that floors her every time. Sometimes her stutter's so bad she has to revert to sign language."

Jessie glared at him, as if stung.

In his office, he slid open a desk drawer and removed a couple of tea bags. "Good to keep your own," he said. "But don't tell anyone where they are, or they'll start disappearing."

"You've just told me," Jessie said.

"But you're the only one, so I'll know who to kill."

In the kitchen, he boiled the kettle. One tea bag each and mugs in hand, he took Jessie to meet DS Nancy Wilson. He introduced Jessie as DS Jessica Janes, who held out her hand and said, "But I answer to Jessie."

Nance shook Jessie's hand. "Call me Nance," she said. "Sorry I never got a chance to talk to you earlier, but Andy's a bit of a tough taskmaster."

"And he also likes his biscuits," Gilchrist said.

Nance held out her hands, palms up. "Sorry. All gone."

"Don't tell me it's my turn."

"It's your turn."

"Damn." He sipped his tea. "Any luck tracking down Craig Farmer?"

"Not yet."

"It's interesting that he denied knowing Donnelly, whereas Donnelly's prepared to swear on the Bible that they're the best of mates."

"As if that would mean anything," Nance said.

"You think he's lying?"

"Well it's clear Farmer is. Fake B and B, fake license, false name—"

"Am I missing something?" Jessie asked.

Gilchrist brought Jessie up to speed and said, "Don't know what it all means, but it would be good to talk to him."

Jessie said, "Have you checked out Donnelly's mobile?"

"Strictly speaking, we're not allowed to access it," Nance said.

"And unstrictly?"

Nance smiled at her but said nothing.

Gilchrist instructed Nance to get facials of the Coastal Path girl to Jackie, then spent the next fifteen minutes familiarizing Jessie with the station layout.

"You won't get lost," he said, pushing through the exit. He pulled up his collar and strode to his Merc. "You think it'll snow?" he asked her.

"You got a bet on for a white Christmas or something?"

"I'm not a betting man," he said. "But if the snow sticks, it'll make finding these heels more difficult."

*

PC Mhairi McBride found the heels before 3:00 PM, fifteen minutes before Gilchrist was preparing to call off the search because of poor light. They lay in long grass over a stone dyke that ran the length of Back Stile, within three feet of each other, two red exclamation marks as plain as day between patches of snow, as if they had been placed there.

Gilchrist faced the wind. Back Stile ran to the seafront, less than two hundred yards from where they stood, where it opened to a gravel car park from which the Coastal Path ran off either side. In the distance behind him, the village of Kingsbarns nestled in midwinter silence, lights glowing from windows, beckoning him to the warmth within.

"Anything planned for this evening, Mhairi?"

"Only *EastEnders* and *Corrie*. But I've got them set for recording. What would you like me to do, sir?"

"Contact the local estate agents. Find out which houses are rented. The longer the term, the better," he said. "Call as soon as you find anything."

She beamed as she pulled out her mobile. "Angus works with Patterson and McLeod. I'll have him jump-start it for me."

When Mhairi drove off, Gilchrist faced Jessie. "In the meantime?" he asked her.

"A good start would be the Watkins," she said, removing her notebook and flipping through the pages. "Can't be too difficult to find them in a one-horse town like this."

It took them less than ten minutes.

Clive and Jayne Watkins lived in an end cottage with a crowstepped gable end and a single chimney from which trailed wisps of gray smoke. The grass looked neat and tidy, the garden black and bare, as if all the plants had been uplifted for the winter.

Gilchrist rapped the brass knocker.

Jayne Watkins welcomed them in with a surprised smile, while Skip pushed past Gilchrist's legs and onto the gravel path to take advantage of an unscheduled airing.

The small living room was overstuffed with dark furniture, its walls brightened with abstract paintings of seascapes and fishing boats, which seemed to cover every vertical square inch. Jayne invited them to sit and offered them tea.

"All tea-ed out," Gilchrist said. "And I'd rather stand. Is Mr. Watkins around?"

"He's in the spare bedroom," she said. "I'll fetch him."

Gilchrist heated his hands by a weak fire smothered black by a pair of briquettes.

A minute later, Clive came through, wearing paint-stained clothes Gilchrist could only describe as rags. He held up palms that could have doubled for palettes. "I won't shake hands, unless you want paint all over you," he said, then explained his attire with, "Hobby. Oils can be expensive. So we've got to watch the pennies. Anyway, I'm sure you've not come here to ask about my paintings."

Outside, the winter dusk was blotting out the walled garden. On a dark night, with the moon sheltered by clouds, a young woman in high heels could walk past without being seen. Gilchrist turned his back to the window. "The young woman you found on the Coastal Path might have lived in this area."

Jayne shook her head. "I'm sure I would have heard if someone had gone missing."

"Do you know everyone who lives around here?"

"Not really, I suppose. We bump into people from time to time. Although most tend to keep to themselves, I'm sure we would have heard something."

When Gilchrist had been growing up, it seemed that every-one knew their neighbors, and popped in and out of houses that were never locked from one year to the next. Nowadays, they would walk past a man dying in the street rather than help. Changed days indeed.

"How long have you lived here?" he asked.

"Coming up on five years," Clive said.

"You said you hadn't taken Skip along the Coastal Path since November."

"That's right."

"Where did you take him instead?"

"Sometimes through the golf course. Got to have Skip on a leash to do that, of course. But mostly we'd take him straight to the beach, let him wade in and out of the sea. Labradors love the water."

"And you would walk to the sea? Not drive, take the car?"

"No. Walk."

"Along the road?"

"Yes."

"Would you ever step over the wall and walk to the sea that way?"

Clive shook his head. "We wouldn't. But sometimes Skip would. Once he'd got his nose buried in the grass it would be the devil of a job to bring him to heel."

Gilchrist wondered if Skip had caught scent of the dis-carded heels and followed it off the Coastal Path to the wom-an's body. Or maybe it was more likely that simple chance had caused Skip to sniff his way across it.

"Do you ever come across other people walking their dogs?" Jessie asked.

"From time to time."

"Know any of them?"

"Those who live around here, yes. Others on nodding terms only."

"Visitors, you mean?"

"Yes. But you don't see too many in the winter. It's too cold."

"Tell me about it." Jessie shivered, as if to prove her point.

Gilchrist said, "Are any houses up for rent?"

"One or two," Clive said, and shook his head.

"Don't pay much attention to any of that," Jayne added.

"How about foreigners?" Jessie again. "As in non-English speakers."

"You see the occasional busload of—"

"No, I mean living in Kingsbarns."

Jayne frowned. "Now you mention it, I did see a man and a woman in the garden of one of the cottages on Seagate. He was darker skinned. Not black. More Indian looking. But not Indian, if you get my meaning."

Gilchrist nodded. "Go on."

"And he seemed angry. He had his hand on the woman's arm. I wasn't really paying attention. I was driving back from the shops. But I thought he was a bit rough."

"Needing a shave? Badly dressed?"

"No. Rough with the woman. The way he handled her."

"Would you recognize him again?"

Her jowls shuddered. "I wouldn't think so."

"So what did you do? After you saw them?"

"Nothing. I thought it was none of my business. Besides, it was just a glance."

"Do you remember which house?" Gilchrist asked.

"I don't know the address. But I can show you."

"Please."

"Let me get my coat, then. It's only a five-minute walk."

But it took closer to ten minutes to find the place by the time they doubled back along a path that Jayne confused with some other walkway. Night had fallen, and the cottage stood in darkness. Either side of it, other homes sat in their own hedged gardens, as if the owners liked the idea of having neighbors, as long as they did not have to see them.

"We'll take it from here," Gilchrist said to Jayne. "DS Janes can escort you home."

"Not at all. I can find my own way back. When you're finished," she said, "why don't you come back for a cup of tea to heat you up? It's shivering out here."

"Thank you," said Gilchrist, as his mobile went off.

Mhairi's name came up on the screen.

"Got one that fits the bill," Mhairi said without introduction. "Two year's rent. Three-bedroom cottage. And it was Angus who set it up in August. Said the tenant didn't want to meet, but he insisted. He thought he was a foreign student on some postgraduate course."

The word *foreign* had Gilchrist eyeing the cottage. "Address?" he asked, and noted the number on the wall by the door as she told him. "Could Angus identify the tenant?"

"I'll ask him."

"Ask him right now," Gilchrist said. "We're at the front door."

8

The cottage appeared abandoned.

The front door was closed, but it opened when Gilchrist twisted the handle, a signal for him to slip on a pair of latex gloves. Jessie did likewise. He pushed the door wide, rubbed his hand over the wall, found the light switch, flicked it on.

Nothing.

He leaned inside, shouted into the darkness, "Hello? Anyone?"

"What's that smell?" Jessie said.

Gilchrist caught the staleness on his tongue. "Something's off."

"I don't like this, Andy. Let me get backup."

Gilchrist moved deeper into the hallway.

The house felt cold. Well, it would be if the electricity was turned off.

But the air also possessed a hint of movement in it, as if . . .

From somewhere ahead and off to his right, he thought he heard the steady stream of water running. Burst pipe? It had been cold enough. Behind him, the sibilant hiss of Jessie's voice as she spoke into her mobile disturbed the silence. And

Jessie had been right. He now caught a guff of foul air and lifted his hand to cover his nose and mouth.

He stepped off the hallway and into the blackness of the kitchen, the soles of his feet pulling on something spilled on the floor. By the dimmed silhouette of the kitchen window he caught the dull silver flash of water running from the tap, spilling into the sink. By the corner of the window a curtain fluttered, and a cold wind blew in through a broken pane.

He reached forward, turned off the tap.

The kitchen fell into silence.

He stood still, cocked his head in the darkness, strained to catch any sounds, no longer within earshot of Jessie. His eyes were developing their night vision, and shape by shape the kitchen came into view—the sink unit, overhead cabinets, dark blots for pictures on walls, a table, chairs, and—

His blood chilled. His breath locked.

He gripped the sink unit to steady himself, his eyes straining at the shape on—

A lock clicked.

The door burst open.

He dropped to the floor.

A light flickered, flashed at his eyes.

"Andy?" Jessie stepped across the threshold. "You all right?"

"Bloody hell," Gilchrist snarled, pulling himself upright. "You scared the . . ." But his voice trailed off as the light from Jessie's mobile shivered around the room and settled on a body slumped on the kitchen table.

"Fuck sake," Jessie said. "I thought I was moving up to Fife for a life of handing out speeding tickets. That's two, and we're not even through the first day yet."

Gilchrist shuffled to the kitchen table and almost stumbled.

He looked down at his feet. "Make that three," he said.

They found the fuse box in a cupboard off the hall, under the attic staircase, and switched on the lights to a scene straight from hell.

The knees of Gilchrist's jeans were stained with days' old blood that spread across the kitchen floor, semi-congealed, thick and dark as treacle.

Both victims were young women, about the same age as the woman off the Coastal Path, as best Gilchrist could tell. And both appeared to have been killed by multiple stab wounds to the chest and neck.

The woman on the floor lay supine, her eyes half-closed, her blouse as bloodied as a butcher's apron. Her long blonde hair lay wrapped around her neck like a blood-soaked rag. Through the mess, Gilchrist counted eight stab wounds. Cooper would likely find more when the body was stripped of clothing that looked familiar—white blouse, short black skirt, burgundy high heels to match a leather belt, and bare legs sufficiently parted to confirm no knickers. Tattoos around both ankles in the shape of barbed wire had him frowning for an explanation, and failing. But they might help confirm identification.

The woman slumped against the table appeared to have fewer wounds, but with her body pressed to the table, Gilchrist was not sure. She was dressed as if ready for bed, and other than the flimsiest of negligees was naked.

"You seen this?" Jessie said to him.

Gilchrist bent closer to the body on the floor.

Jessie traced the scuff marks on the skin. "Rope burns," she said, then pointed to four raised welts on the inner arm, close to the elbow. One looked fresher than the others, still glistening with a blister. "And how about these, too?"

"Cigarette burns?"

"Human ashtray."

Gilchrist returned to the dead woman by the table, lifted her left arm from her side. Rigor mortis had come and gone, so the body was at least twenty-four hours old. "No rope burns or stub marks," he said, "but plenty of needle wounds." He walked around the back of the chair, did the same with her right arm—no burn marks—then let it dangle once more by her side. He cocked his head to the sound of approaching sirens.

"Keystone Kops are on their way," Jessie said.

Gilchrist opened the back door, reveled in the icy freshness of lungfuls of cold air. The smell of blood coated his tongue. He coughed up, spat onto the back lawn. From the front of the cottage, he heard the squealing of tires. Then behind him, the heavy trundle of footsteps running along the hall.

Nance burst into the kitchen, followed by a uniformed constable.

She stopped when she saw the mess.

She glared at Jessie, then Gilchrist. "Anybody hurt?" she demanded.

Jessie pulled herself to her feet, looking short and flabby next to Nance's lithe figure. "Could've been sliced and diced by the time you got here."

"Did you call it in?" Nance said.

"I did."

"Next time don't say it's an emergency when it isn't."

"Didn't know it wasn't when I called."

"It looks friendly enough."

"We haven't checked upstairs yet," Jessie said.

Without taking her eyes from Jessie, Nance turned her head to the PC behind her and said, "Check it out."

Jessie snorted.

Nance stepped forward, eyes to the floor, making sure she did not step in any blood. She leaned down for a closer look and eased back a clotted strand of bloodied hair. Then she gasped and pushed herself upright. "Ah, fuck. She's been decapitated."

Gilchrist frowned. "And her head replaced?"

"Why would he do that?"

"Christmas present?" Jessie said.

Gilchrist and Nance stared at her.

"Surprise surprise, is what I mean. But it also explains the mess." Jessie stared at the floor as if to emphasize her point. "All ten pints by the looks of things," she said, then crouched down for a closer inspection.

Gilchrist turned away. Cooper would send him the details. Overhead, the sound of creaking floorboards gave an indication of the PC's progress. Gilchrist scuffed his shoes on a rug, clearing the tackiness from his soles, then left the kitchen.

Although tight, the attic had been built out to create a bedroom of sloped ceilings low enough to force Gilchrist to duck. The air was thick enough to taste—a stale mixture of body odor and urine, with a fecal undertone. A plain quilt, nailed to the floor, ceiling, and walls of a bay window, was edged with heavy binding tape, as good as any blackout curtain. Four single mattresses, stripped of sheets and stained with urine and bloodied spots, lined a wooden floor as bare as an army barracks. Crushed bedsheets that had not seen the inside of a washing machine for weeks, maybe months, lay crumpled in the far corner.

The young constable—Gilchrist now recognized PC Dan Morton—was on his knees between the first two mattresses. He looked up as Gilchrist approached. "Look at this, sir."

Screwed into the floorboards was a metal ring, heavy and thick enough to moor a fair-sized yacht in Crail harbor. A frayed rope end was knotted around it. Despite its apparent sturdiness, PC Morton gripped the ring and twisted it against its base, managing to ease it from the floorboards by a quarter of an inch or so to reveal a rough-edged rim.

Gilchrist brushed his fingers on the floor beside the ring, collected frayed pieces of rope fiber, and came to see that someone—the Coastal Path woman?—had rubbed her way free from this bed. He pushed to his feet, almost bumped his head on the ceiling. Between the other two mattresses, an identical ring was screwed into the floor. He kneeled down, gave it a tug, but it was fastened to the floorboards as securely as a metal-to-metal weld. He eyed the mess, already computing the obvious.

Four mattresses. Three bodies. One missing?

"For crying out loud, can someone open the window?" Jessie stood framed in the doorway. "This place smells like a hooker's jockstrap."

Morton looked at her as if she had spoken in Chinese.

Jessie stepped into the attic room. "Rugby, son. I'm sure you've heard of it."

From downstairs, Gilchrist heard the subdued shuffle of feet.

The SOCOs had arrived.

"What've you found?" Jessie asked him.

"This." He showed her the metal ring.

She fingered it, her touch light, as if considering a piece of jewelry. Then she stood up, and even as short as she was, that close to the wall she had to duck her head. "Is there another one of these between the other two mattresses?" she asked.

"There is," said Gilchrist. "Why?"

Jessie stared off to some spot over Gilchrist's shoulder, then came back to him with a burning look. "Two years ago we infiltrated a trafficking gang run by the Krukov twins, a pair of Russian gangsters. As big as the Klitschko brothers, they were, only they didn't believe in the Queensbury rules. Whatever they wanted, they took. And whoever stood in their way, they killed."

"Infiltrated?"

She nodded. "One of our team worked undercover for almost a year, gave us names, addresses, how many women they were bringing in, when, and where from, the works. We had everything set up to take them down, and enough evidence to lock them in Barlinnie and throw away the key. But the day before we were planning to move in, our man turned up in the Clyde with his head missing and his tongue crammed into his arsehole. Talk about hitting the fan. We went ahead and raided the place, forty-four of us, everyone ready to gut the brothers from their balls to their throats, except . . ."

Gilchrist waited while she stared at the metal ring on the floor.

". . . he beat us to it."

"He?"

"Kumar. That's all we know about him. Could be his first name or his last, no one really knows for sure. Could even be a nickname."

"Beat you to it . . . ?" Gilchrist asked.

"The brothers," she said. "They owned a farm in Duntocher, just west of Glasgow, and kept the women chained up in a

barn which used to house cattle over the winter." She nodded to the metal ring. "These rings are for shackling cows to
the walls."

Gilchrist felt his gaze being pulled to the ring on the floor,
the knotted end of rope still looped around it. Not yachts,
he thought. But cows.

And now girls. Shackled like animals.

"The barn was used as a kind of holding area," Jessie continued, "while photos were taken, documents forged, passports,
driving licenses, fake addresses, even fake electricity and phone
bills were produced. And all of it was added to the already
exorbitant costs of setting them up in a new country. Illegal
aliens, no longer illegal, who had to spend the next five years
on their backs with their legs behind their ears before they
had any chance of getting back to square one.

"Brutal, the Krukovs were. When the girls first arrived,
they were locked in the barn. No heating, no running water,
just cheap, nasty mattresses like these, spread on the concrete
floor. The week before the raid we thought we were about to
land the mother lode. But when we broke in, the girls were
gone and the barn deserted, except for the Krukov brothers,
lying on their backs, stark naked, with their heads sitting on
their laps, sucking their cocks."

Gilchrist let out a rush of air. "Kumar killed them?"

"It's his calling card, his modus operandi. Head on lap.
Cock in mouth. Tongue in arse. That sort of thing. The guy's
a freak and a half."

"But you don't know for sure—"

"Oh we know it's him," she said. "He recorded the behead-
ings, then sent the disc as a present. Our man, Gordie, and
the brothers getting their heads cut off. But you never see
his face. You only hear his voice, telling us he's teaching us

a lesson." Her lips pressed together in a white line as tight as a scar. "I learned a lesson, all right," she said. "I learned never to delay. I learned to just go in with guns blazing and worry about the consequences later."

"Could get you in trouble," Gilchrist offered.

"Could've saved Gordie's life," she said, and moved to the door.

Silent, Gilchrist followed.

At the doorway, she stopped and faced him. "But d'you know what I couldn't work out?" she asked, her eyes dancing as if on fire. "The metal rings," she said. "When we broke into the barn six of them had been removed from the walls. I always wondered why." She nodded to the floor.

"I'd say that's two of them right there."

9

Jessie did not return home until after 10:15 that night. Angie was still awake but looked like she was on her second bottle, maybe even her third. She took a sip from a champagne flute and said, "Long first day?"

Jessie kicked off her shoes, slumped into the sofa. She shook her head when Angie held the bottle out to her. "I'm buggered," she said. "How was Robert?"

"No trouble at all. In his bedroom. On his computer. It seems to be all kids do these days. All day long—"

"And night," Jessie chipped in.

"But he's been fed and watered. Pizza and chips. Hope you don't mind."

"Why would I mind?"

"Not exactly proper food, is it? But I was knackered. Left you some pizza. Chips got scoffed, I'm afraid."

"I'll have a slice for breakfast."

Angie took another sip. "So how was your first day at the office?"

"You don't want to know."

"No, really, I do. Tell me."

"Three bodies. Two murdered, one frozen to death."

Angie guffawed. "I can see a joke coming out of this."

"No joke."

"You serious?"

"As I said, you don't want to know."

"Jesus, Jessie. I don't know how you can do that job of yours."

"Well, I won't be doing it for much longer if Robert can get my comedy routine up to snuff."

"How's that coming along?"

Jessie snorted, then shook her head at the reality of it. "More or less shite."

Angie chuckled. "Seriously."

"I am being serious. I don't think I'm any bloody use at it. But I'm really doing it for Robert. Trying out his jokes for him." She felt a smile tug her lips at the thought of Robert having his hearing fixed and being able to follow his dream. Her smile stretched to a yawn, and she said, "I'll stick my head in and see Robert before I hit the hay."

"Want me to waken you in the morning?"

"Don't bother. I'll be up before you. Andy wants me in at 7:00."

"Andy?"

"Fife Constabulary's Detective Chief Inspector Andrew James Gilchrist of St. Andrews Crime Management Division."

"At 7:00 in the morning? The slave driver. You sure he's not going to try you out for an early morning knee-trembler?"

"Once he sees my dog's balls for eyes," Jessie said, "he'll be trembling all right."

"What's he like? Could you fancy him?"

"Not half. He's a looker, even for his age. But I'm not his type. Dr. Rebecca look-at-me-posing-like-a-haddy-in-my-green-wellies Cooper call-me-Becky," Jessie chimed, "is more his type. He doesn't have the time of day for someone like me."

Angie lifted her fluted glass. "Away with you. A bit of eye shadow, some lipstick, and those sultry eyes of yours'll have him eating out of your hand, or anywhere else you'd like."

"Give up, Angie."

"That's what I do."

Jessie looked at her, waiting for the punch line. But Angie returned her look with an impish grin. "That's what you do?" Jessie said.

Angie nodded. "Want some details?"

"Got any more of that champoo then?"

Angie pushed herself to her feet, stuttered for a moment as if working out whether to sit or stand, then said, "It's not real champoo, just Cava."

"Perfect."

Jessie's morning arrived with a start and a snorted grunt.

She fumbled for the light switch, scrunched her eyes from a burst of brightness, then picked up her mobile. She peered at it through eyes that hurt—6:25. Bloody hell. How can you sleep through an alarm?

She slapped her feet to the floor and staggered to the bathroom.

The mirror almost gave her a fright, but she ran her fingers through her hair, working out if she could go another day without washing it. This late, she had two choices—go to the station with straw hair, or have a shower with no time to blow dry, and go with rattails.

Rattails won, and ten minutes later she was toweling herself down.

She pulled on black denim jeans, the ones with the elastic waist, tucked her blouse and her stomach in, zipped up, and turned sideways. Not as bad as in the nude. She exhaled, slid her feet into black suede kitten heels, hoped it wasn't raining—a peek out the curtains to reveal a morning as black as midnight, so was none the wiser—then pulled on her gray turtleneck cashmere sweater she bought for a fiver. Well, it felt like cashmere. A dab of lipstick, a smudged finger stroke of kohl pencil, and DS Jessie Janes was good to go.

Except she felt like shit warmed up.

She stuck her head into Robert's room—sound asleep—and couldn't resist creeping in and giving him a kiss on his cheek. His skin felt damp and clammy, and she worried that he might be developing a cold. She pushed her fingers through his hair, with a whispered promise to text him later.

She was only eleven minutes late when she reached the station, and Gilchrist was already briefing his team. She expected him to say something like *Good of you to turn up this afternoon, DS Janes*, the way Lachie always did, but Gilchrist gave her a smile and a nod without missing a beat.

". . . and Mhairi, bring Angus in and sit him down and go through the pile, see if he can ID our man. He's our best shot. We need him to make that ID." He searched the faces, found who he was looking for, and referred to his notes. "Right, Baxter, you take McIver, Wilkes, and Rennie and do house-to-house through Kingsbarns. Somebody's seen something, heard something, thought something. They must have. And if you come up empty-handed, spread out. Focus on hotels, restaurants, shops, anywhere our man might have shown his face. He has to eat, so he has to shop, and he'll likely drink alcohol, regardless of his denomination. Nance is in charge of putting names to the faces and fingerprints. AFIS for starters."

"If they've got no criminal records, sir, AFIS wouldn't have their fingerprints registered, would it?"

"We have to start somewhere, Jo. And who knows, we might get lucky." He scanned the room. "Any other questions?" A pause, then, "Good. Debriefing's back here at 6:00." He turned and walked past Jessie. "Let's go," he said to her.

Outside, dawn was still a good hour away. North Street glistened damp under the streetlights. St. Salvator's Tower reared into the sky like some giant sentinel. Side by side they strode toward Gilchrist's Merc.

"You had breakfast?" Gilchrist asked her.

"Gave it a miss this morning."

"Sleep in?"

"Not really."

"Hard night last night?"

"Too tired to get tanked."

He grinned. "Thought you looked a bit peely-wally."

So much for a knee-trembler.

"Fancy a coffee?" Gilchrist said. "That should help jump-start you. My treat."

"I think I might just be able to keep one down, sir."

"Cut the sir. I answer to Andy."

"Yes, sir, Andy."

"And I've not been knighted and never will."

Starbucks was already open for business.

"What's your flavor?" Gilchrist asked. "I'm having a grande latte."

"That sounds good," Jessie said, although the heat of the place had her body threatening to break out in a flush.

"Skinny or regular?"

"You choose," she said, shooting him a look.

"Share a muffin?"

"Whatever."

She found a table through the back, where it wasn't so stifling, and slumped into a sofa that was in better nick than the one she'd had in her flat in Bishopbriggs. She slipped off her gloves, loosened her down jacket, then took it off just in time to catch the full force of a hot flush. She was unfurling her scarf when Gilchrist placed her cup in front of her.

"I got you a regular," he said. "That should sort you out," and broke a blueberry muffin in two. "Excuse the fingers."

Somehow the fact that he had not ordered her a skinny latte pleased her on one hand but annoyed her on the other— too many calories. Why hadn't she just asked for a skinny? She sipped her coffee as Gilchrist devoured his half of the muffin, and more for politeness than hunger, she fingered a piece of muffin—how many more calories was she about to have?

She glanced at him and stretched a smile when she saw he was looking at her.

She took another sip, pretended to look around the small room, then back to Gilchrist with, "Have I got something stuck in my teeth?"

"Sorry. I don't mean to stare. In a way you remind me of Maureen, my daughter. Same shape of face, same color of hair, same color of eyes—"

"Same big tits?"

Gilchrist chuckled, shook his head. "I wish."

Jessie felt a flush of anger surge through her, the hot nip of annoyance that he thought he had the right, as her boss, to make fun of her. She readied to blast him with—

"Mo suffered from anorexia and bulimia," Gilchrist pressed on. "She's past the worst of it now and putting some weight back on. But she's still far too skinny. So, yes, it would be nice if she . . . eh . . . filled out."

Jessie felt the heat of embarrassment warm her face, or maybe it was another flush. He was trying to help her settle into her new job, and she should make it easy for him, ask him about his family, but she said, "So what's on the agenda today?"

"A visit to the postmortem room."

"The land of the green wellies?" she said, then wished she'd kept her trap shut.

But Gilchrist seemed not to notice. "Rebecca's good at her job. She took over when old Bert retired." Another sip of coffee. "Where Bert was old school, Rebecca's one of the new breed."

Jessie pretended to show interest, but it pissed her off that he kept referring to her as Rebecca, not Dr. Cooper.

"She called later," Gilchrist added. "Said she's found something that might be of interest."

"Like what?"

"Said she would rather show than tell."

Jessie sipped her coffee. Already she was feeling better, her stomach not so queasy, her head not so painful. "Why?"

"I suppose she thought it might spoil the fun."

"Fun? What the fuck's funny about a murder victim being cut up on a table?" She shook her head. "I'm sorry. I shouldn't have spoken like that. I'm still struggling from too much to drink last night."

"At last," said Gilchrist. "There's that honesty I've been promised." He finished his coffee, pushed himself to his feet. "Come on," he said. "Bring that with you."

10

An accident on the exit of the Tay Road Bridge had them sitting in traffic for the best part of forty minutes.

"What are they doing up ahead?" Jessie grumbled. "Operating on the spot?"

"Patience is a virtue."

"So's consideration for others."

By the time they worked their way to Bell Street and entered Dr. Cooper's postmortem room it was after 9:00.

Cooper glanced up as Gilchrist entered, Jessie beside him, and he thought he caught a hint of disappointment in Cooper's eyes as she returned her attention to the body on the table—the woman in the negligee. On the next table lay the body of the woman from the kitchen floor, a white sheet draped over her, her head on a tray by her feet. The body from the Coastal Path had to be in the storage room.

Cooper penciled marks on a sketch, tapped her finger over the page as she counted, then said, "Eleven stab wounds, all in the upper chest, four of which could have caused death in and of themselves."

Jessie snorted.

Cooper glanced at her.

"Sorry. Was about to sneeze."

"So what are we looking at?" Gilchrist said, more to focus attention.

Cooper leaned closer. "See here?" she said. "And here? All the wounds are the same width at the entry point, the only variance being in the depth, strike angle, and the location on the chest. But if you look closely at the shape of the wound, see . . . ?" She eased one of the wounds open with her fingers. "Notice how both ends have been cut—"

"Double-edged blade?" Jessie said.

Cooper nodded. "I would say so."

"That's another one of Kumar's trademarks, Andy."

"You never mentioned that last night."

"Didn't want to plant the wrong seed. I wanted to see what Dr. Cooper came up with first."

"Who's Kumar?" Cooper asked.

"Possible suspect. What else have you found that might be of interest to us?"

Cooper turned and walked from the table.

They followed her through a swing door, across a short corridor, and into another room that looked like a store for zombies. Gilchrist counted seven bodies, some covered in sheets, others wearing the clothes in which they had died, their death wounds exposed in their clotted glory for all to see.

Cooper lowered her face mask—Gilchrist and Jessie did likewise—and peeled back a sheet to expose the blue-white body of a young woman, with stitches in the shape of a Y that ran from her shoulders between a pair of small breasts, down to blonde pubic hair. Gilchrist put her age anywhere between fifteen and twenty. She had been pretty, too, with an attractive shape to her face. But her right eye—half-open in the glazed look of the dead—as well as her lips and nose, were twisted to one side, from lying facedown on a frozen slope, suggesting she had lain there for days.

"Cause of death?" Gilchrist asked.

Cooper reached across the woman's head and pointed to an open wound on the right temple, through which the white bone of her skull could be seen. "She had blood on her hair, which tells me she was alive when she cracked her skull. I'd say she knocked herself unconscious and died from hypothermia."

"Can you tell when death occurred?"

"Best estimate would be three to five days ago. But in the middle of winter, body frozen in the snow, and with no entomological interference, I'm just guessing."

"Assuming all three died on the same day," he offered, "you might be able to determine time of death from the others."

"I'm working on that." Cooper pointed to four raised welts on the inside of the right arm. "Cigarette burns. The others have them on the same place, same arm, same number. I didn't realize that last night with only the one body, of course, not until I tackled the other two. It's odd, don't you think? Maybe some sort of branding mark?"

"Like she was cattle," Jessie said.

Cooper raised the girl's left arm, as if Jessie had not spoken. "In addition to a number of tattoos," she said, "it's interesting to note that all three bodies have the same pair of tattoos in the same place."

Gilchrist leaned closer. Where the underarm had been shaved, two dark-blue identical tattoos, no larger than the width of a small fingernail, stained the skin like twin moles.

"Is it the number eleven?" Jessie asked.

Gilchrist peered at them. "Could be," he said, and glanced at Cooper.

"They're not two tattoos of a numeral one," Cooper said. "Under the microscope they seem more rounded, more like symbols of some sort. But together they could be meant to represent the number eleven."

"Did the Krukov twins have tattoos like these?" Gilchrist asked Jessie.

"Not tattoos per se. But they did have the letter *K* cut into their flesh in eleven different places."

"What's the fascination with the number eleven?" Cooper asked.

"*K*'s the eleventh letter of the alphabet," Jessie said. "And *K* is for *Kumar*, in case you didn't get—"

"How many stab wounds on the one remaining body?" Gilchrist said.

"Not got that far yet," Cooper said. "Have you seen enough?"

Gilchrist nodded.

"How about you, DS Janes?"

"Me, too."

Gilchrist gave Jessie a warning glare as Cooper pulled the sheet back over the body.

Back in the PM room, Cooper replaced her mask and removed the sheet to reveal the body of the woman they had found on the floor. Her stump of a neck caused Gilchrist to have a moment of disorientation.

Cooper lifted the left arm and pointed to an identical pair of tattoos.

Jessie leaned closer and studied them. Then without a word, she walked to the other PM table and raised the woman's left arm. Seemingly satisfied, she let it drop back onto the table with a dead slap.

"Excuse me," Cooper objected. "They may be dead, but I would be grateful if you showed a little respect."

"Sorry," Jessie said, then added, "Today's what? Thursday? So if it's five days, we're looking at probable time of death some time on Sunday?"

"Clever you," said Cooper. "But as no one saw anyone running along the Coastal Path, we could assume it was dark, which would suggest night." She eyed Gilchrist. "Does that work with any theories you have?"

"Won't know for sure until debriefing this evening," Gilchrist said. "But it's a good start. Thanks, Rebecca."

"My pleasure. I should have all postmortems with you later today."

"Could you also include an enlargement of the tattoos?"

"Of course."

Gilchrist had just let Jessie precede him through the door when Cooper said, "Do you have a minute, Andy?"

He turned, caught her nodding in the direction of her office. "I'll catch up with you," he said to Jessie. But she walked on without a break in stride.

Gilchrist entered Cooper's office.

She removed her mask. "Close the door, please."

Gilchrist did as she asked, then moved to the closer of two chairs that fronted her desk. He gripped the back of it.

She smiled at him. "Quite the little spitfire you've got there."

"Doesn't mince her words, springs to mind."

She returned his gaze with a steady look of her own. "I'm having a small gathering at home this evening and wonder if you'd like to come along."

"I take it Mr. Cooper's on his way to Italy?"

"To spend five days with a sultry mistress or two, no doubt."

Gilchrist searched for some way to let her down gently. What Cooper was suggesting could come back to hurt both of them professionally. "This case will probably keep me late."

"Come after," she said.

"I mean, really late."

"Really late is fine. I'll be in bed before midnight. Come and join me."

"What about the others?"

"Small gathering means just the two of us."

"Ah," said Gilchrist.

Cooper pushed herself to her feet and, with an action that he knew she was doing for his benefit, combed her fingers through her hair, tossing it at the nape of her neck.

They faced each other. At five-ten she was not much shorter than his six-one.

Then, as if some decision had been reached, she reached for the door handle. "I'm a busy woman," she said, "and you're a busy man. I'm sure we can find some way that fits both of our schedules." She twisted the handle but kept the door closed. "I feel it only fair to warn you about one failing I have, which is that I tend not to be patient."

"Ah." It seemed to be all he could think to say.

"And I suspect my patience will expire with the return of Mr. Cooper," she said. "I'll send you a missed call. That way you'll have my personal number."

He was about to ask how she had obtained his mobile number, when she twisted the handle, opened the door, and invited him to lead the way.

"After you," he said.

She winked at him. "A gentleman to the last."

11

Gilchrist found Jessie pacing the car park, too deep into her text messaging to notice his arrival. He beeped the remote, and the Merc's lights flashed. Even then, Jessie did not look up. He turned the ignition, reversed the car from its space, and eased toward her.

She finally looked up with a frown when he almost nudged her with the bumper, then recognizing the car, mouthed *One minute.*

When she eventually slid into the passenger seat, he said, "Everything all right?"

"Just talking to Robert. Don't know how we'd communicate without text messages."

"Do you need to go home?"

"No. He's fine. Says he's fine-tuned the sheep piss in the whisky joke for me," she said, and chuckled. "Can't wait to read it."

As Gilchrist pulled into traffic, his mobile beeped once in his pocket. He made a point of looking puzzled, then continued to drive on.

"Is that Cooper giving you her number?" Jessie said.

Gilchrist glanced at her, then decided silence was the best response.

"You're all the same," she said, shaking her head.

"What's that supposed to mean?"

"Shouldn't you be asking, Is it that obvious? Yes it's that obvious." A pause, then, "It was her, wasn't it?"

"How would I know?" he said. "I haven't checked."

"Where's that honesty you're always talking to me about?"

"Well, how's this for honesty? Next time you're at a post-mortem, I want you to show some professional respect for—"

"I don't believe it," she said. "You're protecting her. You fancy her."

"I don't fancy her, for crying out loud. I would be saying exactly the same if it was Quasimodo performing the post-mortems."

"Quasimodo? Now there's a thought."

"We're supposed to be professionals. Not some, some, some . . . Ah, *fuck*."

Jessie waited until they were across the Tay Road Bridge and on the A92 before she said, "I've been giving the tattoos some thought. I don't think they've been done by hand."

"Meaning?"

"I don't know. They just don't seem right to me somehow. I thought they looked too regular, too identical to be done by hand. It's more like they've been stamped on."

"You mean, so they can be rubbed off?"

"No. They're proper tattoos, but done by a machine. Not a machine, but more like a stamping thingie. You know, you lift the arm, smack the stamper onto the skin, and hey presto, there's your tattoo."

Gilchrist gave the idea some thought. Did it matter if the tattoos were hand done or not? He could not see that it made any difference, but he would give Cooper a call regardless, on her office phone, which might also send the message that he did not think it wise to visit her home. On the other hand, he could keep a low profile until after Sunday—

"Earth to Gilchrist?"

"Sorry," he said. "I was thinking."

"Does it hurt?"

He pulled out to overtake a group of cars and had to swerve back in as a farm tractor with a wooden trailer loaded with turnips exited a field gate on the opposite side of the road.

"Steady on," Jessie said. "Do you have any idea how much a new pair of knickers costs these days? And why do they always call them a pair of knickers? Can I buy a pair of knickers, please? And they give you one. I don't get it."

Gilchrist waited until a clear stretch opened up, then overtook the tractor. When he hit eighty, he said, "So what difference would it make if the tattoo was stamped on by a machine thingie versus being hand done?"

She shrugged. "Buggered if I know."

"Why suggest it then?"

"Aren't we supposed to brainstorm? You know, stick our heads together and come up with something out of left field." She chuckled. "And that's another one. What does that mean anyway? Left field."

"It's a baseball term."

"I know that, but what does it mean?"

"Left field is someplace on the baseball park where the ball does not normally go."

"OK, Babe."

"Babe?"

"Babe Ruth? The baseball player? Where's your general knowledge?"

Neither of them spoke for a couple of miles, until Jessie said, "Your face goes kind of red when you're angry. Not *red* red but more of a kind of deeper tan red. Did you know that?"

"No. But I'm glad you've pointed it out." They arrived at an intersection, and for the first time since leaving Dundee, Jessie took an interest in where they were heading.

"Haven't you taken a wrong turn?" she asked him.

"Thought we'd take a look at some videos."

They arrived at Strathclyde Police HQ in Pitt Street, Glasgow, just after midday. DCI Peter "Dainty" Small greeted Gilchrist with a firm handshake that defied the man's size. He nodded at Jessie. "Didn't expect to see you again so soon."

"Likewise."

"This way. Got Tam to set it up. Quality's not great, but it's not quality the bastard was trying to achieve." Dainty pushed through a door, held it open for Gilchrist and Jessie to step through, and said, "It's not for the fainthearted."

"It never is," said Gilchrist.

"No, Andy. This is grim. I mean it." And something in the tone of Dainty's voice warned him to expect the worst.

But in truth, no one could have prepared themselves for the worst.

Tam turned the screen so Gilchrist and Jessie could watch. "I can zoom in, if you'd like. But it's grainy as fuck."

"It's fine as is, Tam, thank you."

The sound was tinny, too, a man's voice talking in the background, mixed with the sibilant hissing from cheap sound equipment. The camera held steady on another man seated on a chair, arms behind him, body and legs wrapped into almost mummified immobility by what looked like duct tape. Only his head was free to move, although his mouth was taped, behind which his lips could be seen writhing.

"I'm going for a smoke and to say another prayer for Gordie's soul." Tam pushed himself to his feet and exited the room without another word.

"Gordie?" Gilchrist asked Jessie, remembering her earlier comment.

She nodded at the screen. "DS Gordon McArthur."

Gilchrist moved the mouse, tried to fiddle with the sound, but Tam already had it set at the best quality. Even so, it was difficult to make out what was being said.

". . . I would not notice? Do you . . . my business and pretend to be . . . think I am a fool? No . . ." The voice rose, as its tone deepened despite the sibilance. ". . . you who are the fools . . ."

"Here it comes." Jessie pressed closer.

The screen blackened, and Gilchrist thought they had lost the image, until the dark void turned into the back of a man walking toward the seated figure, then morphed into the body and legs of someone moving to the side of the chair. Even with the recording's poor quality, Gilchrist caught the fear in Gordie's eyes, which had widened to the point of popping. Taped as he was, he was able only to tilt his head and rock the chair, and Gilchrist realized that the chair must be bolted to the floor, otherwise it would surely tumble. He was also conscious of Jessie's face next to his, her breathing light and low in an expectant pant, like a sprinter trying to steady the nerves before leaving the blocks.

"Here we go," Jessie whispered.

The screen zoomed in so that Gordie's face half-filled it. "There has to be two of them," Gilchrist said.

But Jessie did not answer. Her breath stilled, locked in her throat.

Then a sudden intake by his ear told Gilchrist the moment had arrived.

Gordie's eyes widened more, impossible though it seemed, and even though his mouth was gagged, his roaring scream was unmistakeable. A large hand, clearly that of a dark-skinned man, gripped the top of Gordie's head, while the other sawed what looked like a long boning knife beneath and behind his right jaw, more to the back of the neck.

Five seconds into it, the screaming had not subsided. The blade glinted in the lights as the knife continued to saw, as if the butcher was having difficulty cutting through the gristle. And Gilchrist came to understand that the execution was never intended to be clean and swift, the first cut away from the carotid artery telling him that the killing was being staged, to deepen the horror of the viewer, and Gordie's torture.

Ten seconds in, and the sawing had moved to the back of Gordie's head.

Gilchrist felt his breath leave him as a wave of light-headedness swept over him. He pressed his hand to his mouth. "Dear God," he whispered.

And still Gordie's eyes popped and his breathless scream continued, until it seemed as if all that filled the room was—

Silence.

Gordie's eyes had closed as if a switch had been clicked.

The camera zoomed out, so that the viewer could see the upper half of the victim and the action of the executioner. Gilchrist sensed an urgency in the movements then, as if the best part was over and the need to bring it all to a sorry conclusion was the driving force.

The blade shifted to the throat, cut in deep.

Gilchrist groaned.

The hand gripped Gordie's head by the hair, lifted it up and, with one final jerking tug, cut through all that was left of the neck and pulled the head free.

The executioner carried the head, its neck dripping blood, toward the camera until the screen was filled with Gordie's closed eyes, which looked remarkably peaceful despite the horror of moments earlier.

"Next one's the brothers," Jessie said.

Gilchrist pushed his chair back and stood. "I'll give it a miss," he said, and strode straight to the door, except that he bumped into the wall on the way.

"Andy?"

He fumbled with the door handle, then stepped into the corridor.

Outside, Tam caught his eye as Gilchrist walked toward him, and had a cigarette out of the packet by the time he reached him. Even then, the tremors in Gilchrist's fingers caused him to drop it, and he watched in despair as it rolled into a puddle.

Tam removed another, lit it for him, and planted it between Gilchrist's lips.

Gilchrist inhaled as if his life depended on it. Christ, the way he felt at that moment, it probably did.

"Gordie left a wife and an eighteen-month-old daughter," Tam said.

Two more hard pulls had the inside of his cheeks touching his tongue and the cigarette almost done.

"Another one?"

Although his fingers still shivered, Gilchrist shook his head. "Gave up smoking."

Tam nodded, dropped his dout to the pavement, ground it out with his shoe. "Years ago," he said, "when I was a stupid teenager, I used to be a ban-the-bomber." He narrowed his eyes, stared at some imaginary event over Gilchrist's shoulder. "Now? After seeing what they done to Gordie?" Tam's eyes returned to Gilchrist, cold and hard. "We should nuke the fucking lot of them."

12

"You look queasy," Jessie said.

"That's how I feel." Gilchrist powered up to fifty. Ahead, a steady stream of traffic lined the inside lanes of the M80. He eased out, accelerated to sixty, tried to pull his thoughts together, force himself to concentrate on the case. "Did anyone follow up with the ring?"

"What ring?"

"On his right hand."

"I don't remember seeing a ring," Jessie said.

Gilchrist frowned. The recording had been grainy, the action blurred, but he thought he had caught the glint of a ring on one of the fingers. Or maybe a glint of light on the knife's blade had made him think it was a ring. He struggled to pull it up in his mind's eye, but his brain seemed unwilling to cooperate.

"Maybe I've got it wrong," he said.

"Let me call Tam," she said, and fiddled with her mobile.

While Jessie called Tam, Gilchrist's mind swelled with images of Gordie's execution. He tried to shift his thoughts, but the sawing knife, and the hand steadying the head, refused to leave. And the guttural screaming, too, the sound of an adult man howling in pain and for his life, would not leave his senses.

Jessie hung up. "Tam says they clocked the ring but couldn't make nothing out of it."

"Couldn't make *any*thing out of it."

"That's what I said."

"What about the other recording? Of the brothers?" he asked, and hoped she would not suggest he sit through it just to prove a point. "Can you get a better image of it there?"

"That's what puzzled me," she said. "When he sticks their cocks into their mouths, you can see both his hands, and there's no rings anywhere."

"So he must have taken it off?" Gilchrist said.

"Maybe he put it on."

Jessie's remark puzzled Gilchrist, until he realized that the brothers' executions could predate Gordie's beheading. But why had Kumar decided to wear a ring for the second video? And did it make any difference if he had? Or maybe he was searching for clues where there were none.

"And you're sure it's the same person?" he tried.

Jessie nodded. "Same voice, same suit, same size, same shape."

"There had to be at least two of them. One to work the camera, one to—"

"For all we know there could be a team of them. An audience, too." Jessie snorted. "Maybe he's selling tickets by the busload."

An image of an audience-filled studio surged into Gilchrist's mind with a clarity that had him struggling to find his breath. He pressed a button, and his window cracked open. Even with just an inch, he felt the heat evaporate from his face. "Going back to the other recording," he said. "The one with the brothers. Is it the same knife?"

Jessie nodded. "We tried to tie it to some manufacturer. But it's like trying to figure out which farm a blade of straw came from."

"It looked like a boning knife," he offered.

"General consensus is carving knife, with the blade worn down by repeated sharpening."

"Hotels? Butchers?"

"Been there. Done that. Got the T-shirt."

"What about the voice?"

"Quality's shite."

"Accent?"

"Maybe Middle Eastern. Maybe not. Maybe European, Mediterranean. But male and foreign is about as close as we've come."

"Right," said Gilchrist. "Which leaves the ring."

"Which is unidentifiable and brings us back to Go." She scowled at her mobile and said, "Hang on," then placed it to her ear. "Yeah?"

Gilchrist caught the metallic crackle of a woman's voice, too faint to hear what was being said but loud enough to catch the anger. Without saying a word, Jessie listened for ten, maybe fifteen seconds, then powered her mobile down and stared at the passing fields.

The miles and the minutes passed by in silence.

Not until they reached the backup for the Kincardine Bridge did Gilchrist attempt to open the conversation. "What did your mother say?" he asked her.

Jessie looked at him, her eyes red-rimmed. "I don't listen to your conversations, so I don't want you listening to mine."

"I didn't listen," he explained. "Just guessed."

"Well how about making yourself useful and guessing what the Rangers-Kilmarnock score will be this Sunday?" She returned her gaze to the window.

Gilchrist followed her line of sight, let his gaze drift across the sludge-like waters of the River Forth, its banks slick and slimy with mud. Several boats in dire need of repainting, or more probably scuttling, lay tilted on their hulls, high and dry. Rotted wooden moorings stood from the thick gunge-like dead stumps, black and lifeless. He let several seconds pass before saying, "At the risk of repeating myself, I can't help if I don't know the problem."

"At the risk of repeating *my*self, why don't you mind your own effing business?"

It took another five miles of silence for Jessie to say, "I'm sorry."

Gilchrist thought silence was probably his best response, but memories of his late wife, Gail, and more recently, the inherited brooding silences of his daughter, Maureen, persuaded him to search for dialogue.

"Cooper said the tattoos looked more like symbols than numbers," he offered.

"Oh, it's Cooper now. What happened to Rebecca?"

Well, maybe silence was best.

Jessie shuffled in the passenger seat. "You'll be thinking I'm the bitch from hell."

"Maybe not from hell."

She chuckled, sniffed, chuckled some more. "You've got to laugh."

"Laughing helps."

"Do you know why wellies were invented?" she asked.

He glanced at her, saw she was grinning. "Give in."

"To stick the sheep's back legs in when you're shagging them." She chuckled again. "That image always makes me smile."

"That one's before Robert's time," he said.

"It's a golden oldie. But he's good, is Robert. Got a great sense of humor, despite being stone deaf."

"You make him laugh," he said. "I think having you as his mum is good for him."

She snorted. "What do I know? I was sixteen when it happened. Went to a party, and fancied this guy like mad. Spent most of the night trying to get off with the useless turd." She snorted again. "I've always been on the tubby side, and the bird he was with was some skinny blonde bimbo with the big eyes and the posh Bearsden accent. So what chance did I have? In the end, I got blitzed and screwed to the floor by some guy who was so drunk he could hardly keep it up. Amazing I got pregnant at all, when you think about it."

"Some guy?" Gilchrist said. "So you don't keep in touch?"

"That'd be the day. Said he would call me. But he never did. Months later, I came across a scrunched up piece of paper in the bottom of my purse, with a name and a phone number on it. I had a wee memory flash of him slipping me his address before slipping me the bit. By this time I was out to here, but I thought to myself, you know, maybe he cared. Maybe he would want to know. So I called him."

"Let me guess."

"Right first time." She shook her head, cursed under her breath. "Said he didn't know what I was talking about. Denied everything. I told him I wasn't asking him to marry me or anything, just that I thought, you know, that he might want to know." She snorted. "Lead balloon doesn't come close."

"I'm sorry," Gilchrist said.

"I called him once more," she pressed on, "after Robert was born. Just to tell him he had a son, and if he ever wanted to visit, I wouldn't stop him. But the stupid prick accused me of coming after him for money, and hung up. I thought, right, fuck you, so I tore up his number and that was the end of that."

Gilchrist tightened his grip on the steering wheel, frustrated at the unfairness of it all. How many other women suffered the same fate, walked out on after being taken advantage of, left to fend for themselves, raise a child they never intended to have in the first place? He glanced at Jessie, surprised to see she was smiling.

"He's never visited," she said. "But I didn't expect him to."

"Will you tell Robert who his father is?"

"Maybe one day."

Gilchrist let her words simmer. If he knew he had an illegitimate son, he would want to see him. But only if the mother agreed. Turning up on the boy's doorstep and announcing that he was his biological father could cause serious psychological damage and expose the mother as someone who had lied to her son throughout his life. How could he ever rebuild that trust—

"You know what?" Jessie said. "Even though it's been tough, Robert's father doesn't know what he's missing."

"Not everyone could do what you're doing, being a single parent, and a good mother to a . . ." He caught himself before saying *handicapped child* and said, ". . . to Robert."

"Anybody ever tell you you're a smooth-talking bastard?"

"Not in so many words, no."

"That phone call?" she said. "My bitch for a mother says she's going to take legal action for custody of Robert."

"If it's any consolation," Gilchrist replied, "from first appearances, and from what I know of the law, I'd say her chances of succeeding are zero to a hundred below."

"She doesn't want Robert to live with her. That would cost money. All she wants is for me not to have him."

"Still zero to a hundred below."

"She's got witnesses to me hitting him."

"You hit Robert?"

"See?" she said. "See how easy it is to make someone question the truth? I've never hit Robert in my life, you twerp. But dear old mum's got my two fuckheads for brothers ready to go to court to testify to that. And they're stupid enough to do that."

"Robert would deny that?"

"I'm not going to have Robert go to any family hearing. He's just a wee boy."

"Well, the social services wouldn't—"

"Have you seen how these bastards in the social services work? They swan in, wave a bit of paper, and cart him away. It's eff all to do with what he wants, or what I want, it's what they decide is best for us. Best for *us* . . . ?" Her voice had risen, and she stared out the window for a long moment. But when she came back her low grumble told it all. "I'll kill first before I let anyone take Robert from me."

"It won't come to that," Gilchrist said, then tried to make light of it. "Besides, if you're locked up, you won't be around for Robert when he needs you most." But when she looked away, he knew he was missing something, perhaps some dark family secret, some *thing* that was deeply personal to her. But what it was, he could not say.

"Can you tell me why?" he asked.

"Why what?"

"Why your mother wants to take Robert from you."

"It's personal. I already told you that."

"Yes, you did," he said. And as these words passed his lips, he resolved to make a point of finding out.

13

No sooner were they back in the station than Jessie was collared by Alex of Human Resources. Gilchrist knew from experience that she could spend the rest of the day filling out forms to become an official employee of Fife Constabulary, so he spent time catching up and reading the latest reports from DIs Wilkes and Rennie.

Three other households in Kingsbarns had reported strange goings-on in the cottage, with the lights being left on night and day and a dark-blue Volvo—model and registration number that no one seemed to have noticed—coming and going at all hours. But no one could confirm seeing any women or girls, or men of ethnic background, enter or exit the cottage. One couple even went so far as to suggest the house was haunted—activity was present, that was true, but not necessarily in human form.

A check with the post office in Main Street confirmed that mail—mostly utility bills and advertising leaflets—was being delivered to the cottage under the name of the registered owner, not the tenant. A search on the PNC revealed that a 1998 Volvo, dark blue, originally registered in Birmingham, had been stolen from a Tesco multistory car park in Hull. The car's owner was working overseas in Al Khobar, Saudi Arabia, and had been out of the country since August, which tied up with the rental agreement Angus contracted and the theft from Tesco. An APB—"all ports broadcast"— was put out on the Volvo through the PNC, only to confirm that an abandoned Volvo matching the description of the one stolen in Hull, or rather, what was left of it, had been found torched in a field in the outskirts of Stirling three days earlier.

It seemed to Gilchrist that if he wanted to work his way to a dead end, he was going about it the right way. So he stuck his head into Jackie's office.

"Did Nance give you crime scene photos?" he asked her.

Jackie nodded.

"Any luck?"

She wobbled her head—yes and no—and reached for her crutches.

"I've got them, Jackie," he said, and removed the printouts from her printer.

He flipped through each of the images, faces of young women, some no older than children, it seemed, with forlorn eyes devoid of hope. He stopped at one, the headshot and profile of a scruffy-haired blonde, eyes aged beyond her years, charged with stealing a van and driving without insurance or a license. He was intrigued by her face, its wide eyes, small mouth, and pointed chin giving an almost alien-like triangular shape to her head, which somehow seemed familiar.

Was this the girl on the Coastal Path?

He checked her date of birth, which put her at seventeen, and her height—1.70 meters. He still thought in feet and inches and did a quick mental calculation to five foot seven.

He covered one half of her face with his left hand, to account for the twisted eye and lips on the body in Cooper's PM room, but could not be sure.

Despite that, he felt it was a better than good start.

"This one," he said to Jackie. "See if you can find anything else on her."

Jackie's mouth opened.

"Send me a text when you do," he said.

On the way back to his office, his mobile rang—ID Cooper.

"You sound busy," she said.

"I am."

"Am I to understand you won't be able to make our small gathering this evening?"

"It's unlikely, I'm afraid. Sorry."

Cooper gave out a throaty chuckle, which had him pulling up a memory of her settling onto him, her hair curling over his face as she gasped in his ear. If he inhaled at that moment, he swore he could still smell her fragrance—

"Bones," she said.

"Pardon?"

"The tattoos appear to be two bones. Side by side. Like the number eleven."

"Bones?" He tried to picture them. "Why bones?"

"African witch doctor?"

Gilchrist wondered if she was onto something. But the video of Gordie's beheading, the cock-sucking finale of the Georgian gangsters, the tinny sound of the man's accent, even the name Kumar, all seemed to point away from Africa.

"And I've also found traces of benzodiazepines in their blood," she continued.

"All three of them?"

"Only the two who were killed in the cottage."

Gilchrist stared out over North Street. Benzodiazepines, more commonly known as date-rape drugs—sleep inducing, hypnotic, muscle relaxing, all of the above—were cheap, easy to find, and just as easy to administer.

"It's how he kept them captive," he said at length. "How he controlled them."

"It also might explain how one of them managed to flee." A pause, then, "Any names yet?" she asked.

"We're working on it."

"Let me know when you do. It's bad enough that they were kidnapped, raped, and killed, without them having to be buried anonymously."

"You'll be the first to know."

"I'll send images of the tattoos to you," she said, "and I won't embarrass you by asking if you'd like to come to another small gathering tomorrow evening. You have my number." She paused for a couple of beats, as if to give him time to agree, then said, "Ciao."

He held onto his mobile for a long second before breaking the connection.

The way Cooper teased him told him she knew he was smitten. He would be lying if he said he was not. Having once given in to her seductive charms, he found himself thinking of her at the most inappropriate moments. But Cooper was married, and had been for seven years, and that single night brought back memories of his own failed marriage.

Having lost Gail first to her infidelity and finally to cancer, Gilchrist never remarried. Not that he mourned after Gail—he had done enough mourning for several Gails—rather, he did not want to become involved again. It seemed as simple an explanation as any. And on top of his work, and the never-ending maintenance of his cottage, he seemed to—

"Sir?"

Gilchrist jolted. "Yes, Mhairi."

"Brain's fried," she said. "Going to call it a day. Angus passed on all of them. He's still sitting with the artist, but he's gasping for a pint."

"Can't blame him," Gilchrist said, pulling out his wallet. He peeled off a twenty. "Tell Angus to stick it out for a wee bit longer. He's nearly done. Then why don't you go and have a pint with him. On me."

Mhairi took the twenty and pocketed it with a sleight of hand that could be the envy of any self-respecting pickpocket. "Thanks, sir. We'll be in Lafferty's later, if you'd like to join us."

"Once I battle my way through some more stuff," he said. "And tell Angus I'm grateful for all his effort."

Back at his computer, Gilchrist made a mental note to follow up with Angus. He did not normally hand out cash to potential witnesses, but Angus might have spoken to Kumar in person and could possibly give a positive ID. He clicked the mouse and opened his mailbox, to find one from Dainty— subject heading "DS Janes: Attachment," one scanned PDF with an incomprehensible file name.

He read Dainty's message—Info on JJ call if need more— short and to the point, just like the man, he thought. He sent the file to the printer, resigned for some bedtime reading.

Dainty's attachment was printing when Cooper's e-mail arrived.

He read her message—Call with questions. RC—no kiss this time. Maybe she was beginning to see that small gatherings could be problematic professionally.

He opened Cooper's file attachments, photographs of the left underarm of each of the three women, and printed them out. The three sets of tattooed bones intrigued him—neat, tiny, identical. But the more he looked at them, the more he came to see that although they might be a pair of bones, he was looking at the number eleven—

Jessie pushed through the door. "He could talk for Scotland, that Alex could. And walk away with the gold every time." She leaned over his desk. "Cooper send them to you?"

Gilchrist shoved the printouts across his desk. "Any ideas?"

She gave them a cursory scan. "None that can't wait until tomorrow." She frowned, then said, "I know we're at the start of an investigation and I've been off all afternoon filling in stupid forms, but I've hardly spoken to my wee boy since I've been here, and I'm planning to take him out to The Grill House; they do an early evening meal for two, less than twenty quid, which is a good deal, I think." She grimaced. "D'you mind if I head off?"

Gilchrist pushed his chair back and reached for his leather jacket. "Only if you can squeeze in a pint at Lafferty's."

"I'm always up for a quickie," she said, then added, "A quickie drink, I mean. Sir. Andy. Sorry. Shit. You know what I mean."

"Come on," he said. "I'd like you to meet Angus."

"Angus who?"

"Exactly."

14

Lafferty's bustled with a festive, seasonal buzz. Glasses chinked, voices rose, seemed to hang for a moment, then burst into laughter. TV screens, tucked high in the ceiling corners, flickered sports images in muted silence. Gilchrist managed to claim a spot at the bar by squeezing in between two couples.

"Busy little place," Jessie said to him.

"St. Andrews is a student town."

"Aren't students supposed to be skint?"

"Not here, they're not." Gilchrist spotted Mhairi and Angus at a table in the back, but they were too deep in conversation to notice him. He caught Fast Eddy's eye behind the bar and said, "Deuchars IPA, Eddy."

"One Deuchars IPA for the lady," Fast Eddy said. "And a pint of Eighty for—"

"The Deuchars is for me," Gilchrist corrected.

Fast Eddy raised both eyebrows as he shoved a mug under the tap. "Is the Pope a Catholic? Will the sun rise in the morning? Will Andy have a pint of Eighty? I could have bet my life savings on any one of these bankers. Now you've rocked my world to the core. Are you not well, Andy?"

"Thought I'd try a change, Eddy."

"A change? At your age? That's sacrilege."

While Fast Eddy pulled the Deuchars, Gilchrist turned to Jessie. "What are you having?"

"Deuchars sounds good."

"Make that two, Eddy."

"Another Deuchars for the lovely lady, and are you not going to introduce me?"

"Jessie," Gilchrist said, "I'd like you to meet Fast Eddy. Eddy, meet Jessie."

"I'd shake your hand, darling, but from the look of those wonderful brown eyes of yours, I don't think I could ever let go."

Jessie laughed. "The time you're taking to pull two pints makes me wonder why you're called Fast Eddy."

"You can never rush a good pint, darling, now can you?"

"So why the Fast?"

"You'd have to come out on a date to find out," Fast Eddy said. "So, tell me, darling, what are you doing tomorrow night?"

"You're not that fast, Eddy. What's wrong with tonight?"

For once, Fast Eddy seemed lost for words. "Well . . . in that case—"

"Too slow. I'm already booked."

Fast Eddy chuckled. "Ah, you've a heart of steel," he said, "and a wit as fast as an arrow through it." He slid two Deuchars across the counter. "There you go, my darling. On the house, for the beautiful woman with a lovely smile and eyes that could break a lonely Irishman's heart."

Jessie lifted her pint, tilted it to Fast Eddy, and received a wink in response before he moved to the end of the bar with, "Same again, my lovely?"

She turned to Gilchrist. "Quite the charmer."

"He's certainly that."

"Genuine compliments I can take. But bullshit flat-tery . . . ?" She lifted her glass to her lips, then smiled. "I can take that, too. Cheers," she said, and took a long sip.

Gilchrist did likewise.

"Bloody hell," Jessie said. "I was ready for that. But that's me blown my calorie intake for the day." She glanced beyond him. "Shoes are killing me. Fancy a seat?"

"This way," he said, and walked to Mhairi's table.

Mhairi and Angus were huddled close, all the better for arguing out of earshot, it seemed. Gilchrist interrupted with, "Mind if we join you?"

Mhairi's flicker for a smile did little to shift the transpar-ency of her mood, but she introduced Gilchrist as "the boss" and Jessie as "the new girl in town" and grimaced as Jessie squeezed in beside Angus, splashing drink onto the table as she tried to shake his hand.

Angus tilted his glass to Gilchrist. "Thanks for the drinks."

"So I would know where to find you."

Angus sipped his pint, his gaze shifting from Mhairi to Gilchrist and back again.

"So, you spent the day with our artist?" Gilchrist began.

"Wasted the day, more like. You see it on the telly, these artists sketching faces as someone describes them. And out they come, the perfect look-alike." He shook his head. "Bloody hopeless at it, so I was."

"Did you try Mr. Potato Head?" Jessie quipped.

Angus guffawed, as if he was already on his way to a full house. "I think that's who I ended up with. A man with a face like a well-skelped tattie. If you come across him, wrap him in foil and stick him in the oven." Mhairi chuckled to accompany him.

Gilchrist leaned closer. "Sometimes it's better not to think about features at all," he said. "Tell me how the cottage came to be on the market."

So Angus did, in his roundabout way, interjecting details of the housing market, how rentals were on the uptake, and how he was going to start his own business. Gilchrist nudged him back on course and livened when Angus mentioned that first call from the tenant-to-be.

"Did he give a name?" Gilchrist asked.

Angus sneered. "Mr. Smith."

"Did he say who he was with? Name of a company? Anything like that?"

"He didn't, and I didn't ask. I should of, I suppose."

"Any accent?"

"English. The plonker."

"Any dialect? Cockney? Brummie?" Gilchrist pressed.

"Upper-class. Posh. Almost like it was put on."

Gilchrist caught Jessie's eye, and she nodded.

"And then what?" Gilchrist pressed Angus.

"Said he would mail a check if I sent him the keys. I told him that's not how we do business." Angus finished his pint as if to emphasize that point.

"And?"

"So I met him. I insisted."

Sometimes the way to get answers was not to ask questions, so Gilchrist held Angus's gaze and nodded at his worldly wisdom.

"Met him only the once," Angus continued. "At the cottage. Showed him around, but I got the feeling he wasn't interested. Kept looking out the window. I figured he liked the open view, so I focused on that. Told him the view was great, all the way to the sea, beyond the golf course." He tried a smart smile, but it came off as more of a scowl. "So I jacked up the price, just enough not to scare him off, like, and he went for it." He nodded, to show how clever he was.

"Ethnic background?" Gilchrist asked.

"I thought he was from India or Pakistan, at first. Or maybe an Arab. In the end, I just put him down as foreign looking, maybe even Spanish. I don't know."

"Who spoke perfect English," Jessie confirmed.

"Yes."

"How tall?" Gilchrist asked.

Angus frowned. "Average height. Look, I've given all these details to the—"

"As senior investigating officer, I like to check facts first-hand." Gilchrist nodded to Angus's empty glass. "What is it? Fosters?"

"Why not?"

"Mhairi?"

"Go on then. G and T. Slimline tonic."

Gilchrist walked to the bar and placed the order.

When he returned he said, "Did he wear any rings?"

"Like a wedding ring or something?"

"Something like that."

Angus shook his head. "I didn't notice."

Gilchrist said, "The strange thing is, no one we've spoken to remembers seeing the cottage up for rent. Did you place an ad in the *Courier*?" He thought he sensed the first ripple of unease. "The reason I ask," he added, about to pry deeper by lying, "is that we couldn't find a copy of an ad in any of the local newspapers."

"I don't think we placed an ad."

"You don't think?"

"No. I'm sure we didn't."

It struck Gilchrist that the property could have been advertised on the office window, the same way other estate agents did around town. But his question seemed to have thrown Angus, so he pressed deeper. "So how did you manage to rent the property?"

"Word of mouth."

Gilchrist took another sip of his beer. "So how does that work?"

"How does what work?"

"Word of mouth."

Angus laughed, alone as it turned out. "Exactly like it says on the packet. We were going to place an ad. But I suppose we just never got around to it."

"We?" Jessie said.

"Well, me."

"Did you forget, like?"

"I suppose I must of." Angus beamed, rescued by a fresh pint of Fosters, which he grabbed with both hands. He took a hefty swallow. "Anyway, we need to put it back on the market," he said to Gilchrist. "So once you've completed your investigation, let me know when."

"What about the existing agreement?" Gilchrist pried.

"That's null and void, that is. And he can pish in the wind for his deposit. From what I'm hearing, we'll need to gut the place. New linoleum, carpets, paint throughout, which won't be cheap. I might need to think about suing him for the balance." Angus nodded, all businessman once more.

Gilchrist took another sip, returned his glass to the table. "Whose mouth?"

"What?"

"Word of mouth," Gilchrist said. "Who started it?"

"I don't know. It just starts. And spreads. You know, by word of—"

"So who did you talk to?"

"No one."

Gilchrist sensed Mhairi's unease. Jessie was all ears. Gilchrist pressed on. "But you must have spoken to someone. You had a property to rent. It's money lost if you don't rent it out. You didn't place an ad. You never put up a sign."

Angus hid his response in his beer, draining it halfway.

Gilchrist took that moment to glance at Mhairi, relieved when she got his message.

"Excuse me," she said, pushing herself to her feet. "Nature calls."

Gilchrist waited until Mhairi squeezed past him and was out of earshot before saying, "So what did you tell her?"

"Tell Mhairi?"

"No, Mr. Businessman," Jessie interrupted. "The woman whose name you don't want to mention in front of Mhairi." She slid closer. "Are you giving her one?"

"Giving who one?"

"Is that butter I see melting in your mouth?"

"Three women are dead," Gilchrist reasoned.

Jessie added, "And if you've been dishing out beef injections behind Mhairi's back, you'd better cough up now, or . . . you know . . ." She nodded to the Ladies.

"Look," Angus said. "It's . . . if I . . ."

"We won't tell Mhairi," Gilchrist said—she could read it in his report.

Angus lifted his pint, gave a nervous look toward the Ladies, then said, "Look. It was only a one-nighter. That's all. It meant nothing. I've never seen her—"

"What's her name?"

Angus shook his head. "I can't remember. Honest, I can't."

"That's it," Jessie said, preparing to stand. "Where did you say the loo was?"

"Caryl," Angus said. "She told me her name was Caryl Dillanos."

"Phone number?"

Angus shook his head.

"She give you a business card?"

Angus grabbed his pint. "Here's Mhairi. You gave me your word." He took a mouthful as Mhairi reached across Gilchrist to her seat. "Feeling better?" he tried, and gave her a smile that could have cracked porcelain.

Mhairi retrieved her scarf and coat, bundled them together and, without a word, turned and walked from the bar.

"Mhairi . . . ?"

Jessie glanced at her wristwatch. "Shit, I'm late for Robert." She pushed to her feet.

Panic swelled across Angus's face as his mind worked out the obvious. "You said you wouldn't tell her—"

"I'm going home to take my son out for a meal," Jessie snapped at him. "And I swear that if I ever think he's going to turn into a lying, shagging cheat like you, I will cut his balls off and shove them down his throat." She patted Gilchrist on the shoulder. "Toodle-do."

Gilchrist caught sight of Jessie scurrying past the bar window and wondered if she would catch up with Mhairi, or tell her tomorrow. He faced Angus.

"And then there were two," he said.

Angus lifted his pint, almost drained it.

Now they were alone, Gilchrist did not want him to leave. "Do you have a solicitor?"

"What? Look, I forgot all about her. I never even remembered until—"

"That's it." Gilchrist said, louder than intended. Four people at the adjacent table stilled for a hushed moment, and he waited until they started talking again. "If you want me to charge you with obstructing an investigation, you're going about it the right way. Now let me ask you one more time. Do you have a solicitor?"

"I have. Yes." Angus almost pleaded, "Do I need her?"

"Depends."

"On what?"

"On whether or not I believe what you're about to tell me. And if I get so much as a whiff that you're withholding the truth, I will charge you, and once I do, you can give your solicitor your checkbook, because by the time I'm finished you won't have anything left to start up any kind of business." He sat back and gave a dead smile. "Understood?"

Angus nodded.

"Right," Gilchrist said. "I'll have her business card for starters."

15

Back in the station, Gilchrist ran his fingers over the business card.

Not your run-of-the-mill business card but glossy, colored, quality stock, with DILLANOS FURNITURE embossed in a swirling Victorian gold scroll, beneath which was printed the name CARYL V. DILLANOS and job title INTERNATIONAL BUYER—which would have elevated her professional status in Angus's eyes—and a free-phone and fax number.

The flip side was blank. Did Dillanos Furniture exist, or was the card only a fake to be handed out to impress eager-to-please come-ons like Angus? Or was there some other way he could reach Caryl V. Dillanos, International Buyer for Dillanos Furniture, directly?

Rather than call her office number, he googled Caryl V. Dillanos and came up with zero hits. Caryl Dillanos came up empty, too. He tried the company name, Dillanos Furniture, and received a number of hits, excerpts from newspaper and magazine articles that gave the sales pitch—*specializing in micropocketed spring technology for improved comfort, shape retention, and long-term durability.* One link led him to the company website, but it turned out to be little more than eyewash, with only a few pages of stock photographs, and again no physical address.

But the phone number was the same as on the business card.

He checked the time—9:08 PM—too late, he knew, but he dialed it anyway.

"Dillanos Furniture Showroom. How can I help you?"

The chirpy voice surprised him—English accent, too. "Caryl Dillanos, please?"

"Caryl's not here at the moment. Can I take a message?"

Gilchrist pushed himself to his feet, his mind racing. "When do you expect her?"

"I couldn't say. Who shall I say is calling?"

"It's a personal call. Do you have another number for her?"

"We're not allowed to give it out, sir."

Well, it had been worth a try. "Caryl said she might be in tomorrow," he lied. "Can you give me your address, please?" He scribbled it down, but the street name meant nothing to him. "And which showroom is this?" he asked.

"We only have the one showroom, sir."

He gambled with, "I thought Caryl had another one in London."

"Only Glasgow, sir."

That's better. "I'll call back tomorrow," he said, and hung up.

Out of nothing comes something? He eyed the scribbled address—Glasgow—and thought it was worth a question, at least. He dialed Jessie's number, but it punted him into voice mail, and he left a message telling her she needed to be reachable 24/7.

No sooner had he ended the call than his mobile rang.

"Just missed you," Jessie said. "I was in the loo."

"Caryl Dillanos," he said. "The name mean anything to you?"

"Dillanos Furniture rings a bell. Is that her?"

"Could be."

"They've got a showroom in Glasgow. On the south side, I think. But other than that, I know nothing about them."

"Right. I'll pick you up at 7:30 in the morning."

Gilchrist paid Stan a short visit in the Memorial, pleased to see that he was up and about, albeit shuffling around the ward in pain.

"What's the new DS like?" Stan asked him.

"Your job's safe, old son, don't you worry about that."

"Any news on the missing Craig Farmer?"

Gilchrist raised an eyebrow. "Who told you Farmer was missing?"

"Got to keep my eye in, boss. Can't let the world pass me by. But Nance popped her head in yesterday. Gave me an opportunity to grill her."

Gilchrist nodded. "So, you bought my Christmas present yet?"

Stan rolled his eyes and said, "Why don't you help me back into bed, boss, and once I get out of here I'll put two pints behind the bar. How does that sound?"

"Sounds like a deal."

Back at his cottage, Gilchrist poured himself a full measure, more than was probably good for him, and carried his glass through to the front room. He settled down in front of the gas fire, took a sip, let the whisky swill around his mouth.

In bars, he stuck to pints, but in the privacy of his cottage he would try the occasional whisky, and the Balvenie

Doublewood was like finding a seam of smooth gold in the fiery world of Scotch. He eyed the lowball glass, then picked up Dainty's printout.

Jeannie Janes.

DOB—October 20, 1958. A quick mental calculation put her at forty-seven, twenty years younger than she looked, and thirteen years younger than the required age for a bus pass.

Maybe he should just report her to the authorities and let them deal with it.

He read on.

Jessie's mother lived in Easterhouse, which he knew was more underprivileged than upmarket. He scanned a catalog of offenses, nothing serious in terms of crime, but all of it breaking the law. Most incidents occurred near the infamous Blythswood Square District, an area of Glasgow once renowned for its prostitutes, Jeannie being picked up three times in as many days during a busy spell over one festive season. He found no mention of a Mr. Janes and suspected Jessie's father was like Robert's, another man who abandoned responsibilities before they blossomed.

He took another sip of the Balvenie, returned the almost-finished glass to the side table and, despite the weight of his eyelids, forced himself to read on. But he soon found himself glazing over the same sentence, the heat and the alcohol working their magic . . .

Dainty's printout slipped from his grip onto his lap . . .

He came to, four hours later—3:11 AM—confused for a sleeping moment, until he saw the remains of his unfinished whisky on the table beside him. He eased himself to his feet, spilling Dainty's printout to the floor, and knew from painful experience not to bend down and pick it up until his back loosened up.

He carried his whisky through to the kitchen and sat it on a shelf in the fridge—waste not, want not—then returned to the lounge and switched off the fire. He risked picking up the printout and placed it on a chair under the dining table.

He managed to remove his trousers and shirt before he tumbled onto the top of his bed in his underpants and let sleep take him.

The walk to his Merc could have been at the Arctic Circle.

Sunrise was still a good two hours away, and a stiff wind felt as if the air was cold enough to crack brass balls. Stars pinpricked a black sky. A half-moon gave off a hazy glow. He breathed in the frozen air, felt its crystal freshness clear his lungs and his head. Somehow, just the chill of the early morning darkness reminded him of his childhood days at Christmas, when his big brother, Jack, would lead him through to the living room in the small hours of a Christmas morning, both of them shivering with excitement or cold, he could never tell, then switch on the lights to the stunning thrill of presents beneath the tree, only to have the wrappings ripped open minutes later in the bitter cold of an unheated room.

Although Gilchrist loved Fisherman's Cottage and the coastal town of Crail, he hated that he had no garage and had to park his car in the elements. He switched on the engine, turned the heat up full, and closed the door while he scraped frost from the windows.

Several freezing minutes later he was ready to go.

Outside Crail, he switched to full-beam, the car's headlights reflecting the frost off the road like a million miniature cat's-eyes. He checked the time—7:05, ahead of schedule—and dialed Jessie's number.

"Hello?"

He ignored the grumpiness in her voice and said, "Good morning."

"What d'you want?"

"I'm running early. Should be with you around 7:20."

"You'll have a ten-minute wait then," she said, and hung up.

And he had.

He checked the time on the dash when her front door opened—7:29. Jessie tumbled onto the pathway and strode toward his car, clapping her gloved hands to warm up.

A rush of cold air followed her inside.

She strapped on her seat belt in silence, and he said, "Everything OK?"

"Just drive."

He pulled away from the curb and did not venture a word until he drove beyond the town limits, the Strathtyrum Golf Course on the right. Beyond, the Eden Estuary gave a cloud-laden blush and a hint of the coming day.

"Whatever's upsetting you," he said. "Let's have it."

"It's personal, Andy."

"Not anymore it's not."

"Fire me, then."

"The thought has crossed my mind, I have to tell you. But I like what I've seen so far, and I think you have much to contribute to the—"

"Much to contribute?" she said. "What the fuck does that mean? Here Jessie, have a look at this dead body, and let's have your contribution. Jesus Christ, Andy, it's not a game of charades we're playing, it's a full-bloodied—"

"Exactly." He tightened his grip on the steering wheel. "And if you let your personal life interfere with my murder investigation, then yes, I will fire you. On the spot. Today. Right now, if you want. And happily, too. Got that?"

His anger took him by surprise and seemed to have shocked Jessie into silence. He gave her ten seconds in which to bomb him with her retaliation. But it never came, and he risked a glance, only to find she was staring into the blackness of the passing countryside. For tuppence, he could turn the car around and take her back home, it was nice knowing you—

"Did you talk to anyone about extending the non-harassment order?" she said.

"I did."

She turned to face him then, and he saw that she had been crying, not because he had snapped at her, but at some point during the night. "You never told me that," she said.

"I never had a chance."

She paused for a moment, then said, "Why don't we start again? Good morning, Andy."

"Good morning, Jessie. And how was last night?"

"Shite. How was yours?"

"Better than yours, by the sound of it."

"So why are we heading to Glasgow?" she asked, and a subtle shifting of her position in the seat told him that the joking was over, and so was last night's trauma.

He told her about his interrogation of Angus, how Angus had confessed to having met Caryl Dillanos twice only—he had no reason not to believe that—and that they had sex both times, which extracted a "What is it with men and their cocks?" He handed her Caryl's business card and told her how he had searched the Internet, and that the website looked like it was there as a front only.

"I'm not convinced Caryl Dillanos is her real name," Gil-christ said.

"It sounds too, what's the word . . . ?" she said. "Cinematic."

"Cinematic? Maybe you should take up writing instead of stand-up comedy."

"And maybe you should stick to being a detective instead of a smart-arse."

"Touché."

"So you think this Caryl might have a criminal record?" she asked.

"We'll soon find out," he said, then thought he would try again. "So, how's Robert?"

At the mention of her son's name, her mood changed. A cold wind chilled the air between them.

This time, he had the common sense not to press.

16

They hit the backup to Glasgow city center just before 8:55 AM, but by the time they crossed the Kingston Bridge onto the south side, it was 9:16.

Ten minutes later, after following Jessie's directions, Gilchrist pulled up to the street address, nothing more than a windowless brick building fronted by a pavement littered with the remains of last night's carryout—three crushed cans of Carlsberg Special and a sodden brown paper bag from which two chapatis peeked. A dilapidated sign in need of a blowtorch scraping and a coat of paint, maybe several, announced DIL-LANOS FURNITURE SHOWROOM. To the side, an adjacent plot, wired off with a rusting chain-link fence, displayed the name of some security firm—and not a security guard in sight.

The first thought that crossed Gilchrist's mind was, What would Angus think of his cinematic Caryl Dillanos if he ever saw this? He opened the door and stepped into the damp Glasgow air. The sky hung low with gray clouds that threatened rain or even snow. What odds were the bookies offering this year for a white Christmas? A heavy-duty padlock hung from a double door painted the color of rust. He palmed the

surface to confirm that the door was indeed wood, then gave
the padlock a hard tug. But it was secure.

"Welcome to upmarket Glasgow," Jessie said.

"Not quite what I expected," Gilchrist had to concede.
"What's that sign say?"

"Business hours, Monday to Saturday 10:00 AM to 10:00
PM; Sunday 10:00 AM to 5:00 PM."

"Looks like we have a thirty-minute wait."

"Fancy a coffee? I'm starving."

"Hungry," he said. "People in famines are starving."

"Is that today's English lesson over?"

They found a café on Paisley Road West, and Gilchrist
ordered two lattes. "Will that be all, sir?"

"Share a blueberry muffin?" he asked Jessie.

"These berries look like bluebottles."

"And a muffin," he said. "Cranberry."

Outside, Gilchrist held the muffin out to Jessie. She
tugged a glove off with her teeth and said, "Excuse the fingers," and tore off a piece. Crumbs scattered to the pavement
as she pressed it to her mouth. "Cranberries are nice."

"Better than bluebottles?"

"You get more meat with bluebottles."

For the first time that morning, she smiled, and Gilchrist
was surprised by how white her teeth were—nice and even,
too. He tried to tear off a piece of muffin, but with a coffee
in the other hand he almost dropped the lot. He managed
a small piece, then followed Jessie as she strolled along the
pavement.

Then she stopped and looked the length of the street.
"You can't imagine how busy this street used to be," she said.
"You look at old photographs of Glasgow and the place is just

heaving with buses and trams and people. You ever been on a trolleybus?" she asked.

"Once," he lied.

"I thought you were old enough," she said, then added. "They'll probably bring them back, the way the price of petrol is going." She took another sip of coffee. "You going to eat that thing or stand there like a doo-wally looking at it all day?"

He held it out to her.

"I shouldn't," she said. "But as I said, you're a smooth-talking bastard."

"Did you grow up here?"

She shook her head and mumbled, "Easterhouse. Other side of the city." One more mouthful finished the muffin, and she brushed her hand on her coat, leaving a trail of crumbs. "I needed that," she said.

He sipped his coffee, his breath steaming in the cold air. "Your parents from here?"

"Once a detective . . . ?" She looked at him and smiled.

Her eyes were the darkest brown, and glistened damp from the cold, as if they could well at any moment. The tip of her thin nose had reddened in the cold, and her flawless skin had chilled to the palest of whites.

"Just asking," he said.

She nodded, then looked away, as if her gaze was drawn to some phantom image in her mind. "One of my mother's boyfriends lived around here," she said. "That's another one of the reasons I hate her."

Silent, Gilchrist waited.

"I was four or five, or thereabouts. I remember being dragged from one bus to the next, then being tugged along this street. At that age, I didn't have a clue where I was, but it wasn't till years later that I recognized the street." She turned in the direction of the Clyde. "It was the dockyard cranes that I remembered. The Clydeside used to be full of them, ugly black monstrosities that stood above everything else." She chuckled. "I read *The War of the Worlds* when I was in my early teens, and I always pictured these cranes as the Martians." She fell silent then, but Gilchrist did not want to lose her.

"Another one of the reasons?" he prompted.

Again, the speed with which her emotions changed puzzled him.

Her lips pursed, and she narrowed her eyes, and he had a sense that she was about to open up to him. A tear swelled, trickled down her cheek. She dabbed it dry. "The boyfriend she was going to meet was an artist," she said, then scanned the tenement buildings as if searching for his address. "Never could find out where he used to live."

"Got a name?"

She shook her head. "Bob, I think. But I never really knew. Not like she introduced me to him, or anything. But I remember liking the smell of his house. Turps and oils. And there were no carpets on the floors, just newspapers spread around to catch the drips. I used to kick my feet through it, you know, the way you used to with autumn leaves." She fixed her gaze on a memory in the distance, and something dark and dangerous seemed to shift behind her eyes. "He had a whisky breath," she said, "but his hands were as smooth as polished stone. When he ran them down my face, he would tell me how lovely I looked."

Gilchrist felt a cold chill slip through him. He wanted to tell her to stop, it really was too personal, but part of him—

"My mother would let him do it to her in front of me, standing up against the wall, or on the floor, among the newspapers." Tears dripped to the ground.

"You don't need to say any more." He reached out to her, squeezed her shoulder.

She frowned up at him, then shook her head. "I've never told anyone about this."

Gilchrist lowered his arm, hid his face in another sip of coffee.

"My mother told him . . ." She shook her head. "She told him . . . he could have me if he wanted."

"Jesus . . ."

"I didn't know what she meant."

"Jessie . . ."

"And when they were doing it, Bob with his twisted face and his arse going twenty to the dozen, she would sometimes hold her hand out to me, wanting me to come closer . . ."

Gilchrist caught the giveaway word—*sometimes*—which told him all.

Jessie sniffed, lifted her head, stared across the Clyde as if willing the alien machines to turn their ray-guns her mother's way. "What kind of a mother would do that to a child?"

Gilchrist had no answer. He had been brought up in a lower-middle-income family, but in secure and healthy sur- roundings, with parents who by Scottish nature did not dote on their two sons but taught them the strict rights and wrongs of their own firm moral beliefs. How would his own life have turned out if he had been exposed to the same—

"Come on," Jessie said. "That showroom should be open- ing soon."

From childhood memories to police business in zero sec- onds flat? But Gilchrist just nodded, knowing that pressing for more would likely shut her down for good.

With the car's engine running, and parked fifty yards from the showroom, they waited and watched.

Ten o'clock came and went. As did 10:15.

"Not exactly Sauchiehall Street," Jessie said.

It took until 10:39 before a skinny blonde, with back-combed hair, tight denim jeans over stick-thin legs, and a black Michelin-man anorak, walked around the corner, crossed the street, and stopped at the door. From her handbag she removed what looked like a set of jailer's keys.

"About bloody time," Jessie said.

Cigarette smoke spiraled around the woman's face as she struggled to work the keys. Then she jerked the padlock off and, with one final draw and a flick of her fingers, cast her dout to the wind and pushed the doors open.

"Let's go," Jessie said. "I'm bursting."

17

Inside, the furniture display surprised Gilchrist. The size of the place was confusing, too, as if they had stepped into the TARDIS. Three- and four-piece suites were arranged on raised plinths the size of living rooms. Family-sized signs hung from a ceiling of exposed metal beams and pipes, announcing autumn and winter sales with prices slashed as deep as 75 percent.

"Can ah help youse?"

The accent was thick Glaswegian. Up close, the woman's bloodshot eyes looked as if she'd been up all night. Mascaraed eyelashes seemed in danger of falling off. Lavender perfume failed to smother the throat-catching decay of cigarette ash.

Gilchrist flashed his warrant card. Jessie did likewise.

"Aw fuck," the woman said.

"Caryl Dillanos," Gilchrist said.

"Loo?" Jessie added.

"Loo's that way," the woman said with a nod of her head. Jessie walked away.

"Whit about Caryl?"

"Have you seen her?" Gilchrist asked.

"No for weeks."

"Does she work here?"

"Naw. Uses it as a call center."

"Why Dillanos?"

"Whit?"

"Is she related to the owner?"

"Dillanos is a made-up name," she said. "Gives the place a right Mediterranean-come-Italian flavor, so it does."

"So, who owns this place, then?"

"Big Jock Shepherd. You might've heard of him. Big businessman. Restaurants and pubs all over the place. Minted, so he is."

"And he knows Caryl?"

"He must, if he named the place after her."

"And he gives her permission to use it as a call center?" She shrugged.

Gilchrist said nothing. Cash paid under the table for a receptionist and an address to add to a business card was one of a thousand ways to keep costs down and beat the tax man, as well as giving a moneyed reality to spongers like Angus.

"Can we talk outside?" she said. "I'm gasping for a fag."

Gilchrist followed her back through the double doors and onto the pavement, where she stood sans Michelin-man anorak, shivering in the chill, cigarette already lit and in her mouth, cheeks pulling in as if her life depended on it—

"It's Dot, isn't it? Dot Bonar."

The woman turned as Jessie joined them, took another draw that looked as if it hurt.

"Thought I'd seen you before," Jessie said. "Your man runs a taxi business."

"If you can call it that."

"You bailed him out last month, if my memory serves me."

"And the month afore," she said, and held the packet out. "Want one?"

Jessie seemed tempted. "Giving it up."

"Wish I had your willpower," Dot said, and removed another cigarette.

Gilchrist wondered what she had done with the first one, then located a smoking stub on the pavement about ten feet away. He also noticed she was visibly shaking.

"It's cold," he said. "Why don't we go back inside?"

"Let me finish this first," she said, and sucked her money's worth.

"I won't tell anyone," he tried.

She tilted her head, blew a stream of smoke over his shoulder. "I'm still on my three months' probation with this job. One fuck-up and I'm out on my ear. Excuse the English."

Gilchrist thought that opening the store almost forty-five minutes late counted as a fuck-up, but he said, "So how do you contact Caryl?"

"I don't."

"If she uses this place as her call center, how does she get her messages?"

"She phones in for them."

"Every day?"

Another shrug, another draw.

"Who does she speak to?"

"Whoever's answering the phone."

"So if she called right now, that would be you?"

"It would."

Gilchrist glanced at Jessie, but she beat him to it. "Nip that fag, and let's go back inside and you can show us."

The receptionist's was nothing more than a glassed-off desk near the entrance. Dot stepped into the area, took a seat by a phone. The walls and glass panels were plastered with scribbled Post-its.

"Is this it?" Jessie asked. "The telephone reception?"

"Classy, isn't it. Not." Dot fluttered her fingers through a spiral notebook and said, "Here we are. There's only two. Someone called last night—*9:10 PM, male, no name or number, will call later.* I hate when they do that. And here's the other one, the day afore yesterday—*10:30 AM, Freddie wants you to call back.*" She looked up. "That's it."

"Who's Freddie?" Jessie asked.

Dot gave another disinterested shrug.

Gilchrist took the notebook from her, flipped through it, searching for other messages, but found none. "What do you do with the old messages?"

"Bin them."

Jessie kneeled to the floor, tipped the rubbish bin, and leafed through the pile, none of which were pages from the notebook. She pulled herself to her feet, leaving the mess on the floor. "When was the last refuse collection?" she asked.

"Are you kidding? We've got a dumpster out the back, and that's it."

"When was it last moved?"

She shook her head. "A day or so ago. I widnae know."

"We'll have a look through it on the way out," Gilchrist said. "You said you haven't seen Caryl for weeks?"

"That's right."

"She came here?"

"Aye."

"What for?"

"To check out the furniture, what d'you think what for?"

"Who keeps your sales records?"

"Jock's accountant."

"Who is?"

"A firm in Govan."

"Name?" It was like pulling teeth.

She removed a tack from a card on a corkboard over the desk and handed the card to him. "That good enough?"

Murdock and Roberts CA Ltd. The company name meant nothing to him, but if necessary, he could obtain a warrant for Dillanos Furniture's sales records. Not that it would ever come to that, he thought.

He pocketed the card. "So what does this Caryl Dillanos look like?"

"Like she's minted."

"Blonde brunette tall small thin fat?"

She looked at Jessie. "Blonde. About your height, but thinner. And wears only brand names, all expensive."

"Car?" Gilchrist pressed.

She nodded.

"I meant, what make?"

"Mercedes. One of the sports ones, with the big Mercedes thingie on the front."

"On the bonnet?"

"Naw. The front. On the radiator grille thingie."

"Two-seater? Or four?"

"How would I know?"

"What color?" Gilchrist asked.

"Silver."

"Registration number plate?"

"Are you joking? Takes me all my time to remember my own phone number."

"It's not a personalized number plate, is it?"

Dot thought for a moment, then said, "I widnae know for sure."

"We'll check it out. Anything else you can remember about the car? Any dents, scratches?" he prompted.

"Only that she complained it was getting old and was thinking of putting it up for sale."

"And did she?"

"I've no seen her in weeks, like I told you."

Gilchrist returned the spiral notebook. "Write this down," he said, and waited while she removed a ballpoint from a mug with LOVERS LEAP printed across it, choked with pens, pencils, highlighters. "11:00 AM," he said. "Jessica. Mercedes 350 SLK for sale. Fully loaded. Low mileage. Spotless." Then he read out Jessie's mobile number and said, "You never saw us. We weren't here today. All right?"

Dot eyed Gilchrist, her look shifting with indecision.

"I'll make sure your man doesn't get lifted next month," Jessie said to her.

Something passed behind Dot's eyes, then she revealed a Stonehenge-row of stained teeth. "Forget that," she said. "Lift the dozy bastard, and keep him in for the weekend. Can youse do that?"

"I'll try."

"Good," she said. "I never seen youse then."

In a vacant plot to the rear of the building, Gilchrist inspected the dumpster, but it contained no more than a day's worth of cardboard boxes and plastic wrapping.

"So what's a 350 LKS when it's at home?" Jessie asked him.

"It's a 350 SLK, and it's your boyfriend's car."

"And he's just done the dirty on me," she said. "Which is why I'm giving it away to the first reasonable offer."

Again, the speed of Jessie's mind surprised him.

Then she looked at him as if he'd grown horns. "You sure you weren't a bitch in an earlier life?"

18

As Gilchrist accelerated onto the M8, Jessie said, "D'you mind doing a detour?"

"Where to?"

"Easterhouse."

"Anyone I know?"

"You wouldn't want to," she said.

Silent, he followed Jessie's directions as she guided him off the motorway and into the mazelike depths of a sixties housing development, which he knew, from reading Dainty's e-mail before crashing out, was where Jessie's mother lived.

"Next on the left," Jessie said.

Gilchrist eased into Wellhouse Crescent.

"Nearly there."

"Is this where you grew up?" he asked.

"If you could call it that."

Rows of three-story flats ran along one side of a narrow street lined with parked cars that had seen better days. Derelict open space filled the other side.

"Anywhere here'll do," Jessie said.

He drew in behind a battered Ford Mondeo.

Jessie had her seat belt off and the door open before Gilchrist stopped. "I'll only be a minute," she said.

Gilchrist watched her walk along the pavement, her head low, then turn and walk down a concrete path to a single access door, which she pushed open. She entered, and he removed his mobile and dialed Nance.

"Any luck with Farmer?"

"Not yet. I've got Dan checking out CCTV footage. I'll keep you posted."

"How about the tattoos? You get anywhere with these?"

"Nada. Baxter and McIvie are doing the rounds, but so far no one's owning up. It's a real long shot, Andy, if you don't mind me saying so."

Jessie's suggestion that the tattoos were done by some kind of a tattoo stamp, rather than from the needlework of a tattoo artist, had him almost telling her to call it off. "Give them to the end of the day," he said. "Then bring them in."

"Anything else?"

"Yes. I need you to find the registered owner of a Mercedes Sports. Several years old. Silver. Assume high mileage."

"Is that it?"

"And it might be registered under the name Caryl V. Dillanos, but then again, maybe not. So try personalized registration numbers along the lines of CVD something, or anything else that someone called Caryl-with-a-y Dillanos might find personal enough."

"If it's not registered under Caryl Dillanos, why would the plate be her initials?"

"If Dillanos is not her real name, then it might have to mean something to her. She drives around in it after all. You know, like Cheryl Victoria Dunbar, or some such thing."

"This sounds like another long shot, Andy."

"It's the best I can do," he said. "But I might have something more for you by the end of the day. I'll call then." He hung up, annoyed that his investigation seemed to be stalling. But sometimes you just have to plug away.

Just then, Jessie emerged from the entrance to the flats, her face pale, her lips tight. She marched toward the Merc, and he glimpsed movement at the top window on the block of flats from which she had just left. He peered up at Jeannie Janes mouthing off to Jessie.

The door opened. Jessie slid in.

"Drive."

"Seat belt."

"Oh for fuck sake, Andy, you can be a right plonker at times."

"Who's this?" he asked, as a young man burst into the open.

"Ah, fuck it."

Although stripped to the waist, the man's body was covered with so many tattoos he could have been clothed. He reached the pavement, jerked his head both ways, then saw Jessie. His face twisted with anger as he rushed toward the car.

Gilchrist had the door open and was on his feet by the time the young man reached them, and was striding around the bonnet as the man opened Jessie's door.

"Close the door, sonny."

The young man spun around, hatred twisting his features. "Who the fuck're you?"

"I'm the guy who's going to arrest you for spilling blood all over his nice car."

"Blood? What blood? I've no laid a fucking finger on her yet."

"I'm not talking about her," Gilchrist said.

Something seemed to dawn on the young man then, and he grinned, more grimace than smile. He flexed his muscles, stretched the tendons in his neck, as if readying to charge.

"Don't get yourself in serious trouble, sonny."

"The name's Terry," he said, "and ah've been in serious trouble afore."

"You tell him, Terry," Jessie said, shaking her head. "Just close the door and go back upstairs, will you?"

Terry turned to Jessie. "You ever set one foot in this street again, just one foot, and I'm warning you Jessie, I'll fucking have you, cop or no cop. Got that?"

"Sure, Terry."

He slammed the door, hard enough for Jessie to wince, then turned and strode toward Gilchrist who did the honorable thing and tried to step out of the way. Not quick enough, as Terry shouldered him on the way past.

Gilchrist turned, grabbed Terry's arm, twisted it, and knocked the legs out from under him. As Terry tumbled, Gilchrist spun him so that Terry hit the ground facedown with his arm jammed up between his shoulder blades. A knee into the middle of his back had Terry howling with pain and gasping for breath.

"Let him go, Andy." Jessie now stood at the front of the Merc.

Gilchrist looked up at her. "Are you all right?"

"I'm fine."

A high-pitched voice from the top-floor window had them both lifting their heads.

"I seen that, you fuckers. Police brutality's what it is. Youse'll be hearing from my solicitor. I'll be making a formal complaint. I'll get you flung out the Force, you fucking wee bitch."

"Let's go, Andy. I shouldn't have come."

Gilchrist shifted his knee, eased Terry's arm down his back. He stood back as Terry pulled himself to his feet, his bare chest grazed and oozing blood where he had landed on the pavement. Terry slid an arm under his nose, then spat to the ground.

"Go home, Terry. This is nothing to do with you."

"It's *everything* to do with me."

"Give it up, Terry. I'm through with you lot."

Terry pointed at her, his lean arm as tattooed as a yakuza's. "I'm warning you—"

"Are you threatening a police officer?" Gilchrist asked.

Terry's jaw rippled with anger, his eyes danced with indecision. Then he said, "Ach, away and fuck, the pair of youse."

Gilchrist waited until Terry was stomping his way back to his flat before he turned to Jessie. She shrugged a grimace, then retreated to the car.

As Gilchrist opened the car door, he glanced at the upper-floor window. But Jeannie with her matriarchal vitriol was gone. Silent, he retraced their route back to the M8.

As he accelerated down the slip road, he said, "Who's Terry?"

"My brother."

"Mr. Angry."

She snorted. "Here's hoping you never meet Tommy."

Gilchrist gave her words some thought, then said, "So what's going on is more than just you and your mother not liking each other."

"I'm not ready for this."

"That doesn't cut it, Jessie. I was attacked by—"

"Terry bumped into you, Andy. You didn't need to take him down like that."

"If I hadn't been there, would he have hit you?"

Jessie shrugged. "You overreacted."

"You're not answering the question."

"Maybe."

"Even though he knows you're police?"

Another snort. "That's like a red rag to a bull."

Gilchrist pulled into the fast lane and eased up to sixty. "Terry seemed proud that he'd been in serious trouble before. Do you know the details?"

"Eighteen months in Barlinnie for GBH. But he was lucky."

Gilchrist let her words settle. GBH—grievous bodily harm. Mr. Angry lashes out. "So he's good with his fists," he said.

"Terry doesn't think it's a fair fight until it's two of them against one of him," Jessie said. "You've no idea how lucky you were, Andy."

Gilchrist gripped the steering wheel. *You've no idea how lucky you were.* How true those words were. Bigger, harder, tougher men than he could ever be had taken on criminals filled with hatred for the police, and come off the worse for it. But luck often favored he who struck first, a lesson worth remembering.

"So where's your other brother, Tommy?"

"Back in Barlinnie. For stabbing someone. He's the nutcase of the family."

"Jesus, Jessie."

"Jesus Jessie right enough," she said, and looked at him. "Now you're beginning to understand. Welcome to happy families."

19

Gilchrist was driving through Auchtermuchty when Jessie's mobile rang.

"Could I speak to Jessica?" In the car's cabin, the voice was as clear as if she was on speakerphone.

"Who's this?" Jessie said.

"Caryl Dillanos."

Jessie flapped her hand for Gilchrist to pull over. "Hang on a minute," she said. "I'm driving. Let me stop the car." She waited until Gilchrist pulled down a side street and drew to a halt. "That's me pulled over. So you got my message?"

"I did. It sounds interesting."

The voice sounded fragile and tinny from the mobile's mic, but Gilchrist thought he caught an accent, not English but foreign—maybe Eastern European. But he could not be sure.

"I'd like to see it. Where is it?"

"St. Andrews. D'you know it?"

"Yeah. How'd you get my mobile number?"

Gilchrist caught the serious tone, the underlying suspicion.

"From Angus McCarron," Jessie said.

"You know him?"

"He drinks with my boyfriend. Well, more like man-friend," she said, then grimaced, embarrassed by her rambling.

"So, what's the car like?"

"It's silver. My favorite color. It's a Mercedes. A 350 SKL," she said, and frowned when Gilchrist put his hand to his forehead. "And it's six months old."

"Mileage?"

"Mileage is, let me see . . ." Gilchrist drew the figure three in the air and mouthed *Three thousand*. "Three thousand," she said.

"What's the price?"

"That's up to you."

Caryl laughed, a high-pitched cackle that sounded forced.

"First reasonable offer I get," Jessie said, "then I'm dumping it." She looked over at Gilchrist, and he read the panic in her eyes. He drew 20K on the dashboard and mouthed *Twenty thousand*.

A pause, then, "Why are you selling it?"

"Hell hath no fury like a woman scorned," Jessie said. "I've just found out my man-friend's been boinking his twenty-year-old secretary for the last three months. So, I'm going to sell his car, then tell him to fuck off." She held onto her mobile. "Is that a good enough reason?"

"Six months old? Three thousand miles? No dents, dings, or scratches?"

"It could be straight out the showroom. Doughball polishes it every weekend. Pays it more attention than he pays me. He's even given it a nickname. Tinkerbell."

Gilchrist frowned at her. *Tinkerbell?*

Jessie shrugged, as if to say she had no idea where Tinkerbell came from either.

"How does ten thousand sound?"

"I want to get back at him, not bankrupt the bastard. First *reasonable* offer is what I said. If you're looking for a freebie, then you're looking in the wrong place."

"Do you have anything in mind, then?"

"Won't let it go for a penny below twenty."

An intake of breath, followed by a long whistle. "Do you have all the paperwork?"

"I do."

"Isn't the car his?"

"It is. But I have power of attorney. Don't ask."

"When can I see it?"

"He's flying to London tomorrow for the day. I'd like to give him his going away present tomorrow night, followed by the big heave-ho. Think you can do that?"

"Whereabouts in St. Andrews?"

For a moment Gilchrist thought Jessie looked lost, then she recovered with, "You know the cathedral ruins? I'll meet you there. You can't miss them."

"What time?"

"Hang on, let me check." Gilchrist mouthed *Eleven.* "How does 11:00 in the morning sound?"

"Perfect."

"Cash only."

"What other way is there to do business?"

The line died.

Jessie let out a rush of air. "Jeez-oh. That was worse than a Saturday night gig in the Students' Union." Then she said, "You'd better get hold of Angus. That bitch'll call him to check my story."

Gilchrist poked at his mobile, held it to his ear. "Mhairi? Have you got Angus's mobile number?" He repeated it out loud as she read it off, then he hung up and dialed. He gave

Jessie a wink of reassurance, then said, "Angus? DCI Gilchrist. You might get a call from your friend Caryl. If she does, here's what you're going to tell her . . ."

Without complaint, Angus listened to Gilchrist tell him about Jessie's imaginary man-friend, and how he and Angus were good mates, close enough to exchange mobile numbers. When he hung up, Jessie said, "What now?"

"We need to find a six-month-old silver Mercedes 350 *SLK*," he said, emphasizing the initials. "You had them the wrong way round. It's an SLK, not an SKL."

"Bugger off."

They cleared the town of Auchtermuchty in silence, and Gilchrist pushed the speed up to seventy, before he said, "I thought you handled it well."

"I thought I kind of fluffed my way through it," she said, then asked, "So where are we going to find a 350 . . . a silver Mercedes?"

"That could be a bit of a problem," he said at length. "We're going to be hard pressed to set this up."

"*We're* going to be hard pressed? You're the one getting paid the big bucks."

"Clearly you've never seen my payslip."

But a visit to a dealership in Cupar, and four phone calls later, warned Gilchrist that he might have overstepped his act—until the fifth call. He gave Jessie a victory smile and said, "Shuggie's going to pick one up in Perth and trailer it over. It'll be in St. Andrews this evening. But it needs to be back in the dealership tomorrow night, or it starts costing us. I'll have Nance work out its safe return."

"Why trailer?"

"It's brand new."

"So how much does a brand-new SKL thingie cost, any-way?"

"You've still got it the wrong way round. It's an SLK. And for a 350 . . . ? Upwards of thirty thousand."

"And that cheeky bitch offered me ten?" Jessie gasped.

"That would have been the deal of the decade."

"How about the deal of the century? Who did she think she was talking to?" She looked at her watch, then said, "Can you run me to a mobile phone shop, then drop me at home? I need to give Robert his lunch."

From anger to concern in zero seconds flat. As if she clicked a switch. "What age did you say he was?" he asked.

"Old enough to masturbate, and young enough to need his mum to cook his meals."

"Well, let's hope you never get *that* the wrong way round." Jessie glared at him.

"Sorry," he said. "A joke that came out—"

"The wrong way round?"

"Exactly."

20

He double-parked while Jessie ran in and out of Orange on South Street.

Then he drove her home and agreed to pick her up after 3:00.

Back at the station, he checked his e-mails, saw he had another one from Cooper—Can you call? Not urgent. R xx—back to the two kisses, which meant . . . ?

He waded through the rest of his e-mails, stopped at one from Jackie, and skimmed through it.

Galyna Grabowski. Polish citizen. Nineteen years old. A year ago in March, failed to turn up for her job as a waitress in Trattoria Guidi, Airdrie. Reported missing by her two flatmates. Her body was found in Clydebank, Dunbartonshire, six months later, severely emaciated, with evidence of drug abuse . . .

He clicked on the JPEG attachment.

An image of a young woman, as blonde as a Scandinavian, with the glazed stare of the dead, looked out at him.

He would have put her in her midthirties, not twenty. Her skin reflected her poor diet and health—pockmark scars and the roseate glare of infected spots. A dark bruise tinted her right cheekbone and dulled the skin under her eye. Here was a young woman who had ended at the bottom of the drug-pile and died before she ever had the chance to live. She had been attractive, too, with eyes set wide apart and a face that narrowed to . . .

He leaned closer, enlarged the image.

It was her jaw that intrigued him, how her face had an almost triangular shape that led the eye to a small chin verging on the pointed.

He pulled up Jackie's e-mail again and continued reading.

> . . . evidence of drug abuse and vaginal infection. She died from a single stab wound to the heart. Suspected weapon an ice pick. Her body had a total of seventeen tattoos, ranging from a pair of wings that spread across her shoulders, to a tiny number eleven in her left armpit, less than half an inch in size . . .

Two tattoos in particular caught his attention—the pair of shoulder wings and the number eleven in her left armpit. He opened the JPEG again, placed one hand over the left side of her face. He would not bet on it, but was he stretching coincidence too far?

Was he looking at the sister of the woman on the Coastal Path?

He printed out the image, pushed from his chair, and walked along the hall to Jackie's room. He held up the photo. "Galyna Grabowski," he said. "What drew you to her?"

Jackie opened her mouth, then raised her left arm and patted her armpit.

"The number eleven tattoo?"

She nodded.

"Did you find any others with the same tattoo?"

She moaned a no and shook her head.

"OK, get me a copy of her full report, postmortem, investigation file."

She tried OK but nodded instead.

"Great work, Jackie. Keep me posted."

Back in his office, he found Cooper's mobile number and dialed it.

"So you got my e-mail?" she said.

He kept her on track with, "I might have a lead that could help us ID our Coastal Path woman. I'll have Jackie send you DNA from another victim—"

"You think they're related?"

"Could be. They have similar facial features. So it's a long shot." He gave her Jackie's e-mail address, then said, "You wanted me to call?"

"Yes, I thought you might consider letting me buy you a pint tomorrow night. It is Saturday, after all."

Gilchrist thought of just saying he was busy. But despite his workload, he always tried to keep Saturday night open. "Where did you have in mind?"

"Somewhere noisy and full of students, like the Central. Isn't that your local?"

"One of them, but . . ."

"So we have a date?"

"A date?"

"Yes, boy meets girl, girl meets boy." She chuckled, a throaty growl that sent a signal to his groin. "Bring others along, if you'd prefer. Safety in numbers. We'll probably all want to talk shop anyway. Say, seven o'clock? I'll contact you when I get there." The line died.

Gilchrist returned his mobile to his jacket, trying to shift the feeling that he had just been manipulated, and resisting the petty urge to call back and cancel their date. But just the sound of that word—*date*—pulled a wry smile to his face. It would be Saturday, after all.

Before leaving the station, he made another copy of the photograph.

He collected Jessie from her home and said, "How is he?"

"He didn't masturbate, if that's what you're asking."

"Jesus, Jessie, it was a slip of the—"

"Lighten up, Andy. Where's your sense of humor?"

"That was a joke?"

"Dry delivery. So, where are we off to?"

Again, her change in tack almost threw him. He showed her Galyna's photo, but she was unable to help. She remembered the body being found in a back street on the outskirts of Clydebank, a stone's throw from Duntocher and the Krukovs' barn. But she could not recall a tattoo in the shape of an eleven.

"I'd need to revisit Strathclyde's records," she said.

"Jackie's already ordered them."

"If she was found in September last year, that was before we raided the Krukovs. Which might explain why we never picked up on the significance of the tattoo."

Gilchrist nodded. How often were clues not noticed through poor timing? "Do you think we're missing something?" he said. "I mean, we look at the tattoo and the first thing we see is the number eleven. Then bones. But maybe it's not bones or the number eleven we should be concentrating on. Maybe it's something else," he said.

"Like what?"

He chewed through his rationale but could not push it forward. "I don't know."

"Therein lies the problem."

"Indeed."

Gilchrist spent the next ten minutes contacting each member of his investigation team and asking them to report for debriefing at 5:00 PM. The occasional early night was good for morale, particularly at the start of the weekend. Besides, they were beginning to make some real progress. They had Dillanos driving up to St. Andrews tomorrow morning, which could give them their first lead to the renter of the cottage. They had a possible connection to the girl on the Coastal Path, with a DNA comparative sample ordered, which might—and it was a big might—ID her. But one thing still worried him, which was not related to any crime.

His *date* with Rebecca Cooper.

Having an affair with a married woman was one thing. Flaunting it in a busy pub for all to see was something else entirely. Not that it was unusual for colleagues to share a drink after work or on celebratory occasions. That went on all the time the world over. He was about to drive off when his mobile rang—ID Nance.

"Let me guess," he said. "You've finally got something on Craig Farmer?"

"Not quite."

The tone of her voice had Gilchrist pressing his mobile to his ear. "I'm listening."

"Donnelly's dead. Shot through the back of the head."

Gilchrist stared out the window. On the other side of the road, two women in heavy overcoats, shopping bags clutched in fingers chaffed and reddened by a cold Scottish wind, conversed with each other, unaware of the criminal mayhem around them.

"Where is he?" he asked Nance.

"In an abandoned car at the entrance to Strathvithie Country Estate."

"No witnesses?"

"It's a professional killing."

"I'm on my way."

By the time Gilchrist arrived, the SOCOs were already there.

Not yet 4:00 PM, and dragonlights lit up the scene.

He pulled off the B9131 and parked behind two police vehicles.

The wind had risen, whipping the fields with an arctic chill.

"It's not pretty," Nance said, leading Gilchrist and Jessie to a white Ford that had reversed through a field entrance, now blocked off by crime scene tape. Nance held up the tape to let Gilchrist and Jessie slip under.

The driver's door and the passenger back door on the same side lay open. At first glance, the shattered windscreen looked as if it had been smeared with paint, but as they neared Gilchrist prepared himself for the worst.

Not pretty was an understatement.

The entrance wound in the back of the head was clean enough—a tidy hole that could have been made by a surgeon's drill—with scorch marks to the hair and surrounding flesh that confirmed the muzzle had been pressed to the skin.

The exit wound was another matter. Donnelly was almost unrecognizable.

The bullet—SOCOs' best estimate was 9 mm caliber—had taken most of Donnelly's nose and one of his eyes with it, splattering flesh and blood over the windscreen in a mess like curried vomit. Donnelly's body lay slumped over the steering wheel, his lifeless fingers still clutching a mobile phone.

"You think they'll have a closed coffin?" Jessie said.

"Give it up," Gilchrist said.

Even though he recognized Donnelly's clothes—the same light denim jeans, black V-neck sweater—the tattoo on the nape of his neck confirmed ID. Gilchrist leaned into the back seat of the car. It smelled fresh, suggesting it had been cleaned recently, but not by Donnelly—he had looked too rough to show interest in maintaining appearances.

"The car's a rental, right?" he asked.

Nance said, "Enterprise in Dundee. Already called. They've confirmed it was rented to a Stewart Donnelly this morning for a week. Paid cash in advance."

"Thought he'd just been released," Gilchrist said. "Where'd the money come from?"

"We'll check local banks."

"Maybe we need to be asking why he came to St. Andrews in the first place. I mean, there are plenty of pubs in Dundee. Why here? Can we check the mileage?"

"Already done that," Nance said. "He's clocked up a total of sixty-two miles."

Gilchrist did a quick mental calculation. "The shortest drive from Dundee is twenty miles, so it's forty there and back. As he's still on the St. Andrews side of the Tay, then he must have driven around here for a bit."

"Maybe he drove around Dundee."

Gilchrist grimaced. His gut was telling him that Donnelly rented the car to cross the River Tay and come to St. Andrews. If he had wanted to see Dundee, he could have walked around the place. No, the car was rented for travel. He felt sure of that.

"See if we can find any CCTV on the car," he said to Nance, and returned his attention to the back seat. From the direction of the blood and brain spatter, and the clean entry wound, the killer must have been seated directly behind Donnelly.

"What do you think?" he asked Jessie.

"I'd say there had to have been at least two of them," she said. "A passenger in the front to keep his attention, and another in the back to shoot him."

Gilchrist nodded. "What about his mobile? Why didn't they take it?"

"Maybe he was calling for help."

"Or someone called as a distraction?"

"Which would mean there was a third involved," Jessie said, and walked to the front of the car.

"Not necessarily."

"We'll get our technicians onto it," Nance said.

Gilchrist thought the mobile could give them a lead. At the very least, they should be able to retrieve Donnelly's contacts, view records of his last phone calls. But as he worked through the logic, he came to see that the killers had not taken Donnelly's mobile because they had known it could offer nothing—

"Check this out," Jessie shouted from the other side of the car.

Gilchrist walked around the hood to the front passenger door.

Jessie was crouched on the ground. "Looks like we've got a partial imprint," she said. "And a couple of slip marks, which makes me think our man left in a hurry. But again, who wouldn't when the guy next to you gets his head blown off?" She pushed to her feet. "He'll definitely have some blood spatter on him. And there's no footprints by the rear passenger door this side, which suggests there were only two of them."

"Or the passengers in the rear exited from the same near-side door," Gilchrist offered.

Jessie glared at him, as if irritated at being challenged.

"But I agree," Gilchrist said. "I think there were two of them, and we need to find Farmer." He turned to Nance. "Can we prioritize that?"

Nance nodded, and spoke into her mobile.

Having just scheduled an early debriefing, he ordered Nance to call everyone on the team and postpone it for a couple of hours. Starting up a fresh investigation on a Friday night was not the way to win a popularity contest and would not go down well. But if he offered to buy a few rounds later, that might soften the upset.

21

Gilchrist came to, struggling to work out where he was. Skylight windows looked down at him like black observation strips.

Rain as heavy as a monsoon thudded the rooftop, rattled the glass.

A tongue that tasted like the bottom of a parrot's cage, and a glance at his bedside clock—8:04—reminded him that he'd had too much to drink last night. He pulled himself from bed, still in his shirt and underpants, and eyed his socks, trousers, belt, jacket, and scarf on the floor, like a trail that led back to the hallway.

In the dining room, Dainty's printed e-mail spread across the table like an abandoned letter. Had he tried to read that last night? A long shower, hot enough to cook shrimp, did little to shift the pain, and a couple of Panadol chased with two glasses of Diet Sprite tried to make a start at clearing the fog.

By the time he drove to St. Andrews, the skies had worsened, dumping rain as thick as slush onto roads that seemed naked without traffic. An ice-cold wind that could strip meat from a bone sliced along North Street like a lunatic looking for a way out.

"You think she'll turn up?" Jessie said.

"The weather's not like this in Glasgow," Gilchrist replied. "So she'll be on her way." He checked his watch—9:30. "Probably leaving about now."

As arranged, Shuggie had trailered the Mercedes into St. Andrews, where it now sat curbside in Free Parking at the top of North Street, within easy sight of the cathedral ruins. Rain slid off its shining paintwork in sheets of sleet. Gilchrist found himself resisting the urge to sit behind the wheel, start it up, and just take it for a spin. He handed the keys to Jessie.

"We've got over an hour before she turns up," he said. "How about a coffee?"

"Thought you were never going to ask."

Starbucks heaved and steamed like a cattle market, the cramped floor space more crowded than Marks and Sparks on a weekend sales day.

"Let's go," Gilchrist said, and together he and Jessie ran across Market Street.

Beyond the brief respite in the pend of Logie's Lane, they scurried along South Street and found a couple of seats in Con Panna. Gilchrist ordered two lattes—one skinny, one fatty—which failed to crack the waitress's face.

Having skipped breakfast on the grounds that his stomach could not face it, the warm aroma of cooked food teased saliva to his mouth. "Like a bacon sarnie?" he asked Jessie.

"You trying to fatten me up?"

He smiled at the waitress. "And two rolls and bacon."

When the waitress left, Jessie said, "What's up with her?"

"Hungover?"

"Just like you?"

Gilchrist grimaced. "Does it show?"

"I'm glad I left after two."

"I wasn't far behind you," he lied.

Six pints of Deuchars were four more than he allowed himself as a maximum. But it had been a Friday night, the end of the working week—whatever a working week was—and he had convinced himself that he needed more than a couple to drown the horror of it all. It had not helped that his son, Jack, had turned up when he was finishing his third, and well, what could he say? He had to have a few pints with his boy, and he left with a promise to visit Jack's studio and see some of his new work.

The bacon was salted, the fat verging on crisp—perfect—and the rolls baked fresh that morning. Two bites had Gilchrist signaling for another before Jessie had even finished peppering hers.

"I thought Robert could eat for Scotland," she said. "Looks like he'd take the silver."

"Didn't realize I was so hungry."

Jessie nibbled at her roll, followed it with a sip of coffee, and said, "So what do you want me to tell this bimbo when she turns up?"

"You're going to tell her nothing. Just lead her to the Merc as if you're going to show it to her, then act surprised when I turn up—"

"If you're going to arrest her, I'd rather arrest her myself," she said. "I won't feel like I've settled in until I arrest some-one."

Gilchrist eyed his second roll, contemplating where to bite first. "Better to stay out of it," he said. "You'll have plenty of time to arrest someone later."

Jessie looked at him, as if a thought had just come to her. "Do you think this Dillanos bird'll bring someone along to check out the Merc?"

"I doubt it. By the way she talked numbers, she knows what's what."

Jessie took another sip of her coffee, then said, "If she's rented the cottage from Angus, then I'm willing to bet she knows Kumar."

"But maybe not what he does," Gilchrist said. "A commission for finding a quiet cottage for long-term rent on the Fife Coast could be another way of getting some pocket money."

"She knows Kumar," Jessie persisted. "And she knows what he does. You just need to hear the man's voice to know he's not renting property to watch birds. Well, not the feathered type anyway."

Gilchrist bit into his roll. For Kumar to decapitate a pair of Russian gangsters, he must have no fear of reprisal, no respect for human life. An image of Gordie's eyes widening with fear from the knowledge of what was about to happen, being murdered in the most horrific manner, surged through his brain like an electric jolt.

The psychopathic mentality truly was frightening. Most psychopaths looked like your next-door neighbor, the man you had a chat with in the pub, easy-going, gregarious, would buy you a beer, crack a joke, act as if they were getting on with everyday living, the same as everyone else. But behind that innocent facade lay the complex mind and thoughts of one of mankind's most evil and dangerous killers.

What set psychopaths apart was their lack of compassion for their victims, lack of remorse for their crimes, and a mind-blowing inability to consider themselves responsible for their actions. He recalled interrogating his first convicted murderer and being stunned by the rationale—*If she hadn't told lies about me, I wouldn't have had to kill her*—

"You going to eat that or play with it?"

Gilchrist looked at his roll, pushed it to the side of his plate. "I'm full."

Jessie sipped her coffee, eyed him with suspicion. "Empty to full in five seconds? I wish Robert could do that."

He tried a smile, not sure he pulled it off, then forced his thoughts on a new tack. "Did you give Robert his new SIM card?"

"Who said anything about a new SIM card?"

"Why else would you rush into Orange?"

Silent, Jessie bit into her roll.

"You're just making sure that his grandmother can't text him because you've changed his number," he said.

Jessie pushed her empty plate to the side, as if to clear the way between them. "So I got him a new SIM card," she said. "What's the big deal?"

"The big deal is, why would you deny having bought one?"

"It's personal. OK?"

"Not wanting to talk about it yet?"

Jessie discarded his question with a shake of her head and glanced outside. "Looks like it's settling. Probably be hot enough to wear a bikini this afternoon." She snorted. "Me in a bikini? You'd better hope it starts snowing."

"I should have arrested your brother," Gilchrist said.

"Don't go there, Andy," she snapped, and the fire in her eyes warned him to keep out of it. "My family doesn't exist. My mother, my brothers, all of them, don't exist in my life. Not anymore. Got that?"

"Got it," he said. But if she thought he had, she did not know him.

22

Outside, the wind had dropped and the clouds shifted, leaving a blue sky as clear and cold as a polar morning. Nowhere near bikini weather, but it sure beat slush for rain. They strode along South Street in silence, and at the far end turned left toward Deans Court. The cathedral ruins spilled off to the right. Straight ahead, the 350 SLK Mercedes glinted in the sunlight.

A woman with brown hair appeared to be inspecting it.

"That might be Dillanos," Gilchrist said, and crossed the road, leaving Jessie to walk toward the woman by herself. He cursed at his carelessness. He should have anticipated her arriving early. It was the weekend after all, so why wait for an 11:00 appointment if you had nothing else to do except buy a car in a giveaway deal?

He reached the entrance to the cathedral ruins, stepped inside, and veered off the pathway, pretending to show interest in weatherworn gravestones that littered the damp grass. Through the metal railing, he watched Jessie walk to the car, his sixth sense telling him that all was not as it seemed.

Jessie shielded her face from a blast of icy air as she crossed North Street. The Merc sat parked between a Volkswagen Beetle and a Ford hatchback, its silver paintwork reflecting the cold sunlight like a steel mirror. The woman did not notice Jessie bearing down on her, her attention taken up with peering through the side window, as if trying to read the mileage from the dashboard.

Jessie had almost reached the Mercedes when the woman looked up.

"Hi," Jessie said. "Are you Caryl?"

The woman pushed a gloved hand through her hair and said, "Yeah."

"I'm Jessie." She held out her hand.

Dillanos took it without removing her gloves.

"What do you think?" Jessie offered, turning to the car.

Dillanos nodded. "Not bad."

Jessie took her in—same height, thinner, light-brown hair, not exactly the blonde Showroom Dot had described, but maybe her hair had been dyed. And well dressed, with a thick, woollen jacket and skirt, black woollen tights, and gray shoes that matched her scarf and gloves and turtleneck sweater. But she looked younger than Jessie had expected, in her twenties she guessed, not thirties, far too young to be carrying all that cash around. And it struck Jessie that they should perhaps have called in Angus, just to make sure.

"You got ID?" Jessie asked.

"I've got twenty thousand IDs."

"I mean proper ID. Like a driving license."

"I've got a driving license."

"I'm not asking if you've got one," Jessie said. "I'm asking to see it."

"What for?"

"ID."

"Have you got the keys and the registration documents?"

Jessie looked hard into Dillanos's eyes. No sign of fear there. This was not going as she had anticipated. She had never bought a car before. The deal for her Fiat 500 had been done by Lachie. Jessie had come up with the money, signed the paperwork, of course, but had taken no part in the negotiations. Lachie had done that, worked out a sweetheart deal on her behalf, to show what a caring partner he could be or, even more scary, a loving husband.

Dillanos unbuttoned her jacket, tapped a white envelope that poked from the top of an inside pocket. "I'm not handing this over without checking the registration documents and seeing *your* ID."

Two things struck Jessie. The first—that although she had never seen twenty thousand pounds in cash, the envelope looked too thin. If they were all one hundred pound notes, there would be two hundred. If they were in five hundreds, forty. Was there such a thing as a one thousand pound note? Even so, how thick would twenty notes be? And the second— if this woman was Caryl Dillanos, then Jessie was Marilyn Monroe.

"So," Jessie said. "What do you think?"

The woman shifted her gaze over Jessie's shoulder as she let the wind blow the hair from her eyes. "Look," she said to Jessie. "I don't have all day. I need to see the registration documents." Another glance.

Was she searching for someone?

Jessie nodded. "The documents are in the glove compartment," she said, removing the key fob from her pocket. She pressed it, and the boot lid popped open. She walked to the back and, as nonchalant as you like, closed it.

Off to her side, beyond the cathedral railings, to the right of the war memorial, she caught Gilchrist mulling around the gravestones, mobile to his ear, body angled so that she was within his field of vision. She pressed the fob again, and the door locks clicked.

She reached for the door handle, glanced at the woman—

Another tilt of the head.

Was that a signal?

Along North Street—lights at green; a couple walking their dog; three cars easing toward the cathedral corner, the car in front, a Porsche SUV, almost at a crawl, as if looking for a parking space.

Or . . . ?

Another glance from the woman, and this time Jessie saw it. The eye contact. The Porsche SUV.

Jessie faced the Porsche, registered only that the driver was a blonde-haired woman. She strode onto the street and flagged the Porsche down, but it accelerated toward her with an easy growl from its engine. Jessie tried to grab the door handle, almost caught it, but was spun off by a sudden burst of acceleration.

She fell to the ground, landed with a heavy thud, then pulled herself to her knees in time to catch Gilchrist running full pelt from the cathedral grounds onto the road. He stood his ground, warrant card high in the air, and the Porsche pulled to a halt less than two feet from him, its engine revving, as if the driver was in two minds whether to get on with it and just run him over.

Jessie turned back to the woman at the Merc, who stood with her mouth open, her eyes shifting, not sure whether to make a dash for it or not.

"Don't even think about it," Jessie shouted to her, as she walked toward her. "I've had enough exercise for one day."

23

Jessie pressed a button on the recorder on the table and announced that the interview was being recorded, then listed who was present—DCI Andy Gilchrist and DS Jessie Janes of Fife Constabulary, and Caryl Dillanos. She read Dillanos her rights and said, "You have also been advised that you have the right to have a solicitor present, but you have turned that down. Is that correct?"

"What do I need a solicitor for? Buying a car's not a crime."

"Reckless driving is," Jessie said.

"So I pay a fine and lose my license. Big deal. I'll hire a driver."

"It's not quite as simple as that," Gilchrist said.

"It is to me."

"How about murder?"

Dillanos let out a laugh. "Murder? Who am I supposed to have murdered?"

"Would you like to have your solicitor present now?" Jessie pressed.

"I don't want a solicitor present. OK? I don't need one for a traffic violation. And I've not murdered anyone. But if you lot continue to threaten me like this, you will be hearing from my solicitor. And it won't be about traffic violations."

Gilchrist pressed forward. Time to take over. "For the record," he said, "please state your full name, date of birth, and address."

"Caryl Versace Dillanos, September 23, 1968, Glasgow."

"Address in Glasgow?"

She told them, and Gilchrist thought it was somewhere in the city center.

"Caryl Versace Dillanos," he said. "Is that the name on your birth certificate?"

"Deed poll."

"What's your birth name?"

"Megan Murphy."

Jessie snorted. Gilchrist glanced at her. "Middle names?" he said.

"None."

"When did you change your name?"

"Years ago."

"When exactly?"

"Can't remember."

"Best guess. Ten years? Twenty?"

"Nineties. I was in my early twenties, something like that."

"Why change your name?"

"Are you serious?"

"Very."

"Let me see." She held both palms out, as if weighing one imaginary item against the other. "Megan Murphy? Caryl Dillanos?" She lowered her left hand. "Dillanos walked it."

"And the Versace?"

"Thought it sounded good."

"What do you do for a living?"

"Import export," she said. "But officially I'm an international buyer."

"And unofficially?"

"There youse go. Trying to put words into my mouth. I'm an international buyer full time then. Is that better?"

"An international buyer in what?"

"In whatever you want me to buy." She showed him a set of teeth that had to have set her back several thousand pounds, maybe more.

"Working for?"

"Myself?"

"Trading as?"

"Myself."

"And you'll be registered for VAT?"

"That's right. Check it out with my accountants."

"Murdock and Roberts?"

Surprise shifted to suspicion, then on to irritation. "Have you been checking me out?"

"Are you current with your tax returns?"

"What's this? Do I need a solicitor?"

"Would you like to stop this interview and call one?"

"Just get on with it, will you? I've an appointment in the West End at two."

And with these words, Gilchrist came to see that Caryl Versace Dillanos had lived her entire life on the wrong side of the law. The police were little more than an annoyance to be dealt with every now and then, an interview here, a visit to the police station there, maybe even slipping the odd hundred quid or three to have the boys in blue turn a blind eye while Ms. International Buyer shifted her stolen goods. Who knew? But one thing Gilchrist did know was that Dillanos had no idea of the seriousness of her situation. Or perhaps she thought she could brass her way through it.

Best to go straight to the core.

"Do you know a Mr. McCarron?"

"Never heard of him."

"Angus McCarron?"

She paused, as if making the faintest connection. "Barely," she said.

"Answer yes or no."

"Yes."

"How would you describe your relationship with Mr.—"

"There was no relationship—"

"No *professional* relationship?"

"Yeah, well."

Gilchrist returned her firm gaze, thought he caught the tiniest flicker of understanding, as if she was only now putting two and two together. "Go on," he said.

"He's an estate agent. He showed me some property."

"Whereabouts?"

"All over the place."

"Where, exactly."

She puffed up her cheeks, then blew out. "St. Andrews, Pittenweem, Anstruther, and some other places with names I can't remember."

Gilchrist noted the absence of Kingsbarns. "And did you buy any of them?"

"Wasn't buying. Just looking to rent."

"So as well as being an international buyer, you're also a domestic renter?"

"Very funny," she said. "I buy, I sell, I rent, I wheel and deal. In other words, I make money. Lots of it."

Gilchrist ignored the taunt. "Did any of the rental properties Mr. McCarron showed you interest you?"

"Not for me. For a client."

Gilchrist leaned forward. Now they were coming down to it. "Name?"

She shook her head. "Can't remember."

"Phone records? Notes? Anything that might jog your memory?" he asked.

"Don't keep records."

"So it's all cash, no sales receipts, no records of any kind?"

"I'm not into paperwork."

"Even for Murdock and Roberts?"

"That's different. I'm legit."

Gilchrist offered a dry smile. Being *legit* meant that she filed tax returns through a firm of accountants who probably did not ask too many questions or dig too deep. Having them file her company's annual tax returns was just eyewash to give the impression of being a professional business.

"So what about the 350 SLK?" he asked. "Going to pay cash for that, too?"

"How else?"

Jessie lifted a custody folder from the floor, placed it on her lap, and said, "DS Janes exhibiting two items booked in when Ms. Dillanos was first detained." She slapped two thick envelopes onto the table and said, "There's nine thousand pounds in each. I thought we agreed twenty."

Dillanos shrugged. "That's all I was going to offer."

"And you sent that wee bimbo to check me out?"

"Who is she?" Gilchrist asked.

"Jana."

"Surname?"

"Just Jana."

"Polish?"

Dillanos's eyes stilled, as if realizing Gilchrist would always be one step ahead of her, maybe two. "Could be," she said.

"She have a visa?" Jessie asked.

"Don't know. Ask her."

"So what does she do for you?" Gilchrist again.

"Trainee."

"Trainee what?"

"Trainee international buyer."

Jessie snorted. "Going to take over when you retire?" she said.

"Yeah."

"You'd better train her quick, then," Jessie sniped.

"What's that supposed to mean?"

Gilchrist raised his hand, like a referee stepping in between two opponents. "DCI Gilchrist leaving the interview," he said.

Time to talk to Jana, he thought, and see how her lies compared to Dillanos's.

He pushed to his feet and left the interview room.

24

Gilchrist found Nance and PC Dan Morton in interview room 3.

He introduced himself, noted the time, and sat next to Nance, who shoved her handwritten notes to him. He read the girl's name—Jana Judkowski—then smiled at her.

"Yana Jookofski?" he said. "Is that how you pronounce it?"

"Uh-huh."

"Your boss, Caryl, she says you're a trainee."

"That's right."

"Trainee what?"

"Just trainee."

"I see," he said. "Is she a good boss?"

"She's all right."

"And you've declined your right to have a solicitor present?"

"Uh-huh."

The change in tack seemed not to faze her. "I would remind you that anything you say can be used against you in a court of law," he said. "You do understand that, don't you?"

"I've done nothing wrong."

"I'm not saying you have, Jana. I'm only asking if you understand that any lies you say now could come back to bite you."

"I'm telling the truth."

Gilchrist held her gaze. "Do you have any tattoos?"

"Uh-huh."

"How many?"

"Four."

"Can I see them?"

She gave a knowing smirk, her wounded-girl image evaporating to reveal a temptress trained in the ways of easing money from men's fingers with the oily charm of a seductress. "It'll cost you," she said, lowering her head, raising her eyebrows.

"Can you point to where they are?" he said. "If you feel uncomfortable answering that question, PC Morton and I can leave the room."

She leaned back in her chair, lifted her arm and tapped the back of her neck.

"For the record," said Nance, "The interviewee is indicating that she has a tattoo on the back of her neck." A pause, then, "And another tattoo on her left breast. And her right breast. And one near her genitalia."

"I have a butterfly tattooed on my labia," Jana said, and smiled at Gilchrist. "Want to see it?"

"Any others?" he asked.

She shook her head.

"Yes or no."

"No."

Gilchrist said, "Again, I would remind you of your need to tell the truth."

She shrugged. "That's all," she said.

"You don't have another one here?" He raised his left arm, tapped his armpit.

"No."

Dillanos had taught her well, he thought, taught her how to look someone in the eye and tell a lie as if it were the truth, the whole truth, and nothing but the truth. Or maybe that was why she had been selected as a trainee. He thought back to Dillanos, the cocky manner, the way she shifted in her chair, revealing more thigh than necessary—albeit woollen-tight-covered thigh, but thigh nonetheless. If she smoked a cigarette, she would exhale straight into your face.

"What does the number eleven mean to you?" he asked.

She frowned, as if baffled by his question. "Eleven?"

He nodded. "Does it mean anything to you?"

"Nothing."

Maybe he had it all wrong. "How about bones?" he tried.

"Bones?" She looked at Nance as if seeking relief from this lunatic, then back to Gilchrist. "Bones? What bones?"

"Small bones."

She sniffed, shook her head. "No bones."

Now was as good a time as any to trip her, he thought. "And Kumar?"

"What about him?"

"Him?" Gilchrist leaned closer. "Who said Kumar was a man?"

Jana blinked once, twice, deer caught in headlights, then rubbed her eye, as if something was irritating it. "Kumar's a man's name," she said.

"Not always." He didn't know if it was or not, but sometimes you have to press.

"Well, I thought it was." She lowered her hand. "I don't know anybody by the name of Kumar," she said.

"You didn't meet anyone by the name of Kumar in the cottage in Kingsbarns?"

"No."

Gilchrist stifled a smile. "So you've been to the cottage in Kingsbarns?" he said. "How long did you stay there?"

"I didn't stay there. I just visited it."

"With Caryl?"

"Uh-huh."

"Caryl said she knows Kumar." He sat back to watch her reaction.

"I don't believe you."

"You don't believe Caryl said that?"

"That's not her style."

"What's not her style?"

"Talking to the police."

"She's in trouble, Caryl is," Gilchrist pressed. "Do you want to go down with her?"

Jana's throat bobbed, and she tried to hold his gaze.

"I'll tell you what I'm going to do," Gilchrist said to her. "I'm going to get myself a cup of tea, and while I'm doing that I would like you to tell Detective Sergeant Wilson here all you know about Kumar."

Jana sniffed.

"And if I were you, Jana, I would want off this sinking ship while I still can."

"Ship?"

"Figure of speech." He held her eyes, seeing in their worried look the little girl she had once been. "Do you understand what I'm saying, Jana? Your boss, Caryl, is in trouble. She's going down. She'll probably go to jail. Do you want that to happen to you?"

Silent, she returned his hard stare with a blank one of her own.

Gilchrist wondered if she would open up to Nance if he was not there. So he excused himself and returned to interview room 1.

Dillanos barely glanced at him as he entered.

Jessie's mobile beeped as he took his seat, and she read its message.

Gilchrist reintroduced himself and said, "Jana's not as experienced as you."

"That's why she's a trainee."

Not a blink. Nothing. "She's coughing it all out in the other room," he tried.

Dillanos smirked at him. "Must have a cold, then. Maybe the flu."

Jessie placed her mobile on the table and leaned forward. "Does Bankenson Insurance mean anything to you?" she asked.

"Should it?"

"You've made four insurance claims in the last five years," Jessie pressed on. "Goods lost in transit. Each shipment from Dubai." She picked up her mobile, read the screen. "The largest claim was for three hundred and twenty-seven thousand. That's pounds sterling."

"That's right," Dillanos said. "Stuff's expensive."

"What sort of stuff?" Gilchrist chipped in.

"You name it."

He shook his head.

"They're all the same, these insurance companies," Dillanos went on. "Extortionate rates, and quick to take your payments. But not so quick to pay out."

"But they did in the end," Jessie said. "For all four of them, netting you, hang on a minute . . ." She mumbled as she added it up, then said, "Nine hundred and fifty thousand, give or take. All cash."

"Checks, actually."

"Did you report that to Murdock and Roberts?"

"Of course. Check it out. Phone them up. I had to cough up for the stuff. Which isn't cheap, let me tell you. And after the deductible's paid, you'll see I made a loss."

"Tax write-off?"

"Loss. Tax write-off. Same difference. It still cost me a ton."

"Where were the shipments lost?" Gilchrist asked.

"At sea," Dillanos replied. "Indian Ocean."

"All of them?"

"Yeah."

"They sank?"

"Vanished. The shipments, I mean. Not the ships."

"Pirated?"

"Could be. Off-loaded in Somalia. Who knows. I don't know the details."

"Where did the shipments originate from?"

"Dubai."

"And sailed from there?"

"Qatar," she explained. "Doha."

Gilchrist's Middle Eastern geography was not the best, but he said, "So they were transported by truck from Dubai through Saudi Arabia and into Qatar? Then loaded onto a ship and never turned up at the other end?"

Dillanos said, "It's a bitch."

Gilchrist almost smiled at the scam. The shipments were probably never loaded at Doha but sold on the black market before they reached the docks. You could cover anything you wanted with paperwork—an official stamp here, another there, proof that the cargo had been safely loaded. Who could argue with that? An insurance company would try, for sure. But in the face of compelling evidence, signed documentation, missing cargo, what could they do but pay out?

"You ever been to Dubai?" Gilchrist asked.

"Loads of times."

"Doha?"

"Once or twice."

Gilchrist smiled. "Kumar's an Arabic name, isn't it?" He was guessing, just putting the question out there. But for the first time that day, he thought he detected a shimmer of uncertainty.

25

One hour later, Gilchrist knew he was getting nowhere. Dillanos continued to claim that she was only on a finder's fee for the cottage in Kingsbarns and kept no records of the man she dealt with. She continued to swear—literally—that she did not know, had never met, nor ever spoken to anyone by the name of Kumar. Gilchrist threatened to check CCTV footage. But that drew a blank look of innocence.

Jana played just as dumb, maintaining she was only a trainee.

PC Morton confirmed that the Porsche SUV was registered in the name of Dillanos Ltd—Gilchrist had hoped it might give them a lead to Kumar. But with nothing to hold them, he had no option but to let Dillanos and Jana go.

He left Jessie to charge Dillanos with reckless driving, then placed a call to Dick—a retired policeman who now made a living building websites and troubleshooting IT problems, and who was content to flit across the legal boundaries from time to time, for a fee, of course, a fact that Gilchrist kept hidden from his colleagues.

"Got a number I need you to monitor," he said.

"Shoot."

Gilchrist recited Dillanos's mobile number. "I want numbers and names of every outgoing call from the moment I hang up."

"How long do you want me to stay on it?"

"Couple of days should do it. But I'll get back to you."

Gilchrist then called Shuggie and arranged for the Mercedes to be hauled away.

"That was quick," Shuggie said.

"Gives me time for a liquid lunch."

Jessie caught up with him in the Central Bar.

She eyed the empty plate on his table, the almost-finished pint of Deuchars IPA in his hand. "How come you don't put on weight?" she complained.

"Who said I don't?"

She nodded to his pint. "I put on two pounds every time I look at one of these," she grumbled, and shuffled in beside him.

"How did Miss Versace take it?"

"Bitch couldn't have given a toss. For two pins, I could have stabbed her through the heart. You know, when she left the station she was laughing."

"You get a lot of that." He pushed himself to his feet. "What're you having?"

"Oh, go on then. One of them two-pounders."

At the bar, he asked for a couple of Deuchars IPA and was about to pay for them when his mobile rang—a number he did not recognize. But with the background noise, he was struggling to tell if the caller was a man or a woman.

"I'll need to step outside," Gilchrist said into his mobile. "I can't hear you." He left by the side door onto College Street, then said, "Run that past me one more time."

"Are you interested in information?" A woman's voice.

"Who's this?" Electronic silence filled the line long enough for Gilchrist to think he had been disconnected. "Who gave you my number?" he tried.

"A mutual friend."

"Does our mutual friend have a name?"

A pause, then, "Everyone has a name."

Gilchrist watched his breath cloud the air. The temperature was close to zero, forecast to drop lower for the next day or two—

"It's about Stewart Donnelly."

Gilchrist felt the hairs on the nape of his neck stir. He pressed his mobile to his ear. "Do you know Donnelly?" he asked her.

"Stewart's dead."

Stewart—not Donnelly—the first name spoken without the slightest sign of emotion. Gilchrist had been thinking girlfriend, but the ice in the voice suggested maybe not. "How do you know him?" he asked.

"You've not answered my question." A hint of urgency in her voice, as if someone was cajoling her from the side. "Are you interested?"

"I'm interested in anything that can help me solve Donnelly's murder," he said. "Can we meet?"

"Do you have a pen?"

"I've a good memory."

"Call this number." She rattled off a phone number which he recognized as a mobile number—the same service provider as his own—but when he asked again for a name, the line disconnected.

He dialed the number from memory, but it rang out, did not dump him into voice mail, or cut off. He tried again, but it still rang out, and he cursed himself for trusting his memory. Had he misheard or confused the numbers? So he found the woman's number in his mobile, and called her back.

But her number was no longer available. Disconnected?

He made a mental note to try again later, and returned to the bar.

Back inside, he paid for his pints and carried them to their table. "Got you a lightweight one," he said to Jessie, and placed a frothy pint in front of her.

She gave him a tired smile and mouthed a silent thanks.

"Don't let them get to you," Gilchrist said, and tilted his pint. "Cheers." He waited until she returned her glass to the table, then said, "You look as if you didn't enjoy that."

"It's probably pulling in millions of fat nodules on its way to my stomach."

"I shouldn't worry," he tried.

"It's all right for you," she complained. "If you were a woman you'd be one of these bone-thin models."

Gilchrist almost grimaced. She could have been talking about his daughter, Maureen, who could do with putting on another ten pounds, even twenty. He shoved these thoughts to the back of his mind and said, "So, what are you doing tonight?"

"Are you asking me out?"

"Some of the station come here on a Saturday night. Nothing fancy. Just a few pints, a bit of craic, then off home. I usually give it a miss, but as it's your first weekend here, I'm happy to come along and introduce you to some of the others."

"Thanks but no thanks," she said. "I promised Robert I'd be home early."

"Checking out some new jokes?"

"Something like that."

"Hear anything more from your mother?"

A quick glare to remind him it was off limits, followed with, "So what are we going to do with this Dillanos bitch?"

"Wait," he said.

"For what?"

"I'll tell you tomorrow."

"Tomorrow's Sunday."

"Correct."

"And Sunday's usually my day off."

"Mine, too," he said. "But I usually end up working it."

"You have children, right?"

"Two," he said. "Jack and Maureen."

"Grown-up?"

He nodded. "And living in St. Andrews."

"Well I've got a teenage son who needs to see his mum from time to time. And I'll be buggered if I'm going to let the job take that away from me."

The look on her face told Gilchrist that she was regretting her outburst, that she might have made her point too strongly.

"Look," she said, "I'm happy to put in a full shift, do whatever overtime is necessary like everyone else. But when it comes down to it, St. Andrews Crime Management Division will still be here when I'm not and Robert's all grown-up with no mum to make his dinners for him."

"Noted," he said, and sipped his beer.

"Have I pissed you off?"

Gilchrist replaced his beer on the table. "I need to know I can count on you."

"Didn't I just say that?"

"That's not what I heard."

"Well that's what I meant," she said. "So let me know what you need me to do about this Dillanos bimbo." She took a long swallow from her pint, then added, "I wouldn't miss nailing her for the world."

Gilchrist tilted his glass to her, took a swallow of his own.

He felt sadness sweep through him, and niggling disappointment at what he had said. Jessie was a single mother, a woman who was not only struggling to raise a disabled child by herself but was doing so against the background of a vicious family. Years ago, if he had paid more attention to the needs of his own family, instead of trying to solve the case of the day, would Gail not have had her affair? Would she have remained in St. Andrews instead of scurrying off to Glasgow with their children, to set up home with her newfound lover?

He thought not.

So who was he to dictate hours of work? Jessie had her priorities right. She would put in a full shift, do what was needed. Wasn't that what Dainty had said?—*reliable, rock solid, won't let you down*. Which was what Gilchrist was asking for. So what was his complaint? Jessie's son needed time with his mum. And Sunday was a day off. Which meant he had a lot to take care of before close of business that afternoon.

He almost finished his pint and shoved the glass away from him. "Ready?" he asked.

"Whoah there. Slow down, big boy. I've only just started."

"Let me make a call," he said, and pushed through the swing doors into Market Street.

The sky hung low, and a wind that could have blown in from northern Siberia chilled his lungs and watered his eyes. He caught a flutter of snow, the flakes small enough to make him think he was only imagining it. When she answered, he went straight in without introduction.

"Any luck with the DNA comparison?" he said.

"And here was me thinking you must have me on *Candid Camera*."

"I'm sorry," he said. "You've lost me."

"I'm about to step into the shower," she explained. "I'm in the nude."

"Ah. Right. Would you like me to call back?"

She chuckled, the sound husky, inviting. "My shower can wait."

She was toying with him. He knew that. But try as he might, he could not move his memory away from the image of her straddling him. Perhaps it was because Mr. Cooper was away for the weekend. Or maybe his subconscious was already calculating possibilities for later that night. He crossed the cobbles of Market Street. Against the granite stones, snowflakes seemed to grow in size, dots of white that thickened the air, beginning to accumulate—

"Are you still there?"

"Sorry. Yes. I'm still here. The DNA comparison," he said. "Any luck?"

"It's too early, Andy. I should have something for Monday."

Or perhaps it was because he had known it was too early for the DNA results, and he had called just to hear the huskiness of her voice and let his mind stir with the possibility of having just one more night . . .

"OK," he said. "Good."

"Anything else?"

"No."

"See you later, then." She gave what sounded like a kiss, then said, "Ciao."

He almost said Ciao in response. But she had already hung up.

He pocketed his mobile and walked back to the Central. He stepped onto the pavement as Jessie emerged. She looked at him from the doorway and gave a knowing grin.

"I'd say she's under your skin."

"Come on," he grumbled. "We've got work to do."

26

But the remainder of the day brought nothing new.
No leads to Kumar, no updates from Strathclyde, no information on anything that might move the case forward or help ID any of the murdered women.

Which troubled Gilchrist.

Why would no one report them missing? Had they no family? But a short memory jag of Jessie's mother and brother told him that perhaps they had no family who *cared*. An image of shackles screwed to the cottage floor only added to his concern. The girls had been treated as nonhumans, animals, nothing more than assets to be pimped by captors who used and abused them.

By 6:00 PM he was at a dead end.

Jessie and the others had gone to the Central to start their Saturday night, with Jessie assuring him she was only staying for the one. Before he joined them, he stuck his head into Jackie's office, surprised to see her still there.

"Shouldn't you be at home," he said, "getting all dolled up to hit the town?" He could have been speaking in Chinese from the look she gave him. "It *is* Saturday night," he added.

"Like to join me?" He held up two fingers and smiled at her. "I'm only having one pint."

Her face broke into a grin, and she managed to say, "Me too."

"Finish up, and I'll meet you in the hallway," he said.

When Jackie joined him, struggling on her crutches, it struck him that he had only ever spoken with her when she was seated at her computer. Although she could scoot around the office as if her crutches were legs, dressed for winter her mobility was hindered by a coat and scarf and a handbag looped around her neck, which swung in front of her like a dead weight. A thick pair of mittens hid the handles of her crutches.

He held the door open as she hobbled outside.

The temperature felt too cold for snow. A cutting wind pulled tears from his eyes. Under the streetlights the pavement glistened damp with ice. A sky as black as soot melded into the roofline. He pulled his collar up, tightened his scarf, breath gasping in white puffs. The temperature felt as if it was dropping by the second.

He walked at Jackie's pace, as she wobbled by his side in silence, her eyes to the ground, her look determined, crutches prodding the way like a blind man's white stick. He thought of holding her arm to give support but could see that doing so would only hinder her movement. An image of her slipping on the ice hit him with such clarity that he said, "Here. Let me take these," and managed to remove one of the crutches from her grip.

"Hold onto my arm," he said, as he finagled the other crutch from her.

Even through her mittens, her grip felt like talons that dug into his sleeve. They set off, slowly at first, both crutches in his left hand, Jackie gripping his right hand for all she was worth, lumbering into Muttoes Lane in silent concentration.

Her clumsy gait caused her to bump into him with every second step, but they soon found their stride—one step, bump, one step, bump, a bit like their own dance—and by the time they entered the Central Bar, he thought they had managed to work it out quite nicely between the pair of them.

They found the others—Jessie, Nance, McCauley, Baxter, and Rennie—seated at the rear of the bar, and it intrigued him to see how Jessie and Nance had chosen to sit diagonally opposite each other, as far away as the table permitted. Jackie maneuvered her way next to Nance, who took her crutches from Gilchrist and laid them on the floor against the seat.

"I see you're getting to know everyone," he said to Jessie.

"It's amazing how the words *my round* win instant friend-ship."

"My round?" said Gilchrist, and he could not suppress a grin when Baxter tried to finish his pint in immediate acknowledgment. Nance surprised him by asking for a Cointreau with plenty of ice and a slice of lemon for Jackie. "A double?" he asked Jackie.

Yes please, she nodded.

Round purchased, and thirty quid lighter, Gilchrist managed to squeeze in between Jessie and McCauley on the bench seat. He thought Nance's glare was uncalled for, but ever since she'd split up with John she seemed less tolerant, not quite bitter, he thought, but more like she was beginning to realize that despite her looks and sex appeal, she could not sustain any meaningful relationship, and that life was passing her by. But Gilchrist often surmised that her take-no-prisoners attitude could hold men at bay, even push them away.

He triggered some fresh banter by venturing, "No Mhairi?"

"Angus asked her out."

"And she said yes?"

"I think she's giving him one more chance."

"That's two more chances than he deserves."

"What is it with guys and their dicks?"

"What is it with women and their one-more-chances?"

"She should have told him to piss off."

"Yeah, take a hike, fatman."

"I mean, what an absolute spastic."

The banter hushed, while hands reached for their drinks, all eyes away from Jackie.

"Talking of spastics," Jessie chirped. "Jackie says she can always tell when she's had too much to drink, because when she staggers home she slots the key in the lock first time."

No one laughed, reminding Gilchrist of her routine in the Stand Comedy Club.

Jackie hid behind her drink but could not suppress a chuckle.

"Did you hear the one about the sailor with the wooden leg?" Jessie said.

"Why don't you tell us the one about the fat bimbo from Glasgow?" Nance said.

"Don't know that one, Nance. Like to run it past me?"

Nance picked up her drink, and for an unsteady moment, Gilchrist thought she was going to throw it over Jessie. But she cast Jessie off with a mouth-twisting smirk and said to Rennie, "How's your wife keeping?" and took a sip.

"Four weeks to go," Rennie said. "We're hoping for a boy."

"We hope so, too," Baxter said. "With an ugly mug like yours, a daughter wouldnae stand a chance of getting herself a man."

Rennie grinned, a flash of teeth that looked too big for his mouth. And as Gilchrist listened to the others chip in, Jessie's silence felt like a physical presence that sat by his side as unforgiving as a cold wind. Watching the group liven, he could almost feel her hurt from Nance's barbed comment, like some stranger alone in a new land. He lifted his pint, tilted his drink to hers, but she was looking to the side, her attention drawn to her mobile, already pulling away, shuffling to her feet. She made the connection and walked toward the side entrance for some privacy.

"Where did you dig her up?" Nance said to him.

"Give her a chance," Gilchrist replied, conscious of a quietening at the table. "She's sorting out some issues."

"She needs to sort out her tongue first."

"That cuts both ways," Gilchrist said.

No one spoke, as if his words had chastised them all. He was saved by Jessie's return.

She lifted her pint, took a parting swill, and said, "Got to go."

"I'll put a pint for you behind the bar," Baxter offered.

"Don't worry. I'll catch you next time." She grinned at Jackie, stabbed an imaginary key into an imaginary lock, then gave a twist followed by a thumbs-up. "Toodle-do."

Jackie chuckled, gave a thumbs-up in response.

As Jessie squeezed her way toward the Market Street door, Nance whispered, "What a bitch," causing Jackie to look to the floor.

Like the others, Gilchrist chose not to say anything.

McCauley and Baxter stayed for only one more, and Jackie hobbled off after finishing her double Cointreau. Rennie had gone to the bar to order a round, where he now stood, deep into an argument with someone over the rise in transfer fees—

"Where's it gonnie end?"—how sports agents are lining their pockets—"They're ruining the game"—and what a season ticket for Dundee United would cost next year—"Fucking out of order, so it is."

Seated alone at the table with Nance, he found it odd that she had nothing to say to him. Where they had once shared more than casual conversation, she now seemed intent on avoiding eye contact. Her attention was focused on her mobile, texting a message. He was nursing his second pint, taking his time, catching snippets of Rennie's argument, when he heard, "Any room in there for me?"

He had not noticed Cooper enter, and as she leaned forward and placed her glass on the table—a surprising filled-to-the-brim whisky and crushed ice—loose curls swirled by her shoulders like a shampoo ad. Her eyes were darkened with a touch of kohl—another surprise—and when she gave a hint of a smile and a flicker for a wink, they sparkled with a blue fire. Nance shifted her chair, an invitation for Cooper to sit next to her. But Cooper ignored the gesture, squeezed between the tables, and took a seat next to Gilchrist.

That close, her presence felt like electricity pulsing the air. A fragrance—soap and shampoo with a hint of some perfume he had smelled before but could not place—filled his senses with the freshness of a spring morning.

She lifted her glass, chinked it against his.

"Welcome to Saturday night in the Central," he said to her.

"Busy little place."

"You should see it when it's full," he joked, strangely relieved to see her return his smile. He took a sip of his beer, conscious of Nance watching them, like a student checking to see if her teacher is going to try the same old tricks on someone new. He was aware, too, of Cooper's closeness as she searched her purse and sidled closer, not much, but enough to let him feel the press of her thigh against his.

"What brings you here?" Nance said to her.

Cooper gave a narrow smile. "Excuse me?"

"I haven't seen you here before."

"Me neither. So tell me, Andy, anything new on the case?"

Gilchrist thought he had never seen Nance look so put out. He sipped his pint, and from the corner of his eye watched Nance ease her seat back and, with a "See you Monday," push to her feet and slide into the throng. Rennie glanced at her as she bumped past, and gave a belated "See you."

"So where were we?" Cooper said to him.

"I think I was about to order a drink," he said.

"Put it on my tab. And I'll have another one of these."

"Which is?"

"Rusty Nail."

"Would you like to see a menu?"

"I've booked a table for two at the Doll's House." She glanced at her watch, which hung on her wrist as loose as a bangle. "Which gives you about thirty minutes to finish your pint."

"Ah. Right."

He ordered the round, handed over a tenner, niggled by the thought that Cooper had assumed he would go along with whatever she planned. He was happy enough to have a pint with her in a busy bar, but somehow the thought of being caught in the more intimate setting of a restaurant irked.

"There you go," he said to her, placing her Rusty Nail on a coaster, while she returned her mobile to her handbag. He took a quick sip of his Deuchars, then said, "I think I'm more of a pint and a pie kind of a guy. So you might want to cancel that table."

"Already done that." She patted her purse.

"You have?"

"You're an easy man to read, Andy."

He lifted his pint and took another sip. Any libidinous thoughts he had about that evening's liaison evaporated in the Saturday night hubbub.

27

His escape came by mobile phone.

"Got a few names and numbers for you," Dick said. "Five in total. But a couple she called several times. I can e-mail them to you."

"I'm not in the station."

"I'll send them to your mobile."

"I'm hopeless with that stuff, Dick. Just read them out to me. I've got an old-fashioned pen and paper." He slid a pen and notepad from his pocket and, with his mobile tucked under his chin, scribbled as fast as Dick could recite them.

"Couldn't put a name to the last number," Dick said. "Probably one of those dodgy SIM cards, prepaid. They're almost advertising them in the supermarkets down south. Buy your SIM, slot it in, use it until the credit runs out, then throw it away and slot in the next one. By the time you trace the call, the punter's on his way to France or wherever."

"Untraceable?"

"You might be able to locate the source, but these guys are in the moving business. One day here, another there. You'd never pin it to anyone. I checked the transmission data and was able to get a bearing on it. It's local."

Gilchrist pressed his mobile to his ear. "St. Andrews?"

"Dundee," Dick said. "And another farther south."

"Kingsbarns?"

"Could be. I'll keep looking and get back to you with anything new."

Gilchrist thanked Dick and hung up, his mind firing with possibilities.

Dillanos was calling someone in Dundee? Was that where the rat's nest was? If so, renting a cottage in Kingsbarns made sense. Not exactly shitting on your own doorstep, but Dundee was close enough to keep an eye on it, and far enough away to deny any connection.

He eyed his scribbled notes and scanned through the names and numbers. He thought he understood a couple. Dexter Murphy, an address in Greenock, could be Megan Murphy's—*call me Caryl*—brother or father; Siobhan Murphy, an address in Altrincham, could be her sister; Murdock and Roberts, her accountant in Glasgow. Why call them? Oh, and here's a surprise, McKinlay Iqbal Solicitors, an address in St. Vincent Street, Glasgow, which told him that she might have reported that morning's incident, no doubt exaggerating the way she had been treated by the local constabulary, and in particular by a certain DCI Gilchrist.

And finally, the number with neither name nor address—just Dick's confirmation that it was local. Gilchrist toyed with the idea of calling it. But would doing so only alert them that someone could be on to them?

He checked the details of the calls and saw that Dick had read out the list to him in chronological order. Caryl Dillanos had called Dexter Murphy first—3 minutes 24 seconds, short and to the point. Which meant . . . ? Could mean any-thing. Then Siobhan Murphy for a shorter 37 seconds—left a voice mail?—followed by another 29-second call . . . to leave another message? Then a longer call, 6 minutes 22 seconds, some twenty-five minutes later—sisters' heart-to-heart? Some-how, an image of Dillanos taking solace from anyone, let alone a sibling, failed to materialize. Murdock and Roberts were next—1 minute 43 seconds—which had Gilchrist thinking she had called to set up a meeting. But that call niggled him. A call to an accountant after being grilled for a couple of hours by the police was out of place.

Would she not have called her solicitor first?

He picked up his pint, took a sip, and wondered if the call to Murdock and Roberts was about the twenty thousand, sorry, the *eighteen* thousand she had brought with her. Who had that amount of cash just sitting around? Caryl Versace Dillanos had, of course.

But the calls to McKinlay Iqbal, all three of them, held his attention.

In his haste to scribble them down he had not picked up their significance, and he now saw a certain sense in their order—a short call of 54 seconds to ask to speak to her solici-tor; two minutes later, almost to the second, another short call of 38 seconds to be told that they had not yet found him; followed by the final call another two minutes later, which lasted all of 15 minutes 29 seconds. Long enough to give a detailed account of her grilling in the station, and to receive legal advice in return?

It seemed as good an explanation as any.

Then the final call, the one with no name and address, that lasted all of 2 minutes 31 seconds.

And that was it—

"Should I book a table for one?"

"Sorry," he said. "It's just . . ."

"To do with the case we're working on?"

"In a way, yes."

She smiled then and chinked her glass to his. "Don't let me keep you," she said. "It's lovely to watch."

"What's lovely to watch?"

"You on the job. You light up. Your whole being becomes energized. Has anyone told you that?"

He shook his head. "I'm sorry, I really do have—"

"Don't be sorry, Andy. Go. I can find my own way home."

He thought it strange how quickly emotions can change. Ten minutes earlier he had felt irritated at being expected to wine and dine to order. Now he felt regret at leaving. On the spur of the moment, he leaned over and pecked her on the cheek. "I'll call later." He prepared to stand, but her hand gripped his arm.

"I'll call you," she said.

Outside, the cold hit him anew, a bitter chill that flapped at his scarf and had him bowing his head as he strode into it. Snow now covered the cobbles and drifted over the stones in flurried gusts. He walked down College Street and into North Street. He thought of driving home, but he was a couple of pints over the limit, and he had a few things to check at the station, which would help him work the alcohol from his system.

Or so he told himself.

Back at his desk he powered up his computer and googled McKinlay Iqbal Solicitors. Their office was a corner building in the city center, which looked as if it could do with a coat of paint, maybe three, not exactly the way to advertise legal services. He checked his watch—7:53. No one would be at work on a Saturday night, well, if you did not include DCIs who'd had a couple of pints, that is. He was about to dial the number on his screen when he paused. He removed his notebook from his pocket, checked the website number against the number Dillanos had called, and confirmed they were different.

Which meant . . . ?

Had Dillanos called a direct line to her solicitor?

He dialed that number.

He counted six rings, expecting it to shunt him into voice mail, but it kept ringing on to ten, fifteen, then twenty before he hung up. He stared at the phone, then dialed again, and after ten rings was about to hang up when—

The ringing stopped.

Someone had picked up.

He held his breath, thought he caught muffled breathing on the other end, nothing definitive, more like a palpable sense that someone was listening. Should he say nothing, or could he persuade whoever was on the other end to say something?

But before he reached a decision, the connection died.

He dialed back, but the line was engaged.

He tried the main switchboard number—the one on the website—and was put through to voice mail on the second ring. He returned to the original number.

But the line was still engaged.

He replaced the handset to its cradle and stared at his phone. Someone had picked up. But why had they not spoken? Had his number come up on their phone screen? Were they already checking out the source of the persistent caller?

Which would not be good. On the other hand, it could be.

Out of nothing comes something?

He googled Murdock and Roberts and checked the main number against that in his notebook. Well, would you look at that? Different, too. Was this a direct line to Mr. Murdock or Mr. Roberts? Gilchrist dialed it, but it rolled over to voice mail on the fifth ring, and a man's voice with an accent telling him he had reached the desk of Osgar Murdock. He hung up, not sure if he had caught the name correctly, then tried again.

Sure enough, Osgar Murdock.

Osgar? Middle Eastern? Turkish, perhaps?

He found it interesting that he was uncovering some foreign connection—Kumar, Osgar, Iqbal—names with a Middle Eastern ring to them. And his mind replayed his earlier calls to McKinlay Iqbal. Had Dillanos's number gone straight through to the desk of Iqbal? Had it been Iqbal on the other end of the line? But more troubling, by calling had he set in motion some reaction to find out who the caller was?

And with that thought, he decided to take a chance.

He dialed the last number, the mobile number with no name or address. It rang out to twenty, which he thought was odd—no voice mail. He hung up, dialed it again, and again counted to twenty. He dialed the number four more times, before replacing the handset, then stared at the phone and smiled.

If they would not speak to him, then maybe his calls would flush them out.

28

Sunday arrived with a fog as fine as haar.

Snow covered the ground in a thin blanket of white.

Rather than walk straight to the newsagents, Gilchrist decided to jog, take a long road for a shortcut—down by the harbor, out to the end of the pier, then back up Shoregate onto High Street. He slipped on his track suit and trainers and wrapped up well, winding a scarf around his neck and tucking it in. He pulled on a pair of gloves, then stepped outside into Rose Wynd.

The fog had thinned, exposing a winter sun that sat low on the horizon, a watery pink that threatened to peel back a sky as white and fine as gauze. A cold wind carried the promise of a white Christmas and had his breath gusting in visible puffs as he got into his stride.

By the harbor, he slowed down to a walk and breathed in the smell of salt and kelp. Sheltered by the pier walls, the harbor lay as flat and motionless as slush, as if the cold had frozen it into immobility. He eyed a flock of raucous gulls on the hunt for food, and watched a couple of them fight over a scrap, a dirty rag by the looks of it, then tumble over the harbor's edge only to be beaten to the winnings by a herring gull that flew in and caught it, then let it fall midflight into the black waters. As he strolled seaward, fishing boats in need of a good painting and a better gutting, floated in cold silence by his side.

At the end of the pier, Gilchrist faced the wind, breathed it in.

Beyond the stone walls, the sea heaved and swelled like some beast stirring awake. Terns skimmed the dark surface in synchronized flight. Waves rose as if to peak, then settled again as if overcome by the effort. His mobile rang, its electronic tone out of place, like modern day interfering with the timelessness of nature.

He eyed the screen. The incoming number meant nothing to him, and he puzzled as to who would call at that time on a Sunday morning.

"Hello?"

The line disconnected.

He dialed back and, phone to his ear, turned from the end of the pier.

Where Shoregate met the harbor, he caught the burst of exhaust from a white car—a ubiquitous look-alike—and a man sliding into the passenger seat. He heard the door slam, the soft roar of the engine as the car slipped from view.

A recorded voice told him the person he was calling was unavailable.

More from instinctive curiosity, he started back along the pier, walking quickly to begin with, then breaking into a jog. He tried the number again.

No answer.

He reached the harbor front and managed to catch the tail end of the white car as it rounded a corner, too far away to

identify the make and model, but close enough to make out
a dent in the back bumper.

On impulse, he dialed Dick.

"Bloody hell, Andy, what time is it?"

"Early. Got another number for you."

"You sound like you've been running."

"Morning exercise."

"Let's have it," Dick said, wide awake now.

Gilchrist recited the number. "And if it's one of these
untraceable ones, get me a location on it, will you?"

"I'll get back to you."

Gilchrist ended the call, then put his head down and gritted his teeth as he ran up Shoregate. If he was quick enough,
he might catch another glimpse of it.

But by the time he reached High Street, the car was gone.

The hard jog had his heart racing, and despite the cold
wind, sweat warmed his brow. He walked along the pavement, and by the time he entered the Co-op, his breathing
had returned to normal.

He bought a *Mail on Sunday*, half a dozen large eggs—
brown for a change—bacon, and four morning rolls. The jog
to the seafront had done wonders for his appetite, and the
thought of grilled bacon and a poached egg on a fresh roll
had his mouth watering.

As a child, his Sundays had always started with a full,
cooked breakfast, as if that was the only morning his father
had time to eat, instead of having to rush off to work. But
back then, everything was cooked in lard, served up swimming in fat, eggs fried hard, not soft-poached or scrambled,
and bacon strips from which you could wring your weekly
intake of oil. And in true Scottish fashion—waste not, want
not—bread slices fried to soak up the remains of the frying

pan, served dripping with fat hot enough to blister your lips. And they wonder why Scotland was the heart-attack capital of the world.

On the walk back to his cottage, he held his shopping in a plastic bag with one hand, while he did what he could with the other as he flipped through the newspaper—Dundee United lost 0–1 away to Livingstone; both Bush and Blair were standing by the decision to invade Iraq.

He stepped off High Street and walked into Castle Street.

A glance downhill to a row of parked cars, and not one of them white. What was he expecting? But over the years he had come to trust his gut. Which was why he stopped, his back against the wall of the corner building, plastic bag at his feet, newspaper opened, as he pretended to be caught up in some interesting article.

He did not have long to wait, less than a minute as best he could tell.

A white Toyota, distinguishable by its logo, slowed down at the entrance to Castle Street, indicator flashing, then accelerated off in the pretense of a wrong turning. But Gilchrist had caught the look of surprise on the driver's face, the silent curse as the car accelerated away, and the dent on the rear bumper. But the passenger looked vaguely familiar, although for the life of him Gilchrist could not place him.

He slipped his newspaper inside the plastic bag and dialed the station.

He introduced himself and said, "Put me through to CID." When a woman's voice introduced herself as Liz, he said, "I need you to run a number through the PNC." He recited it from memory, then said "I'll wait."

In less than thirty seconds, she said, "Here we are, sir. Just pulling it up now. Hang on. Run that number past me again?"

He did.

"You sure, sir?"

He was.

"That number's registered to an Alfa Romeo in Bourne-mouth, a Mr. Fleming."

For a confusing moment, Gilchrist wondered if he'd mud-dled the letters, but a quick run through the mnemonic phrase reassured him he had it right. And the numbers were easy, four letters that were as good as a date. No mistake. Fake plates.

"Initiate a lookout for that number on a white Toyota," he said. "Apprehend the passengers, two males. Driver's foreign-looking." He had wanted to say Arabic but did not want to taint anyone's opinion. "Maybe Spanish, Mediterranean. You get the picture. Black hair, tanned complexion." He pulled up an image of the man slipping into the car down by the har-bor, again puzzled by a sense of familiarity. But he had been too far away to make an ID. "Passenger's a white male," he said. "Approach with extreme caution. They may be armed."

"Will do, sir. Anything else?"

"Have someone call Fleming in Bournemouth. And get back to me."

He hung up, picked up his shopping, and trotted to his Merc parked at the corner. It was the fake registration plate that did it. Anyone who went to the trouble of switching plates had to have a good reason to run from the law.

He clicked the key fob, threw the shopping onto the pas-senger footwell.

He powered up, backed into Castle Street, and acceler-ated onto High Street with a squeal from the tires. On the A917, he pushed up to eighty, braking hard as he pressed into corners, accelerating through them, the steering wheel jerking in his hands as the Merc clipped the road edge. On the straight, foot to the floor and back against the seat as the 2.3-liter engine let loose with a rush of power.

Hedges, grass verges, stone walls, whipped past in a snow-white blur.

He cursed himself for not thinking ahead. He should not have been pretending to read his newspaper. He should have been in his Merc, key in the ignition, ready for the chase the moment the Toyota showed itself.

He slowed down to a sedate forty as he entered the town of Kingsbarns. He glanced up side streets, considered for an idiotic second driving to the cottage, then realized that if they were who he thought they were, even the dumbest brain on the planet would not risk going anywhere near there.

Through Kingsbarns and up to ninety at one point. He over-took a convoy of cars with a blare from his horn, through another corner touching seventy. He felt the wheels give a flicker, and eased back at the thought of black ice, as he neared the Boarhills cutoff.

Straight ahead for Boarhills. Left for St. Andrews.

With a lookout being requested from St. Andrews, the white car would be intercepted before it reached St. Andrews. The downside to that argument was that the A917 had any number of side roads that led into the country, through farm-land, over hills, to connect with some other road. You might be lost for a while, but you would hook up with civilization eventually.

He chose straight on.

He felt his body lift from the seat as he powered over the brow of the hill toward Boarhills. He slowed to little more than a crawl as the road narrowed, and followed it as it wound through the small village. He nodded to a woman walking her dog, pulled to a halt to let an elderly couple cross in front of him, all the while searching side roads, parked cars, driveways to garages and homes, for a white car with a dent in its bumper.

He eased uphill, past a well-kept farm that faded in disrepair to a collection of derelict stone buildings, then downhill to open fields on the right and an old brick ruin on the left. The unpaved road opened up to a turning area, then branched off to the right, toward the sea.

He pulled over, stepped out. The air felt colder here, straight off the North Sea.

The narrow road stretched ahead, nothing more than two rutted tracks separated by a row of grass high enough to snag a car's axles. And lying white and pristine with untouched snow as fine as powdered sugar.

Back into his Merc, a quick reverse, a spin of his wheels, then powering uphill.

He called the station.

"Anything?" he asked Liz.

"One moment, sir."

He wound back through the village, speed at a minimum, the car's engine burbling beneath the bonnet. Driving in that direction gave a different view into homes, a variation in the angle, a sight line past a trimmed hedge, a peek into a distant corner of a gravel driveway. He eased into a corner, slowed to a crawl as a tractor approached him, taking up most of the road, its oversized rear tires spitting up slush and dirt in a spattered spray—

"Nothing to report, sir."

Gilchrist thanked her, asked her to call the moment she heard anything, then threw his mobile onto the passenger seat. When the tractor passed, he tugged the wheel, depressed the accelerator then slammed on the brakes. He clipped into reverse, backed up ten feet, and eyed the driveway.

He was not mistaken.

From the back corner of a single bungalow at the end of a long gravel drive, poked the tail end of a car, parked at an angle that permitted him to see the dent in the bumper.

He pulled over the curb and onto the pavement.

He kept the engine running and reached for his mobile.

But even from where he sat, he worked out that he was too late.

A pair of almost identical tracks in the snow-covered driveway told him the Toyota had driven out, then returned. But a single line of tracks, slightly wider, the last set to be laid down, told him that a larger vehicle, maybe an SUV, had driven off.

He stepped onto the pavement and stood at the entrance to the property. The house looked as if it had closed for the winter. Curtains were drawn in all windows, and the roof was covered with a fresh layer of snow. An expansive lawn fell away from the front door, its unmarked surface as smooth as a white bowling lawn. He studied the tracks on the driveway and confirmed his thoughts. The third set overlaid the others, and twin strips of ice in the form of skid marks told him that whoever had been driving had left in a hurry.

Had he just missed them?

He eyed the road that led uphill to the A917, tried to remember what vehicles he had passed. But it was no use. His whole focus had been on chasing a white car to the exclusion of all others. He tried the station, just in case.

"Nothing yet, sir."

He called off the lookout and told Liz to send someone to—he read out the address on the wall—and said, "See if you can find out who owns it," then walked toward the entrance gateway. He had warned the station that they might be armed.

Despite that, he marched up the driveway to the half-hidden car.

29

Gilchrist's instincts had been spot on.

He had his white Toyota, dent in the rear bumper, and a number plate that told him his gray matter was not dying after all. On the ground, the tell-tale trail of footprints showed him how someone had walked from the Toyota straight to the other vehicle, the driveway clear where it had been parked overnight. The other man had entered the house, then returned to the car. A couple of slide marks on the back step showed where he had slipped.

Gilchrist called the station again, told Liz he had located the car, no passengers, but they might manage to lift prints. And even as he was saying that, he realized they could have an entire house-load of fingerprints from which to lift.

"Mr. and Mrs. Ramsay," Liz said to him. "That's whose name the house is in."

The back door was closed but unlocked.

Gilchrist opened it using the tips of his gloved fingers.

The kitchen blinds were drawn. Light from the open door cast a bright beam over a terra-cotta-tiled floor and reached into the room like a painted line that ran up and over pine cabinets. The air held a hint of disinfectant, as if the place had been scrubbed clean.

"Hello?" He pushed the door wider. "Hello?" He stepped inside.

He opened the blinds, feeling as if he was letting daylight into the house for the first time in weeks. As he scanned the work surfaces, the sparkling stainless steel sink, the drying tray to the side with nothing in it, he thought the place had been kept overly tidy for a pair of thugs. The walls, too, a light beige that blended with darker doors and frames, were devoid of pictures, as if whoever lived here had failed to turn the house into a home.

An opened door led into a dark hallway. At the far end, a heavy velvet curtain hung over the front door, doubling as a draught excluder.

He found a light switch and clicked it on to reveal an empty hall, furnished only by a beige runner that covered a wooden floor.

"Hello?" he shouted.

Silence.

A quick look into other rooms confirmed the house was deserted.

Outside again, he was halfway down the drive when his mobile rang.

"No luck," said Dick. "Somewhere in Crail, as best I could tell. But the number's untraceable."

Gilchrist was about to thank him, when Dick said, "I also did another check on that mobile you gave me."

Gilchrist reached the end of the driveway, stepped around the skid marks.

"I didn't mention it yesterday," Dick said. "But the funny thing is, that it's not made any more calls, other than to the numbers I gave you yesterday."

"Incoming?"

"Nada. Zilch. Outgoing only."

"Powered down?"

"More likely SIM card removed and thrown away."

"So, it might be safe to conclude that the person Dillanos spoke to on the last number she called, the one you couldn't trace or identify, might have given her a warning?" It seemed the only logical answer.

"That would be a sensible bet, I'd say."

Gilchrist eyed the neighboring bungalow to the left, then a two-story semidetached to the right, and wondered if anyone had noticed anything in the Ramsays' bungalow, or if they might be able to give an ID.

"There's no way you can trace the number?" he tried again.

"Not with an iffy SIM card. Ten a penny. Use them and ditch them."

A squad car rounded the corner, and Gilchrist recognized DC Bill McCauley at the wheel, PC Mhairi McBride in the passenger seat. He thanked Dick and disconnected. By the time he reached the car, McCauley was on his feet blowing into his hands.

"Bloody freezing," McCauley said.

Gilchrist nodded. The temperature felt as if it had dropped more than a couple of degrees. Overhead, the sky had dulled to a darker gray, the morning threat of sunshine now only a fading memory. Mhairi made her way around the front of the car to join them.

"What have we got, sir?" she asked.

Maybe it was seeing Mhairi again, or the memory of why she had not joined them last night, but it seemed so obvious that he wondered why he had not thought of it sooner. "Are you and Angus still on speaking terms?" he said.

"Not anymore, sir."

"That sounds serious."

"I'd rather live in the Antarctic, sir."

"Good," he said, and smiled at her. "Phone Angus, and find out if this house is on his books. And if it is, lift him."

Mhairi grinned and walked off, mobile at her ear.

Gilchrist put his hand on McCauley's shoulder. "You look rough, Bill."

"After the Central, I had a date with Eilidh." He smiled. "Stayed up too late."

Gilchrist nodded. He did not believe a word of it. McCauley was well known for his binge drinking, and the minty smell of his breath told Gilchrist that Eilidh was being used as an alibi. He gave McCauley's shoulder an avuncular squeeze and said, "I'd like you to give the keys to Mhairi, and make sure she drives for the rest of the day. OK?"

McCauley grimaced.

"And I don't want to have this conversation again, Bill. Is that clear?"

"Yes, sir."

"When you get back to the station," Gilchrist pressed on, "start the ball rolling for a warrant to search this house."

"Yes, sir,"

"Is Baxter in today?"

"Day off, sir."

"That's more sensible," he said, and stared McCauley down until he got the message and returned to the car and slid into the passenger seat.

Mhairi returned, her eyes sparkling from anger, or the cold air, he could not say.

"Problems?" he tried.

"None that clapping a pair of bricks to his gooleys wouldn't solve."

"Ouch." He eyed her. "I'm listening."

"He denied it, of course."

"Of course. And you think he might have rented it out?"

She shook her head. "Don't know any more, sir."

Gilchrist saw that Mhairi was still hurting, and he now regretted asking her to call. But a glance at McCauley told him that only one of them had turned up for work that day.

"How was it left?" he asked her.

"I told him to get himself to his office in an hour, or I'd have him arrested."

"How did that go down?"

"He told me to eff off."

"What's his number?"

"Sir?"

"I'd like to call him, tell him what's what—"

"I can handle it, sir."

He held her gaze and sensed her panic. "Something you're not telling me, Mhairi?"

"No, sir, I just . . . I just need to do this myself."

"Even the arrest?"

She took a deep breath, let it out. "If I have to, yes, sir."

Gilchrist glanced at the squad car, thought McCauley looked ill. Probably just the mention of a bacon sandwich would have him throwing up. "Drop Bill off at the station," he said to her, "and I'll catch up with you at Patterson and McLeod."

30

G ilchrist waited another fifteen minutes for the SOCOs to arrive.

Their white Transit van pulled up behind his Merc.

Colin was first out and shook Gilchrist's hand. "Christ, it's chilly," he said.

Gilchrist eyed the van, expecting to see others follow. "On your own?"

"Roddie's with me. Finishing off a call to his bird. He's coming to the good bit." He winked at Gilchrist, then eyed the driveway. "So what've we got?"

Gilchrist showed him the tire tracks. Despite the low temperature, the asphalt was beginning to show through in blackening patches. He nodded to the car. "And see what you can find on that Toyota. But don't enter the house until we have a warrant."

"Is the Toyota unlocked?"

Gilchrist grimaced. "Didn't check that."

"Don't worry. If it's got a lock and a handle, Robbie's your man." He marched to the front of the van and smacked the windscreen with the flat of his hand. "Out," he shouted. "Come on, we've got work to do."

Gilchrist grimaced, then left them to it.

The neighbor's driveway was shorter and led to an almost identical bungalow. The garden lay white with snow, thicker in places protected by the shadow of a garden wall that ran the length of the boundary—a perfect winter's scene, he thought. Smoke rose from the chimney in a gray column that thinned in a light wind. Either side of the front door, windows glistened, through which he caught the silhouette of someone deep in the room.

He pressed the doorbell, a small lighted button with the name CLARKE beneath it.

A few seconds later, the door opened to the sound of clicking locks and a bright-faced woman who reminded him of his late wife, Gail, before she turned bitter.

He held up his warrant card and introduced himself.

The woman stepped into the vestibule and pulled the door behind her, as if to keep her home and her personal belongings safe from his prying eyes.

"How well do you know the Ramsays?" he asked.

"I've known Lennie and Jean all my life," she said, then as if realizing why he was standing on her doorstep, pressed her hand to her mouth. "Has something happened to them?"

He shook his head. "I need to talk to them. That's all. Do you know where they are?"

"British Grand Cayman. They visit their son every Christmas and New Year. They always stay for at least three months, sometimes four."

"Anyone look after the house while they're away?"

"They leave a key with me," she said, "but they also have it registered with a property management company who sometimes let it out over the festive season."

"Patterson and McLeod?" he tried, just itching to bring Angus into the equation.

"I don't think so," she said.

Well, maybe Angus was clean after all. "Can you tell me anything about the people who are renting it out at the moment?"

"Not really," she said. "They keep themselves to themselves."

A few more innocent questions got him nowhere, until he said, "Have you noticed what they drive?"

"One of their cars is the same as ours," she said, "which is the only reason I would know."

Gilchrist eyed the sleek body of a BMW X8 SUV. Snow clung to the roof and bonnet, but along the side its black paintwork glistened showroom new. "Same color?"

"Silver."

"Registration number?" He was pushing the boat out, but you could never tell.

She shook her head. "I don't know my own. If the lights didn't flash when you press the button, I'd never find it." She chuckled, and Gilchrist smiled in support.

He asked if she could describe the renters, perhaps give some idea of ethnicity, but she had paid no attention—why should she? She's not nosy. He asked when she had last seen the renters, how long she thought they had been there, and if she knew when Mr. and Mrs. Ramsay were expected to return. But her answers were only filling up his notebook, not really gaining any ground.

He had just about run out of questions, when he said, "Do you have any way of contacting the Ramsays? In an emergency, say?"

"I've got their son's number."

"That'll work," he said.

As he waited while she returned indoors, he thought of the call to his mobile earlier that morning, and the glimpse of the man getting into the Toyota, which in turn had led him to the Ramsays' house—

The door snapped open.

"Here you are." She handed him a slip of paper. "I've included the international code."

He exchanged the slip for one of his cards and asked her to call him anytime, day or night, if she ever thought of anything else. He crunched his way back down the driveway, called the station, and asked Liz to request a lookout on a silver BMW X8 SUV, two passengers, one white, one Arabic-looking. There, he had said it.

He just hoped he had it correct.

Next, he eyed the printed phone number.

He had spent a week in British Grand Cayman once, when Gail first left and he took himself off to the Caribbean for a few days of sunshine, rum cocktails, and the hope of some quickly forgotten holiday romance. But a shrimp cocktail on his first night put him in bed for the next three days with food poisoning. All things Caribbean after that were eaten or drunk with halfhearted enthusiasm.

He glanced at his watch—10:33—which, if his memory and arithmetic were correct, put it at 6:33 on a Grand Cayman morning, sunny, no doubt. Time they were up, he thought, and dialed the number.

He got through to a man's voice on the second ring and asked for Mr. Ramsay.

"Speaking."

Gilchrist had expected an older-sounding voice, then realized he might have their son on the line. "Mr. Ramsay Senior?" he asked.

"Lennie's still in bed. Can I help?"

Gilchrist gave a belated apology for disturbing them at such an early hour.

"No problem. We're all usually up by now. But Lennie had one too many last night."

What is it with Scotsmen and Saturday nights? Gilchrist explained the reason for his call and asked if Lennie could give him a call back.

"Jean's around," the man said. "She might know."

When a frail-sounding voice came onto the phone, Gilchrist worried that he had woken the entire Caribbean neighborhood. But Jean could not remember the name of the property management company. "And I warned Lennie not to go with him. I didn't like the look of his eyes."

"Whose eyes?"

"The man who came around to look at the property."

"From the property management company?"

"That's what I said, didn't I?"

For a moment, Gilchrist thought he was going to land lucky, but he'd really been asking too much. "And you can't remember the name of the company?"

"Hold on a minute, I'll check with Lennie."

"I thought he was . . ." But from the clatter of the phone, he realized that she had laid it down. Another glance at his watch confirmed it was 6:42, and just the thought of a sun-filled morning and a walk along Seven Mile Beach was enough to have him toying with the idea of trying the Caribbean again—but without shellfish dishes.

A sudden wind shift had him pulling his collar up. Ice brushed his hair, and he caught the black forms of carrion crows landing en masse in the leafless branches of a nearby tree—chestnut, he thought—a silent group, with black, invisible eyes that watched everything, as if conspiring to commit a crime. A murder of crows seemed apt. Starlings lined an overhead telephone cable, as if deciding whether or not to migrate. Should they not have flown the country before now—

"McCarron and Co.," a man's voice said.

"Excuse me?"

"The name of the property management company is McCarron and Co."

Gilchrist fired awake. "Are you sure?"

"As sure as my name's Lennie Whatsisname," he said, followed by a guffaw that had Gilchrist pulling his mobile from his ear. "Touch wood," Lennie continued. "We're still all here."

"Can you describe Mr. McCarron?"

"Not really. Blue suit, white shirt, tie. The usual. A bit young, I thought. But friendly enough. And a bit on the chubby side. That's about all I can remember."

"Phone number?"

"I've got a business card somewhere. But it could take me some time to find it. Can you wait?"

Gilchrist's lips felt as if they were about to turn blue. "Don't bother. I'll find it."

Back in his car, he turned on the engine, the heater to full, and rubbed his hands.

Mr. McCarron—a bit on the chubby side, blue suit, white shirt, tie, the usual.

And a liar to the bloody hilt.

Gilchrist looked along the driveway to the white Toyota. It sat with its boot open, Robbie half-hidden, his head and shoulders buried inside. He thought of checking with Colin, see what they had found. But he would catch him later.

He eased his Merc off the pavement and accelerated onto the road.

He did not want to spoil Mhairi's fun.

But if she had not arrested Angus by now, she had missed her chance.

31

Gilchrist managed to find a parking spot in South Street and arrived at Patterson and McLeod's just after 11:00. The door was locked to the public, but through the window he saw Angus with a scowl on his face mouthing off to Mhairi. From the look on Mhairi's face, all was not going well.

He rapped the window with his key fob.

Angus started, then opened the door.

Gilchrist ignored the glaring welcome and brushed past him. Inside, the office felt as cold as an open-air stall. Mhairi returned his gaze with a hard look of her own.

"Everything all right?" he asked her.

"I was trying to—"

"No," Angus interrupted. "Everything's not all right."

Gilchrist faced Angus. An uneven flush colored stubbled cheeks, and a redness in his eyes gave the impression that he might have had more to drink last night than McCauley and Baxter combined. "I'm listening," Gilchrist said.

"I've offered to help," Angus complained. "I've done my bit as a good citizen. I've wasted hours of my time being dragged along to the station and looking through a gazillion photographs, and, and . . ." He turned the full heat of his thousand-watt glare onto Mhairi. "And now I've been cautioned and treated like some . . . some piece of shite?" He dabbed a hand to his mouth, wiped spittle from his lips.

"Finished?"

"I've a right good mind to call my solicitor."

"Do that."

"You'll be hearing from her too. I'm just about—"

"Take a seat." The words came out louder than intended, but seemed to stun Angus into silence. Gilchrist turned to Mhairi. "So Patterson and McLeod have nothing on their books with respect to that property in Boarhills?"

"Apparently not, sir."

"I've already told her—"

"When I want you to speak I'll ask you a question. Now shut it and take a seat."

Angus paused, as if unsure how far to push. "I'll stand." His anger pulsed like a force field, and Gilchrist came to see that Angus had abused Mhairi in their past relationship, that he was just one of a million other men around the world who may not use physical violence but who played on their masculine presence as a threat.

Gilchrist said, "Would you like your solicitor present?"

"Just get on with it."

"How long have you worked with Patterson and McLeod?"

"Eight years."

"Straight from school?"

"From uni."

"Which one?"

"Aberdeen."

"And you've worked nowhere else?"

"Look, what is this?"

"Don't make me ask again."

Angus gritted his teeth. "No."

"You were thinking about starting up on your own. Wasn't that what you said?"

Wary now, as if he knew he was being herded to some cliff face but could not see the drop. "So?"

"When were you planning to start up on your own?"

"Soon."

"How about business cards?"

"What about them?"

"Get any printed?"

Something seemed to dawn on Angus then, a revelation of sorts that spread across his face and ended with him opening his mouth in an "Ah."

Gilchrist waited.

Angus scratched his head, looked at Mhairi, then back to Gilchrist. "Years ago I got some business cards made up," he said. "That's what this is about. Isn't it?"

"How many years ago?"

He shrugged. "Six, seven. I was new to the game, keen to break out." He gave a smile of success. "McCarron and Co. That's what I was going to call my new business. Didn't know who the Co. was going to be, though. But I liked the sound of it."

Mhairi said, "So what happened?"

"Didn't have the money to rent anywhere."

"With you in the know?" she said. "A finger in every pie, you used to tell me? You couldn't locate a property to rent for a reasonable price?"

"Not in town. No."

"So you gave up?" She seemed flabbergasted.

Angus clenched his fists, as if reassuring her that he could slip into bullying mode in a heartbeat. "I decided to put the business venture back a few years. Wait until I saved up a few bob. You know, had some capital to invest." He nodded his head, all businessman once more.

Gilchrist forced them back on track with, "So you rent out property on the side using your own business cards—"

"No way," Angus said. "That would get me fired."

Gilchrist held Angus's shocked look. "So how do you explain your business card turning up at the Ramsays'?"

"Who?"

"Lennie and Jean Ramsay. They live in Boarhills."

Angus twisted his mouth with failed memory recall. "Don't know them."

"I didn't say you did." Keeping Angus on track was like trying to hold a fish with oiled hands.

"They must have been stolen," Angus said.

"All of them?"

"Yeah. From the office."

"You kept your own business cards in the office?" Mhairi said. "Here? In Patterson and McLeod?"

Angus shrugged. "Stupid, eh?"

"Anything else stolen?" Gilchrist tried.

Angus shook his head. "Not that I remember."

"I see." Gilchrist walked to the middle of the floor. Outside, a young couple, oblivious to his presence, were eyeing sales advertisements taped to the window, faces flushed from the cold, or perhaps at the prospect of trying to save for a down payment on a home of their own.

He turned back to Angus.

"The Ramsays are on holiday," he said. "The Caribbean."

"All right for some."

"And while they're away, they rent their home on a short-term lease."

"Yeah, Christmas and New Year in the East Neuk is beginning to catch on."

"They gave a description of the property manager they dealt with."

Angus seemed to tense, like a schoolboy preparing for six of the best.

"And they described you to a T."

Angus shrugged, shook his head. "They couldn't have. I don't know them."

Anyone would think the man did not have a care in the world. And at that moment, Gilchrist came to see that Caryl Versace Dillanos, with her Mercedes sports cars and Porsche Cayennes and her boy toy on the side, had probably twisted Angus's mind with the promise of the good life and plenty of nookie on tap—as long as he did as he was told.

"Caryl Dillanos?" Gilchrist said, more to gauge a reaction than generate a further line of inquiry. And he thought it interesting how Angus's eyes darted first to Mhairi, then flitted around the room to settle, in the end, on Gilchrist.

"What about her?"

"Did you give her any business cards?" he asked. "The McCarron and Co. ones?"

And Angus, as if leaping at his way out of a deepening hole said, "Yeah. I think I might have. Maybe one or two. You know, from a few spare I had lying around."

Gilchrist grinned and turned to Mhairi. "Would you like me to do the necessary?"

"I've got it, sir," she said, reaching to her belt.

Gilchrist cautioned Angus while Mhairi unclipped a pair of handcuffs from her belt and approached Angus like a Rottweiler to meat.

"Turn around," she ordered.

"Hang on, Mhairi. What's going on? What am I being lifted for?"

"Resisting arrest," said Gilchrist, "if you don't do as the lovely lady says."

"Ah, fuck this."

"Indeed," said Gilchrist.

32

By midafternoon, the lookout on the BMW X8 SUV resulted in his team pulling over eight silver-colored X8s. But none with two male passengers. So, Gilchrist checked back with the SOCOs to see if the white Toyota with the dent in the bumper had offered any clues.

"Checking the VIN on the PNC confirmed it was stolen in Nottingham," Colin told him. "And it's been wiped clean—"

"No fingerprints at all?" Gilchrist asked, unable to mask his disbelief.

"Cleaner than a baby's bum. The steering wheel, dashboard, door handles, seats, doors, windows—we found nothing."

"What about the house?"

"Nothing there, too."

"Not even the kitchen?" He felt sure they would have found something there.

"It's not that difficult to do," Colin said, "if you think about it, if you start out with the intention of not leaving any fingerprints. You could wear latex gloves—"

"All day, every day?" Gilchrist argued. It seemed far-fetched.

"And carry a rag or a cloth in your pocket to wipe—"

"All right, I get the picture."

And he did. He was dealing with professionals who knew how to evade detection, not leave evidence, not draw attention to themselves, and who had contacts south of the border who could knock off cars in Nottingham—

His mobile rang—ID Dainty.

He pushed back from his desk, flexed his shoulders, and connected with, "Gilchrist."

"Got some news for you," Dainty said without introduction. "Don't know if it's good or bad, but I've just got a report of a double killing. Two women. Megan Murphy, a.k.a. Caryl Versace Dillanos. Born and bred in Glasgow. And Jana Judkowski, Polish. Heard of them?"

Gilchrist closed his eyes. He had tried to convince Jana that Dillanos was trouble. But trouble enough to have her killed? He pressed his mobile to his ear, stared out the window, and dreaded asking. But he had to know.

"How were they killed?"

"Single shot to the head," Dainty said, "then dumped at the edge of Greenock Road to make sure we'd find them."

"CCTV?"

"Not at that spot. Bodies weren't discovered until around midday, but we're thinking they were dumped in the wee hours. It was pissing down last night. And on that stretch, cars are hitting seventy or eighty, even the ton. You'd have to be looking straight at them to see them. These guys knew what they were doing. We're thinking professional team, someone with a grudge against Big Jock Shepherd."

The name had Gilchrist gripping his mobile tighter. "Why Shepherd?"

"Dillanos was known to do some ducking and diving for the big man."

"Like Dillanos Furniture?"

"And more."

"Enough to get her killed?"

"Big Jock's been in the family business all his life. He's powerful. Like the patriarch of Glasgow crime. There's more than a few punters down here would like to see him turn up in the Clyde wearing a pair of concrete boots. But he's not the kind of guy you'd ever want to cross. Maybe these bullets to the head will be the start of something. Who knows."

The bullets to the head had Gilchrist thinking of Donnelly's murder. "I'll have our SOCOs send you a ballistics report. Could you check it for comparison?"

"I thought you were investigating stabbings."

"We had a separate shooting yesterday," Gilchrist said. "Does the name Stewart Donnelly mean anything to you?"

"Not ringing any bells. You think it's connected?"

Probably not, Gilchrist wanted to say. But the murder of Dillanos and her trainee, Jana, felt as if they were two killings too many. "Just want to tick all the boxes."

"Keep me posted, Andy."

Gilchrist was about to hang up, when a thought struck him. "Why did you call me?"

Dainty chuckled. "I wondered how long it would take you to ask," he said. "Dillanos had Jessie's name and number written on a note in her purse. And yours, too, circled half a dozen times."

"Like a reminder?"

Dainty snorted. "Like she'd never want to forget."

When Gilchrist disconnected, he tried to work through the rationale of how his mobile number ended up on a note in Dillanos's purse. But if he thought about it, it made sense. The call to his mobile at Crail harbor earlier that morning could be the link. Had Dillanos given his number to them? But even so, why would they have called him, then driven off?

He was missing something, but what he could not say.

But one thing was clear.

Angus McCarron was about to cough up.

Snow was falling by the time Jessie found her way back onto the A917.

The afternoon had been a huge success. Angie had arranged an informal meeting for Jessie and Robert with a doctor friend of hers, who supposedly had some serious contacts in the medical profession. So Jessie had gone along, not really expecting much—Angie could be an airhead at times—and been surprised to learn that he'd already arranged for Robert to have a consultation with a Mr. Amir Mbeke—one of the top five ENT consultants in Britain—on Wednesday morning at Ninewells Hospital in Dundee for a hearing test. Jessie made a note to ask for time off work. She was determined for Robert to have a cochlear implant. And if he could not have it done on the National Health, she would go private and worry about the costs later.

She would find some way to settle the bill. She always did.

She felt a smile crease her lips at the thought of taking Robert to a football game and watching his face light up at the deafening roar of a goal-happy crowd, or listening to "Hotel California," "Brown Sugar," or how about "Waterloo Sunset"? Now there was a song. None of this modern-day hip-hop crap—

Her mobile rang. She removed it from her pocket, eyed the display, and cursed. She thought of letting it ring out, but he would only call back. Lachie was like that—a persistent bastard when he put his mind to it.

She made the connection and said, "Hello?"

"Jessica?"

"Who's this?"

"Got a new phone number, I see."

"Oh, it's you, Lachie."

He chuckled in that pig-grunting way of his that shook his jowls and narrowed his eyes to needle slits. "Couldn't get through to you on the old one," he said. "If I didn't know any better, I'd say you were trying to avoid me."

"Who, *moi?*"

"Jessica, doll. I know I'm not the greatest catch in the world, but—"

"I'm driving, Lachie. I shouldn't be on my—"

"—I've fallen in love."

Jessie cringed from the memory and the knowledge of what was to come. "Anyone I know?" she said.

"I've got a few days accrued," he pressed on. "Thought we might go away—"

"Fuck sake, Lachie, I've just started a new job. I won't be taking a few days off any time soon."

"I can pull a few strings," he said. "I wouldn't worry about that."

This had always been the troubling side of Lachie, the willingness with which he was prepared to abuse his own position to secure personal favors. He'd be fiddling his overtime next, if he was not already doing so. She turned from Robert—he did not need to be face-on to lip-read—and said, "I've got Robert to think of."

"Bring him along."

"I'll ask him," she said. "I'm sure he'll jump at it."

"I'm serious," Lachie said. "He should come with us. I need to get to know him."

Jessie pulled the phone from her ear and glared at it. She thought of hanging up, then came back with, "I've got too much baggage for you, Lachie. You don't want to get involved with me. I've told you before."

"Not a problem, my lovely," he said, his voice warming to the possibility that at long last he might be winning her over.

"And so do you," she said.

"I'm getting a divorce."

"You filed for it yet?"

"It's in the works," he replied, which told her nothing had changed. The only reason Lachie had not left his wife was because she was the heiress, or rather one of four heirs, to a national biscuit manufacturing fortune.

"Well, my baggage has just got bigger," she said.

The line fell silent, long enough for Jessie to think she had lost the connection. Then she heard the rush of traffic, someone's voice in the background, and realized Lachie had been talking to someone else.

"What's that, doll?"

She thought of hanging up, but he would only call her right back. No, she had to bring this to a head. But how? She had tried to end sexual relations with him before. God, how could she have let her guard down—or her knickers, for that matter? Depression and drink, came the answer. But Lachie had just tried harder, sent her flowers, flooded her with love cards, almost to the point of her dropping her knickers herself just to stop them coming.

Once he'd even turned up in a stretch limo, wearing a new suit that had to have cost his wife over a thousand pounds, and refused to budge until she agreed to accompany him to the Rogano in Royal Exchange Square, where he'd reserved a table for two. Rather than have the limo block her street for the rest of the night, she had relented. Later, he tried to entice her to bed with a promise of a week's holiday in the Swiss Alps over Christmas. She thought he finally got the message when she tore up the plane ticket in front of him. In response, he had suggested they try Spain in the summer. But in all that time, never a concern for Robert.

Until now.

"I was saying my baggage has just gotten bigger."

"Don't worry about that."

"Nice to know you care."

"Of course, I care, Jessica, but—"

"It's not about me," she snapped. "It's Robert."

The line fell silent again, and she had a sense of Robert turning her way, as if he had picked up the sound vibrations of his own name in the air.

"So how is the wee man?" Lachie asked.

"Oh, like you care all of a sudden?"

"Of course I care, Jessica—"

"Enough to fork out a hundred grand for an operation?"

"How much?"

"You heard."

A chuckle that had her fighting off another image of Jabba the Hutt. "Did you say one hundred thousand pounds?"

"I did."

"That's a lot of money."

"That's what the operation's going to cost." She had no idea how much a cochlear implant would cost. But she hoped that one hundred thousand was enough to scare Lachie away. Mumbling in the background told her he was talking to someone again.

She broke the connection, stuffed the phone into her pocket.

Part of her wanted to scream at the man, claw out his eyes, while another part wanted to pin him to a wall and say, *Your only concern was for the money. You never once asked why Robert needed an operation.* And as her mind replayed their conversation, she knew for certain—if she had not already known—that whatever relationship Lachie thought he had with her was over.

And over for good.

33

Gilchrist spent ten minutes reading Angus's written statement, then looked at Mhairi and said, "He still maintains he didn't rent out the Ramsays' home. Do you believe him?"

Mhairi shook her head. "I don't know what to believe anymore, sir."

"Right," he said, "let's talk to him."

He arranged for Angus to be escorted to interview room 1, while Mhairi went off and organized some tea and biscuits—Angus used to be her boyfriend, after all.

Angus was brought in and slumped into a chair on the opposite side of the table, and declined Mhairi's offer of a cuppa. Gilchrist poured a mug of tea for himself, took a sip, then said, "Have you spoken to your solicitor?"

Angus gave a disinterested shrug. "I've done nothing wrong. I don't need one."

"If you can't afford one," Gilchrist said, "we can arrange—"

"Has anybody told you you're a right cheeky bastard?" Angus snarled, then glared at Mhairi to include her in that comment. "I've got money. But I don't need to waste it on some legal rep to sit here like a doo-wally and say fuck all, then send me a bill that would choke a fucking horse."

"Finished?"

"Just get on with it."

"For the record," Gilchrist said, addressing the recorder on the table, "Mr. McCarron has declined his right to have his solicitor present." He nodded to Angus. "Is that correct?"

"Yeah."

"OK," Gilchrist began, "I'm going to ask you some questions, and I want you to tell me the truth about—"

"Read my statement. It's all there."

Gilchrist waited several seconds while Angus shifted and shuffled on his seat. Once he settled again, Gilchrist said, "Do you know Jana Judkowski?"

Angus frowned at him. "Who?"

"The young brunette who accompanies Caryl."

"Oh, her. I never knew her name."

"She's dead."

Angus stilled for one, two, three seconds, then his gaze danced between Gilchrist and Mhairi. "Dead? What d'you mean she's dead?"

"She was shot in the head last night, then dumped on some street in the outskirts of Glasgow. Strathclyde Police suspect it's a contract killing."

Angus frowned, looked away, looked back. "What're you telling me this for?" he gasped. "What's this got to do with me?"

"You said you knew her—"

"But I only seen her with Caryl. That's all—"

"Caryl's also dead."

Angus stilled, as if struck by a stun gun.

"Shot in the head, too. Her body was found with Jana's." Gilchrist leaned forward. "Three women dead from the cottage in Kingsbarns," he pressed on. "And another two within twelve hours of us locating the house in Boarhills. Both houses rented through you."

Angus fixed his gaze on Gilchrist. "What're you telling me?"

"That you could be next."

"*What?*" Angus shook his head. "No way, *no way*—"

"You rented both houses to Caryl—"

"But . . . I . . . I . . ."

"No buts, Angus. I believe you're innocent," Gilchrist added.

Angus's mouth hung open. He glanced at Mhairi, then stared at Gilchrist, as if pleading for an explanation.

"I believe you were duped," Gilchrist said. "I think Caryl tricked you."

As if seeing the wisdom in Gilchrist's words, Angus nodded.

"Along she comes," Gilchrist said, "looking beautiful, with plenty of money"—with Mhairi seated next to him, he chose not to mention sex—"and persuades you to go along with whatever she wants. It wouldn't take much to agree, I have to say."

"All I did was—" Angus stopped, as if realizing he was about to set off his own trap.

"I'm listening," Gilchrist urged. "All you did was . . . what?"

Angus wrung his hands, stared at the floor, shook his head. "I didn't do anything wrong," he pleaded. "She said she would be looking for another couple of cottages out in the wilds in the next few weeks or so—"

"Caryl said?"

Angus nodded, eager to let it all spill out. "She didn't want to go through Patterson and McLeod. Said she would rather do business with me directly. I saw it as an easy way to make a few quid on the side. I mean, anyone would. Right?"

"So you showed her the Ramsays' house and dropped off one of your McCarron and Co. cards."

"We'd had it on the books for some time—"

"Patterson and McLeod's books?"

"Yeah. But they weren't interested in short-term rents. Six months was about as short as they wanted. Not enough profit in it. So I took it on myself—"

"Behind Patterson and McLeod's back."

"It's a company, not two people. I run the St. Andrews branch."

"So when you say *they* weren't interested in short-term rents, you mean *you* chose not to put it through their books."

Angus wrung his hands, then pushed his fingers through his hair. "Look," he said. "Can I have a smoke?"

"No." It was Mhairi.

"I'm not asking you," Angus snapped.

"I've only got a few more questions," Gilchrist said, "then you're free to go."

Angus looked at him. "You're not charging me?"

"I told you I think you're innocent." Gilchrist smiled, and said, "Of course, it all depends on whether or not I believe your answers to my remaining questions."

Angus swallowed a lump in his throat, then nodded, eager to prove his innocence.

Gilchrist took another sip of tea, replaced the mug on the table with deliberation. He was in two minds whether to charge Angus with obstructing an investigation, perverting the course of justice, or just let him go. As he watched Angus watch him, he came to realize that Angus was little more than a fly-by-night salesman, a common con man who could see no farther than the next deal, who lived only from day to day, with unrealistic aspirations of making it on his own. A toss of the coin might better decide on which side of the law he would earn a living. Gilchrist felt saddened for Mhairi and hoped she now saw that, too.

He leaned forward, narrowing the gap between him and Angus. "How many other cottages in the wilds was Caryl looking to rent from you?"

"Two or three."

"Did you show her any?"

Another glance at Mhairi told Gilchrist that Angus had been seeing Dillanos behind Mhairi's back for longer than a couple of months. "One or two," Angus said.

"Maybe four or five?"

"Maybe."

Gilchrist reached forward and switched off the recorder.

Angus looked at him, then Mhairi, a smile twitching his lips. "Is that it?"

Gilchrist slapped the table with a move so sudden that both Mhairi and Angus jolted. Then he reached out, grabbed Angus by the neck of his shirt, and said, "Now you listen to me, sonny Jim. When I ask you a question you tell me the truth, and nothing but the truth. I don't want to hear any more of your lies. Got that?" He shoved Angus back onto his seat with a force that almost toppled it over.

Angus tugged his shirt, adjusted the neck, ran a hand through his hair, eyes fired with an anger of his own, as if readying to tell Gilchrist where to get off.

"And before you think of filing a complaint," Gilchrist said, "Mhairi saw nothing, and heard nothing, other than your repeated lies." He leaned forward again. "You have one thing going for you, Angus. Do you want to know what that is?"

Angus swallowed a lump in his throat.

"The fact that whoever killed Caryl Dillanos, Jana Judkowski, and the three other women probably doesn't know about your involvement. *Yet*." Gilchrist watched the meaning of his words work their way through Angus's stunned mind. "Do you understand what I'm saying? If you continue to feed me a bunch of shite, then I'm going to feed you to the lions." He waited one beat, two beats, then said, "Do you understand now?"

Angus nodded.

"I didn't hear you."

"I understand."

Gilchrist nodded for Mhairi to switch the recorder back on. A glance at the light to make sure it was recording, then, "Let me ask you that question once again, Mr. McCarron. How many other cottages in the wilds was Caryl Dillanos looking to rent from you?"

"Two, she said, maybe more."

"And did you show her any?"

"I did." Another furtive glance at Mhairi.

"How many did you take her to?"

"Six in total."

"And did she take any on?"

Angus pursed his lips for a moment, then let his breath out with "One."

"Did she sign any paperwork?"

"No."

"Give you any money?"

"Three months' rent in advance."

"Cash?"

Angus nodded, defeated.

Gilchrist thought of pursuing the details and wondered if the owner of the property knew his place was being rented out on the side. Angus McCarron really was flying by the seat of his pants. Cash meant no declaration to the Inland Revenue.

"When did you show her these properties?"

"Last week."

As Gilchrist worked out the significance of that timing, a frisson ran the length of his spine. With three women dead from the cottage in Kingsbarns, the ringleader—this Kumar if that's who it was—would have known it was only a matter of time before their bodies were discovered. Time to move on. A no-brainer. But if Dillanos had been hired to locate a new property, then been killed, the logical conclusion was that Kumar was starting off with a clean slate, getting rid of anyone who could give away his new hideaway. He stared hard at Angus and wondered if he knew how much danger his life was in.

"What day last week?" Gilchrist asked.

Angus lowered his head. "Friday."

Mhairi hissed a quiet curse, now aware why Angus could not make their date.

"Just you, Caryl, and Jana?" Gilchrist continued.

"Yes."

"Are you sure there was no one else?"

"Positive."

"Did Caryl tell anyone she was going through you?"

Angus frowned, shook his head. "I don't think so."

"It's important, Angus."

"How would I know who she talks to?"

"I hope she didn't tell anyone. For your sake. If she did, I wouldn't bet a penny for your life." It troubled Gilchrist that he took such satisfaction from the look of disbelief that crossed Angus's face then shifted to fear. But the man really had jerked his chain.

"Tell me you're joking," Angus blurted.

"No joke. You could be next."

At that, Angus put his hands to his face, his elbows on his knees, and moaned.

Gilchrist glanced at Mhairi, caught her look of disgust. Back to Angus. "Do you have an address for this latest Dillanos rental?" he asked him. "If the person who is behind the killings has already moved in, we might be able to catch him."

Angus sat upright, his tear-filled eyes alive with hope. "I can take you there."

"Address is fine. You shouldn't be seen to be involved."

Angus grimaced, as if not understanding.

"For your own safety," Gilchrist explained.

34

The following morning, Monday, Gilchrist assembled his team.

Rather than burst in and break down the doors, he decided to play it safe. There were too many unknowns, too many variables, and until he knew who and what he was dealing with, he would keep his team to a minimum. With Dillanos and Judkowski dead, he worried that the occupant—if he had indeed moved into the new premises—would not be averse to killing again, if it kept him out of prison.

So, reconnaissance was the order of the day.

Gilchrist and Jessie took the lead, with Mhairi, Nance, and McCauley as secondary.

The address was another cottage in the countryside, between the villages of Tayport and Leuchars; a three-bedroom bungalow with an attic conversion, and a lounge extension with a conservatory out the back that overlooked the four acres of land on which it sat, and which were rented out as pasture to a neighboring farm. A stone-built barn stood fifty feet from the bungalow, a separate building just waiting to be modernized—or perhaps to have shackles installed to secure women for the year. Interestingly, Gilchrist thought, the barn was barely visible from the main road, hidden by the roadside hedgerow and lounge extension.

They established that Joe Bowden, the bungalow's owner, was a geotechnical engineer who worked overseas for an American oil company, and who owned two other properties in the United Kingdom—a two-bedroom flat in Weston-Super-Mare and a four-bedroom semidetached in Hayling Island. Records confirmed that both English properties were rented out long-term, whereas the property in Fife had lain empty for three months—since the end of the summer—after the previous tenant, an elderly author looking for a quiet space, returned to Ireland.

McCauley had managed to track down Joe Bowden, who confirmed over the phone that he was thinking of putting the bungalow on the market as he had been unable to rent it for two years. When Gilchrist heard this, his first thought was to charge Angus with fraud, but he thought it might be better to keep that up his sleeve for the time being.

You could never tell when a little blackmail might be needed.

By 9:30 they set off, Gilchrist and Jessie in Gilchrist's Merc; Mhairi and Nance in an unmarked Fife Constabulary Ford Focus, and assigned to make discreet inquiries of adjacent homes; McCauley in a white Toyota RAV4—courtesy of Shuggie—and assigned to do a series of drive-bys.

Gilchrist and Jessie's first port of call was the adjacent farm.

He pulled his Merc to a halt outside a two-story stone building that faced a three-sided courtyard. To the left was a row of buildings as low-slung as stables. To the right an open-sided metal storage facility half-filled with bales of straw.

Gilchrist stepped from the car, breathed in the bitter smell of silage.

Jessie joined him and screwed up her face. "What the hell is that?"

"Silage," he said. "Cattle fodder."

"Cows eat that?"

"They do."

"That should be deemed cruelty to animals."

A man appeared from behind the storage facility. His face glowed with the weather-beaten tan of a Scottish farmer. Gray stubble dotted his chin. Shirt sleeves were rolled up, as if he were oblivious to the cold. Tattoos writhed on hair-covered, muscular arms. He approached and said, "Can I help you?"

Gilchrist held up his warrant card. Jessie did likewise.

"Are you the owner?" Gilchrist asked him.

"The old man is, but he's in Stirling for the day."

"We'd like to ask a few questions on a case we're involved in."

"Will it take long? I'm in the middle of sorting out cattle feed."

"Shouldn't take long at all," Gilchrist assured him. "Do you work here?"

"I also live here," he said, giving Gilchrist the answer he was looking for. If he was going to ask about the neighboring bungalow, he needed to speak to someone familiar with the vicinity.

"You rent land from the cottage at the other end of the field," Gilchrist asked, nodding to Bowden's bungalow about five hundred yards distant. The barn sat off to the side as if on another property.

"We do. Cattle graze on it. Why?"

"Do you know the owner?"

"Never seen him."

"Him?"

"Could be a her, for all I know."

"Who do you pay your rent to?"

"All done by direct debit from the bank. Pay quarterly, best I remember."

"Into whose account?"

"Property manager's. McCallum, McCannon, a name like that."

Gilchrist grimaced. He would need to check it out, but it sounded like one more nail into Angus's coffin. "Have you seen any unusual activity in the last week or so?" he asked.

"Unusual? Like what?"

"Any contractor vans, maintenance vehicles, lights on in the house, that sort of thing."

"Not a thing. Haven't seen any lights on inside for a few months either. Outside lights come on in the evening. Solar sensitive. Why?"

"Have you seen anyone at all in the last couple of weeks?"

"Can't say that I have. But I've not been looking. The old man should be back this afternoon, if you want to ask him."

"Anybody else living here who might have seen anything?" Jessie asked.

He eyed Jessie as if surprised to hear her talk, then shook his head.

"Wife? Mother?"

"Wife's blind as a bat, and the old dear's been gone for four years last New Year."

"I'm sorry," Gilchrist said, and handed him a business card. "If you happen to notice anything unusual, lights, cars, that sort of thing, give me a call, anytime, day or night."

"Sure thing."

Back in the Merc, Gilchrist hooked his mobile to his car speaker system and said, "Anything, Bill?"

"The first run past, I thought it was deserted. But from the snowfall, it looks like a car has driven in and out. From here I can't see if there are any footprints to the door—"

"Don't go in, Bill. You'll only leave your own tracks. It's important that we leave no evidence that we're looking at this property. You got that?"

"Got it."

"Don't hang about either, in case you get noticed. Do another drive-by at midday, then again in the early afternoon, and once more before it gets dark."

"Got it."

"And no liquid lunches. You're driving."

"Would never dream of it."

"In the meantime, see if you can come up with anything new on Craig Farmer."

Without waiting for a response, Gilchrist ended the call and dialed another number. He let it ring for ten counts and was about to disconnect when Nance's voice said, "Sorry, Andy. Couldn't pick up there. Got tied up with one of the neighbors."

Gilchrist had instructed Nance and Mhairi to knock on doors to a number of houses close to Bowden's bungalow, the nearest one being four hundred yards along the B945.

"Any luck?" he asked her.

"Sort of," Nance said. "A Mrs. Minnie Black said she saw . . . and I'll use her exact words . . . 'one o' thae black apes wi' some blonde wi' a skirt up tae here,' and . . . wait for it . . . 'just seeing the two o' them thigither was enough to make you boak.'" Nance finished with a chuckle.

"When was this?" Gilchrist asked.

"Saturday morning at around nine, when she was hanging out her washing."

"In the winter?"

"Beats tumble drying."

"What car were they driving?"

"A *car* was about as good as she could say. But she did say it was silver, and she never noticed the number plate, of course."

Gilchrist's thoughts crackled with possibilities. Dillanos lived in Glasgow, about ninety minutes from St. Andrews, so around nine would be about right if she drove up that morning. Was it possible Kumar had met her? And if so, once he had sight of this latest property, then maybe Dillanos had served her purpose and could be eliminated.

The whole idea could be ridiculous. But it was an idea nonetheless.

"Check CCTV footage around that time," Gilchrist ordered. "They must have been caught on camera somewhere."

"Will do."

Gilchrist disconnected, then dialed another number.

Cooper answered with a curt, "Cooper."

"It's Andy Gilchrist here, and I've got you on speaker with DS Janes," he added, just in case Cooper had any ideas of turning on the charm. "You got anything of interest for me?"

"I was about to call you," she said, which had Gilchrist turning up the volume. "I've been able to confirm ID from the deceased's fingerprints," she said. "Stewart Donnelly. You were right. But he also had a number of tattoos, several of which might intrigue you."

Gilchrist thought Cooper sounded as if she was slipping into her seductive tone. "We're listening," he said, reminding her that Jessie was listening, too.

"He had a series of teardrop tattoos—"

"Series?"

"Four, to be exact."

"Where?"

"Under his left arm, next to the number eleven."

"Eleven? As in bones?"

"Yes."

Jessie said, "Were they outlines of teardrops, or inked-in solid?"

"Three were solid, and one was an outline."

"The symbolism varies around the world," Jessie said to Gilchrist, "but I'd bet he's killed three people and was still to take revenge on one."

"Revenge being symbolized by the outlined teardrop?" Gilchrist asked her.

Jessie nodded. "Once he's taken revenge, he would have it inked in."

"I looked into the symbolism," Cooper said, as if not to be outdone, "and teardrop tattoos, by definition alone, are typically tattooed on the face, beneath the eye—"

"We're in Scotland," Jessie interrupted. "Openly displaying teardrops might be seen as an invitation to be challenged. Better just to keep the tally hidden."

Cooper ignored Jessie's comment with, "So what are your thoughts, Andy?"

Gilchrist puffed out his cheeks, then exhaled. "I'm guessing," he said, "but I'd say the teardrops being tattooed next to the number eleven bones means something—"

"He killed for Kumar," Jessie said. "Donnelly was Kumar's hit man."

Gilchrist looked at her. "Maybe," he said, then stared across the open fields. Nothing seemed to make sense. Teardrops, numbers, symbolic tattoos, and murders mounting in Fife. Who would ever have thought international crime would find its way to this spot on the East Neuk? But find its way it had.

If Gilchrist could not break the case open soon, many more young women would be kidnapped and chained to walls, branded with bone tattoos, then used and abused.

And in the end, murdered, too.

35

The remainder of the morning turned up nothing new.

Gilchrist and Jessie paid a visit to Minnie Black, and he handed her a business card with instructions to call him the instant she noticed anyone enter Bowden's bungalow. Jessie did likewise, striking out her Strathclyde phone numbers and scribbling down her new mobile number, only to have Black scowl at it.

On the drive back to St. Andrews, Jessie said, "What's the rush? Everywhere we go you've got your foot to the floor."

"Force of habit," he said, and accelerated to eighty just to annoy her.

But driving fast seemed to sharpen his thinking, hone his sense of logic. As he eyed the road ahead, he tried to work out how to find the missing pieces. His gut was telling him that Minnie Black's *blonde* and *black ape* were Caryl Dillanos and Kumar. But with Dillanos dead, the only way to prove it would be to talk to Kumar. And then there was Craig Farmer, Donnelly's so-called mate, who had not been seen or heard from since signing his written statement. If he was able to confront either of these two, he might be able to move the case forward. Black's report intrigued him.

He glanced at Jessie. "I'm going to have Bill keep an eye on Bowden's bungalow. And I want you and Mhairi and Nance to ID Craig Farmer once and for all."

Jessie nodded, then said, "It's odd, don't you think? The attack on Stan. Pulling his mate off. Giving a statement under a false name. I mean, why would he do that? And then to give a false address in St. Andrews? Maybe he drove back to Dundee. Wasn't that where they came from?" She shook her head. "I don't get it."

Neither did Gilchrist. Breaking up a knife attack and stopping someone from being murdered was one thing—you had to have nerves of steel to do that, as well as a willingness to right a wrong—but giving a statement that could assign your *friend* to a term behind bars, then vanishing from the scene thereafter, was another.

"Maybe he didn't want his mate, Donnelly, to be charged with murder," Gilchrist said.

"Maybe they're not mates at all."

"Which is another puzzle. Farmer says they met in the pub for the first time that day." Gilchrist slowed down to thirty as he entered the village of Leuchars. "Check in with Jackie back at the station," he said. "I've got her searching CCTV footage on Stan's attack."

They settled for silence as he eased through Leuchars, and he was about to accelerate when Dainty called.

"You were spot on, Andy," Dainty said without introduction. "The ballistics match. The gun that fired the bullets that killed Caryl Dillanos and Jana Judkowski was the same gun that killed Stewart Donnelly."

Gilchrist mouthed a *Wow*. "So in all probability, they were contract killings."

"I'd bet the house on it. And here's an interesting fact. That same gun was used in two separate incidents last year. One in Manchester in August. Local kingpin Col Feeney, a right bad bastard, and his bodyguard were shot through the head in Feeney's Jaguar in an Asda car park. Feeney was in the backseat, his bodyguard was behind the wheel. In the middle of the fucking day, and no one saw a thing—"

"Or no one was willing to risk their life being a witness," Gilchrist said.

Dainty grunted, then went on. "On top of that, the CCTV cameras weren't working. And the other incident took place in Edinburgh in September—another punter who fancied himself as an up-and-coming big shot, Jerry Best, was shot in the back of the nut as he was about to step into his home. Again, no one saw a thing. But it happened late at night in a quiet residential area."

"Any business connection between Feeney and Best?" Gilchrist asked.

"Both of them were into prostitution and high-priced escorts," Dainty said. "Although Best was more upmarket than Feeney, if you get my drift."

"How about drugs?"

"Feeney dabbled, but not much." The tone of Dainty's voice warned Gilchrist that worse was to come. "But Best was starting to make a name for himself in trafficking," Dainty growled. "Starting to build a thriving business. The mind boggles. It's un-fucking-believable that a modern-day slave trade exists."

"And the girls come from Europe?" Gilchrist asked.

"Everywhere. Poland's popular. So is Belarus, Ukraine, and Romania, and probably all these other fucking places that used to belong to Russia."

"Any leads to the shooter?" Gilchrist asked.

"Dead ends. Every one of them. In and out, and leaves not a clue. They've even got a nickname for him. The Ghost," Dainty said. "Well he's scary enough, that's for fucking sure."

"And now the Ghost has made his way up north," Gilchrist said.

"Looks like it," Dainty confirmed. "Listen, Andy, I'll send you what I've got, and if you need anything else, just give me a buzz."

Gilchrist thanked Dainty and ended the call.

"The Ghost," Jessie said, and chuckled. "If it wasn't so scary it'd be funny."

"Maybe Robert could work it into your comedy routine," Gilchrist said.

But he did not catch Jessie's response. Instead he heard the echo of Colin's voice whisper *cleaner than a baby's bum* as his mind pulled up an image of a man down by the harbor slipping into a white Toyota with a dent in the bumper. He had never worked out why his mobile had rung that Sunday morning or why the man had driven off or why they had driven back while he was standing at the corner reading his newspaper. Then to find the abandoned house in Boarhills, as if he had been led by the hand, with not a fingerprint in sight, no clues, and no farther forward.

It made no logical sense.

But Gilchrist knew logic and sense were nothing to do with it.

That Sunday morning, had he seen the Ghost?

*

CCTV footage confirmed that Donnelly had crossed the Tay Bridge at 8:23 on the morning of Stan's attack. Donnelly had been driving the rented Ford, with one passenger in the front seat, the mysterious Craig Farmer. It seemed as if Farmer had just slipped away, like a ghost, which had Gilchrist's mind firing into overdrive but leaving him with nothing but intangibles and thin air.

On the practical side, Jackie had located other footage of the same car as it appeared in the streets of St. Andrews. As best they could work out, Donnelly first hit North Street at 9:40, which had Gilchrist wondering what took him so long— Dundee to St. Andrews on the A919 was less than fifteen miles, and no more than a thirty-minute drive. Maybe they stopped for breakfast, or visited someone. Or some*where?* Gilchrist's gut stirred at that thought.

Had they stopped off at Bowden's cottage?

Or was he stretching reason too far? Still, the thought niggled.

Nance confirmed that Donnelly and Farmer had two pints in 1 Golf Place. Only one staff member recalled seeing two people who matched their description, but could give no details, only that they both wore hoodies, which they kept pulled up.

"They're avoiding being ID'd on CCTV," Jessie said. "These guys knew what they were doing."

Gilchrist could only agree.

At 11:52 the Ford was recorded leaving St. Andrews on the A917 heading toward Kingsbarns and Crail on the coast, then captured on its return, clocked at 4:22—still with Donnelly driving, still with his solitary passenger, and still with their hoodies pulled up.

At 5:18 it pulled into the car park at Murray Place. The lights were doused, and the engine switched off, while Donnelly waited for Stan to arrive, which was burning proof to Gilchrist—if he ever needed it—that Stan's attack had been premeditated, not provoked as Donnelly had insisted.

Stan had finished for the day and had a bite to eat in the Golf Hotel on The Scores, followed by a pint in Ma Bells. When he walked through the lane to the car park in Murray Place, he was attacked as he was about to enter his car, keys in hand.

Footage showed Stan pulling the door open, then hesitating as Donnelly approached from his left. Stan faced him, and the next second he was flat on his back, legs kicking and arms flailing as Donnelly, still wearing a hoodie, slashed his knife at him. It took three seconds into the attack—Gilchrist counted it—before Farmer emerged from the rental, jerked Donnelly by his hoodie, and pulled him off.

Two things struck Gilchrist as they replayed the footage: one, that Farmer moved with the speed and slickness of a man trained in unarmed combat; and two, that Donnelly put up no resistance to being pulled off and had even sat with his rump on the bonnet of an adjacent car while Farmer attended to Stan—odd, to say the least.

Of course, Jessie noticed one other thing that troubled Gilchrist.

"Zoom in on the back of Stan's car," she said to Jackie.

Jackie did as instructed.

"That's a Mercedes," Jessie said. "Isn't it?"

Jackie nodded, gave a nervous glance at Gilchrist.

"Is there a fire sale on Mercedes in Fife?" Jessie said, before the penny dropped and she turned to Gilchrist with a now-I-get-it gesture. "That's your car," she said to him.

"Stan's was in for repair," he replied. "He borrowed mine for the afternoon."

"Which means . . ."

"That Stan was in the wrong place at the wrong time," Gilchrist conceded.

"And Donnelly was not after Stan. He was after you."

The wrong place at the wrong time.

Gilchrist could only give a defeated nod.

36

After end of business, Jessie and Gilchrist met up in the Central Bar, just the two of them—Nance had a date and had to put on her face; Mhairi was going home for a glass of wine, and an early bed; Bill was assigned to an hourly check of Bowden's cottage.

Jessie chinked her pint to Gilchrist's. "Going back to this mistaken identity attack on Stan," she said. "I'd assume Stan's worked it out for himself."

"I'd be surprised if he hadn't," he agreed.

"So why would Donnelly be after you? You come across him before?"

"Not that I'm aware of."

That was always a policeman's worst fear, that one of the criminals he had helped put away would seek revenge. But as far as Gilchrist knew, his and Donnelly's paths had never crossed. Which introduced a new set of fears, that Donnelly had been contracted to kill him. Why else would he have let Farmer pull him off Stan so easily once he'd been told he was trying to kill the wrong man?

He forced these thoughts to the back of his mind, as Jessie persisted.

"I've had a colleague of mine in Strathclyde check out Donnelly," she said.

"Not DI Lachlan McKellar, I hope."

"Lachie's not DI," she corrected. "He's bribed and screwed and lied all the way to chief super. If he wasn't such a fat useless moron, I might be impressed." She gripped her pint glass as if it were Lachie's balls.

Gilchrist responded by sipping his pint.

Chief superintendent. That's the level of seniority he should have reached by now, if he had not pissed off Fife Constabulary's hierarchy with monotonous regularity. In a moment of drunken weakness, he had once tackled Assistant Chief Constable McVicar about his prospects for promotion and been assured by the big man himself that they could not afford to lose someone with such drive and intuitive energy as Gilchrist had, to the mundane duties of upper management. He had known then that McVicar had been letting him down gently—

"Did you know that Donnelly was born in Dundee," Jessie said, "then moved to Manchester to live with his girlfriend?"

"Can't say that I did. About him living with his girlfriend, I mean."

"She's dead."

"That figures."

Jessie chinked her glass to Gilchrist's. "She didn't die at the hands of Donnelly, you stupid twat. She was killed in a car crash—"

"Was Donnelly driving?"

"You're a right bundle of laughs, I must say. Anything wrong?"

Well, he could tell her how guilty he felt over Stan being stabbed by mistake. Or how he wished he had been more aggressive interviewing Donnelly, maybe threatened him with a stabbing of his own. Or how he felt as if he was failing—it had been, what, six days since the woman was found on the Coastal Path, and they seemed to have achieved sweet eff all. But if the truth be told, he knew it was Jessie's comment about Lachie reaching CS that stung him the most. Or maybe he needed to speak to his children before they forgot all about him.

He chinked his glass against Jessie's. "I'm fine," he said. "Just tired."

He watched her dark eyes dance with his, and her smirk twist into a tight grin. "If I didn't know better," she said, "I'd say you weren't getting enough nookie."

Gilchrist could have sworn the bar stilled for an instant while he struggled to come up with some witty response. "Speak for yourself," was all he could think of, and regretted the words the instant they left his mouth.

But Jessie failed to take insult. "Who the hell would want to be screwed by Jabba the Hutt?" She took another mouthful, almost drained it. "Not me, although . . ."

Gilchrist frowned as her voice trailed off. "Have you heard from him recently?"

"It's nonstop. He texts me at least three times a day, every day. I mean, what is there not to understand about fuck off? If he keeps it up, I'm thinking of forwarding them on to his wife. That would start the shit flying."

"You can do better than Jabba."

"Anyone in mind?"

"Not off the top of my head," he said. "But you're young, attractive, smart, witty—"

"Are you trying to get off with me?" She let out a hacking chuckle that had heads turning their way. It took all of ten seconds for her to settle down. She wiped her eyes and said, "I'm sorry, Andy. You should have seen your face. You shouldn't take what I say so literally." She reached for her purse. "Here, let me get another round. I'm beginning to enjoy this."

Gilchrist was saved by his mobile ringing—ID Bill McCauley.

"Yes, Bill."

"Nothing to report, sir. Just done another drive-by, and the house is still in darkness. No lights on inside, although some landscaping lights are on in the front."

"Solar sensitive," Gilchrist assured him. "Anything on Farmer?"

A pause, then, "I thought you'd already checked out the farm, sir."

"Not the farm, Bill. Craig *Farmer*. Donnelly's sidekick."

"Oh. That. Eh . . . no. Not yet, sir."

"Well, keep at it, and let me know what you come up with. And in between, continue with an hourly drive-by. If you don't see anything by midnight, call it a day."

Gilchrist disconnected, troubled by Bill's forgetfulness. By assigning Bill to drive by every hour through midnight, he hoped it might keep him from the pub. But Bill seemed to have a way of turning up at the station, the overpowering aroma of strong mints giving the game away—as damning as cigarette smoke on wool.

"Problems?" Jessie said, nudging a settling pint his way.

Nothing that a good sacking wouldn't take care of, he thought of saying. But he had done what he could for Bill and knew he would have to bring it to a head. Rather than get into it with Jessie, he lifted his glass and chinked it against hers.

"You're falling behind," she said, then her mobile rang. She glared at the screen, excused herself, and walked outside.

Through the window, Gilchrist watched her breath cloud the air while she let the caller have it full force. Her mother, he thought. Or maybe one of her brothers. He returned to his pint. Maybe it was what Jessie had said to him, or the beer working its magic. Or perhaps he was just feeling lonely. But he took the opportunity to make a call of his own.

"To what do I owe the honor?" Cooper said.

"Calling to find out what's new."

She chuckled, a throaty rasp that cast up memories of silken skin and loose curls, and had him shifting his position on his stool. "Ah," she said, "Mr. Cooper has now returned from his sultry mistress in Italy."

A confusing mixture of disappointment and relief flooded Gilchrist, followed by a surge of regret that he had called in the first place. "That's not . . . I mean . . . I—"

"You called to find out what's new," she interrupted.

"I did. Yes." All business again. He gripped his pint.

"Well," she said, "the latest is that Mr. Cooper is now on his way to London and not expected back until tomorrow evening at the earliest."

He glanced out the window—no Jessie—felt his heart leap to his mouth. "I can't really talk at the moment," he said. "Let me call you back."

"Don't bother," she said.

He gave a wry smile. Well, she had every right to tell him to fuck off—

"I'll leave the front door unlocked," she said. "Come by anytime."

The call ended.

Gilchrist slipped his mobile into his jacket, surprised to find his hands shaking. Even his heart was racing. What the hell was that all about?

"You all right?" Jessie said, sliding herself up and onto the bar stool.

"How about you? You look fired up." He lifted his pint and stared beyond her as he took a sip.

"Just when I was beginning to enjoy myself," she said.

"Lachie?"

"I wish. Then I could just tell him to fuck off."

"Your mother?"

She took a long quiet sip of her beer, then placed the glass on the bartop with a deliberation that had Gilchrist on full alert. "Close," she said. "Her solicitor."

Gilchrist waited several polite seconds before saying, "That doesn't sound good."

"I suppose it had to come in the end."

"She'll never be granted custody of Robert," he assured her. "I can guarantee that."

"Custody?" She snorted. "She doesn't care about custody, or Robert. She only cares that I don't have him. That's what psychos do. She couldn't give a toss about Robert. She hasn't a hope in hell of seeing him, even if she won the grandmother-of-the-year award. And the earth would have to melt before that ever happened." She shoved her pint to the side. "I'm having a G and T. Want one?"

"I'll stick with Deuchars. Here, let me get this," he said, and nodded to the barman. "Large Tanqueray and tonic, Slimline if you've got it, in a tall glass with plenty of ice, and two slices of lime, not lemon."

"You got it," the barman said.

"Holy shit. I'm impressed. Are you sure you're not a gentle-man in disguise?"

"Don't worry," he said to her, and smiled. "We'll work it out."

"We?"

"You're one of the team. And I wouldn't want one of my most promising DSs to let a mere thing like a battle for child custody upset her." He regretted his words the instant they spilled from his mouth. Her smile shifted to a tight-lipped grimace that had her eyes welling. "I'm sorry," he said. "I didn't mean to make light of your problems."

She shook her head, dabbed a finger at her eye. "It's OK. It's not that."

Gilchrist thought silence his best option. He sipped his pint and waited. Neither of them spoke until the barman slid over a tall glass, and Jessie took a sip.

"Bloody hell," she said. "Does that taste good, or what?"

"Better?" he asked, and raised his pint.

She chinked her glass to his. "Getting there. But when the shit hits the fan, I hope you'll stand by me."

Dainty's words came back to him—*reliable, rock solid . . . won't let you down. I'd recommend her.* "Why wouldn't I?" he said.

"Because it looks like I'm going to be charged with resetting."

Resetting—the receiving and keeping of goods known to have been stolen. "Says who?" he asked.

"Heathen-face, and my cunts-for-brothers."

"With their records, I shouldn't think any of it would stand up in court."

"It shouldn't. Except for one teeny-weeny flaw."

He knew what she was going to say, but he had to ask anyway. "Which is?"

"It's true."

"Right," said Gilchrist. "You never said that. And I never heard it."

37

They left after that drink, and Gilchrist dropped off Jessie at home.

He eyed the road ahead, knowing he was over the limit. He knew, too, that if he was ever involved in an accident when he'd had a few pints, it would be his jotters for him, and early retirement. But despite that real and ominous threat, he continued to drink and drive.

It made no sense, and he could not explain why he continued to do it. But what also made no sense to him was driving through a frosted night to the home of a married woman, albeit an unhappily married woman. He glanced at his dashboard—10:32—and thought of just turning around and driving back to his cottage in Crail. But an image of Cooper sliding her hands up her negligee had him reaching for his mobile.

He dialed her number.

"Hello?" she said.

He thought she sounded tired. "I hope I haven't disturbed you."

"Of course you have," she said, then lowered her tone a notch. "But I don't mind being disturbed at this time of night when I'm in bed by myself. Where are you?"

"Driving."

"That tells me what you're doing, not where you are."

"Precision has always been one of your stronger points."

"That's why I'm good at my job." A pause, then, "Are you alone?"

"I am," he said.

"So you're able to speak?"

"Which is why I'm calling."

It seemed a game they played, like a cat toying with a mouse, a precursor to supper, perhaps, although Gilchrist had no doubt which of them was for the eating. And he could not fail to pick up on the subtlest of nips in her comment, a reminder of his earlier call, abbreviated as it was.

"The front door is unlocked."

"I worry that you do that," he said. "It's like inviting crime into—"

"Once a policeman, always a policeman." Another chuckle. "I prefer to think of it as inviting the crime-buster into my home."

Ahead, the road glittered with diamonds of frost, a million tiny lights that sparkled and danced to the tune of his headlights. A hedgerow zipped past, stripped branches white with frost, close enough to remind him that he was over the limit and driving too fast.

He lifted his foot from the accelerator, felt the car slow down.

"Gail was unfaithful," he said at length.

"I know. It's what makes you reluctant to become involved with a married woman, to do to some other husband what was done to you."

"I . . ." He shook his head. What was he trying to say? "I'm sorry . . . I . . ."

"Would it frighten you off if I told you I've filed for divorce?"

"I'm sorry . . ." It seemed to be all he could think to say. "I mean . . ."

"Mr. Cooper doesn't know yet."

Which told him that she had not yet filed for divorce.

He gripped the steering wheel, flexed his fingers. "When Gail left," he said, "I was hurt, confused, angry, vengeful, all of the above. But once the dust settled, and I looked back on what happened, what struck me the most was how many years I had put into my marriage, how much time I'd lost and could never recover. It seemed such a waste. If I hadn't had Jack or Maureen I don't know what I would have done—"

"I don't want any children. Well, certainly not with Mr. Cooper." She laughed then, a high-pitched chuckle that suggested a glass of red wine, maybe two, even more. "Now I've really frightened you off."

"No." He pulled the Merc to the side of the road. "What I'm saying is, that you have a great deal to consider before going ahead with a—"

"I love that about you, your diametric opposites. You're quite the conflict," she said. "Has anyone told you that before? No, I don't suppose they would have, would they?"

He chose silence as his response.

"You can be so considerate and understanding at times." Her voice sounded tinged with the slightest of frustrations. "Yet at times, so utterly unfeeling and cold."

He took the opportunity, and said, "Like now?"

She waited a couple of beats, then said, "You've stopped driving, haven't you?"

He thought of saying he was sitting at a traffic light, but he knew one lie only led to another. "I have," he said.

"You're worried that you're the cause of the breakdown in my marriage." A pause, then, "Well let me assure you that you're not. My marriage was broken long before you and I consummated our relationship. Mr. Cooper saw to that," she said, with a finality that signaled the filing for her divorce was imminent.

He was not sure if he was expected to comment, so he said nothing.

"Oh, Andy. I don't know what I'm going to do with you." Another pause, then, "It's getting late. And I'm sure you have a busy day ahead of you tomorrow. Go home to bed, Andy. Go. I'll be in touch. Ciao."

He gave her a "Ciao" in return, but the line had already died.

He glanced in the rearview mirror—all clear—swung his Merc around in a tight circle, the tires slipping on the icy surface, and accelerated into a vortex of swirling snow. The road no longer danced alive with frost but lay covered by a thickening blanket, as if reflecting the smothering of his own feelings.

Cooper was right in what she had said. She was right in almost all she said.

But one thing struck him.

He did indeed have a busy day ahead of him.

By the time he parked in Castle Street, the snowfall had stopped.

Overhead, stars pierced a black sky. The wind had risen, beating powdered snow along Rose Wynd like white dust.

From the harbor, the sea whispered in a voice as cold as an Arctic winter.

Inside his cottage, he clattered a couple of chunks of ice from the ice maker into a thick Edinburgh Crystal whisky glass and poured himself a double Balvenie Doublewood— well, maybe a triple—and collected Dainty's report on Jeannie Janes from one of the chairs in the kitchen. Sometimes that was the problem with correspondence—if it was not in ready sight, it often lay forgotten.

He switched on the fire, then the TV—TV to mute—and took a sip of whisky as he settled down. He started off by flicking through the pages, looking for words that caught his eye—a list of petty offenses, nothing to write home about, but all of them breaking the law; several visits from the social services resulting in attempts to recover overpayments, mostly to no avail; probation, community service, fines, disturbance of the peace—now where had he heard that?—on and on, as if to abide by the law was a crime in itself.

He took another sip of whisky and returned to the beginning.

He noted the address in Wellhouse Crescent, Easterhouse, Glasgow—the tattooed body of Mr. Angry, and Jessie's mother screaming at them from a third-floor window, flashed into his mind—and her date of birth, October 20, 1958. For occupation, *assistant salesperson* was noted, beneath which was typed

lifelong prostitute who worked Blythswood Square in the '70s and '80s, but now suspected of pimping in the city center.

He had to force himself to take a sip, not drain the glass. It was not uncommon for prostitutes to raise their children to follow in their footsteps, as if they were passing on the baton, the gift of the world's oldest profession.

No wonder Jessie hated her mother.

He read on.

Suspected of supplying Jock Shepherd with underage girls, but that link remains unproven, despite three separate undercover operations.

The name Jock Shepherd stopped him short again, and he recalled an image of the Dillanos Furniture Showroom and a skinny nicotine addict by the name of Dot. The world was becoming smaller. A list of names with which Jeannie Janes was associated, or suspected of being associated, ran for most of one page, and he scanned them for any he might know, and stopped with a grunt—*William Thomson Reid, a.k.a. Bully*, and *James Thomson Reid*, the Reid brothers, Bully and Jimmy. Christ, Planet Earth really was shrinking by the second. Again, Jessie's voice echoed at him—*Tommy's back in Barlinnie. He's the nutcase of the family*. If Jessie's two brothers, Tommy "Nutcase" and Terry "Angry" Janes, were only half as bad as the Reids, then Jessie really was better out of it.

He eyed his whisky, then drained the glass. He stretched for the Balvenie, pulled out the cork, and poured another— only a small double this time. Another sip had him marveling at the honeyed spiciness and toying with the idea of becoming a whisky connoisseur. The only problem with that, he knew, was that he liked beer more—or should he be saying he liked more beer?

He chuckled and returned his attention to Dainty's report. And as he read, the glow from the Balvenie and the heat from the gas fire were working their magic. Concentrating was becoming an effort, and he was about to call it a day, when he jerked awake.

He read the lines again.

> ... has two sons, Thomas and Terence—no middle names—and one daughter, Jessica, whose middle name, Harriet, she claims was for Harry Allen, the executioner who hanged Peter Manuel at Barlinnie Prison in 1958. She also claims that her mother, Dolly Janes, née Ferguson, was raped by Manuel after he murdered the Smart family in January 1958, but escaped being killed when she told Manuel that it was her eighteenth birthday. Jeannie Janes claims she is Peter Manuel's illegitimate daughter. The story has never been verified . . .

Gilchrist pulled himself to his feet.

> . . . Peter Manuel's illegitimate daughter . . .

Which would mean that Jessie was Peter Manuel's grand-daughter.

Was that the secret Jessie wanted to keep from Robert, that his great-grandfather was one of Scotland's most notorious serial killers, whose reign of terror in the '50s came to an end when he was hanged in Barlinnie in 1958? He rechecked Jeannie's date of birth—October 20, 1958—and saw that the dates fit.

Was this true, or just a story put around by Jeannie Janes to add to her own personal infamy, the illegitimate daughter of Peter Manuel? How many extra turns had she done once that bit of information came out, and what, if any, extra underworld respect had she gained as one of Glasgow's madams purporting to have a serial killer's genes? But one more thought struck him, that if Peter Manuel were still alive, he would be in his eighties.

He revisited Dainty's notes.

He did not know Jock Shepherd personally, had never met the man. But he did know he was a fair old age, and one of Glasgow's original thugs who had brawled his way to the top by his bootstraps. Had Jock Shepherd known Peter Manuel? Or had he known Jeannie's mother, known that she'd been raped? If so, it was not a huge stretch of any imagination to see the big man take care of a bastard child with a criminal pedigree already in the making. Had Big Jock been Jeannie's surrogate father, or an avuncular figure who would shove opportunities Jeannie's way?

He scanned the printout again—suspected of supplying Jock Shepherd with underage girls—while these thoughts and more, as far-fetched and illogical as they were, fired at his mind with the speed of a snake strike. He understood Jessie's need to distance herself from her criminal family, her desire to make a new life for herself, her struggle to free her son of all familial rancor. And he came to understand how far Jessie had come, how much she was prepared to do to give her son the upbringing and chance at life that she never had.

He folded Dainty's report, undecided how best to handle it.

He drained his whisky and made his way to his bedroom.

As he stripped off and went through his nightly ablutions, images flickered and flashed on the screen of his mind—Jessie's mother with her foul mouth and white flouncy hair; her brother with his muscled body blackened with tattoos; young women in summer dresses, their half-naked bodies lying white and blue in snow-covered grass.

He had never understood how the subconscious mind worked. Maybe the alcohol loosened it up, or maybe it just churned out answers to avoid breaking down from overload. But whatever it was, or however it worked, it worked. And it worked at the most unexpected moments.

Like at that moment.

He replaced his toothbrush, rinsed his mouth, retrieved his mobile from the top of his bedside cabinet. It took him less than a minute to find the first number—the number given to him by an anonymous female caller—and all of ten seconds to find the other—the number of the person who called him when he jogged down to Crail harbor.

He compared them, ran through their sequences digit by digit, and knew he was not mistaken. But he also knew it would take him longer than the remainder of the night to work out why they were one and the same.

38

Gilchrist dialed the number, pressed his mobile to his ear. He counted ten rings before the line clicked. He waited for someone to say something, but the line hung in silence. Had he been shunted to voice mail? He ended the call and tried again—ten rings, then same result—which suggested he was through to voice mail. He was about to leave a message, when he thought better of it. Whosever phone it was would see his number on the ID screen and know he was calling.

He ended the call and placed his mobile on the table.

By that time, he was wide awake. Sleep would elude him if he went to bed. So, he spent the next hour googling Peter Manuel.

He learned that Manuel murdered the Smart family on January 1, 1958, and was arrested twelve days later. Jessie's grandmother, Dolly Janes, was born on January 10, 1940, so if she was raped by Manuel on her eighteenth birthday, that was three days before Manuel's arrest. With Jeannie's birth in October that year, the dates did indeed agree, and Gilchrist conceded to the possibility that Jessie could be Manuel's granddaughter. Or, more terrifying when you looked at it

261

another way, that her brothers, Tommy and Terry, seemed consigned to carry on in their grandfather's tradition.

Scary did not come close.

He was interrupted by a call on his mobile—ID Bill McCauley; the time, 12:14 AM.

"Thought I should call you, sir, and let you know that I've completed the final drive-by of Bowden's bungalow. The lights are still off, other than those in the garden. Would you like me to arrange for someone else to carry on through the night?"

Gilchrist knew that Bill was phoning this side of midnight in the hope of disturbing his beauty sleep. But he was too long in the tooth to be troubled by petty niggles. As long as Bill did his job, and stayed out of the pub, everything would be fine.

"Thanks, Bill, but I've arranged for an unmarked to drive by through the night. Let me know what you've found on Farmer in the morning." Gilchrist thought he caught a whispered curse as the connection was broken, which told him that Bill had little to offer on Farmer.

Well, Bill could tell him face to face, in the morning.

Gilchrist toyed with the idea of pouring another Balvenie, then decided against it. The trouble with whisky, he was learning, that it was more-ish—the more he drank the more he wanted. Maybe he should just stick to pints. At least his belly and his bladder offered some form of control.

His mobile rang, and he checked the number—not one he knew.

"Is this Detective Chief Inspector Gilchrist?"

"It is."

"This is Minnie Black. You asked me to call if I saw any lights on in the hoose along the road. Well, someone's just driven in."

Gilchrist's first thought was that Bill had decided to have a closer inspection. "Are they still there?" he asked, stripping off his shorts and reaching for his underpants and jeans.

"That's what I'm telling you."

"Don't go anywhere near the house," Gilchrist ordered, not wanting to add *they may be armed* for fear of frightening her.

"Have nae fear of that. The snow's coming doon in bucketloads."

Gilchrist disconnected, then called Bill. "Where are you?" he asked.

"On my way home."

So, if Bill was not at the bungalow, who was? "How close are you to Bowden's?"

"No more than five minutes. Why?"

"Mrs. Black's just called. Someone's there."

"I'm on my way."

"Just watch, Bill. Don't go in. Stay well back. We need to make an ID first." He thought of calling Jessie, but it was after midnight, so he said, "I'll meet you there."

He hung up and pulled on his clothes.

But the snow was beginning to bed, making the road surface slick, and he called Bill as he drove past the entrance to the Castle Course.

"Anything, Bill?"

"Haven't seen anyone yet, sir. The lights are still on, and all the curtains are drawn. But I've got a registration number on a silver BMW X8 SUV." He read out the number, and Gilchrist assigned it to memory.

"Do you need backup?" Gilchrist asked.

"Shouldn't think so. If I see any movement, I'll call you immediately, sir."

Gilchrist ended the call, then phoned the station to order a search on the PNC for the X8. He got through to a woman who identified herself as Pat—Gilchrist could not place her—and said, "Call me the instant you come up with anything."

It took all of five minutes for Pat to call him back, confirming the number tallied with the vehicle. "And it's registered to a Dmitri Krukovskiya with an address in Duntocher, outside Glasgow," she said.

The name niggled, but he could not place it. "Exact street address?" he asked.

But the address meant nothing either, so he asked Pat to forward it to Strathclyde.

He was negotiating the roundabout at Guardbridge when it struck him that the name Krukovskiya might have been shortened to Krukov, the same name as the Georgian twins whose bodies were found with their heads on their laps. And was Duntocher where they had their barn to keep women chained to the walls?

A cold sweat flushed through him.

He dialed Bill's number, but it kicked him into voice mail on connecting.

"Shit," he said, and tried again.

Same result.

He left a curt message. "Bill. Andy. Give me a call."

He then called Minnie Black, who picked up on the second ring. He apologized for the late call and said, "Can you tell me if the lights are still on in the house along the road?"

"They switched them off about ten minutes ago."

"Can you see any vehicles?" he asked. "An SUV. Silver colored?"

"I wouldnae know what an SUV looked like if it came up and ran me over."

"Are there any cars there?"

"It's too dark to tell."

He wondered if the landscape lights had been turned off, too, but rather than push any further, he thanked her, then disconnected. He tried Bill's number again, but it shunted him straight to voice mail. He thumped the steering wheel. He tried upping his speed, but the tires spun on the ice, forcing him to cut back. He dialed Jessie's mobile and was surprised when she picked up on the third ring, sounding wide awake.

"Sorry to call at this time," he said to her.

"Don't worry. I'm past caring about beauty sleep."

"Does the name Krukovskiya mean anything to you?"

"That was the name of the Georgian twins, the gangsters from Duntocher, Dmitri and Yegor. Krukov was easier to say than that Krukovskiya shite and had the added benefit of rhyming with fuck off. Why? What have you got?"

"Don't know yet," Gilchrist said, but now fearing the worst. "What became of the property in Duntocher?"

"Auctioned off."

"Everything?"

"Everything that could be sold."

"Any of it walk?"

"I'm sure some of it did, although we could never prove it. They were supposed to have a stash of cocaine, but we never found it. Cash and jewelry, too. We shut down their bank accounts, recovered about a hundred grand. I think that was about it."

"How about cars?"

"A few, I think. Fancy ones. Why? What's going on?"

He thought of asking her to meet him at Bowden's bungalow, but it was past one o'clock in the morning, the middle of winter, and a snowstorm. Besides, there could be some other explanation for Bill not answering. "Go back to sleep, Jessie. I'll call if I have anything for you." He drove on into the white whirlpool and prayed he was not too late.

His car's headlights picked up the entrance to Bowden's bungalow. Landscape lights lit up the gable end—the side hidden from Minnie Black's view—but the windows lay cold and black.

He slowed to a crawl, and when he reached the entrance, he stopped.

A pair of fairly recent tire tracks swept from the short drive and headed in the direction of Tayport and Dundee. It had been snowing for the best part of two hours, but with that inconsistent fall typical of a Scottish winter—one moment it could be thick enough to blind you, the next as fine as haar. And even though the temperature was close to zero, in some places the ground retained sufficient heat to prevent the snow from sticking.

But that night, the snowfall had laid down a white bed, enabling Gilchrist to work out what happened. He figured that the tire tracks of the car's entrance to the property were already covered. But he took encouragement from the exit tracks, and came to see that Bill might have followed the SUV as it drove off.

He dialed Bill's number again and was shunted straight to voice mail.

He ended the call. He did not like it, not one bit, but did not want to start a panic by requesting a lookout for Bill's car. There could be any number of reasons why Bill was not picking up—his mobile could be switched off or out of juice, or he could be in an area that had no signal. Or Bill could be making another point to piss Gilchrist off, that *it's*

*against the law to talk on the phone while driving and I'll call
back once I've parked.*

He would not put that past Bill.

So he tried to put himself in Bill's position, work out from
where he might have watched the bungalow. He thought back
to their last call and saw that from the length of the drive,
and the layout of the property, Bill had to have been close
to the entrance to read the registration number.

Gilchrist eased the Merc forward, hoping to find evidence
of Bill's presence in the snow, but in accordance with that
irritating rule of Sod's Law, the snowfall thickened, laying
a blanket at least half an inch thick in a matter of minutes.
Gilchrist turned around and drove back, pulling up beside
a farm gate on the opposite side of the road, which offered
a sensible spot from which Bill might have surveyed the
bungalow.

But the snow offered him no tire tracks, footprints, or
anything that would help.

He tried Bill's number again, but this time it was dead.

Nothing. Had the SIM card been removed?

He called the station, got through to the duty officer, and
inquired if she had heard anything from DI Bill McCauley.

She had not.

"Try his home number, and any other numbers we have
on file for him," he ordered. "And if you can't raise him in
the next few minutes, put out a search request for his car.
You have the details?"

"I'll find them, sir."

"And put out a PNC broadcast for a silver BMW X8 SUV."
He read out the number from memory, then added, "Likely en
route to Dundee, so alert Tayside Constabulary right away."

"Will do, sir."

Gilchrist disconnected, did a three-point turn, and headed for the Tay Road Bridge and Dundee beyond. He prayed that he was overreacting, that Bill was just making him suffer for assigning him an hourly drive-by through midnight.

But as he drove on toward the River Tay, he prepared himself for the worst.

39

They found Bill's decapitated body at the first light of dawn that morning, in a turnout off the B946 just west of Tayport. The headless body of a woman was found alongside. They were both lying facedown—in a manner of speaking—and fully clothed for winter, with jackets, jeans, boots, scarves, and gloves. Their wrists had been tied behind their backs with what looked like blue-colored towing rope.

Bill's wallet was still in his inside pocket, credit cards intact, and thirty-five pounds in used notes. Nothing appeared to have been taken. His warrant card was still strapped around the bloodied stump of his neck, making identification a formality.

Gilchrist was able to identify the woman as Eilidh Chambers—Bill's partner of two years—when her head was located twenty yards from the body, in a field down the slope to the River Tay, about as far as an executioner could fling it. He thought she looked calm, not frightened for her life, as she surely would have been, and so lifelike that it seemed all she had to do was open her eyes and everything would be back to normal.

Bill's head was a different story. Blood spatter suggested it had been thrown in the opposite direction, and it was eventually located about the same distance away, in the field on the south side of the B946. Numerous premortem cuts and bruises on the skin and massive bruising around the eyes—his right eye was completed closed—suggested he had been beaten up—call it torture—before having his head hacked off.

Bill's white RAV4 was parked in the turnout, abandoned and unlocked with the keys still in the ignition. Eilidh's purse lay on the floor in the passenger footwell—again, nothing taken—and her ID was conclusively confirmed from the photo on her driving licence. A half-finished bottle of Stolichnaya lay in the back seat. Despite a thorough search, the only things found missing were their mobile phones.

Back by the bodies, Cooper—who had arrived forty-five minutes earlier—was still busy with her preliminary examination.

Gilchrist and Jessie stood well back. "You think it's Kumar?" he said to Jessie.

She stared off across the brown waters of the Tay Estuary, her breath clouding white in the morning chill. "It's certainly got his signature," she said. "But he has his minions to do his dirty work for him now, although I'm sure the sick fuck will lop off the occasional head just to keep his hand in." She cleared her nose, spat a man-sized gob into the snow. "Fuck. I don't know what the world's coming to, Andy. I really don't."

Gilchrist had no response to that. He eyed Bill's body. His jacket and sweater looked as if they had been steeped in dye. Congealed blood in disturbed snow and gravel confirmed that Bill and Eilidh had been executed where their bodies now lay. Gilchrist tried to visualize what had happened, and stared around him. But at that location, in the early hours of a cold winter's morning, no one would have seen a thing. Bill and Eilidh could have screamed for all they were worth and not a soul would have heard them.

"So Bill brought Eilidh along to keep him warm," Jessie said. "And she ends up getting herself killed."

"Looks that way." Gilchrist said. "I think he would have done Eilidh first."

"Beheaded, you mean?"

"As opposed to . . . ?"

"Raped," Jessie snapped. "He's known to do that, too. Sampling the goods, make sure they're up to snuff. If I get the chance, I swear I'll tear the sick fuck's balls out by the roots."

Gilchrist's gaze drifted back to Eilidh's body. Staring at it, without a head, his mind struggled for a moment to work out the reality of what he was seeing. "Her clothes look intact," he said, more to assure himself. "But Cooper will confirm it one way or the other."

He stared off beyond the crime scene. Traffic shuffled across the Tay Road Bridge in a steady stream of cars and vans. He returned his attention to Cooper. She held Bill's head in her hands. He watched her insert her fingers into Bill's mouth, and had to pull his gaze back to Jessie.

"Any thoughts?" he asked her.

She nodded to the disturbed snow around Bill's RAV4, the scuffled tracks that gave some indication as to what happened and led in a muddled disarray to the blood-spattered scene of the slaughter. "It looks like Bill and Eilidh were both dragged from Bill's car," she said. "So who was driving?"

"Bill?"

"How would they have got him to do it? A big strong lad like that? He looked as if he could hold his own."

"A gun is always a good persuader," Gilchrist said. "Particularly if it's to the back of the girlfriend's head."

"He would have put up a fight—"

"Against a gun?"

Jessie gave his words some thought. "The Americans have the right idea, you know. We should all be armed. Every one of us."

"You sound as if you're a gun advocate."

"I'm registered. Got a .22 that I keep under lock and key."

"Does your mother know about it?"

"She will one day."

Gilchrist did not like the way the conversation was going and tried to bring them back on track with, "So, assuming Bill drives, once they're here, their wrists are then tied. I can't see Bill just letting them tie his wrists together."

"But somehow they did."

"Maybe drugged?"

"That's possible."

Gilchrist shifted his gaze to Cooper. If Bill was drugged, she would confirm it.

Jessie clapped her hands, blew into her gloves. "It's freezing. You must've needed brass balls last night. They wouldn't have hung about. They would have had Bill watch Eilidh being beheaded. Or maybe they beat Bill up in front of her."

"What's to be gained from that?" he said, as his mind pulled up an image of Gordie, eyes bulging with the knowledge of what was to come. For a moment, he had to chew back the bitter taste of bile, and thought he was going to throw up. But it passed, and he looked away as he dragged a hand across his mouth.

"How would they have known Bill was a detective?" Jessie said to him. "OK, he's parked outside the bungalow, I know.

But he's with his girlfriend, having a snog and a shag in the backseat. Why would they think that's suspicious enough for a beheading?"

Jessie's rationale made sense, but Gilchrist thought he also knew Bill well enough to understand he could not have sat in his car on the pretense of having it off in the backseat.

"Bill didn't stay in his car," he said. "He left to have a closer look."

"Did you see any footprints to back that up?"

"Only the exit tire tracks. But the snow could have covered Bill's footprints, and he could have been in the X8 when they drove out. Then they stopped for Eilidh in Bill's car parked up Lover's Lane, or wherever."

Jessie nodded, then said, "Uh oh, legs alert."

Gilchrist followed Jessie's line of sight. Cooper had stripped off her forensics clothing and now walked toward them, her hand by her ear, tugging strands of loose hair from her face. She looked good in jeans. Up close, her eyes sparkled sky blue and creased with the tiniest of crow's feet.

"I'd say our killer has medical expertise," she said to Gilchrist.

"Or plenty of practice," Jessie said.

"Why do you say that?" Gilchrist asked Cooper.

"The cuts are precise, the same on each body. And I'm thinking boning knife—"

"Why not scalpel? Smaller, easier to hide," Jessie argued.

"But not to cut through the spinal cord. No," she said. "Boning knife."

Jessie shoved her hands into her pockets, as if chastised.

"Anything else?" Gilchrist said.

"Their throats appear to have been sliced in one steady cut," Cooper said. "From left to right." She lifted her chin, pressed a finger to her neck about a couple of inches below the left earlobe, then dragged it with slow deliberation across her throat in a U-shaped cut, to an equivalent point under her right earlobe.

"So the killer would have been standing behind?"

"Most definitely. And the victims would have been kneeling, or maybe lying down. Then hand to the hair, head back, and just get on with it."

"Boning knife in his right hand?"

"I'd say so. The insertion wound appears to be on the left, with evidence of the exit wound tailing off on the right. But I'd want to reserve a final call on that until I've had a closer examination in the PM room."

"The cuts and bruises on Bill's face," Gilchrist tried. "Pre- or postmortem?"

"Pre-."

"So he was beaten up before being beheaded."

Cooper nodded, then looked at the bodies. The SOCOs were preparing to bag them. Then she faced Gilchrist and said, "Bill's right eyeball was removed. Not cut out but ripped from its socket."

"Fuck." Jessie again.

Gilchrist tried to shove that image way—a hand tugging Bill's eye, teasing it from the socket to aggravate the pain and horror—but failed. He gritted his teeth, wondered if they had thrown Bill's eye into the fields. "Did you find . . . ?"

Cooper nodded. "In his mouth."

Gilchrist felt his whole being deflate. He suffered no illusions over the horrifying extent of men's cruelty to one another. The planet could catalog an entire history of acts so evil and barbaric that they could almost defy imagination. Even the town of St. Andrews had its own historical notori-

ety—men burned alive at the stake; hanged, drawn, and quar-
tered in Market Street; tortured in the castle dungeons—the
list went on. But somehow, being blinded by having your
eye torn from its socket hit Gilchrist with renewed horror—

"Why didn't they rip out his other eye?" Jessie asked.

Gilchrist almost groaned.

"He could have fainted," Cooper said. "The pain would
have been excruciating."

"So they'd want to cut off his head when he was still able
to feel it."

"Possibly."

"More than likely, I'd say. They didn't try to cut off his
balls, did they?"

"They're still intact."

"So, no sexual interference to either of them?"

"None that I can see. But I'll know more later."

"Well, that's something."

Gilchrist was discovering a side to Jessie that was unsettling. From the chirpiness in her voice, she could have been
having a chat about the weather. "Anything else?" he asked
Cooper.

Cooper held his gaze. He thought she looked sad, as if
she had something to tell him that she did not want him to
hear. He swallowed an annoying lump in his throat, forced
the bile from rising.

"The killers would have been covered in blood," she said.

"That's obvious," Jessie said.

"Which they would have transferred to their car. It would
be on the steering wheel, the seats, the doors, anything they're
likely to have touched. A BMW X8, silver, you say?"

"We think so," Gilchrist confirmed.

"I shouldn't think there would too many of those around."

Jessie bristled. "Yeah, we'll just drive over to Dundee and pick him up before he orders lunch," she said, then turned and stomped off.

Together, Gilchrist and Cooper watched Jessie stride up the beach.

"She's a touchy one," Cooper said at length.

Gilchrist could not disagree, but he also felt an odd reluctance to acknowledge his agreement. "She has some issues," he said.

Cooper's teeth glinted white in the cold air. She tugged a strand of hair, ran it behind her ear. "Do you think these decapitations are related to the Kingsbarns killings?"

"I'm positive they are."

Her mouth tightened, and her eyes creased, causing her cheeks to pull in and giving Gilchrist a glimpse of what she might look like in later years. Then she stared off to some point in the snow-covered distance. "I've worked on a number of murder cases," she said, "but this one is disturbing."

Gilchrist could only agree in silence and watch her turn to face him.

"Are you any closer to finding a suspect?" she asked.

He took a deep breath, then let it out. "Yes and no. If we could have carried out more surveillance on the cottage, I might feel better about it." He shook his head. "But they won't come back to it now. I suspect they'll find someplace else, lie low for a while."

He found himself resisting the urge to look at Bill, as if to do so would confirm his thoughts that Bill was to blame. Had Bill slipped up? Had he downed a few slugs of Stollie then decided to take matters into his own hands? Had he been caught checking up on the cottage at close quarters? Was that what had caused Kumar, or whoever he was, to flee? If

Bill had done as Gilchrist had instructed, he and Eilidh would almost certainly still be alive, and the chances of catching Kumar would still be a reality—

"You need to be careful," Cooper said.

The cold air had brought tears to her eyes, and he said, "Am I not always?"

She smiled at his double entendre. "I mean it, Andy. The body count on this one is rising as if there's no tomorrow. I haven't seen anything like it."

Gilchrist nodded, unable to stifle the feelings of failure that stirred deep within him. Was he to blame for Bill's and Eilidh's deaths? If he had not been so intent on keeping Bill out of the pub, would he not have put his life in danger? He tried to work through the logic of that argument but felt as if he was stumbling in the dark—

"You're a good man, Andy. There aren't too many out there."

He opened his mouth to respond. But Cooper turned and walked away, hips swaying in that come-on stride of hers, causing him to watch her in silence until she slid behind the wheel of her Range Rover and drove off, leaving him unsure of what to make of her parting comment.

40

The rest of the day passed by in a flurry of meetings and briefings.

Despite the fact that Fife Constabulary had lost one of its own, the press hounded Gilchrist as if he had personally beheaded Bill and Eilidh. National newspaper, TV, and radio crews made their way to St. Andrews and Dundee in flocks, and the quiet estuary village of Tayport was in danger of losing its charm to the onslaught of camera equipment, sound systems, vehicles, reporters, and a host of spectators more interested in seeing their faces on TV than in providing any meaningful assistance to the investigation.

The apparent newsworthiness of the double decapitation troubled Gilchrist and only emphasized to him how barbaric the human race still was. Put an ordinary stabbing or shooting on the nightly news and people would barely notice. But a decapitation, and a double one at that, seemed better entertainment. The reporting business, and the manner in which the public received it, just sickened him. And by the end of the day he felt as if his investigation had taken three steps backward.

The SOCOs had been unable to lift any fingerprints from Bowden's bungalow. All surfaces had been wiped clean, reminding Gilchrist of the cottage in Boarhills. Fife, Tayside, Grampian, and Lothian and Borders police forces found no trace of a silver-colored BMW X8 SUV with the registration number noted by Bill, though Tayside confirmed that an X8 matching the description crossed the Tay Road Bridge at 2:21 AM, tying in with the timing of Gilchrist's visit to Bowden's cottage. CCTV footage was unable to confirm the registration number plate, as it was covered in slush and snow—the plates would have been changed by now anyway—and beyond Dundee, heading north to Aberdeen, they lost all trace of it.

An examination of the tracks and footprints around Bowden's cottage lent strength to Gilchrist's theory that Bill had disobeyed his instructions and had worked his way around the cottage in an ill-fated attempt at police heroics. No one could say with any certainty how Bill had been caught, as footprints—two distinctly separate pairs—leading to where the X8 had been parked showed no signs of a scuffle having taken place.

It seemed as if Bill and Eilidh had simply driven off.

Jessie said, "I think Bill followed the X8 once they left the cottage."

"But why would they leave the cottage at all?" Gilchrist argued.

"How do I know? Perhaps they were only checking it out so they could move in the next day. Or maybe they saw Bill sniffing around and decided to take care of him. Or maybe they didn't see him until he started to follow them. However it happened, I'm willing to bet that Bill and Eilidh were overpowered someplace other than the cottage."

Again, Jessie's rationale worked with his own, and Gilchrist was beginning to see that behind her bitter Glasgow tongue and her couldn't-care-less attitude hid a detective whose mind was as sharp as any he had worked with.

He decided to check his own logic against hers. Statistically, the last call made on a mobile is important. But his team had already confirmed from phone records that the last call Bill made had been to Gilchrist, and the last call received was the one Gilchrist made later.

"So where's Bill's mobile?" he asked her.

"Bottom of the Tay. Destroyed. Does it matter?"

"Do you think it odd that Bill never used his mobile for three hours before calling me?" he asked.

"What's odd about that? Bill had Eilidh beside him. They were too busy shagging each other senseless. Check Eilidh's mobile records and see if they match."

Gilchrist did that, and the records matched, with Eilidh's last call being one to Bill at 8:14 PM, which in turn matched Bill's records. Feeling as if the mobile records were getting them nowhere, he called Cooper and put her on speaker.

Cooper confirmed that Bill and Eilidh's throats had been cut from left to right, which suggested a right-handed person, probably male, because of the depth of the cut and the strength needed to slice through the spinal cord.

"Strong female?" Jessie tried.

"Could be, but I doubt it."

"Any sexual interference?" Gilchrist asked, cutting off the argument before it started.

"I've recovered seminal remains from Eilidh's vaginal tract, but no sign of rough play, all pointing to consensual sex. Interestingly," she added, "I also found semen in her mouth—"

"Never heard of a blow job?" Jessie fired.

"I won't dignify that with an answer. But if the semen isn't Bill's then it might be the killer's—"

"It was too cold last night to fool around with blow jobs," Jessie said. "By the time they chopped off their heads and ripped out Bill's eye, they would have been bloody freezing."

"Just check out the DNA, Becky," Gilchrist said, "and let me know what you find."

"Already doing that."

He ended the call and said to Jessie, "It would be helpful if you gave Becky and your dead colleague a bit more professional respect."

"Becky? Not Dr. Cooper?"

"Becky," Gilchrist said. "Unless you want to start addressing me as DCI Gilchrist."

"Got it," she said, but Gilchrist doubted it.

By the time Gilchrist finished his debriefing—a difficult meeting because of Bill's and Eilidh's murders—it was almost 8:00 PM. He waited until the bulk of his team left the room, then said to the remaining few—Jessie, Mhairi, Dan, Nance— "I'm done for the day. Anyone fancy a pint?"

They all declined, except for Nance who said, "I'll stay for a quickie," which brought a snorted chuckle from Jessie.

Gilchrist chose the Dunvegan Hotel.

He had not been there for a couple of weeks, and when he pulled up a stool by the bar, Sheena caught his eye with that welcoming white smile of hers and said, "The usual, Andy?"

"You talked me into it."

Nance ordered a Corona and poked the lime down the neck.

Gilchrist took a sip of his pint, then said, "Give Jessie time. She'll grow on you."

"Yeah, like fungus."

"She's a good addition to the team. Brings a lot with her."

"Particularly where weight's concerned."

"Ouch," Gilchrist said, and thought it best just to take a sip. He waited until Nance returned her Corona to the bar-top. "Just tell me to shut up if I'm becoming too personal," he said, "but do you ever see John now?"

"Lost contact with him. Which isn't all bad."

The last Gilchrist had heard of Nance's ex-fiancé was that he had transferred to Northern Constabulary, which policed the Highlands and Islands, only to be suspended within six months. Once an adulterer, always an adulterer, he supposed.

"A bit acrimonious in the end, wasn't it?" he said.

"The understatement of the decade." She tilted her bottle his way. "How about you? How's your love life?"

Well, he supposed he never should have started asking personal questions. "Mostly nonexistent," he said.

"I shouldn't think Jessie would be your type."

"Other than the fact that she's also a member of my team?"

"Didn't stop you before." Nance took a long swig, then shook her head. "I'm sorry, Andy. That was out of order. I shouldn't have said that."

"Forget it, Nance. No offense taken."

She turned to face him then, and he found his face flushing under the directness of her stare. "I'm really sorry," she said.

"I said forget—"

"No, Andy. I'm sorry. Truly sorry. I've never apologized to you before. For the way I treated you. The way I just . . . it was . . . unkind of me." She held his gaze. "I'm sorry for that. You didn't deserve it. You were always a gentleman to me, not . . ." She took another sip.

"Not like John?"

"Definitely not like John," she said, and finished her Corona.

"Would you like another?"

"Only if you're having one."

"I think I can be persuaded." He nodded to Sheena, indicated another round, then turned back to Nance. "If it's any consolation," he said, "I wasn't offended in the least. I enjoyed our time together, but I always knew it would be short lived—"

"Why?"

"Age difference for one, I suppose."

"And for two?"

He sipped his beer, returned it to the bar, and shook his head. "When you put it like that, I suppose there really wasn't a two."

Nance smiled, a clean smile that sent a surge of radiance through her, making him realize he had not seen her happy for weeks, maybe even months.

"You should smile more often," he said. "It suits you."

That comment seemed to knock both of them into silence, until the second round was served, and Nance said, "Did you ever think of leaving the Force?"

"When?"

She shrugged. "It's a hell of a job we do. It's not for the fainthearted." She gripped her beer. "In any normal day at the office, we're exposed to things no human being should ever be exposed to. Sometimes it all seems to be too much."

He did not want to say *You get used to it*, but to survive as a detective you had to view murder victims with a dispassion verging on the inhuman. He eyed Nance over the rim of his glass. "Is that how you feel?" he asked her. "That it's all too much?"

She stared at the gantry. "I can't believe Bill's dead. Eilidh, too. He was only twenty-three. We had a drink in Lafferty's last weekend, and Eilidh came along, too." She dabbed a hand to her eyes. "And to see the pair of them on the beach

with their . . . like that . . . I don't know. It just seems . . ."
She shook her head, then buried her thoughts in her Corona.

Gilchrist said nothing, just turned his attention to his own
pint.

Nance had not been herself the last several months. He
had put it down to the demise of her relationship with John.
Secretly, he had been pleased to learn of their breakup, not
because John had been the reason Nance ended her affair
with Gilchrist—in a strange way, he had been happy that it
had ended—but because he had always seen John as a user of
women, someone who never put into a relationship what he
got out of it. But now Gilchrist realized that Nance's breakup
with John had been only a part of her problems, and he worried
that the job, or rather the gruesome aspect of it, was becoming
too much for her—

"I don't mean to sound so morbid," she said, and eased closer
so that her thigh slid along his. Then she smiled. "Would you
like to come back for a nightcap?" But something in his look
must have surprised her, for she added, "I don't mean in any . . .
I'm sorry . . . it's . . . it's not appropriate . . . I shouldn't have—"

"Nance," he said, and waited until she returned his gaze.
"If any over-keen journalist just happened to snap a picture
of the two of us going back to yours, particularly after the
day we've just had, it wouldn't look good, would it?"

She gave a tight smile, shook her head.

He had never been one for slamming his doors, preferring
to close them quietly, even leave them ajar—just a touch.
"How about sharing a sandwich," he said, "and we can take
a rain check on that nightcap." He raised his pint.

She nodded, sipped her Corona.

But if the truth be told, he really thought he had put his
foot, probably both of them, smack dab in the middle of it.

41

On the A917 to Crail, Gilchrist pushed the Merc up to eighty.

Fields either side glinted white under a clear sky. The road plows and gritter trucks had been out earlier, and the road ahead lay clear and black under his headlights. Kinkell Braes Caravan Park zipped past on his left, a bit too fast, he thought, and he eased his speed back to a sensible sixty. The clock on his dash told him it was 11:37.

He turned up the radio when he caught the guitar strains of a song he had not heard for the longest time. His taste in music tended to be eclectic, and he preferred the '60s and '70s eras—the Eagles, the Kinks, Cream—rather than the mind-numbing hip-hop beats of modern day. He tried to clear his mind, refocus on the murders of Bill and Eilidh.

But try as he might, his mind kept tugging him back to Nance.

It turned out that Nance's fiancé, John, had been calling and texting as often as twenty times a day. He had even turned up on her doorstep one Sunday morning, about three months ago, begging her to take him back. Nance told him in her own

way—she was known for the occasional string of expletives
that could redden the cheeks of even the most time-hardened
policeman—and the next day she had the locks changed, her
Santander bank accounts moved to RBS, and even inquired
about having a panic alarm installed in her bedroom.

Not what Gilchrist wanted to hear. Not at all.

"And has John stayed away?" he had asked her.

"He's getting the message."

Gilchrist had made a mental note to call an old friend of
his, DCI Tommy Coulson of Northern Constabulary, and
have lover-boy John stuffed back into his box. Their evening
had ended with Nance thanking him for listening to her tales
of misery and woe, then leaning forward and giving him a
surprise peck on the cheek.

"Later," she had said.

Not quite the come-on Ciao of Rebecca Cooper, although
Gilchrist had not failed to catch the temptress gleam in her
eye. But Nance was one of his team, a valuable member at
that, and he did not want to take, or be seen to be taking,
advantage of her. He saw, too, how she was not the Nance
of old—the occasional nervous giggle, the way she picked at
her nails—and he came to understand that her psyche was
more fragile than he had ever—

His phone rang.

He felt his heart leap to his mouth when he recognized
the number.

DC Bill McCauley's.

He slammed on his brakes.

The car's tires crunched and slid on the frosted grit as he
jerked to a stop next to a farm gateway that could have been
waiting for him. A jumble of thoughts pulsed through his
mind as he made the connection, his most immediate being

that he did not want to scare the caller off—Bill's mobile could have been picked up by a civilian who was calling the last recorded number in an attempt to return it. They might be able to lift prints off it, if it had not been handled too much.

Well, he had to live in hope, he supposed.

"Andy Gilchrist, here," he said.

Silence filled the line long enough for Gilchrist to think he had been cut off. He was about to ask again, when a voice said, "Detective Chief Inspector Andrew James Gilchrist?"

Ice fingered Gilchrist's neck. But as he tried to work out how the caller knew his full name and rank, his gut was telling him that Bill would have had his number and full name logged into his mobile—another one of Bill's quirks—and that the caller was reading the ID from the screen.

"Speaking," he said. "Who's this?"

"You already know my name." A man's voice, deep and clear, the words pronounced with the deliberation of a foreigner trying not to be misunderstood. "You and I need to meet."

"Who's speaking?" Gilchrist repeated.

"You will remember the house in Kingsbarns," the man said, then gave Gilchrist the correct street address in case he pretended to have forgotten it.

Gilchrist stared at the phone, now in no doubt who was speaking—Kumar.

"You will park your Mercedes at the corner of Back Stile and North Carr. And you will walk to—"

"Why?"

"We need to discuss how to minimize interference from Fife Constabulary, as well as . . . how do I say it . . . find some way to keep you sweet—"

"I don't do bribes," Gilchrist said.

Kumar chuckled. "Everyone has a price, Mr. Gilchrist."

The fact that Kumar knew he drove a Mercedes suggested he had been on Kumar's radar for some time, probably since the discovery of the body on the Coastal Path. Knowing everything about your enemy was one way of staying ahead. And Kumar was a master—Bill's and Eilidh's bodies were evidence of that. Gilchrist was being toyed with, but he had to press, keep Kumar on the line, see if he could find something he could use to his advantage.

"Why don't I just hang up?"

"That is your prerogative, of course. But it would be foolish to do so. You first need to hear what I can give you," Kumar said, with barely a change in tone. "But only you. No one else. Once you've parked your Mercedes, you will walk to the house. We will be watching you, and if I suspect that you have not come alone, or that you have told someone about this call, then you will lose out on a financial arrangement that—"

"You're not listening. I don't do bribes."

"Everyone can be bought, Mr. Gilchrist."

Gilchrist's mind was racing, trying to work out what to do once the call ended. Kumar was a killer, a hunter, someone who knew how wild animals selected their prey, by separating the weak from the pack. Kumar wanted to meet Gilchrist, not to discuss some sweetheart deal that would have Gilchrist turn a blind eye while Kumar continued to kidnap, rape, sell, or murder young girls at his whim. That was not going to happen.

No, Kumar had a different plan, plain and simple.

He wanted Gilchrist alone, so he could kill him.

Lights in the rearview mirror brightened the cabin for a dazzling moment as a van approached from behind, then faded as it passed. Just that momentary burst of light seemed to clear Gilchrist's thinking and tell him that he needed to hear all Kumar had to say before he could work out a plan.

"And what do you think my price will be?" Gilchrist said.

"That is why we need to meet."

"We can do this over the phone."

"Then it would not become, how do I say it . . . personal."

Gilchrist waited several beats, then said, "Where do you want to meet?"

"Not over the phone, Mr. Gilchrist. This has to be between you and me."

"I'm listening."

"At the house in Kingsbarns, at the front door, you will find two flowerpots. Under the flowerpot on the left is an envelope. In the envelope is a note that will tell you where we shall meet."

"How can you trust me to come alone?" Gilchrist said.

Another chuckle, long and deep, with no trace of concern or fear. "You are on your way to your home in Crail. I know where you have been this evening, and I know who you have been with. I know where your children live, too . . ."

A hoof thudded Gilchrist in the gut.

"Jack and Maureen," Kumar added, as if Gilchrist needed another ounce of proof that the man had him where he wanted. "So I think you will find it in your interests to meet me alone. Don't you agree?"

Gilchrist tried to work spittle into his mouth, but his tongue was as dry as cardboard. He dabbed sweat from his brow. He tried to think of some smart riposte, but his mind could have belonged to someone else. "When?" was all he could say.

"You are no more than five minutes from Kingsbarns," Kumar said, which had Gilchrist glaring into the rearview mirror. The road behind lay clear, then his mind kicked alive and told him the van that had just passed must have been one of Kumar's men.

Gilchrist pushed into gear, pressed the accelerator.

"Once you find the note," Kumar continued, "it will take you only ten minutes or so to reach me."

"I'm on my way," Gilchrist said, and killed the call.

Gilchrist suspected he had likely been shadowed for most of the day. They had seen him tackle the media in Tayport, seen him with Nance in the Dunvegan, seen him drop her off at her flat, and followed him on his return home.

He gripped the steering wheel and pressed into the night. He tried to still an awful pounding in his chest which thumped its way to a pain behind his eyes. He jerked the neck of his shirt, tugged it open, took a deep breath. Christ, he had suffered less physical discomfort from running five kilometers.

What was happening?

But he knew what was happening. He was scared. The monotony of Kumar's voice, and the unerring certainty with which he gave instructions, frightened him to his core. He was dealing with a man who knew no fear, who had killed before, and would kill again, a man who could murder someone just to test the blade of a knife, or to satisfy an itch, who took pleasure from watching the life fade from a victim's eyes.

Gilchrist thought of calling for backup but feared that Kumar would keep to his word and seek revenge on Gilchrist's children. He could have his team try to locate where Kumar called from, but he had used Bill's mobile just to let Gilchrist know who was calling. Bill's SIM card would have been removed once again. He also knew that much.

The mention of his children had been the final nail, the one piece of information that Kumar knew would have Gilchrist following any instruction to the ends of the earth. He eyed the dark tunnel of the road ahead, pushed his speed up to seventy, then eighty, and caught the glimmer of taillights of the truck ahead.

He felt his grimace turn into a tight smile.

"OK, you bastard," he said. "I've got you now."

42

But Gilchrist was unarmed, and once he caught up with the van, his fleeting sense of invincibility passed. He slowed down, sat well back, at least a dozen car lengths, and worked through his thoughts.

He now felt certain that Kumar was not working alone—*we will be watching you.* He suspected the van would be driven by the person who had fed information to Kumar on where Gilchrist was—*in your Mercedes . . . on your way to your home in Crail . . . no more than five minutes from Kingsbarns*—all drip-fed to Gilchrist to instill fear. Well, Mr. Kumar, if it's fear you're trying to instill, it's working. You've got me scared, all right. But you've slipped up, and I'm just about to nail you.

Gilchrist devised a plan that was simple. And clear.

He would drive to the cottage in Kingsbarns, collect the note that told him where to meet. But instead of driving to his rendezvous with Kumar, he would send in a team. In the meantime, if he did as Kumar suggested—park his car at the corner of North Carr View, then walk to the cottage alone—Kumar would think his plan was working.

But did Kumar really believe he was that stupid?

The cottage could be a trap, the note under the flowerpot the bait.

Kumar could have no intention of striking any deal with Gilchrist, but just to entrap him so he could kill him. Perhaps he had someone hiding at the cottage, someone who would shoot him the moment he turned up on the doorstep. But as that scenario wormed through his brain, he came to understand that shooting policemen was not Kumar's style, beheading them was—witness Gordie, Bill, and Eilidh—which told him that for Kumar it was all about being personal.

That thought made up his mind for him.

He dialed the station and spoke to the duty officer.

"Check the PNC for a white Transit van," he instructed, then read off the registration number of the van ahead. "And have someone from the Anstruther station pull it over, with extreme caution. The occupants are likely armed and dangerous."

Having taken care of the van, he then called HQ Glenrothes and spoke to the SPOC—the Single Point of Contact, the person in charge of the control room—and instructed him to have an ARV—Armed Response Vehicle Unit—maybe two, ready for quick deployment.

Ahead, the van slowed down as it entered the village of Kingsbarns.

Gilchrist did likewise.

Back Stile was a road that ran all the way to the beach, off the A917 just beyond Kingsbarns. Whoever was in the van would surely know Gilchrist was now behind them and would probably not turn into Back Stile but drive straight on.

Gilchrist followed, his eyes peeled for any other vehicles.

Other than his Merc and the van ahead, the road ran clear, as if the village had locked down for the night. The Barns

Hotel passed by on his left, and moments later the primary school on his right. Gilchrist felt his body tense as he readied to leave the village. With Back Stile coming up on the left, would the van turn left . . . ?

It powered past Back Stile and accelerated into the open country road.

Gilchrist slowed down and turned off the main road.

Although snowplows had cleared Back Stile, subsequent snowfall had laid down another couple of inches. Tire tracks rutted fresh snow. The pavement that ran along the left side of the road all the way to Seagate, after which it became gravel, lay thick with snow, its surface disturbed by a solitary set of footprints. Streetlights cast a hazy glow over the winter scene.

The clock on the dashboard read 11:56 PM. Gilchrist eased the Merc forward, keeping his speed at a steady twenty-five, taking it slow, peering into the dark tunnel ahead, ready to accelerate or slam it into reverse if he happened to see anything suspicious. A glance in his rearview mirror told him no one was following. He turned the radio to low, then switched it off altogether.

He eased through a shallow left-hand bend, then cruised past the entrance to the Steading, then MacKenzie Garden. The road appeared to widen at the branch for North Carr View, taking with it the last of the tire tracks.

Ahead, Back Stile lay white with pristine snow, the entrance to Seagate on the left, lit by the last of the street lighting on the right. Beyond, the road ran on to the sea and the beach parking. The snowplows had not cleared that far, and the road's surface lay in whitened darkness, as if untouched by humans.

Seconds later, Gilchrist turned left and parked against the curb.

He kept the engine running, flicked his headlights to full-beam. Seagate stretched before him, as smooth as a white blanket. Light snow continued to fall, the tiniest of flakes that glinted for a moment, then seemed to melt under the glare of his full beams.

At that moment, Gilchrist realized his luck. If anyone was lying in wait at the cottage, their footprints would give them away, the recent snowfall not heavy enough to obliterate all trace. That thought settled him, and he took one steady three-sixty-degree look around him before turning off the engine. He disconnected his mobile from the car's system, slipped it into his pocket, and opened the door.

His shoes settled into snow no more than three inches deep, his footprints the first disturbance that day, it seemed. He pressed his key fob, and the locks clicked. Ahead, the scene was brightened by streetlights and roadside homes and Christmas lights on bushes and hedges, which flickered and pulsed in blues, reds, whites. He pulled up his collar, shivered off the cold air, and walked toward the abandoned cottage.

He took his time, his senses on full alert, his eyes scanning the ground ahead for the tell-signs of a trap. Lawns and driveways lay thick with snow, parked cars like hibernating beasts huddled under white blankets. A stone-eyed snowman watched him in silence. He stopped twice, turning his head to the wind to catch the tiniest hint of movement.

But the place was graveyard silent.

It took him no more than three minutes before the cottage appeared on his right. The windows of the houses either side glowed with welcoming warmth, as if in invitation to the weary traveler to stay for the night. In contrast, the abandoned cottage lay in complete and utter darkness, putting Gilchrist back on full alert.

If someone was hiding, would he be able to see their foot-prints?

As he stood at its wooden gate, he saw that the path outside was clear of footprints. He eyed his own trail back to the footpath on the opposite side of the road. Other than a pair of tracks on a neighboring driveway, it seemed as if the residents in this housing estate had battened down their homes for the winter storm.

He faced the cottage again, gripped the gate, and pushed it open.

Even in the midnight darkness, the snow reflected suffi-cient light to confirm that the short walkway to the cottage—no more than twelve feet—lay undisturbed. Snow-covered bushes guarded the garden boundary either side. Two flower-pots on the step to a black door held dead conifers cloaked in snow. Strips of yellow police tape—DO NOT CROSS—stretched across the doorway, the cottage's very own Christmas wrap-ping.

Gilchrist removed a pair of latex gloves from his jacket pocket and slipped them on. Next, he pulled out his mobile phone, and swiped it on. The screen lit up, which he used as a light. One more three-sixty scan confirmed he was still alone.

Then he stepped through the gateway and into the property.

He reached the front doorstep, leaned down, and lifted the flowerpot on the left.

Sure enough, there was Kumar's note, a small, white enve-lope, just as he said.

Gilchrist picked it up—

Something fluttered to his left, movement in the dark.

He froze, his breath locked in his throat. His gaze darted around the shrubbery, and he saw with a gut-wrenching sense of helplessness how careless he had been, how they had waited for him in the bushes. His heart pounded in his chest, telling his brain that his lungs had to breathe. He held out his mobile phone, as if that alone could stop the attack, its weak light barely helping him—

Movement. Another flutter.

He saw it that time, snow falling from the branches of an overladen bush.

Not Kumar's men. Not a trap.

Just nature shifting and stirring around him.

His heart and lungs kick-started with a sharp exhalation and intake of air.

Bloody hell, he was too old for this anymore.

He clutched the envelope, retreated along the cottage walkway, retraced his steps across the road until he stood under a street light, his back to the house behind.

Across the street, the cottage stared back at him in dark and derelict silence.

He waited thirty seconds, maybe more, while his lungs and his heart did what they could to settle his nerves. And it struck him then, with a clarity that shook him, how stupid he had been, how easily he could have been attacked, how an aging detective—because that was how he now saw himself—was no match for a gang of killers intent on expanding their criminal activities beyond London, Manchester, and Glasgow into the quieter regions of the Fife countryside.

That thought had him doing another three-sixty.

But he could have been alone on the moon for all the inactivity around him.

He turned his attention to the envelope. It was unsealed. He pulled back the flap, removed the note—handwritten. In addition to any fingerprints they might lift, the printed word might help nail Kumar to the proverbial cross.

He read the note.

Outside the Secret Bunker in 15 minutes.

Gilchrist knew the Secret Bunker, constructed during World War II to house the regional government in the event of a nuclear or biological attack. The only evidence of its existence was the guardhouse in the form of a farmhouse that sat over a labyrinth of heavily reinforced underground offices and tunnels, the size of two football fields, a hundred feet underground. He had taken Jack there, years ago, when security restrictions on the bunker's existence were lifted, and it was opened to the public.

He did another three-sixty scan.

If Kumar was watching him, he could not tell from where.

He dialed HQ Glenrothes again and got through to the SPOC. He arranged for one ARV to take position on the east end of the road that led to the Secret Bunker and another on the west end, and to wait there until he gave further instruction. But time was not on his side. He knew that. Kumar's words came back to him—*only ten minutes or so to reach me.* It would take at least half an hour before the ARVs were in position, maybe much longer. He might be able to stall the meeting in some way, and if he did, the ARVs could move in and make the final arrest.

Maybe not the best of plans, but it was a plan.

And no matter what, Kumar was going down.

Gilchrist ended the call to the SPOC with, "I'll get back to you in fifteen minutes."

He walked toward his car. He still held his mobile in his hand, and despite the hour he thought of calling Jessie to see if she would be interested in making her first formal arrest in

Fife. But he realized he was being inconsiderate. Jessie had just moved to St. Andrews, and with trying to settle into a new job and set up a new home, she needed more time with her son. So, he decided to call her later.

Twenty feet from his car, he clicked the key fob.

The lights flashed as the doors unlocked.

He walked closer, checked that the snow around his car had not been disturbed since he had locked it—only his own footprints. No one had followed, and no one was lying in wait for him. He was about to slip his mobile into his pocket and open the door, when something stung the side of his neck.

He lifted a hand to touch it, felt his blood chill as his fingers brushed the short, hard bristles of a dart. He gripped it, pulled it out, threw it into the snow.

No time to waste.

He reached for the door handle, tugged the door open . . .

The car spun away from him.

He grunted, surprised by the cold slap of snow on his face.

Around him, the air seemed to buzz with muffled silence, broken only by the sound of shoes crunching snow. He tried to lift his head, but it could have been nailed to the road.

From the distance, he thought he heard the revving sound of a car's engine starting up. Then blackness swept over him, his own midnight cloak. And his last waking thoughts were of the pungent smell of garlic, warm hands on his face.

And the deep lazy chuckle of the Devil himself.

43

Jessie crossed the Tay Road Bridge into Fife and followed the sign for Tayport.

Left at the roundabout, then pedal to the metal, followed by a whispered curse at her car's lack of response. Not that she needed to be pressed into the back of her seat, but her Fiat 500 had to have something bigger than a hair dryer under the bonnet, surely.

On one hand, it irked that she had let Lachie work out a deal for her, committing her to a four-year loan through a contact of his. On the other hand, no one could have worked out a better deal for her. And if the truth be known, as fat and ugly as Lachie was, he really only had her best interests at heart.

Maybe she would call him and apologize for her recent behavior.

She thought about that for a moment, then decided maybe not.

She stretched over and squeezed Robert's leg.

He jerked with surprise, and she blew him a kiss and signed that she loved him.

His fingers flickered in return—*You're silly, but I love you, too.*

She pressed her fingers to her lips, then dabbed his cheek. "Love you," she said.

Robert smiled, then returned his attention to his mobile.

Robert's 8:30 appointment at Ninewells Hospital with the ENT consultant—Mr. Amir Mbeke—had gone well, other than having to wait for almost forty minutes despite arriving on time. Mr. Mbeke had told her in a voice as smooth as honey that Robert could be a suitable candidate for a cochlear implant. He would have to carry out more tests, of course, but he felt that an operation could be successful. Even better, they would run a means test on Jessie to see if there was any way she could qualify to have the costs covered by the NHS.

All in all, not a bad morning's effort, she thought.

She waited until they were past the village of Tayport before removing her mobile. A quick look in the rearview mirror confirmed she would not be stopped for talking on the phone while driving. She dialed his number, and the call was picked up on the second ring.

"You'll never guess," she said to him.

"DS Janes?"

Jessie scowled at her mobile. "I thought I dialed Andy's number."

"You did," the voice said.

"Well, put him on."

"There's been a problem."

It struck her with a force that took her breath away, that it must be serious for Andy not to have his mobile. "Don't tell me," she said.

"We're not sure what's happened—"

"Where are you?"

"Outside the Secret Bunker."

"The what? Never mind. How do I get there from Tay-port?" she asked, and nodded as she took in his directions. "Who am I speaking with?"

"DI Davidson."

"Stan?" she said. "I thought you were in hospital."

"I signed myself out a few days ago. Thought I'd pop my head into the station and say hello. And, well . . ."

"Shit. This must be serious."

"Very."

"I'm on my way." She killed the call and tried to acceler-ate. "Come on, come on," she said, and jerked when Robert tapped her thigh.

What's up, mum?

My boss is missing.

Is that a joke?

She scowled at him.

I'm sorry, mum. I hope you find him.

"I hope so, too," she said.

Gilchrist came to.

He eased his eyes open and lifted his head.

Pain as hard as a rabbit punch stunned the back of his neck. He groaned, closed his eyes, and his head slumped back onto his chest. He had the vaguest memory of snow on his face, and realized he had slipped and knocked himself unconscious. He had no idea how long he had been out, and his mind seemed unable to work out why he was no longer in the snow.

He counted to ten. Then started again, on to twenty. He tested his brain a bit harder, multiplied twenty-five by four to get . . . to get . . .

He knew the answer, but could not work—

One hundred. And with that arithmetical revelation, his senses began to clear the dark numbness in his mind. But with it came pain that eased through his body, drip by sensitive drip. And cold. So damn cold. His mouth felt dry, his tongue thick enough to choke him. He risked opening his eyes again, and in the dim light could make out the shape of his thighs.

He was upright, in a sitting position, but . . .

He lifted his head with care.

Pain throbbed in his neck, across his shoulders, and seemed to work down his arms. Even his fingers felt thick and numb, and he flexed them, tried to stir some sensation into them. His mouth and jaw felt odd, too, and seemed not to work the way they should. He tried to say something, but his lips were as good as glued together. He turned his head to the left, then to the right, worked his way beyond the pain. His night vision was improving, his eyes beginning to adapt to the darkness.

Shadows took on shapes. Shapes took on forms.

Forms became . . .

An almost overpowering need to close his eyes, let sleep take him, surged through his body in a warm wave that threatened to pull him into its numbing depths. He forced his eyes to stay open, focus on the shapes, the forms that stood before him, as tall as a man . . .

A short man. Then, not a man, but someone else . . .

Some*thing* else . . .

His head seemed too heavy for his neck, but he refused to let it buckle, and he forced his eyes to focus through the darkness. What was he looking at? What stood before him?

What was that . . . that man, that thing?

His peripheral vision darkened, and once more sleep— or unconsciousness—reached up to pull him down. But he fought off the numbing waves as his eyes recovered their sight, and his brain struggled to piece together the form that was now manifesting from the shadows before him. And at that moment, as he recognized what it was and understood the full extent of his predicament, fear surged through him with a force that killed his breath.

"Stay here," Jessie told Robert.

She recognized Cooper in conversation with a group of four others. Cooper saw her approaching, then whispered to a tall, slim man by her side, who glanced over at Jessie and excused himself from the group.

"DI Davidson," he said to her. "Good to meet you, DS Janes."

She shook his hand and said, "Likewise," then eyed the group. Cooper had returned to her huddled conversation and now stood with her back to Jessie. "So what's the scoop?"

Stan nodded toward a farmhouse, then winced.

"Should you not be in bed?" she said.

"I don't make a good patient." He frowned, as if at another stab of pain. "DCI Gilchrist was—"

"Andy," she snapped. "Let's cut the formal crap." She stared at him.

Stan leveled his gaze at her, as if to stifle annoyance, and said, "Andy called the station just after midnight last night and asked for two ARVs to take position down the road. But he never turned up and never responded to any of his calls, so we moved the ARVs in." He shifted his gaze to focus somewhere in the distance.

"Then?" Jessie demanded.

"They tried calling his home and mobile numbers peri-odically, and just before seven this morning, his mobile was answered. Turned out to be a Mr. Smart in Kingsbarns, who was out walking his dog when he heard a phone ringing. He said his dog found it buried in the snow beside Andy's Merc—"

"Locked?"

"What?"

"Was his Merc locked?"

Stan scratched his head. "Never asked."

"Could be important," Jessie said. "If it was locked, he probably still has his key fob on him. We might be able to track its location through GPS." She glared at him. "Do you know if his fob has that capability?"

Stan shook his head. "Let me get someone onto it." He removed his mobile and spoke briefly, then ended the call.

"Keep going," Jessie said to him.

"We searched the immediate area and followed a set of footprints to the cottage, and a flowerpot which had been shifted. Nothing else appears to have been disturbed, so we're figuring he picked something up from under the flowerpot but was taken when he returned to his car. The snow's disturbed, and it looks as if he was dragged to some other vehicle. Tire tracks can be seen in a three-point turn, and we've put out a search request on a white Transit van."

"Why? Did somebody see it?"

"Andy called in for the Anstruther station to pull it in. But they never found it."

"This isn't looking good," Jessie said.

"We found spots of blood in the snow. Not a lot," Stan added quickly, as if seeing the panic on Jessie's face. "We're running a DNA test on the blood right now." He seemed to lean down to her. "Does any of what I've said bring anything to mind?"

Jessie shook her head. "You've got Andy's mobile?"

"We have. And the last incoming number came from DC McCauley's mobile—"

"Which was used to entice Andy to meet him here. At the bunker."

"We think so. We've managed to triangulate the position of that call, and it came from Kingsbarns, close to where they found Andy's car." Stan paused for a moment as a team of armed men emerged from the bunker. "Looks like they've found nothing," he said.

"He's not here," Jessie said. "You're wasting your time."

Stan returned her hard look with one of his own. "Do you have any ideas?"

"Check the key fob," she said, then stopped as a thought hit her. "Any other numbers on Andy's mobile that look odd?"

Stan smiled, as if seeing her for the first time. "Just the one," he said.

"Do you mind if I call it?"

"Be my guest."

44

Try as he might, Gilchrist could not break free.

His ankles and calves were strapped to the legs of the chair with duct tape, almost tight enough to cut off circulation. His arms were bound to the back of the chair, hands taped together behind him, too, in an unnatural position that caused fire to burn across his chest and shoulders at the slightest movement. But it was the tape around his face and head that warned Gilchrist of his imminent fate.

Gordie's bulging eyes, and his muted scream, reverberated through Gilchrist's mind in flickering images and an endless death cry that refused to fade. But unlike Gordie, the tape around Gilchrist's face was wrapped in a way that left a gap at his mouth, not to help him breathe—he thought he understood that much—but to let him talk.

Gordie had no chance of escaping.

And Gilchrist knew that he, too, was now waiting for the inevitable.

He stared at the form in front of him, which had manifested into some small man-thing. Then he closed his eyes. But like the memory of Gordie, the image before him refused to vanish. Eyes closed or open, it did not matter. And speaking would not help either. The tripod with the video recorder mounted on it, was in position and ready to be put to use.

It would not take long before Gilchrist's bulging eyes, or his final death scream, would be the next nightmare to be imprinted with indelible persistence onto someone else's mind.

He groaned at the thought and tried to will himself to die.

Jessie dialed the number Stan had given her, but it gave a few rings then kicked her into voice mail. She tried again but got the same result. She was about to dial a third time, when she caught Cooper walking toward her.

"It's not looking good," Cooper said to her.

Understatement of the bloody century, Jessie thought.

"I found traces of benzodiazepines in Bill's and Eilidh's blood," Cooper added. "It's probably how they were taken so easily. And likely what happened to Andy."

"So, how would it be administered?" Jessie asked.

"Syringe, perhaps."

"I can't see Andy letting someone approach him and stick a needle in him."

"Depends on the element of surprise."

Jessie grimaced. She had witnessed Andy disarm her brother Terry without missing a beat or putting a hair out of place. "I don't see it."

"He'd had a few in the Dunvegan," Cooper persisted.

"How about a dart gun?" Jessie said.

"That could work."

"Kumar's used it before," she added. "Similar drugs were found in the bodies of the Georgian gangsters, Dmitri and Yegor Krukov. Impact marks from something other than a needle were also found on the necks of both of them."

"Why didn't you mention this before?" Cooper said.

"It's not been relevant to the case so far—"

"But Bill and Eilidh—"

"I mentioned it to Andy," she lied. "If he didn't deem it worthy enough to pass on to you, then that's his decision, not mine."

Cooper held Jessie's gaze, her eyes unflinching, her look unforgiving. Then she tucked a strand of hair behind her ear and turned and walked away.

"Charming," Jessie said to herself, and dialed the number again.

Still no reply.

She found Stan talking to Nance and thought Nance looked as if she'd been crying. "Any luck with the key fob?" Jessie asked Stan.

Stan grimaced, shook his head. "It's not trackable," he said. "But it was worth a try."

Somehow, Stan's response flattened her. "Any luck with CCTV footage on the white Transit van?" she asked.

Stan shook his head. "Nothing."

"We're not doing too well, are we?" Jessie said.

Nance said, "Well as soon as you come up with something, why don't you let us know."

"I didn't mean it that way," Jessie said.

Nance pulled out her mobile and turned away.

Jessie watched her leave and was about to return to her car to take Robert home when she noticed PC Mhairi McBride standing at the back of an SUV with its hatchback open. A large map lay unfolded and spread open across the back floor.

As Jessie approached, Mhairi grimaced. "I can't believe it. He could already be dead."

"Don't think like that," Jessie said. "Andy's alive until we find him otherwise. And it's up to us to figure out where he's at." She nodded to the Ordnance Survey map. "Where are we on this?" she asked.

Mhairi pointed to it.

Jessie stared at the map, not really knowing what she was looking for or expecting to find. What did strike her, though, was how vast and empty Fife looked. Miles of open land seemed to separate towns and villages. Long stretches of coastline lay uninhabited. All of a sudden, the enormity of the task that lay ahead seemed insurmountable, her words—*it's up to us to figure out where he's at*—ridiculous.

Andy could be anywhere. But he had to be *some*where.

She pressed a finger to the village of Tayport. "Bill's and Eilidh's bodies were found here, right?" She leaned closer, ran her finger along the road toward Leuchars. "Bowden's cottage is here," she said. "Show me where Stewart Donnelly's body was found."

It took Mhairi a few seconds to find what she was looking for. "Strathvithie Country Estate," she said. "Here it is."

"And Kingsbarns is here." Jessie poked her finger at it and stared hard at the map. "So if you drove from Kingsbarns to the Strathvithie whatsit, which way would you go?"

Mhairi ran her finger along Station Road to its connection with the B9131, then along that road until she reached the Country Estate. She looked up at Jessie and said, "So what does that tell us?"

Jessie puffed out her cheeks, raised her eyebrows, and exhaled. "That there's a lot of ground to cover," she said. "And a hundred different roads to take. Kumar's not from this area, and with the shit hitting the fan, he won't have gone anywhere near his home. So, he would have gone somewhere else, somewhere where nobody knows him, someplace that's safe. Right?"

"Right."

"So, if you didn't know your way around, where would you go to find someplace safe?" Jessie asked.

Mhairi stared at the map, shook her head. Then something seemed to dawn on her. "I would need help."

Jessie smiled. "You most definitely would," she agreed. "And we know just the boy to help us. Don't we?"

Mhairi pursed her lips, as her eyes danced with some inner rage.

"Come on," Jessie said. "Phone that conniving fuck and tell him we're on our way."

Gilchrist held his breath.

He thought he caught the faintest crunch of shoes in snow. But he could have been mistaken. Then a scraping sound had him peering through the darkness at the door to the barn. Every nerve in his body tensed as he caught the unmistakeable sound of metal on metal—a key being inserted into a lock.

He held his breath as the wooden door creaked, then had to close his eyes and turn his head away from a burst of white light that blinded him.

Then the barn settled into darkness again. He now knew it was a barn, because even in that most fleeting flash of light he had caught the shapes of farm tools hanging on the walls. A flashlight beam wavered toward him, then steadied as it found him, only to blind him again.

"You are awake, I see."

Gilchrist faced away from the glare and mumbled, "Water."

A deep chuckle. "I am sure you must be thirsty."

Then the beam left Gilchrist's face and danced across a dusty concrete floor where it settled on a spot in the corner of the far wall—to the left of where the tripod and its camera stood. The beam shortened as the man walked to the corner, then was lost for a flickering moment as he leaned down and fiddled with something on the ground.

Gilchrist heard a click as the barn opened up to him in a weak yellowish light.

The man pushed himself to his feet and turned to face Gilchrist.

"Well, Mr. Gilchrist. We meet at last."

Gilchrist needed no introduction to know who the man was. Jet-black hair combed back in a thick slick, and eyes as black as the River Styx in a swarthy complexion, told him he was looking at Kumar. Even bound and taped and helpless as he was, he could not help but marvel at how handsome Kumar looked, and well-dressed, too, with tweed jacket and waistcoat, and pleated trousers, nothing at all like the mind's vision of a cold-hearted killer. A solitary ring sat on Kumar's little finger like a bauble, the only jewelry on display.

"My name is Kumar," the man said, leaning down to open a case by his feet. When he stood up, a knife that Gilchrist recognized from Gordie's beheading glinted in the dim light.

"And you, Mr. Gilchrist, are about to feature in your own video."

45

Mhairi rang the doorbell, Jessie by her side. Robert sat alone in the Fiat 500, his whole being absorbed with his mobile, it seemed.

Angus opened the door and stood back with grim resignation.

Jessie pushed past him and said, "Table?"

"Second door on the left."

Jessie followed the directions and entered a small kitchen that smelled of cooked food tainted with the acrid hint of burnt toast. The sink and draining board stood elbow-deep in dishes that could overload her dishwasher. The kitchen table's wooden surface was littered with newspapers, magazines, and envelopes, and she swept her arm across it to clear a space.

Mhairi entered, followed by Angus.

"Put it here," Jessie ordered, and waited while Mhairi unfolded the Ordnance Survey map and patted it flat on the table.

For all the attention Mhairi was giving Angus, he could have been invisible. From the domestic dilapidation around them, Angus seemed to be missing a woman's touch, maybe

Mhairi's in particular. Several days' worth of stubble dirtied his face, and the skin under his eyes was swollen. He could have been on the bottle for years.

Jessie spread her hands across the map. "Right, Angus. No messing. We need your assistance, and we need it now. You showed your blonde bimbo Caryl—"

"I should throw you out right now for what you said, you wee fat tramp."

Jessie glared at him. "It's been a while since I've been called wee."

"Yeah, well, show some respect for the deceased," Angus grumbled.

"Sorry," Jessie said. "You showed your *deceased* blonde bimbo Caryl a number of properties." She slapped the map. "Show me where they are."

"You've already got the addresses—"

"I don't give a fuck what we've already got. I want you to show me where they are on this map. And I want you to show me how you got there—"

"By car. How else?"

Jessie pushed herself to her feet and confronted Angus. She stood a good six inches shorter than him, but as she pressed herself forward she could have been looking him in the eye. "Keep acting the dumb fuck that you are, and I swear, Angus, I really do, cross my heart and hope to die, I will set my brothers on you. And believe me, they will give you a different definition of mincemeat." She stepped back to clear the way for Angus to stand at the table. "Now let's try this once more. Show me on this map which way you drove your fucking blonde bimbo around all day, before she was deceased."

"Anything to get rid of you lot," Angus grumbled, and stepped to the table. "First one here, and the—"

"Describe it."

"What?"

"You thick or what? Describe the property to me. What the fuck does it look like? Ten stories, twenty bedrooms, four swimming pools, or what?"

"Three-bedroom two-bathroom bungalow on an acre of land. Fully modernized to the highest specifications," he said, settling into his sales pitch. "New PVC fascia, double-glazing in all windows, new combi-boiler and radiators throughout, master bathroom with the latest in power showers—"

"Neighbors?"

"Identical bungalows either side—"

"I can see that from the map. How nosy?"

"How would I know? They're elderly, I think. I don't know."

"Does it have a garage?"

"Garage has recently been extended to take two cars," he said, getting back into his sales rhythm, "with a door leading into the kitchen utility room—"

"Any other structures outside? Huts, sheds, chicken coops?"

Angus shook his head.

"Is it vacant?"

"They all were. That's what Caryl was looking for."

Mhairi shuffled her feet, tugged her jacket.

"Next one," Jessie ordered.

Angus pointed to the map. "This one," he said, and gave the address.

"Let's have it."

Angus described that, and another two properties, none stirring much interest until he said, "This one here. Smallholding on two acres. On the downside, needs work done to it, but they're not asking as much as the others—"

"Neighbors?" Jessie asked again.

"A farmhouse across the road."

"How about next door?"

"Another smallholding about a couple of hundred yards away."

"Huts, et cetera?"

"A steading."

"What's that?"

"A stone-built barn that was once used for keeping chickens."

"As big as the barn at the Bowdens' cottage?" Jessie asked.

"About two-thirds the size," Angus said. "But as I said, it needs work done to it."

"Only this one and the Bowdens' has a barn or steading?"

Angus nodded.

"Why would Dillanos take the Bowdens' and not this place?"

"Bowdens' was better maintained, and the barn was larger, too."

Jessie glanced at Mhairi. "What do you think?"

"I think the steading's the key. I think that's what he needs to imprison the girls."

"Keep them out of the house but close enough to check up on them, you mean?"

"Yeah."

"Anything else?" Jessie asked her.

Mhairi glanced at Angus and said, "I feel as if my skin's crawling."

Jessie nodded. "That makes two of us."

Angus stepped toward Mhairi and said, "Come on, Mhairi. Don't be like—"

"Get your filthy hands off me," Mhairi snapped, then turned and left the kitchen.

"That's you been told," Jessie said to Angus. Then she shook her head and gave him a grim smile. "You messed up, Angus. Big time. So take your medicine, and move on. Got it?"

Angus stared at her in silence.

Jessie had her mobile in her hand by the time she reached the end of the hallway. She thought of calling Stan and asking for backup, but she knew it was such a long shot that she might be seen as some fearmonger. Mistakes with police resources were expensive and could stay with you the remainder of your career. But Andy's life was in danger, so what choice did she have? And delays could be deadly. She knew that from experience.

So she decided to follow her hunch and check it out first.

She slid in behind the wheel and signed to Robert in the back, *Are you doing OK?*

Can I have something to eat? he signed in reply.

She thought of driving him home, dropping him off, and ordering a chippie. But that would take her on a detour, cost thirty to forty minutes of time. Besides, she was only going to check the place out, not break in, and she could always call for support if her long shot paid off, and if she needed it.

She signed *I've got to take care of something first, OK?*

Her heart sank as Robert sullenly returned his attention to his mobile.

In the passenger seat next to her, Mhairi sat with her lips pursed in angry silence.

Without another word, Jessie pushed into gear and set off toward the cottage with the steading.

Kumar fiddled with the camera, adjusted the focus, then frowned at the screen, as if unhappy with the image Gilchrist was portraying. He switched on a pair of spotlights that stood on either side of the chair, which Gilchrist had not noticed until that moment.

Light bathed both sides of Gilchrist's face and brought the barn walls and floor into bright view. Overhead, wooden rafters faded into the shadows of the barn's roof, like a ship's ribbing. Fluorescent lights dotted every other beam, their metal casings speckled with rust and covered in spiderwebs as thick and gray as wash-worn rags.

But Gilchrist was now able to confirm the helplessness of his own predicament.

If he had any thoughts of being able to wriggle free from the tape that bound him, they were dashed there and then. The chair to which he was tied was made of wood and metal—wooden seat curved to the shape of your behind, so you could be decapitated in relative comfort, and metal legs bolted to the floor, to avoid the risk of hurting yourself if you happened to topple over in your final frantic moments.

If only hangmen could be as considerate.

The matte black finish on the camera and spotlights made the equipment look at odds with the barn's tired finishings. Whitewashed walls, blistered from lack of care, had peeled back in spots to reveal mortar as gray as ash. Light switches, plug sockets, wall-mounted shelves, even an opened tool kit, looked as if they had not been touched for years.

And Kumar looked at odds with his surroundings, too, as he shuffled around the camera, adjusting this, twiddling that, his polished shoes losing their shine as he kicked up dust. That alone gave Gilchrist hope, for he reasoned that someone as well-dressed and meticulous as Kumar would surely not want his clothes ruined from the unavoidable blood spurting from a manual decapitation.

Gilchrist struggled to make sense of that logic.

Maybe he was going to be filmed tied and bound, and the recording used as some bargaining tool. What would Kumar hope to gain? Money? Safe passage? A plea-bargain deal with the procurator fiscal? But the worry that Kumar might have an associate—yet to make his appearance—who would handle the messy business of sawing through Gilchrist's neck, while Kumar recorded the event from a spatter-free distance, stifled Gilchrist's hope. But it was his recognition of the long carving knife that lay on top of the case by the camera, its blade reshaped into a worn curve from repeated sharpenings—the same one used to cut off Gordie's head—that smothered Gilchrist's hopes altogether.

The human survival instinct is arguably the most powerful of any living species. If Gilchrist could somehow delay the inevitable, perhaps convince Kumar that it made more sense to let him go rather than kill him, maybe even strike a deal of his own, he might yet be saved. But the tape around his lips and chin made speaking difficult, although he could pronounce his words if he took his time.

"You're only digging yourself deeper," Gilchrist managed to say.

"Ah," Kumar said, and glanced at him before ducking behind the recorder again. "Say something else." A red light appeared on the front of the camera.

"You don't have to do this," Gilchrist said.

"That's better," Kumar said. "I think we have the sound working now."

"I can be bought."

"I know you can."

"I can." It felt good to be talking, even if his tongue felt as dry as cardboard.

"I thought you didn't do bribes."

Gilchrist worked up some spittle. "Everyone has their price. That's what you said. Your exact words."

Kumar looked at him as he stepped back from the camera, but said nothing.

"Even me," Gilchrist tried. "And it won't cost much."

"It won't cost me anything, Mr. Gilchrist, because I don't believe you." He leaned down, picked up the carving knife with one hand and a whetstone—which Gilchrist had not noticed until then—with the other. "I am always amused by the change in personality at the recognition of death being only a few moments away. The closer death comes, the more a person is prepared to agree to terms they rejected moments earlier." He worked the blade of the knife in a slicing action, one side other side, one side other side, back and forth, its steel blade ringing, again and again, like a butcher preparing to slice off a cut of meat—which in a sense he was. "But I know from experience that it is only a ploy to delay the inevitable. So I tend not to listen."

Kumar put the whetstone down, dabbed his thumb on the knife's blade.

"I think we're ready," he said, and laid the carving knife next to the whetstone.

Then he removed what looked like a small, white package from the camera case.

A surge of white fear exploded through Gilchrist. His blood thundered, his heart pounded, his peripheral vision darkened, as Kumar unfolded the forensic suit and slipped his legs into it. Then he pulled it up his thighs, inserted his arms, left first, next his right, then up and over his shoulders.

No associate to assist him, Gilchrist saw that now.

And no worries about blood spurts spoiling his nice, tailored suit.

Gilchrist tensed his muscles, jerked his body on the chair, tried to tear free from his bindings. He pulled at his hands until the fire in his chest burned as if torched.

He was tied too securely.

As good as dead.

Steam from his urine lifted in the cold air as he watched Kumar lift the carving knife from the camera bag and walk toward him.

"No," Gilchrist groaned. "No, no, *no* . . ."

46

"How far away are we?" Jessie asked Mhairi.

"About fifteen minutes."

Jessie glanced at the dash, calculated that they should arrive at 1:10 PM, give or take. She gritted her teeth and pressed on, irritated by the sluggish traffic. She was fourth in a plug of cars that trailed a slow-moving tractor. Even with a clear run at it, her Fiat did not have the power to accelerate and overtake all the way to the front—never mind that the cars ahead were so closely bunched together that she would have to wedge her Fiat in between them if she dared to try.

"How much trouble has Angus got himself into?" Mhairi asked.

"If it was up to me," Jessie said, "I would drown him in the deepest shite. But I'm new to these parts, so what do I know?"

"I could never live with myself if he was somehow associated with DCI Gilchrist's death—"

"What is it with everyone in Fife, that they speak to each other in terms of rank? DCI Gilchrist? Andy's Andy, as far as I'm concerned. And he's very much alive, until proven otherwise."

Mhairi cleared her throat. "Do you think so? Do you think he's still alive?"

"I know it. Don't ask me how or why I know. I just do." She glanced at Mhairi, but the worried frown on Mhairi's forehead told her she was not convinced. "Do you know that most people bring on their own suffering by thinking about all the bad things they don't want to happen to them? It's true," Jessie said. "It's in the Bible somewhere, and don't ask me where. Can't remember the last time I saw a bible, let alone read one."

Up ahead, the lead car pulled out and overtook the tractor, sharply followed by the car behind, exhaust belching oily smoke from its sudden surge of power.

"Well thank goodness for small mercies," Jessie said. "That's us second in line. Not that I could pass that thing even if I wanted to." She glanced in her mirror, tried to catch Robert's eye, but his head was still down—focused on his mobile.

She retrieved her mobile from her pocket and passed it to Mhairi. "Here," she said. "Do me a favor and dial the last number I called."

"Whose is it?"

"That's what I'd like you to find out. It was on Andy's mobile and seems to be untraceable. I've called a few times, but it just kicks me into the service provider's voice mail. Try giving it a few calls. Maybe someone'll pick up."

Mhairi fell into silence as she tried to work her way around Jessie's mobile. But being unfamiliar with it, she tutted as the menus refused to open.

"Try swiping your hand across it," Jessie said. "Not poking."

"Got it," Mhairi said.

But from the way she was fiddling with it, Jessie thought it would take some time before Mhairi got it. She glanced at the dash.

Less than ten minutes away.

Kumar positioned himself behind Gilchrist.

He gripped Gilchrist by the hair and tugged his head back.

Gilchrist tried to resist, but Kumar's grip was too strong. He felt his Adam's apple bob in his throat, felt his utter and absolute vulnerability as the razor-sharp blade danced in front of his face, then slid down and under his chin, and moved to the left. And even in that stunned moment of silence before his death, it struck Gilchrist that Cooper had been correct—entry wound to the left, a couple of inches beneath the left earlobe, then across the throat in one smooth stroke—

"*Fuuuck*," Gilchrist screamed, and jerked his head from side to side with every ounce of his strength, tearing himself free from Kumar's grip.

His head jerked forward. Spittle dribbled from his lips. His breath pulled in and out of his lungs as if on fire. He gasped with disbelief as Kumar stepped around the chair to stand in front of him. What was he doing?

Was he going to behead him face-on?

Then Kumar walked back to the camera and laid the knife on the case.

Gilchrist's heart raced as if ready to explode. Blood pounded through his system with a ferocity that could not be good for his health—as if that was of any concern at that moment. He tried to pull his body free, but flames seemed to lick and savor every fiber of his being, their scorching tongues firing every muscle, every sinew, every nerve.

If he closed his eyes, he could already be in hell.

But he focused on Kumar, knowing that he was not in hell. He was still alive. And as long as he had air to breathe, and power to move, he would continue to stay alive. He jerked his body back with all his strength, then jerked forward. He tried it again—back and forward, back and forward, rocking the chair free—

Hope soared as he felt some give in the chair's legs.

Had he loosened the bolts into the concrete?

He glanced at Kumar, but he seemed too focused on whatever he was digging out of the camera case. Gilchrist jerked again, back and forward, his muscles tight, his chest molten. But he had no time to think of the pain. He continued to struggle and fight, the tape cutting into his legs, his arms, his face. He tasted blood on his tongue—

"You're wasting your energy," Kumar said. "You cannot break free."

Gilchrist froze. His chest heaved as if he'd run the four hundred meters. Perspiration blinded his sight. He blinked it free.

"You should use what little time you have left to make peace with your God. You do believe in God," Kumar said, then walked toward Gilchrist like a doctor to a patient. "I do hope so," he added, holding up a syringe half-filled with clear fluid, as if for Gilchrist to approve.

Gilchrist gave a grunt of shock.

"People of many religions ignore their God throughout their lives, yet turn to Him in their darkest hour. Not like Muslims, who pray to Allah five times every day. I wonder if you now wish you had paid more attention to your God, Mr. Gilchrist. Do you? No? You're not an atheist, are you? Never mind." He pressed the syringe, causing a squirt of liquid to ejaculate. "This should help you to relax."

Kumar walked to the back of the chair, out of Gilchrist's sight.

Gilchrist rocked on his chair, hoping to make it difficult, maybe even impossible, for Kumar to inject him.

"This is not potent enough to put you out," Kumar continued, as if Gilchrist were more a willing patient. "We wouldn't want you to miss the fun. Oh, no, Mr. Gilchrist, we wouldn't want to do that."

Despite continuing to struggle, Gilchrist's arms were secured behind the back of the chair with tape as tight as lashing. He could do nothing as he felt Kumar's fingers touch his wrist, push his sleeve back, tap his skin as if in search of a vein. "You won't get away with this," Gilchrist groaned, and grunted a curse as the needle pierced his skin with a sharp nip.

"Whether I get away with it or not, Mr. Gilchrist, will be of no concern to you. That I can promise you." Kumar reappeared at Gilchrist's side.

Helpless, Gilchrist could only watch Kumar walk back to the camera and replace the empty syringe into the case. Whatever drug Kumar had injected was already beginning to work through his system. The fire in his chest was dying down, as if the flames were being smothered with a blanket. His muscles, too, seemed salved in cooling lotion.

Kumar retrieved the carving knife and walked around the camera to stand with his back to it, blocking Gilchrist from the viewfinder. Then he lifted the knife with a determined smile, an executioner keen to get on with the grim reality of business.

"The day is getting late, Mr. Gilchrist."

47

Kumar walked from the camera toward Gilchrist, his step slow and precise, which had Gilchrist's memory pulling up an image of a blank screen that opened up to a man—Kumar—walking away from the viewer to behead a terrified Gordie.

"Detective Chief Inspector Andrew James Gilchrist," Kumar announced, more for the viewers' benefit than for Gilchrist's, "do you have anything to say? Any words of wisdom or advice you would like to pass on to family or colleagues?"

Gilchrist thought of just reciting a description of Kumar, giving his team something to go on. But on top of the drugs coursing through his system—making thinking as difficult as breathing through treacle—he knew Kumar would simply delete whatever Gilchrist said, before sending the video to whomever he intended to send it.

He thought of saying a few parting words to his children, Jack and Maureen. But that would effectively ensure that they would watch a recording of him moments before his death, maybe even the beheading itself. Not the kind of legacy any father would want to leave his children.

"Nothing?" Kumar asked, ever the gentleman.

Gilchrist opened his mouth to tell Kumar to fuck off, but his lips refused to work, and his tongue could have belonged to someone else. Even the carving knife, which had held his fearful attention for so long, seemed to slide away from view, as if Kumar was trying to hide it prior to Gilchrist's decapitation. But Kumar would not be as considerate. Where would be the fun in that?

Gilchrist's dimming brain worked out that much at least.

His head seemed to have gained pounds in weight, making it difficult to keep an eye on Kumar as he neared. He no longer felt the fire in his chest, the pain in his arms, his neck, his legs. Even Kumar's grip as his fingers grabbed Gilchrist's hair from behind and jerked his head back to expose the soft flesh of the neck and throat, the carotid artery pulsing away, like an indicator reminding Kumar where to slice his blade, just in case he had forgotten.

Kumar was talking for the benefit of his viewers. But it could have been in a foreign language for all the sense Gilchrist's numbing brain could make of it. He felt the press of Kumar's body, the warmth of his breath with its hint of garlic, as he leaned closer. An arm encircled his head, the fearsome blade flashing before him, then vanishing beneath his line of vision. An aromatic fragrance filled his senses, like Old Spice aftershave, reminding him of his father—how many years since he had died?

It seemed impossible to work out.

Gilchrist blinked once, twice, expecting each blink to be his last.

Would he feel any pain? The injection should take care of that, he reasoned.

Kumar's voice had taken on an unearthly echo, as if he were whispering in his ear one second, then shouting across an abyss the next. With his head tilted back, rafters seemed to swell from the shadows to take on the shape of the gallows, but for the life of him, Gilchrist could not see the noose with its hangman's knot.

And when had spring arrived? And birdsong, too?

Except the song turned into a sharp tone that beeped with electronic regularity—

The knife flashed, its silver blade slicing the air before his eyes—

Gilchrist gasped.

Kumar cursed, released his grip.

Gilchrist blinked. Was he dead? Dying?

He held his breath as his vision returned to the horizontal, and Kumar walked off to the side. The ringing was coming from the shadows close to the wall on his right, from some point beyond the reach of the spotlights, which had Kumar's irritated attention. Despite his leaden mental powers Gilchrist was still able to work out that Kumar would not want his recording spoiled by the persistent ringing of a mobile.

Another curse as Kumar kneeled down to a large bag on the concrete floor, which Gilchrist had not seen until that moment. He had to grit his teeth and strain his neck to watch Kumar as he tugged at the bag—except it turned out not to be a bag but a body. Kumar tore at the man's clothes, and the body rolled over, its lifeless eyes staring at Gilchrist as if asking *Remember me?*

And Gilchrist did. Even in the drugged fog of his mind, he remembered—Craig Farmer, Stewart Donnelly's mate and the man whose phone number had been given to Gilchrist by an anonymous caller.

Kumar tore open Farmer's jacket, dug deep into the inside pocket, and removed a mobile phone, its screen brightening the shadows.

The ringing rose, crystal clear now—

Then stopped.

Kumar did not speak, just held the mobile, staring at it. He carried it over to Gilchrist and said, "Does this number mean anything to you?" and was halfway through reading out its sequence when the mobile rang again.

Kumar glared at it. Even through the syrup in his mind Gilchrist could see the man was torn between switching it off and just getting on with the beheading, or finding out who was phoning Farmer. Why this was important to Kumar, Gilchrist could only surmise; were the Dillanos, Judkowski, Donnelly— and now Farmer—murders associated in some way to Kumar's criminal activities? That being the case, if you added in the three dead women, along with the Krukov brothers, Gordie, Bill, and Eilidh—plus one more if you included Gilchrist's own imminent beheading—the man before him was a veritable serial killer.

And how many others had he killed before?

The ringing stopped for a few silent seconds, then started again—

Kumar made the connection that time. He placed the mobile to his ear, his black eyes watching Gilchrist as if expecting the caller to ask to speak to him. He listened in silence for about ten seconds, then held the mobile out to Gilchrist, the sibilance of the woman's voice sounding tinny and distant.

". . . there . . . ? Hello . . . ? Hello . . . ? Who's there . . . ? Hello . . . ?"

Gilchrist returned a blank look, which was no more than he could give with the drugs in his system. Just as well, he thought, puzzling at the voice's vague familiarity.

As if realizing Gilchrist was beyond speech, Kumar ended the call. He unclipped the back of the mobile, pulled out the SIM card, then threw the mobile at Farmer's body.

It landed with a metallic clatter and skittered across the concrete floor.

With his heart in his mouth, Gilchrist watched Kumar return to the camera and adjust the settings—to delete the part of the recording with the interrupting call? Kumar could have been alone in the barn for all the attention he was giving Gilchrist. It took several minutes of close concentration before he clicked a switch and the light on the camera turned to green again.

Then, as if satisfied, Kumar picked up the carving knife and looked Gilchrist's way.

Something in the set of Kumar's jaw, the fire in his eyes, the white line around his lips, told Gilchrist there would be no posing for the camera this time. Just grip the hair, back with the head, in with the knife, grit your teeth, and give a right good tug. A bit of digging and hacking through the spinal column, no doubt, but with Kumar's expertise it should not take too long.

Simple, when you think about it, really.

Then what?

Maybe he should have paid more attention to his religious upbringing, prayed to God on a regular basis, even gone to church on occasion. His mother last took him there as a boy—him and his big brother, Jack—but she stopped after Jack was killed, and as far as Gilchrist could recall, none of them crossed a church threshold again. Even for his ex-wife's funeral, Gilchrist had not attended the church service but had driven straight to the crematorium.

Would God hold that against him now?

Kumar approached.

Gilchrist closed his eyes.

And prayed.

"I got through that time," Mhairi said. "Then he hung up."

"He?"

"Figure of speech." She pressed the keypad, tried to redial. "Shit," she said. "Now it's dead."

"No automatic voice mail?"

"Nothing."

"He's removed the SIM card—"

"Next left," Mhairi interrupted.

Jessie jerked her foot to the brake and said, "That one?" as the turnoff zipped past.

"Sorry," Mhairi said. "Wasn't looking."

"Shit happens," Jessie said, eyeing the road ahead, looking for a place to turn around.

"Just pull over here." Mhairi looked over her shoulder. "Do a three-point turn. There's no one behind."

"Been a while since I've tried one of these. Here's hoping I don't back us into a ditch."

"Want me to jump out and guide you?"

Jessie gave a dead-eyed smile, then swung the Fiat across the road and jerked to a stop. Into reverse—a quick look at Robert in the rearview mirror—back it up to the verge, oops, bit of a bump, shift into first, and away we go. The Fiat's tires slipped on the road surface as Jessie floored the accelerator.

Mhairi adjusted her seating. "Didn't know you were a stunt driver."

"There's a lot you don't know about me."

"Like what?"

"Just stuff." Jessie flicked on the indicator. "This it?"

Mhairi nodded.

"How far now?"

"Up there on the left."

Jessie eyed the property as they neared.

The house was a typical Scottish smallholding—one story, square-shaped, but with off-white roughcast walls that could do with a coat of paint, maybe three—*needs work done to it*. The roof lay thick and white with frosted snow, a sign of an unheated interior from lying vacant. The two acres of land fell downhill across snow-covered fields. Trees, hedges, stone dikes marred the white blanket with dots and strips of white-capped blacks.

Beyond the smallholding, and farther from the main road, stood the steading, a lone building which, even seated behind the steering wheel, Jessie could tell was in a more dilapidated state of disrepair.

Directly across the road, and a good fifty yards up a hedge-lined driveway, stood a farmhouse, the smallholding's closest neighbor. A tractor with an oversized fork for a front loader, was dumping straw-like material onto muddied ground behind a metal-framed building. A herd of cows watched from a safe distance, ankle-deep in muddied slush, before hoofing closer when the tractor backed away.

"Is that a car?" Jessie said.

"Where?"

"To the side of the house."

Mhairi narrowed her eyes. "There's nothing wrong with your eyesight."

"Get onto the station," Jessie ordered.

"And say what?"

"I'll tell you in a minute." Jessie felt herself tense as she drove closer to the unmarked entrance. Thirty seconds later, she pulled the Fiat to a halt at the opening and eyed a single set of tire tracks that ran from the road down a narrow driveway, leading her eye to a white car parked outside the steading, no more than twenty yards away.

Her nervous system flipped to red alert. "Fuck," she said. "He's here."

"How can you be sure?" Mhairi said. "It might be someone looking to rent."

"So why look at the steading and not the house?" Jessie replied. Even from where she sat, she could see the snow in front of the steading's wooden door had been disturbed. "He's in there," she said. "Call for backup. ARVs. Helicopters. The works. And find out who owns that car. I'm going to check it out."

Mhairi spoke into her mobile and rattled off the make of car—Vauxhall Astra—and registration number. "And get back to me as fast as you can," she ordered.

All of a sudden, Jessie wished she had not brought Robert along. But backup would be with them shortly. A sudden flash of doubt hit her, and she thought of doing nothing until backup arrived. But she knew from past experience that any delay could be fatal.

She had to check it out. No questions.

She turned to Robert in the back, tapped his leg, and signed, *Stay here. I'll be back in a minute. Then we'll go for something to eat.*

I'm not hungry, he signed, then focused again on his mobile.

Jessie left the keys in the ignition and opened the door, leaving Mhairi ordering the backup—baton guns, dogs, armed teams. As she faced the steading, a stiff wind whipped in from the open fields, blasting her face with grains of snow, clocking a windchill factor that had to pull the temperature well below freezing. Two hours ago it could have been summer compared to this.

She pulled her collar up, made her way down the narrow driveway, keeping her feet on the tire tracks, her shoes crunching gravel beneath the snow. The tracks looked fresh—it had not snowed since the night before—and she locked her eyes on the steading door as she approached. The steading looked larger now that she was almost upon it, maybe a story and a half high. Two narrow slits for windows were boarded over. If the roof had any skylight windows, they were snowed over. The only entrance appeared to be a single wooden door, the color of weatherworn unpainted wood, which was located more or less in the middle of the long facade before her.

Her inner self was warning her that she was unarmed, asking why she did not keep her .22 in the glove compartment. "OK, OK, I'll do that next time," she whispered to herself. The closer she eased to the steading, the harder her heart raced—

A car door slammed.

Jessie turned and glared at Mhairi. "For fuck sake," she hissed. "Why don't you just knock on the door and tell them we're here?"

"Sorry," Mhairi said, "a gust of wind caught it," and scrambled after her.

"Any luck with the car?"

"Not yet."

"Put your mobile on vibrate, and stay behind me. And not another word. Got it?"

"Got it."

Which were two words.

But the look Jessie gave Mhairi made sure she at last got the message.

48

Gilchrist could barely breathe.

His head was pulled so far back he thought his neck was going to break, that he was about to die that way. The rushing in his ears, the sound of his pumping lifeblood, told him he was still alive. But it also helped drown out Kumar's rambling soliloquy, his playacting for the camera.

". . . know nothing about my organization," Kumar announced to the viewers, his voice loud and confident with the arrogance of the undefeated. "You have destroyed this nest, but I have already set up elsewhere. Which is the beauty of my scheme. Demand exceeds supply, and the supply is limitless. Do you know how many young women from Europe cross your country's borders illegally every day? It's in the thousands. And by the time you receive this warning, another thirty women will have been selected, and under my control . . ."

Gilchrist felt Kumar's fingers tighten their grip on his hair. He would beg for his life, if he could. But breathing, just to stay alive long enough to be decapitated, was taking all his attention.

"... I am not an unreasonable man," Kumar continued. "I live by the most basic of laws, the law of reciprocity—a life for a life—the simplest form of fairness that ensures mutual respect across race, religion, and politics ..."

Kumar's breathing deepened. His grip squeezed tighter, pushing Gilchrist's head back even more, stretching his neck almost beyond the point of strangulation. Not that it mattered, he supposed, as his final moments were now upon him.

"... so I will show you how the law of reciprocity works."

Gilchrist felt Kumar's muscles tighten, sensed the deadly stillness in his being. He closed his eyes, held his breath, readying for the blade to pierce his—

A hard thud resounded from outside—a car door slammed shut?

Kumar stilled, looked at the steading's wooden door.

Gilchrist jerked his head, gagged, managed to find air.

Behind him, Kumar shifted, the tip of the knife blade pressing into Gilchrist's skin hard enough for blood to trickle down his neck. Time seemed to stop for a frozen moment. Then Kumar's breath puffed in the cold air, and Gilchrist could almost hear the man's thoughts, empathize with his dilemma.

Proceed with the beheading? Or first make sure all is safe?

Kumar cursed, and chose the latter.

He released his grip from Gilchrist, then moved to the body on the floor. He tugged at the clothes, almost ripping the jacket from Farmer's corpse, and removed something—another mobile? But from where he sat, and at such an angle, Gilchrist could not tell.

Kumar pushed back to his feet, strode to the camera.

He flipped a switch, and the green light went out.

He moved to the corner, leaned down, removed a plug.

The barn fell into darkness.

Gilchrist was not sure if he had become accustomed to the drugs, or if the adrenaline surge from his imminent beheading had helped to flush them from his system. Whatever the reason, he was able to follow Kumar's progress to the barn door, by sight and sound—sight from a flicker of light as a crack in the wooden door was pressed open, and sound from the hard rattle of wood as Kumar released it and hissed another curse.

Gilchrist took his chance. Someone was outside. He shouted for help, but the word came out in a weak groan. So much for the adrenaline flush. He lifted his head to try again, and something as heavy as a hammer hit the side of his head with a force hard enough to crack bone.

"Shut up," Kumar hissed.

Then Kumar was behind him, striding through the barn's darkness with authority, a man who knew exactly where he was going and what he was about to do. Light flickered for a moment, then vanished as a door in the back wall closed.

Drugs or split skulls. It made no difference. Gilchrist could not tell where he was. He seemed to be floating one moment, looking down on himself strapped to the chair, then the next, staring into the black emptiness of a beamed ceiling.

He pulled in air, bringing his senses back to life.

His throat burned from lack of water. His heart pounded like some caged animal. Despite the freezing chill, sweat dripped into his eyes. Or maybe it was blood. He blinked, shook his head to clear it, and felt his world spin for a disorienting moment. He was still drugged up, or maybe half-conscious. But his strength was coming back to him, along with feeling. A sharp pain dug into the back of his neck where Kumar had tried to bend a couple of vertebrae, and a dull ache persisted at the corner of his left eye, keeping in time with the thudding beat of his heart, and making him blink in an effort to see.

But with Kumar gone, Gilchrist realized he had to take this one chance.

He had no time to feel the pain. He had to break free.

He gritted his teeth, tensed his muscles, and with every ounce of his strength tried to tear his limbs from the taping. He felt some movement as the binding stretched, and he held it until he could hold no more. He took another breath, tensed his muscles, giving it his all, held it again, felt the tape bite into his arms, his legs, felt fire sear across his shoulders. But a few seconds later he reached the grim conclusion that it would take a stronger man than he could ever be to tear himself free.

Exhausted, he slumped forward as far as the binding permitted. His head lolled, his chin to his chest. He was done. He was through with it all. Part of him wished Kumar would return and just get on with the job of lopping off his head, while another part wanted to beg for one phone call, to talk to Jack, to Maureen, for just one minute, to tell them he was proud of how they turned out, how he was sorry he would not be around for their own yet-to-be-born children, and that he loved them. Yes, even if he had time enough only for that, to tell them he loved them, that would do.

But he now knew that would never happen.

He would never speak to them, never see them again.

He could do nothing to stop the tears squeezing from his eyes or choke back the heavy sobs that grunted from his very core.

Jessie stopped dead, her arm out to halt Mhairi. "Did you see that?"

"What?"

"The door. I thought it moved."

"Could have been the wind."

As if to prove Mhairi's point, an arctic gust blasted in, stirring up snow, shifting it across the ground like spindrift in a winter storm.

Jessie tugged her collar, blew into her hands. Was it always this cold on the east coast, for Christ's sake? "I don't think it was the wind," she said.

"Well, we know someone's in there."

"And he now knows we're out here."

"He?" Mhairi quipped.

"Here's hoping it's not *they*."

Jessie turned her attention to the car parked outside the steading, a white Vauxhall Astra, the name and address of the rental company in Dundee on an oval sticker on the rear window. But it was the footprints around the car that held her attention.

She stared at them, tried to make sense of the mess.

One clear set ran from the passenger door around the boot and another, not so clear, from the driver's door. Both sets seemed to converge by the rear door only to be lost in a confusion of disturbed snow. But what struck Jessie was the single line that ran in a scuffled trail from the rear door to the barn, as if . . . as if . . .

"Fuck," she said, and faced Mhairi. "Andy's in there," she whispered. "They've dragged him from the back seat. There's two of them at least," she confirmed.

Mhairi hissed a curse of her own, then said, "We need help."

Help was good. But it would take time for help to arrive. And Jessie knew she could not delay. Not this time. Not after losing Gordie. "You go on," she said to Mhairi and pointed to the far corner of the steading. "Nip around the back. See if you can find another way in." Jessie tried to work through the logic, but it was now everything or nothing. "And get onto your phone again, and this time tell them it's an emergency."

"What about you?"

Jessie grimaced. "I'll distract them."

Mhairi held Jessie's gaze for a stunned moment, as if about to ask if she was crazy or what. Jessie was not sure if she could give an honest answer. Then Mhairi pushed past her, crept beyond the barn's door, and on toward the far corner.

49

Jessie watched Mhairi disappear around the end of the steading.

All of a sudden, she realized how vulnerable she was. And how stupid. How really fucking stupid. She was so fucking stupid she was shaking in her shoes. And here she was now, trying to tackle a known killer without a weapon and without backup. The sensible thing to do would be to back away, watch from a safe distance until the others arrived. But she was beyond that, she had taken one step too far—maybe several—and in doing so had endangered not only her own life but the lives of Mhairi and Robert.

With that thought, she glanced at Robert—

What . . . ?

He was standing by the side of the Fiat, looking at her.

Get back inside the car, she signed. *It's too cold.*

There's someone with a gun.

Jessie's heart jumped to her mouth. *Where?*

Behind the wall.

Jessie looked the length of the steading, at snow that lay undisturbed all the way to the near corner. Then she turned back to Robert. *Where?*

Robert flapped a hand at the gable end, then signed, *Behind the wall with a gun only six feet from the corner run mum run he'll shoot you.*

And it struck Jessie that if Robert could see the man, the man could see Robert.

So she ran.

She ran toward the corner.

She ran toward the corner and the man with the gun, knowing that if she was killed, then Robert would be killed, too. She risked a glance at Robert but could not see him, and a surge of relief powered through her that he had the sense at least to hide.

And as she ran, her feet crunched snow, kicked through frosted grass long enough to slow her down. Her breath gushed in front of her. By the near corner, the snow had drifted. With less than ten feet to go, her feet sunk into thicker snow, telling her that she was not going to reach the corner in time, she was too slow, too late—

A man stepped out from the corner of the steading.

Jessie's heart stopped, but her legs kept pushing as her mind tried to work out why he was wearing camouflage fatigues and why the gun looked so long.

The gun swung her way, aimed at her face.

She half-stumbled half-dived as her mind told her they were not military fatigues but forensic coveralls, that the gun was a Makarov fitted with a silencer—

She heard the spit as the Makarov kicked in Kumar's hand.

She felt something slap her shoulder, but her momentum carried her forward, and she landed on her knees as her head butted Kumar's groin and powered him onto his back on the snow-covered ground with a surprised grunt.

Jessie tried to kick herself to her feet, but some part of her was not working the way it should. The Makarov was still gripped in Kumar's hand, and he swung his arm at her to take another shot. But at such close quarters, the length of the barrel with its silencer was more of a hindrance than an advantage.

Jessie heard the angry spit, felt the warm buzz, as a bullet zipped through her hair.

Another bullet spat past, ricocheted off the barn's stone wall.

Then she had Kumar's gun arm gripped in both hands, except that it felt as if it was only one. But Kumar, instead of fighting to recover his gun, rolled onto his side, taking Jessie with him. Before she could work out what had happened, she was on her back with Kumar on top of her, trying to tug his gun arm free.

Jessie held on as long as she could, but it was no use.

The gun slipped from her grip, and Kumar struggled to his feet.

He looked down at her, lowering the barrel as he pointed it at her face. "You stupid bitch," he said, and turned his head at an animal roar by his side.

Something flashed before Jessie.

The silencer spat, the bullet burying itself in the snow by her head.

Kumar toppled over, overpowered by the surprise attack. Even above the animal's roar, Jessie heard the angry spit of another three shots in quick succession.

She pulled herself over, made it to her knees, surprised to see the snow bleeding red.

And why was Robert here, roaring like a madman, swinging his fists?

Jessie struggled to push to her feet, almost made it before slumping back into the snow. "Robert," she shouted, but her voice came out as weak as a gasp. He could not hear her anyway, she knew that. But as he continued to punch she saw that his attack was lightweight, little more than boyish slaps rather than manly punches.

She saw, too, how strong Kumar was—the ring on his little finger told her he was Kumar—for he seemed to be taking no notice of Robert's flailing punches, more intent on finding his feet, which he did with alarming ease.

And Robert, as if realizing at last that he was no match for the man, rushed over to his mother's side, grabbed her by her hands, tried to pull her to her feet to lead her to safety. But his grip slipped on her blood, and his face grimaced in horror as he looked at his bloodied fingers and roared his deaf-man's roar again.

Behind Robert, Kumar rubbed his hand under a bloodied nose, then gave Jessie a red-toothed smile as he leveled the gun at Robert.

Jessie reached up, pulled Robert to her, and threw her arm around him.

"He's only a boy," she pleaded.

"That doesn't matter to me," Kumar replied, his finger tightening around—

The Makarov jerked and spat a bullet at the snow.

Kumar grimaced in pain as his gun arm twisted behind his back, then grunted with surprise as his head butted the steading wall. Then his other arm jerked behind him to the metallic click of handcuffs, and Mhairi saying, "You're under arrest, you fuckhead."

Kumar seemed to recover from his second surprise attack of the day, and put up a struggle to break free. His head rocked back in a reverse head-butt that could have cracked concrete. But Mhairi pulled out of the way just in time, took hold of Kumar's head with both hands, and thudded it into the barn wall—once, twice, three times for luck—with an anger she must have been saving for Angus.

Kumar slumped to the snow, his face leaving a bloody trail down the stone wall. Mhairi retrieved his gun and, with an expertise that surprised Jessie, removed the magazine clip and slipped it into her pocket.

Then she was kneeling by Jessie's side. "You've been shot."

"Forget me. Take Robert to the car."

"It's OK—"

"There's two of them."

"Not anymore."

"Bloody hell, Mhairi . . ."

But Mhairi already had Jessie's jacket unzipped and her arm freed from her sleeve, and was ripping her sweater open at the neck, tearing the buttons from her blouse.

"What about Andy?" Jessie asked. "Is he there?"

"You were right."

"Is he . . . ?"

"Andy's inside," Mhairi said. "There's a door at the back. He's alive. That's all I know. I've not had time to check him out." She dabbed Jessie's wound. "You're OK. Looks like the bullet went through." She slipped a key ring from her pocket and opened the blade of a Swiss Army knife, then sliced the sleeve from Jessie's sweater to use as a makeshift sling.

"Didn't know you were a field medic," Jessie said, "and a karate queen."

"There's a lot you don't know about me."

"Want to talk about it over a drink?"

"Or three?"

Jessie tried a smile. "You're all right, Mhairi. Angus doesn't deserve you."

"Fuck Angus."

"No thank you."

Mhairi gave a short smile and pulled Jessie's jacket back over her shoulder. "That should do until the real medics arrive." Then she turned to Robert, touched her lips, and said, "You're mum is going to be OK."

Robert looked at Jessie for reassurance.

Jessie tried a smile, but it felt all wrong. Then she reached up with her good arm and pulled him to her. She buried her lips in his hair and realized that without her son, she had nothing. She shook him with mock anger. "You wee rascal," she said to him. "I told you to stay in the car."

He pulled back and frowned at her, as if puzzled by her change in mood.

But she gave him a cleaner smile and said, "I love you."

His eyes filled, and he said, "I love you too."

50

Gilchrist pushed himself to his feet and stumbled into Mhairi. "Leg's numb," he said to her, as she pulled his arm over and around her shoulder and took most of his weight.

"You don't have to walk, sir," she said. "You can sit."

If he moved his head, his world spun, and he realized it would take some time before the drugs cleared his system. He was also having difficulty remembering exactly what had happened, although the urge to be on his feet and away from the steading was so strong as to be almost overpowering. "I don't want to sit on that chair," he said, pleased that he was able to pronounce his words, even though his tongue felt like a cotton ball.

He worked up some spittle, shuffled his left foot forward, then his right. The tape had cut off the circulation, and his legs could have been connected to someone else's nervous system. But just moving around, and breathing without physical restriction, was already doing wonders for his spirit and his strength.

Still, walking and trying to stay upright required concentration.

"Pretend you're going for a pint, sir. That's what my father used to say. The day I cannae walk to the pub is the day they're gonnie put me in my coffin."

Gilchrist chuckled. Having a pint or a half. The Scotsman's answer to all ailments. He tried lengthening his stride—well, pushing one foot farther forward than the other. "Did he pass away at the bar?" he managed to ask her.

"Run over by a bus."

Gilchrist halted. "Sorry, I . . ."

"Only joking, sir. He smoked like a lum and died of lung cancer."

Through the open steading door, the snow lay as white as a sheet under the blue blanket of a cloudless sky. The wind gave a sudden gust, buffeting Gilchrist as he stepped into the cold. If not for Mhairi's grip, he would have been bowled over.

"Bit chilly," he said, breathing in the freezing air and marveling at the clarity of the countryside, as if seeing it for the first time through eyes that could focus on the finest of details. Maybe you really had to stare death in the eye before you appreciated life.

"We can go back inside," she said.

"Outside's fine."

Gilchrist had come to—he could not remember the moments before passing out—as Mhairi was slicing through the duct tape, and it had taken her several seconds to convince him that Kumar was not going to break through the door and kill them both.

Once freed, all Gilchrist had wanted to do was get off that chair.

Mhairi glanced at the corner of the steading, and Gilchrist did likewise. "I've called for backup," she said. "And an ambulance. They should be here any time."

Robert was on his knees in the snow, stroking his mother's hair. Jessie's face was as white as her surroundings. When she saw Gilchrist and Mhairi, she could not resist quipping, "The pair of you look like you're going out on a date."

"I wish," Mhairi said.

Gilchrist jerked his arm. "Why's Jessie sitting in the snow?"

"She's been shot, sir."

Gilchrist blinked, wondered what he was missing. His mind was not functioning the way it should, and he was struggling to make his memory work. "Shot?" he said. "Where?"

"In the shoulder. Looks worse than it is."

"Take me to her."

"The snow's deep."

"And your point is . . . ?"

Gilchrist shuffled his feet, tried to turn around, when he heard the distant sound of sirens. And a memory came back to him then, of a man with a knife. "Kumar," he said.

"He's handcuffed."

"Where?"

"Behind the barn, sir."

"Right." He was sure he was missing something, but he could not say what. Rather than continue to ask questions and receive answers that failed him, he thought it best to keep quiet.

"You're shivering, sir." Mhairi helped turn him around. "We should go back into the steading," she ordered. "It's sheltered, and warmer."

"But not that chair," he said, relieved he at least remembered that.

The sirens were closer now, and Gilchrist caught the blue flashes of a line of police cars—a convoy, it looked like—racing at speed toward the smallholding.

He blinked, at least he thought that was all he did, and was surprised to find himself inside the steading on his back on the floor, with a paramedic checking his heartbeat. Other parts of his memory seemed to have evaporated, too, as if he was watching them on an old film reel that stopped and started out of sequence.

"Close your left eye," the paramedic said.

Gilchrist did as he was told.

"No, your left eye."

"Right," he said, and got it that time, only to have his eye blinded by a pencil torch and irritated by a pair of fingers that pulled at his eyelids.

"Follow my finger."

Gilchrist did, but seemed not to impress the paramedic.

"We'll take him to Ninewells for observation," the para-medic said to a tall man with blond hair, who appeared beside them as if from nowhere.

Had he passed out again?

Against the black overcoat with its upturned collar, the man's face looked as pale as the snow. Even from where he was, Gilchrist could tell the man's crown was thinning. Then his memory returned as Stan peered down at him.

"Help me up, Stan. There's a good lad."

"No can do, boss. You look too peely-wally to be on your feet."

"You sure you're not looking in a mirror?"

Stan grinned and leaned closer. "His full name is Kumar al Baradi, per his British driving license. But that's likely an alias. He also has driving licenses in the names of Kumar Bretford, Kumar Blumenthal, and Kumar Brukowski."

Gilchrist noted all first names Kumar and surnames beginning with the letter *B*. Did that mean anything? Or did it just make it easier to remember if you lived under permanent deception? But just the mention of the case was doing wonders for his memory. Faces flickered before him, and he felt his heart slump at the recollection of Bill and Eilidh—

"I'm sure we'll find other aliases when we look through his home," Stan said.

"You know where he lives?"

"His mobile phone. It's a gold mine. Addresses, bank accounts, phone numbers . . ."

When Stan said nothing more but just looked down at him, Gilchrist said, "What have I missed?"

"Phone numbers?"

"What about them?"

"Your number is in Kumar's mobile."

"Why?" Gilchrist shook his head. "I don't remember talking to him." Had he? Or was his memory still failing him?

Stan shrugged. "Our technicians will try to recover data."

An image flashed into Gilchrist's mind of Kumar tearing open a bag. "There was another body," he said. "Over by the wall."

Stan nodded. "Craig Farmer. Shot through the back of the head." Stan paused, then said, "We also recovered Farmer's mobile and SIM card. Your number's on there, too."

Gilchrist had a vague recollection of something at Crail harbor but could not pull it up. "The gun," he said. "I think it's Farmer's."

"Why?"

Gilchrist dabbed the side of his head, at a lump above and in front of his ear. His hair felt clotted, and when he looked at his hand, he was surprised to see blood. "I don't know," he said to Stan. Then he closed his eyes and opened them again, and waited until his world steadied. "I tell you, Stan, I don't know how anyone can function on drugs."

"They don't. That's the point." Stan turned his head at the sound of a woman's voice, then said, "Catch you later, boss."

The stop-start film reel kicked in again, and when he next blinked Dr. Cooper was by his side, holding his hand, squeezing his fingers. "How's my boy?" she said.

Gilchrist surprised himself by squeezing back. Maybe it was the word *boy* or the sight of a woman that fired his brain, but some part of his memory surged back to him.

"Where's Jessie?" he asked. "And Robert?"

"Jessie's being transported to Ninewells. She's lost a lot of blood, but all her signs are stable. They'll probably keep her in for a few days." Cooper smiled down at him, then turned to the side as a pair of paramedics pushed a gurney alongside and fiddled with the settings.

"Whoa," said Gilchrist.

"We have the ambulance outside," one of the paramedics said.

"I'll walk," he said, and pulled on Cooper's hand. "Help me up."

"Are you sure about this?"

"Definitely. I don't like being horizontal."

"Pity," Cooper said. "I like you horizontal."

Gilchrist frowned, not seeing the joke, and wondering if there even was one.

Cooper helped him to his feet and steadied him by placing her arm through his.

"I could get used to this," she said.

Through the open steading door, the place thrived. Radio static crackled. An engine revved. Lights flashed. Voices mumbled. Bodies shuffled past. Busier than Market Street at the Lammas Fair, he thought.

As Cooper helped him into the ambulance, she said, "Mr. Cooper called this morning."

Mr. Cooper rang a bell, brought back memories. "Called?" he said.

"He's leaving me."

"I'm sorry to hear that."

"I was hoping that might please you."

He looked at her and smiled, and a memory of golden hair slipping through his fingers, tumbling over his face, flashed into his mind. "I think it does," he said to her.

She placed her hand by her ear. "I'll give you a call."

Gilchrist had time only to nod before the door closed.

51

Two days later
Ninewells Hospital

She was asleep when Gilchrist arrived.

He tried not to waken her, give her a few more minutes of rest, but she opened her eyes as he was removing the cardboard wrapping.

"For me?" she said.

"Thought I'd bring them in to brighten up your day."

She tilted her head, lifted her chin. "Let me smell."

He held the flowerpot out to her.

She closed her eyes as she inhaled. "How did you know I love hyacinths? Did Robert text you?"

Gilchrist shook his head. "My daughter loves them, too," he said. "Their fragrance always reminds me of New Year."

"Is Robert OK?" she asked.

"He'll be in later with Angie."

Jessie slumped back into the pillow. "He's too young to see what he saw. I hope he won't be haunted."

"Kids are more resilient than we give them credit for." He returned her look. "It's you I'm worried about."

"Me? I'll be on my feet in a day or so. Don't know why they won't let me out."

"You've been shot."

"In my shoulder. Not my foot."

Gilchrist pulled the conversation back on track with, "Do you remember saying you wanted to leave?"

Jessie frowned. "Leave what?"

"The job. St. Andrews. Scotland. You never spelled it out." He tried to give her a smile of reassurance, but her eyes danced with his, as if she was preparing to challenge him. "You were doped up," he explained, "but even so, it's your subconscious releasing these thoughts."

Jessie pursed her lips, stared at some point high up on the wall. Tears squeezed from her eyes. She sniffed, wiped a hand across her cheeks.

He waited a polite five seconds, then said, "You can't keep running away."

"I will, if it keeps that heathen bitch from Robert."

"I spoke to Dainty," Gilchrist said. "He thinks highly of you." He thought she looked vulnerable as she stared up at him, as if he was seeing what she looked like as a young girl. "Dainty pulled in your brothers, Tommy and Terry, told them that if they concocted a story about you taking stolen goods, he would charge them both—"

"Even if it's true?"

"It's not true." He held up his hand. "No buts. That's it." He thought it odd that she felt such a need to be punished for having broken the law, and he wondered if it had something to do with her recognition of her criminal heritage, or a desire to remove all trace of it from her family tree. "I understand now why you asked for a transfer," he said.

"To keep Robert away from my bitch-for-a-mother and my mental brothers," she said.

"Mostly," he agreed, then after a couple of beats said, "But more significantly, you want to keep the identity of your mother's father from him."

Jessie stilled, as if her heart had stopped. Then she glared at him. "Who told you?"

"I read it in your mother's police report."

She whispered a curse, then said, "It just follows me."

"It'll go no further."

She shook her head. "And I don't even know if it's true, or just something that bitch dreamed up." Her look of disappointment held for a long moment, then shifted to panic. "You can't tell anyone," she said to him. "You can't tell Robert—"

"No one will know."

She stared at him, her eyes searching his. "Not even Stan?"

"It's between us," he said. "Just you and me." He waited until he felt she believed him, then tried to change the subject with, "I've spoken to Mhairi. She told me what happened, how you put two and two together and—"

"Mhairi took Kumar down single-handedly," she said. "Don't let her try to tell you different. She saved my life. And Robert's, too."

Gilchrist nodded. If not for Mhairi, Kumar could have bagged another few bodies to his list, his own included. "But it was you who made the initial connection," he said, "then challenged Angus—"

"And almost got us all killed."

"But you didn't. And you saved my life, too." He had seen the partial recording of his execution-to-be and watched with mesmerizing horror how close he had come to being killed. "I haven't thanked you for that," he added, removing an envelope from his pocket.

He held it out to her.

"What's that?"

"It's for you."

"I asked what it was, not who it was for."

"It's a pity that bullet never nipped a bit of your tongue."

She shook her head. "Some habits die hard, I suppose. I'm sorry." She flinched as she shifted her elbow. "But this bloody shoulder still hurts."

"It'll be sore for a while, so I'm told. But you'll live."

"Regrettably, I hear you say?"

He shook his head. "You've made a bit of a name for yourself. And Stan is worried I'm going to ease him out for you."

"Musical partners, is that the way it works up here?" She nodded to the envelope. "Are you going to keep it, or tell me what it is?"

"It's your non-harassment order," he said. "Extended to cover Fife."

"How did you . . . ?"

"Go on. Take it," he said, and flapped the envelope at her.

She took it from him, nothing more than a handwritten note on sheriff's letterhead, a single piece of paper that looked at odds with its legal potency.

"I got them to widen the scope, too," Gilchrist said. "No doubt your mother will try to challenge it in court, but with her record, she has next to no hope of having it overturned."

"The bitch'll breach it."

"Then the bitch will go to jail."

"Here, what's this?" Jessie said, and removed a voucher. "The Doll's House?"

"One of my favorite restaurants."

"It's for a hundred quid." She looked up at him.

"Happy Christmas," he said. "It's the least I can do."

"How about putting me forward for a salary upgrade, then?"

"Already have. Of course, CS Greaves is as tight as they come, but once he takes the credit for bringing Kumar to justice, his purse strings will loosen up a bit."

She stared at his neck, scrunched her eyes to focus, and said, "Is that a dressing?"

Gilchrist tapped a finger to his neck, to the cut where Kumar's blade had pressed too hard. No sutures required, but it had bled heavily and still stung. "Had a close shave with a boring knife," he said.

"Jesus," Jessie said, as if realizing the seriousness of it all for the first time. "I thought we were too late."

"You almost were."

She gave that comment some thought, then said, "What about Angus?"

"It's not looking good. He's been charged as an accessory, and Mhairi has contacted Patterson and McLeod's head office. They're thinking of taking legal action against him for fraud. She's also dropped him in it with the tax man."

"Ouch. Remind me never to get on that woman's bad side. So, she's not getting back with him, is what you're telling me?"

"She's well shot of him." Gilchrist confirmed. "And Mhairi spoke highly of you."

"I didn't do anything."

"Modesty doesn't suit you." He turned as the door opened.

Robert walked in and hesitated for a moment when he saw Gilchrist, or perhaps at the look of panic in his mother's face. But Gilchrist smiled at Jessie and winked at her, and

Robert stepped around him and leaned down to his mum in bed, to give her a hug.

"Steady on, love," she said. "I'm still stitched up."

Gilchrist's mobile vibrated, and he pulled it from his pocket—a number not logged in his system. He thought of just ignoring it, then said, "Duty calls."

"Andy?"

Gilchrist paused for a moment, then reassured her with a smile and a wink, and nodded to Angie as he pushed through the door to take the call.

He did not give his name, but said, "Hello?"

"Mr. Gilchrist?" A woman's voice, as rough as Glasgow gravel.

"Who's this?"

"You don't know me, but we need to meet."

Gilchrist stepped past the lift and headed for the stairs. "Why do we need to meet?"

"Do you know the King's Bar in Nethergate—"

"You're not answering my question—"

"Meet me there in an hour, and I'll answer it then."

"And if I—"

"And come alone, or you'll regret it."

The line died.

Gilchrist tried calling back, but the caller had powered down her phone. Although he had visited Dundee often in the past, he now found his way about town with only sightseeing familiarity. He had the vaguest recollection of the King's Bar but no memory of ever having a pint there.

He phoned Nance as he walked to his car. Since their evening at the Dunvegan they had said not more than a dozen words to each other, as if Nance now regretted her invitation to him that night.

She answered as he slid behind the wheel.

"Sir?" she said, even making that single word sound cold.

"The name's Andy, Nance."

"I can't really talk right now. I'm in the middle of stuff."

Which sounded like the brush-off it really was. "I'll only take a minute, maybe less," he said. "Have you heard from John?"

Silence for several beats, then, "Look, Andy, I shouldn't have mentioned—"

"Because if you do, report him to DCI Tommy Coulson." He waited another couple of beats, but silence seemed to be order of the day, so he added, "John is now officially walking on thin ice." He fired up the ignition, slipped into gear giving Nance time to answer. But when the line remained silent, he said, "You still there?"

"I've given this some thought," she said at length, "and I've decided to submit a formal request for a transfer."

Out of the blue did not come close. Struck by a comet would be more like it.

He pressed his mobile hard to his ear and said, "Can we talk about this . . . ?" before realizing she had hung up. He thought of calling back, but common sense told him to wait a few . . . minutes, hours, days? With Nance, he could never say.

His mobile rang again—ID Stan.

Gilchrist tried to sound chirpy. "How's the interview going, Stan?"

"Frustrating, boss. He's not coughing up."

The battle for jurisdictional rights over Kumar was now in full flow, and it had taken the intervention of ACC McVicar to secure him in Fife, at least for the time being. Four of Greater Manchester Police's CID were currently on their way to have an interrogation of their own, expected later that afternoon, and two senior detectives from the Metropolitan Police were scheduled for the following morning. Although Gilchrist had spent the best part of that morning questioning Kumar for the second straight day, an idea had since come to him.

"I'll be with you in fifteen minutes, Stan," he said.

"Good. I need a break."

"But I can't stay long," he said, adding, "I'd like you to check something out for me."

"Shoot."

"Can you find out who owns the King's Bar in Dundee?"

Gilchrist closed his mobile and thought of the possibilities. He was stretching it too far, he suspected. Sometimes you had to. But if his idea had any substance, the day really had consisted of comet strikes.

And maybe even shooting stars.

52

One glance through the two-way mirror that looked into the interview room told Gilchrist that nothing had changed since he had left. He was about to enter, when Stan walked in, waving a handwritten note.

"Hot off the press, boss."

Gilchrist read it. "The plot thickens," he said.

"A finger in every pie?"

"Something like that."

It took Stan less than a few minutes to update Gilchrist on Kumar's interrogation, the conclusion being that they were getting nowhere with him answering everything with "No comment." Still, Gilchrist thought it would be worth asking the question just to gauge a reaction. Even no reaction might give him an answer.

He reentered the interview room, said, "DCI Gilchrist returning," and noted the exact time for the record. As he took his seat, Kumar raised his eyes and gave a dead-eyed stare, before returning his attention to some spot on the table between them.

Handcuffed, no longer in his bespoke suit, and with a couple of days' worth of salt-and-pepper stubble on his face, Kumar looked less the businessman that he once purported himself to be, and more the pedophiliac pimp and serial killer that he now indisputably was—still to be proven in a court of law, of course.

Numerous cuts and bruises added to the change in image.

His forehead sported two bruised lumps that peaked in crusted grazes, and the swollen bridge of his nose was as thick as a boxer's. A nasty-looking cut sliced through his upper lip. He could have gone five rounds against Vitali Klitschko and looked better. Mhairi had denied using unreasonable force making her arrest, maintaining that Kumar slipped in the snow. Her story had been confirmed by Jessie, and Robert had been too traumatized to witness anything. Kumar also denied the charge of attempting to murder Gilchrist, but the half-finished recording told a different story and nailed him to the wall—not to mention the boring knife with its razor-sharp blade, or the Makarov with its silencer and half-spent magazine.

Although the Makarov had been handled by both Kumar and Mhairi, forensics had lifted a perfect set of Craig Farmer's fingerprints from the barrel of the silencer from his having screwed it on. The bullets in the magazine matched those retrieved from the bodies of Caryl Dillanos, Jana Judkowski, and Stewart Donnelly, laying these murders at Farmer's feet but with the finger of suspicion pointing to Kumar as the man who gave the orders.

But trying to obtain any confession from Kumar was as good as talking to a rock.

Kumar's solicitor—Matthew Johnson of Johnson, Petrie, and Associates, Edinburgh—sat next to him, fresh-faced and oil-haired, wearing a suit that had to have cost the best part of one thousand pounds, maybe two. Perhaps they shared the same tailor.

Gilchrist faced Johnson. "Your client has not been forthcoming in his answers."

Johnson said, "That's his prerogative under the law."

"Under the law," Gilchrist said, and gave Johnson a dry smile. "Right." Then he faced Kumar. "Are you a religious man?"

"No comment." Kumar's voice sounded strong. No sign of any nerves there.

"I'm not going to ask what religion you believe in, although I think voodooism might be close to the bone." Kumar seemed not to notice his emphasis on the word *bone* or appear insulted by his reference to witch-doctor magic. Johnson appeared to take more offense and stirred in his seat. So Gilchrist pressed on with, "But my question is, when did *you* last pray to *your* God?"

"No comment."

"A couple of days ago, you told me you were always amazed that people turned to their God in their darkest hour."

Nothing.

"Your darkest hour is almost upon you," Gilchrist said. "Do you not feel a need to turn to your God now?"

"No comment."

Johnson stirred again, and Gilchrist held up his hand in a stay-out-of-it gesture. Then he said to Kumar, "The Lord is my shepherd. I shall not want. He maketh me to lie down in green pastures. He leadeth me beside the—"

"Is there a question in there? Or does my client have to listen to your ridiculous religious soliloquy all day?"

Gilchrist ignored Johnson, kept his focus on Kumar's eyes. He did not want to miss any reaction, no matter how slight.

"He leadeth me beside the still waters," he continued. "He restoreth my soul." He waited a couple of beats. "The twenty-third psalm," he explained. "The Lord is my shepherd. Do you know it?"

"No comment."

"So, you don't know it?" Gilchrist said.

"No comment."

"We've identified you and Craig Farmer from CCTV footage of your car crossing the Tay Road Bridge. Although you've already denied it, I'm ready to put a bet on that you live in Dundee, or in the outskirts."

"No comment."

"That wasn't a question."

Kumar said nothing, moved nothing. He could have been a cardboard cutout.

"But this is," Gilchrist said, "and it's associated with a somewhat buggered version of the twenty-third psalm. Do you know the words to this?" He leaned closer, focused hard on Kumar's eyes. "Shepherd is my Lord," he said.

Kumar blinked once, twice, then lifted his gaze to hold Gilchrist's eyes for one dark moment, before looking away.

Gilchrist had his answer.

He pushed himself to his feet and excused himself from the interview.

Gilchrist arrived in Dundee with less than ten minutes to spare. But by the time he found a parking spot and walked to the King's Bar he arrived just over five minutes late.

Inside, the ambient din from around the bar made ordering a shouting match. But he managed to buy himself a pint of Deuchars IPA and find a seat that backed against the wall, one that gave him a good view of the interior of the bar—well, as clear a view as the hubbub would allow. He picked up a discarded *Daily Record* from the seat, flipped it open to the back page, and watched the bar's clientele from behind the sports news.

No bankers or businessmen here; mostly working men in their twenties to sixties, who stood or sat in groups of threes, fours, or more around the bar. In the tight space behind the counter, three barmen slipped past each other with the artful grace of dancers, intent on not spilling a drop. Gilchrist noticed a woman sitting by herself at the opposite end in an alcove as tight as a snug.

He retrieved his mobile, recovered the phone number from its memory, and dialed it. His gaze never moved from the woman's face, but the number was still powered down, or the phone disconnected, and the woman never so much as blinked.

Twenty minutes later, he downed his pint. He walked up to the bar, having made the decision on a deadline. If the woman did not appear by the time he finished his second pint, he would call it a day. But even so, that made no sense. She had not arranged to meet him in Dundee so she could have a chat with him. No, he suspected he had been summoned to meet someone else, the man who ran Kumar. He was sure of that.

At the bar, several groups had dispersed, and the general noise level had dropped a touch. Ordering was no longer the shouting match it once was, but the scowl on the barman's face did not encourage striking up conversation. Even Gilchrist's "Thanks" on receipt of his pint seemed as good as an insult.

Back in his seat, he resisted the urge to text Stan. If the woman was going to turn up and take him to her leader, she might have someone watching him, to make sure he really was alone. Better to read his paper, sip his beer, a lonely man waiting for someone to join him—or stand him up.

The crowd in the bar continued to thin, the noise level dropping from the party din of thirty minutes earlier. Two of the barmen had finished their shifts, or stepped out the back for a smoke, and a few stragglers ignored the scowls of the remaining barman, more intent on finishing their pints before heading back to work or off to some other bar.

Gilchrist glanced at the alcove.

The woman was no longer there.

Not long to go now?

He was almost halfway through his second pint, when he realized that he was alone in the bar—well, other than the barman who appeared to find interest in cleaning glasses all of a sudden, and the two hardmen who stood facing him from opposite ends of the counter. The bar's entrance was blocked by two more hardmen-come-bodyguards who twitched their muscled shoulders, as if in prefight anticipation, under black leather jackets that hid the odd weapon or two.

Gilchrist returned his pint to the table, slid his hand into his inside jacket pocket, which had the nearer of the two hardmen taking a step toward him. He removed his mobile and placed it on the table, face up, and gave the hardman an innocent smile.

Then he sat back.

The Lord is my shepherd . . .

Gilchrist almost smiled. Maybe he needed to pray—well, at least pray that he had not miscalculated. He bounced a look off the hardman on his left and received a cold-eyed stare in return. Any thoughts of chickening out and leaving were wiped out there and then. Part of him wished he had never been so foolish, while another part assured him that he needed to do this to get to the truth. He had to know.

On a positive note, he did not have long to wait.

Forty seconds, in fact, forewarned by the door bodyguards stepping to the side as if to clear space for a bull to barge through. Behind the bar, the barman gave Gilchrist a parting scowl, then slipped off to join his work associates for a smoke.

The sound of hard heels announced the man's arrival.

All six-foot-six of him if he was an inch, with shoulders widened by the raglan style of his black, woollen coat, stood silhouetted for a long moment in the doorway, as if to give Gilchrist time to shit himself.

It almost worked.

The Lord is my shepherd . . .

Gilchrist reached for his pint and took a sip, not surprised—rather, disappointed—to find his hand shaking. He had every reason to, of course. If a killer like Kumar flinched at the mention of the big man's name, then Gilchrist should not be ashamed of his own rising fear.

The Lord is my shepherd . . .

As the man approached his table, both hardmen stepped back in criminal deference.

And Gilchrist came to see that Dainty had been correct in all he said.

Big Jock Shepherd really was the Lord.

53

Shepherd pulled out the chair opposite Gilchrist, tugged his black coat around him, the woollen material swinging from the weight of something in the inside pocket—a gun? No doubt a man of Shepherd's standing and reputation would come equipped to protect himself, whether or not he was protected by a team of heavies.

Even seated on one chair, it seemed as if Big Jock Shepherd filled enough space for two. He might be formidable in size, but Gilchrist knew from Dainty that Shepherd was also formidable in life, and at the grand old patriarchal age of eighty-four could still hold his own against a couple of men half his age.

Shepherd nodded to Gilchrist's mobile. "You expecting a call, son?" The accent was raw Glaswegian reared on sixty Capstan a day.

"I didn't want to miss her," Gilchrist said.

"Switch the fucker off."

Gilchrist picked up his mobile and powered it down.

Shepherd narrowed his eyes, turned his head to the side, and without shifting his gaze from Gilchrist, shouted, "What's keeping youse?"

The hardman on Gilchrist's right nodded to the other who lifted the counter gate and stepped behind the bar.

"Can I get you anything?" Shepherd said. "A wee one for the road, perhaps?"

Gilchrist did not like the sound of *for the road*, Shepherd's less-than-subtle suggestion that he was about to take a trip, perhaps? Or maybe he was telling him that he did not intend to stay long. Gilchrist settled on the latter. He was still a detective chief inspector with Fife Constabulary after all, and no matter how big you were in the criminal underworld, longevity in that business was guaranteed to be shortened for a cop-killer.

Still, a good kicking was not unheard of. A glance at the muscled bulk of the hardman glaring at him from his spot at the bar told Gilchrist that he had to dance with extreme care.

"I'll stick with this," he said. "I'm driving."

Shepherd held up his hand, and a glass of whisky was placed in it. He took it, drew it under his nose like a wine connoisseur testing the bouquet, then killed it in one. He held up the empty glass. "Don't gie me a fucking mouthwash this time. Gie me a measure."

Gilchrist eyed his half-empty pint, conscious of Shepherd's eyes on him. He wanted to take a sip, but did not think he could do so without his hands shaking. He reached out, clasped the pint tumbler with both hands, then said, "You wanted to meet."

Shepherd returned Gilchrist's look with a stare as hard as stone, saying nothing until another tumbler, glowing to the brim with amber liquid, was handed to him. He scowled at it, held it up to the light, as if checking the glass was clean. "They don't know the meaning of a measure these days." He tilted the glass, splashed whisky onto the floor, then held it up for all to see. "You see this?" he growled. "This is a fucking measure. Got it?"

The hardman behind the bar grimaced.

"Got it?" roared Shepherd.

"Got it, Mr. Shepherd, sir."

Shepherd narrowed his eyes at Gilchrist, as if to say *You see what the fuck I have to put up with?* then took a sip of his whisky. He coughed, ran a hand across his lips. "Nectar of the fucking gods, let me tell you."

Gilchrist lifted his pint, took a sip of his own, relieved to see that his nerves were holding. Witnessing hardmen being downsized seemed to settle him. "I'd join you," he said, "but on top of driving, I've got to get back to the station."

Shepherd nodded, as if at the wisdom of Gilchrist's words, or in acknowledgment of his sharing a friendly drink, if only. Ripples of emotion seemed to shift across the big man's face, then he lifted his tumbler, took another sip, and scowled at Gilchrist.

"Them behind us?" he said, and gave a backward nod. "That's the fucking future for you. Think they know it all. Think they know what it takes." He grimaced as if in pain. "But they know fuck all. They're young, stupid, drunk as fuck when they see money. And every now and then, one of them floats to the top of the shite and thinks they can take you on." He tried another sip, but from the look on his face the nectar of the gods had turned sour. "But they fuck it up and it's bad for business." He stared at Gilchrist. "You get my meaning?"

Gilchrist thought he did, and nodded. "Kumar?"

"Aye," Shepherd grumbled. "Fucking Kumar."

"He's one of yours?"

Shepherd narrowed his eyes. "Careful now, son. I wouldn't want you getting any ideas that I'm involved with that wee bastard."

Gilchrist thought silence his best option.

"Kumar came up here from down south. Chased over the fucking border more like." He sipped his whisky with a grimace that told Gilchrist being chased over the border was not considered good. "London, Manchester, Birmingham. He set himself up there. Next thing, he's on our doorstep trying it on, thinking he's gonnie start up on his fucking ownie-oh." Shepherd shook his head, wiped spittle from his lips. "I think fucking not."

Gilchrist leaned forward, chose his words carefully. "He was being disrespectful of family boundaries?"

Shepherd gave Gilchrist a slit-eyed scowl for a long moment, which had Gilchrist thinking he had overstepped the mark. He heard the shifting of someone's feet to his right. Then the hard look evaporated, and Shepherd finished his whisky with an angry grunt.

He held up the glass. "A correct fucking measure, this time." He pulled his hand over his lips and said, "Disrespectful?" He raised an eyebrow. "That's putting it mildly, son." Then he leaned closer and, in a softer voice, said, "But you're right about the family. That's what's fucking important." He sat back. "I know you keep in touch with that gobshite, Dainty. He's so fucking wee it'd be an embarrassment to be seen kicking his cunt in. But he's got a good head on his shoulders. Know what I'm saying, son? Knows when to hold and when to fold, as the saying goes." Shepherd nodded at his own sage words, then growled over his shoulder, "What's keeping youse?"

"Can't find any more of the Macallan 10, Mr. Shepherd."

"Go and tell that fucking numptie to get it then." He turned back to Gilchrist and said, "See what I mean, son? No one cares a fuck anymore. That's what's missing in the world these days. Discipline. And fucking respect."

The words were pronounced with the gravity and finality of a black-capped judge pronouncing sentence, and Gilchrist watched the barman—no longer scowling—scurry to the bar with a full bottle of whisky and hand it over—the Macallan 10, no doubt.

Shepherd seemed content to wait in silence until his glass was replenished. But his stone-hard eyes drilled into Gilchrist with a direct stare that he found unsettling. Gilchrist said, "So, you own this pub?" more to break the stare than start a conversation.

"You know I do, son. That's why you're here."

Footsteps announced the arrival of another tumbler, which Shepherd took without thanks or acknowledgment. He held it up in front of Gilchrist. "That's better," he said, and took a sip. Then he looked at him, and Gilchrist sensed that the moment of revelation, the reason he had been summoned, was now upon him.

"I'm a businessman, son. I run a family business. That's what I do." He paused, as if waiting for Gilchrist's nod of approval. But Gilchrist returned the stony look with one of his own. "And do you know what I'm good at?" Shepherd said, pressing closer.

"Tell me," Gilchrist said, just to keep up his side of the conversation.

"I'm good at taking care of business. And I look after my own." He sat back. "You follow what I'm saying, son?"

Gilchrist thought he saw where Shepherd was going with this, although any form of confession would be beyond reality. He knew that, at least. Again, he chose his words with care. "You're saying that if anyone interferes in your family business, you . . ." He grimaced, trying to give the impression of finding some kind way to say it. ". . . you sort them out."

"Aye, son. I do indeed." He grinned. "I sort them out."

"Is that what happened to Caryl Dillanos?"

Shepherd stilled. Every muscle and fiber and hair and tissue on his eighty-four-year-old face and body froze, as if the name had triggered some button that stopped the universe. Then the scene rebooted, and the big man groaned and slid his hand inside his coat pocket for his gun.

And Gilchrist knew, this time he was surely going to die.

54

But Shepherd did not pull out a gun.

Instead, he withdrew a brown envelope and slapped it onto the table.

Gilchrist stared at it, his heart pounding. He swallowed a lump in his throat, tried to look composed. But he was fooling no one, least of all himself.

Shepherd nodded for him to open the envelope.

Gilchrist reached out, picked it up. The flap was not sealed, and he peeled it back. He glanced at Shepherd, but for once the big man seemed unable to return his look. He pushed his hand inside, flicked through half a dozen or so ten-by-eight color photographs.

He removed the first one.

A head shot of Caryl Dillanos.

She stared back at him, vacant, dead-eyed, her blonde hair no longer coiffed perfectly but spread across her bruised cheek like rats' tails. Her skin shone with a mixture of blood and rainwater that glistened on her face like plastic.

He slid out another—a full-length of Dillanos on her back on rain-soaked grass, her short skirt high enough to show tanned thighs and the V of white knickers. He pulled out another, and another, all the while his mind racing, his blood turning colder by the second, until he flipped his way through all of them—nine in total—and realized that not one of them showed Jana Judkowski.

Did that mean Caryl Dillanos was a special person in Big Jock Shepherd's life? Was she part of the business? Part of the family? All of a sudden the word *godfather* took on a different meaning. Did Shepherd somehow blame Gilchrist for her death? Was that what this was about, the meeting, the talk, the hardmen, a gentlemen's discussion over a lunchtime drink to explain why he was about to be killed?

The manner of when and where raised other issues.

They would not kill him in the pub, certainly not one that was owned by Shepherd. That was too close to home. So not now but later. The memory of Shepherd's words—*a wee one for the road*—sent a subzero chill the length of Gilchrist's spine.

It could, of course, mean something else entirely.

So Gilchrist clung to that straw and eased into it with, "Caryl meant a lot to you."

Shepherd glared at him, the stony look back full force. His lips tightened in a fearsome grimace, as if he was about to tell Gilchrist when, where, and by how many of the thousand cuts he was going to kill him. But he reached for his drink, and Gilchrist came to understand that the man was in too much pain to speak—not physical pain but pain of a kind that could hurt much more. And it slowly dawned on Gilchrist why he was here, what Jock Shepherd really wanted.

He wanted revenge. But not on Gilchrist.

He wanted revenge on Kumar for killing Caryl Dillanos, the young woman in the big man's life. But even so, as these thoughts fired though Gilchrist's mind, he knew that he was missing something. Kumar was alive and locked up in a cell in St. Andrews, waiting to be interrogated by half the police forces in the United Kingdom. So, how could he help Shepherd?

Gilchrist restacked the photographs in a pile, tapped the edges flush, then returned them to the envelope. "Tell me about Caryl," he said.

Shepherd stared at Gilchrist, his look as forlorn as that of a childless parent. Then he gazed around him, as if admiring the interior design, his face softening with the memory of something close to his heart. "This place was gonnie be hers," he said. "And everything else. She was gonnie take over the family business. All of it. When I go."

Gilchrist thought back to his interview with Dillanos, the cocky manner, the lack of fear, the disrespect for the law, the absolute and utter disregard of the consequences. What had she to be frightened of, when she had Big Jock Shepherd, Scotland's crime patriarch, looking out for her? It put a different perspective on the word *trainee*.

"She was smart," Shepherd pressed on. "A woman of the world, so she was, son."

Gilchrist nodded. Dubai, Qatar, Poland. She certainly was.

"Said she was gonnie sort out that fucker Kumar for me. Set him up, then shut him down for good."

Gilchrist's ears perked. "How was she going to do that, exactly?"

"Kumar was a fly wee cunt." Shepherd's eyes narrowed at the thought. "He played his cards close to his chest, trusted no one. That's how he survived for so long." Shepherd took another sip, then scowled at Gilchrist. "But he didnae treat women right, son. He treated them with disrespect."

If Gilchrist had any thoughts that he might be winning the big man over, they were shot down there and then. Shepherd's eyes flared, his lips quivered. As he lifted the glass to his lips his hand shook with the sheer force of a suppressed rage that Gilchrist could only imagine.

Then the moment passed.

"Don't get me wrong, son," Shepherd growled. "A woman needs to know her place. And a man needs to knock it into her once in a while." He shook his head, and his eyes glistened. "But no to be treated like some fucking animal. No that, son. No one deserves that."

Gilchrist saw his opening and took it. "But that's all women were to Kumar," he said. "Nothing more than animals to be chained, fed, watered, and used when the mood fit." He waited until Shepherd looked up from his whisky. "Which is not your style."

Shepherd lowered his head and eyed Gilchrist, like a bull preparing to charge a red flag. "Watch that tongue of yours, son. I don't do women slaves. End of. That's my fucking style. Got it, son?"

Got it, Mr. Shepherd, sir, flitted through Gilchrist's mind. But he held up both hands in a gesture of apology and said, "That's what I meant."

Shepherd stared Gilchrist down, then snapped his whisky over, and held up the glass. The hardman at the corner of the bar took it without a word, and silence reigned until the glass was returned with a measure that received Shepherd's nod of approval.

While Shepherd took another sip, Gilchrist decided to press on before the man was too drunk to speak. "So Caryl teamed up with a local estate agent," he said, choosing to keep

Angus's name out of it, just in case, "and started searching for properties suitable for Kumar to live in—"

"Aye, and suitable to chain his women slaves to a wall."

"So, how would renting properties help shut Kumar down?" Gilchrist pleaded. "You said he was chased north of the border, to set up shop. But that interfered with your family business, and you would have none of it."

Shepherd grinned at Gilchrist, like a man of the world to a boy-child. "You're no quite as smart as I was told you were, son," he growled, leaning closer. "And you're no listening. I don't do women slaves. Period. And I wouldnae stand for some wee bastard breezing into Scotland and thinking he can fucking take over my territory, no matter what fucking line he's in. First women, then afore you know it, you're out on your ear." He dabbed spittle from his lips. "But here's how the takedown was gonnie work."

Gilchrist found himself leaning closer, wished he could record what he was about to hear.

Shepherd lowered his voice. "Caryl got wind that a shipment was due in."

"Shipment?"

"Women. Girls. In their teens. Forty of them. All gonnie be driven up in a convoy of lorries from England, like fucking cattle. In simple language, son, he was moving shop to set up here. Caryl offered to help by finding properties. For a fee, of course. Nothing fancy. One here, one there, none that would draw attention to herself."

Gilchrist watched Shepherd take another sip, surprised to see the big man appearing to liven, rather than slide beneath the table like any normal person would.

"And once the wee cunt was all set up and ready to go, we were gonnie fuck him, and shop him to the polis."

"Why not just . . ." Again, he chose his words with care. ". . . sort him out?"

Shepherd narrowed his eyes, giving Gilchrist's words some thought. He could have been a businessman analyzing market strategy. "That would be just the head of the snake, son. Another piece of shite would float to the top and try to take over where that wee cunt left off." He shook his head. "No, son, if you're gonnie get rid of a nest of snakes, you take out the whole fucking lot. Catch them red-fucking-handed. That's what Caryl was gonnie do."

"And Kumar found out?" Gilchrist said.

"Aye, he did."

"Who told him?"

"That stupid wee fucker, Donnelly."

"So Craig Farmer killed Donnelly."

Shepherd eyed Gilchrist, as if seeing something smart in him for the first time. "You don't expect me to acknowledge any association with that now, do you, son?"

Gilchrist shook his head. "Of course not. But off the record?"

"This fucking meeting never took place, son. Got it?"

He had indeed. "Got it," he said.

Shepherd stared hard into Gilchrist's eyes as if willing himself into his mind and explaining the consequences of a loose tongue. As if satisfied, he said, "Donnelly was a loose cannon. Not to be trusted. One of them up-and-coming youngsters I told you about. Getting too fucking big for his boots."

"Donnelly attacked one of my team in a car park," Gilchrist said. "DI Davidson. Could have killed him, if Farmer hadn't pulled him off in time." He waited a beat. "But Donnelly got the wrong man. DI Davidson had borrowed my car for the day."

Silent, Shepherd returned Gilchrist's look.

"Why would Donnelly want to kill me?"

Shepherd narrowed his eyes. "Maybe you're asking the wrong question, son. Maybe you should be asking yourself why Farmer pulled him off." He took another sip of whisky, and Gilchrist caught a sense that the meeting was coming to an end. "None of my men do cops, son. You can trust me on that."

Gilchrist would like to take comfort from that, but talk was nothing but words. "Kumar killed Farmer," he said. "Was Farmer one of your boys?"

"I thought he was one of Caryl's, but until I get to the bottom of why he didnae take Kumar out, I'll never know for sure." Shepherd snapped back the remains of his whisky and cracked the glass onto the table with a force that should have shattered it.

The meeting was over.

"So you want me to do what?" Gilchrist said. "Kumar's been charged and will be tried through a court of law."

Shepherd pushed his chair back and himself to his feet. He slipped his hand into his coat again and removed another envelope, white this time, to avoid confusion. "Caryl was good at what she done. Which is why I trusted her to run the business." He nodded to the envelope. "That's from her," he said. "You never got it from me, and we never met." He waited until he had Gilchrist's nod of agreement, then said, "That'll help you fuck him."

Gilchrist waited until Shepherd and his four hardmen waded through the door and into the afternoon daylight before he picked up the envelope and slid it into his jacket pocket. Then he pushed the remains of his pint to the side and walked from the bar.

55

The contents of Big Jock Shepherd's envelope were sufficient for the procurator fiscal to charge Kumar with multiple murders, and to expect the full force of the law to put him behind bars for life—with no chance of parole. Ten other members of his gang were charged with kidnapping, rape, and drug distribution and expected to be put away for ten to twenty years each, a pittance compared to the many young lives they helped destroy.

A disc that contained footage of women being raped, tortured, then killed, and featuring a blood-soaked Kumar, slaughterer's knife in hand—the same knife with which he had intended to decapitate Gilchrist—caught in profile and face-on, his voice distinguishable from all others, was irrefutable evidence that Kumar was a serial killer of the first order, and would ensure he would never see this side of a prison cell ever again. And the ring removed from his little finger on his left hand proved to be the tattoo branding stamp, with its own ink pad embedded inside—two quick stabs under the arm, side by side, and you had your double bones, or number eleven.

But it had been the contents of the flash drive copied from Kumar's personal laptop—Gilchrist later confirmed with Big Jock that Craig Farmer had stolen it as supposed protection against Kumar's burgeoning business activities—that pulled Kumar's empire to the ground and tore it up by the foundations.

Properties in six English counties were seized, and a total of sixty-seven girls were released from barns, attics, basements, and in one case, an outside toilet. The conditions that many of these girls were kept in were described in one national newspaper as "hell on earth." Two of the young women, both from Gdansk in Poland, died in hospital from drug abuse, their systems simply shutting down in the end from the onslaught. A folder containing photos and full details of every girl under Kumar's control provided conclusive ID—Marysia Grabowski, the Coastal Path girl, was indeed the sister of Galyna, whose triangular chin had edged Gilchrist closer to the truth. The other two found in the house in Kingsbarns were identified as Anna Kowalski from the town of Rzeszow in southeast Poland, and Zosia Walczak from Elblag in the north. A team of Policja detectives flew to Scotland for formal identification and commencement of repatriation proceedings.

A separate investigation by Stan revealed that Stewart Donnelly once shared a cell in HM Prison Peterhead with Big Jimmy Fisher, a serial rapist originally from Dundee who was found hanging in his garden shed on the morning a warrant for his arrest had been issued for alleged sexual offenses against three preschoolers. The senior investigating officer about to make the arrest had been DCI Andrew Gilchrist of Fife Constabulary.

"That's the reason for the attack right there," Stan had said.

"Revenge?"

"For you causing the death of his mate, boss."

Well, it seemed as good an explanation as any.

But Jock Shepherd's words—*None of my men do cops, son. You can trust me on that*—sounded weak against the big man's uncertainty over Craig Farmer's allegiance. If Stan had not borrowed Gilchrist's Merc that day, would Donnelly have been permitted to finish the job?

"I think you were lucky," Stan said.

Gilchrist could only nod in agreement.

And Gilchrist had one more surprise when CS Greaves called him to his office and introduced him to a clean-cut man in a pristine business suit.

"Reginald Hardcourt," the man said, as he shook Gilchrist's hand. "Home Office."

Greaves said, "Take a seat, Andy."

Gilchrist did as he was told.

Hardcourt removed a folder from a leather case and handed it to Gilchrist. "Can't let you take this away with you," he said, "but it should make for interesting reading."

Gilchrist opened the folder to a photograph of Craig Farmer, the clarity of the image tickling his memory, telling him he had seen that face in a car driving past him one Sunday morning in Crail. He read the name, then frowned at Hardcourt. "Martin Fletcher?"

Hardcourt nodded. "Fletcher went by a number of pseudonyms. But he was with the Serious Organized Crime Agency," he said. "Worked undercover and managed to infiltrate Kumar's trafficking organization. He was about to take him down when . . . well, when it all went to hell in a handbasket, quite frankly." Hardcourt returned Gilchrist's stare with an inquisitive look, as if wondering why it had taken him so long to work it out.

Big Jock Shepherd's voice came back to Gilchrist—*you should be asking yourself why Farmer pulled him off*—and he said, "Did Jock Shepherd know?"

Hardcourt shrugged. "I shouldn't think so."

Gilchrist thought back to the phone call that morning at Crail harbor, to the Toyota and the trail that led to the house in Boarhills. He thought he now saw some sense in it all, that Farmer—Fletcher—had been feeding them breadcrumbs, leading them to the steading where Kumar was going to relocate his trafficking enterprise.

But something did not fit.

"If Fletcher was with SOCA," he said, "why were we not kept informed?"

"We had concerns he'd been compromised," Hardcourt told him. "We were about to call him in, bring the operation to an end. But Fletcher had invested too much of himself into it by then, so regrettably he went even deeper." Hardcourt shook his head. "Informing anyone that we had an undercover agent on the case could have got him killed."

"Which happened anyway," Gilchrist pointed out.

"But not before he befriended Caryl Dillanos."

Gilchrist almost gasped. "She was in on it?"

Hardcourt grimaced, shook his head. "I doubt it. But when you're undercover, you make friends with unusual bedfellows. Fletcher trusted her, he told us. Something to do with having a common interest."

"Like taking Kumar down?"

Hardcourt nodded. "Fletcher managed to access Kumar's personal files, but he failed to pass them to his controller. Instead, we realize now that he passed them to Dillanos."

"Why?" It was all Gilchrist could think to say.

"Again, conjecture, but we believe by that time Fletcher wanted Shepherd's men to handle Kumar, maybe even terminate him, rather than have him spend the remainder of his life in prison." Hardcourt grimaced. "But it turned into a right sorry mess, I regret to say."

"And Kumar somehow found out about SOCA's involvement and killed him?"

"Again, not sure. More likely that Fletcher knew too much about his operation, and Kumar was preparing to move forward with a clean slate. No need to have anyone close to him. That seemed to be his MO. But we'll never know for sure." Hardcourt held out his hand for the folder. "May I?"

Gilchrist handed it back and said nothing as Hardcourt returned it to the confines of his leather case. Then he looked at Gilchrist and held out his hand. "I've already spoken to the chief constable and told him that you and your team did one hell of a job. Well done."

Gilchrist shook Hardcourt's hand, his head still spinning with it all. But he had one more question. "Col Feeney in Manchester," he said, "and Jerry Best in Edinburgh. Two major traffickers who were supposedly murdered at the hands of the Ghost."

Hardcourt narrowed his eyes, wary all of a sudden. "I believe they were," he agreed.

To his side, CS Greaves pushed himself to his feet. "That'll be all, Andy."

Well, there he had it. Not high enough up the chain to talk shop with the big boys.

Gilchrist turned to leave, when Hardcourt said, "Needless to say, Fletcher and SOCA's involvement will need to remain in the dark."

"And the Ghost, too?" Gilchrist asked.

Hardcourt gave him a narrow smile. "As I said, needless to say."

Gilchrist nodded, then left the office.

56

One week later
6:00 PM, December 23

With the procurator fiscal going forward with the full set of charges, with rock-solid evidence before her, Gilchrist took his team out to mark the end of a successful case, at least in terms of nailing the bad guys. With one more shopping day before Christmas, no one was intending to stay long. But it always helped to lift team spirits, particularly after the murders of Bill and Eilidh, whose bodies were not to be released for cremation until after New Year.

The Central Bar in Market Street was a suitable venue, as always.

"So, what's with Nance handing in her transfer request?" Jessie asked Gilchrist.

"Time to move on, I suppose."

"Is she after my old position in Strathclyde?"

"I shouldn't think so," Gilchrist said, and gave her a look that said *Let's change the subject*, then added, "So, have you heard from your mother?"

Jessie got the message and turned away to talk to Dan.

Gilchrist looked at Stan, who was in full flow with Mhairi—now there's a thought that had never crossed his mind—and said, "How are your wounds, Stan old son?"

"Doing fine, boss," Stan said, then returned his attention to Mhairi.

Gilchrist seemed unable to participate in any conversation. One pint later, he felt like the odd man out, and he slipped out his mobile, checked his e-mails. But his inbox was empty, which was becoming a bit of a rarity of late—

"Look, it's started snowing," said Mhairi, which had all heads turning to the window, and Jessie singing, "I'm dreaming of a white Christmas—"

"Give it up," Mhairi said, and smacked Jessie across the thigh.

"Careful," said Stan, grimacing from her sudden movement. "I'm still tender—"

"My poor pet," Jessie smooched. "Like me to kiss them all better?"

As Gilchrist listened to the camaraderie banter, he was struck by how young his team looked. Even Stan with his thinning crown and healing wounds looked in better shape than Gilchrist felt. And Jessie, too, looked as if she had never been wounded, although she did give the occasional flinch. He really was beginning to age. He seized an opportunity in a lull in the conversation by pushing to his feet and saying, "Anyone like one for the road?"

"What are you having?" Jessie asked him.

"Maybe a pint."

"Maybe a pint?" she said. "That sounds like you're ducking out for an early bath."

He grinned and said, "Same again, then?" and stepped to the bar without waiting for their response. He bought another round and asked for a receipt. CS Greaves would choke on his porridge when Gilchrist turned in his expenses, but it was the festive season after all, and Greaves was still basking in the glorified aftermath of Kumar's international trafficking organization being blown wide open.

Back at the table, Gilchrist said, "Merry Christmas, everyone. I'm heading off," and was bombarded with a mixture of festive wishes and complaints to stay for another pint. He waved them all away and walked to the door, only to find Jessie gripping him by the arm.

"You can't go just yet," she said. "Stay for another."

He shook his head. "An early bed is what I need."

She squeezed his arm and said, "Thanks for everything."

He frowned.

"You know, keeping my family secret a secret." Then some idea seemed to cross her mind, and she said, "Stay put for one more minute. I've got a surprise for you."

"But I haven't bought you a Christmas present," he complained.

"That's not what I'm talking about. Well, not exactly. Wait outside," she ordered, and almost pushed him through the door.

Snow was falling, beginning to stick. Thickening flurries clouded the streetlamps.

Through the window, he watched Jessie talking on her mobile. Then she looked up at him and smiled, and placed her first finger and pinkie to her ear. He played along, slipped his hand in his pocket to retrieve his mobile, when it rang.

He glanced at Jessie, but she was seated with the others, grinning at him with a smug look on her face. Then he looked at the incoming number—ID Cooper.

"Hello?" he said, and caught Jessie giving him the thumbs-up. "Becky? This is a surprise. Or do I have that the wrong way round?"

She chuckled. "Thought I would drive into town and see who I might bump into."

"Well, I was just about to head home," he said. "But I suppose I could be persuaded to stay a little longer." He frowned when the connection was cut, and was about to redial when he felt an arm slip through his.

"Where would you like me to take you?" Cooper said.

Gilchrist's smile turned into a chuckle. He glanced at Jessie, and she blew him a kiss and gave him one of her toodle-do waves.

He winked at her, then walked onto Market Street, Cooper on his arm.

"We could try the Doll's House," he said, "if we can find a table. Will that do?"

She leaned into him, her thigh bumping his as they crossed the cobbled street.

"I think that'll do quite nicely," she said. "For starters."